From Grandeville - A Tale
Book Four

I0634594

Not Again.

Being A Tale of What Happens

When You Decide To Help A Friend.

George R. Mead

E-Cat Worlds Press

Not Again

Library of Congress Control Number: 2007929317

Mead, George R.
    Not Again; being a tale of what happens when you
    decide to help a friend./George R. Mead
    p. cm. – (From Grandeville, a tale; Tale 4)
    ISBN-13 978-0-9741973-6-4

1. Fantasy. I. Title. II. Series.

E-Cat Worlds established its publishing program as a reaction to the large commercial publishing houses currently dominating the book industry and the smaller intellectual clones. It is interested in publishing works of fiction and non-fiction that are often deemed insufficiently profitable or commercial or that are not necessarily reflective of literary trends and fads.

E-Cat Worlds, 57744 Foothill Road, La Grande OR 97850
ecatworldspress [dot] com
SAN 255-6383

First Edition: October 2007, revised 2018
Printed in the United States of America

Fiction

From Grandeville.
Portal, 2nd edition
Lair, 2nd edition
Search
Not Again
And Again.
Magiwitch
Rebirth
Offspring
Holiday
Treasure
E'Nilt
Braidna
Seemna and Chyndra

A Tale of The Feyra
Jonathon and Dee
Dee Of The Fontala
Dee and The People
Dee and The Golden Cartouche

The Seven Lands
Seventeen Siblings (assisted by Zakke L. Zacog)

Stream
Special Investigator
Dark Souls

Non-fiction

A History of Union County
The Ethnobotany of the California Indians, 2nd Edition
A History of The Chinese in The West: 1848-1880
Yachats. The Town Called "Dark Water at the Foot of the Mountains."
The War On Poverty. A Short History - Kennedy to Reagan
A Different Look At Stress. Stress and Culture Change

Some adventures begin deliberately.

Some begin when you are not looking.

This one began with a phone call.

Small Pieces.

Grandeville. Tinker's Place. Early Morning.

"NEPHEW! PHONE!"

The intercom blasted in his ear. He hit the button. "O. K., Chen, I'll be right there."

It was mid-morning and John Tinker was halfway through the rough draft of a new book. This one was on the history of the martial arts in China. The martial arts was an area he specialized in, and one in which he was well known by that small population of people who shared a common interest. He had been sitting and staring at a blank page for several minutes now. So, he didn't really mind being interrupted this time.

He walked from his "office" and out into hall, grabbed the phone and leaned against the wall.

"Hello," he said cautiously, wondering what was going on. Normally Chen wouldn't interrupt him when he was working.

"Tinker, it's me, J. C. I need your help."

"To do what?" That didn't sound right. J. C. never needed or asked for help with anything.

"Well, I don't actually need your help. It's Hard. He needs our help. Or something."

"What exactly does Hard need our help for? Or something?"

There was a long pause. That was also very uncharacteristic of J. C.

"Well . . . ?" prompted Tinker.

"Hard is dying . I think we should go over to his house and visit. NOW! RIGHT NOW!"

"O.K., I'll be right there."

As a conversation this one didn't make any sense at all. The last time he had seen Hard he had been robust and radiantly healthy. But, if J. C. said something was so, then it was so. Tinker started to hang up.

"Ah, Tinker?"

"What?"

"You all right? You recovered?"

"Yep. We just looked worse than we were, that's all. I've started work on a new book. See you in twenty minutes, more or less."

"Fine." The phone banged loud in Tinker's ear.

Slowly he hung up the instrument. And walked into the kitchen where a small Chinese gentleman was puttering around.

He was Master Adam Liu Chen, owner of *Chen's Chinese*, a restaurant in downtown Grandeville, Tinker's first friend in Grandeville, and his martial arts teacher.

"I'm going into town and I don't know when I will be back. That was J. C. He said that Hard is dying."

"Bad news. Give my condolences to his parents. Eat something in town."

Chen began to put away the kitchen things. And nodded. That single nod indicated that he knew that whatever Tinker found out would be shared as soon as possible.

"I will. Both."

Tinker walked from the kitchen and outside, puzzling over why J. C. would think that Hard could be dying.

Chicken and Smoke were standing next to the extended-cab pickup, holding the passenger-side door open. Messenger and Fair Morn hurtled around the corner of the house, racing toward them. Messenger was tucking in her shirt.

"We do with thee be a'going, My Lord!@" stated Chicken in her usual twisted syntax.

They all looked grim and determined. They had all

caught his thoughts and his mood as he had hung up the telephone.

The four clambered into the truck and waited for him to get behind the wheel. They were all dressed in similar attire. It was what they called their "local costume." Cowboy boots, blue jeans, checkered flannel shirts.

Smoke and Messenger grabbed sunglasses from the glove compartment and put them on.

Tinker jumped behind the wheel, started the truck and headed to town.

As they started down the long slope of the driveway, the valley opened before them. Eighteen miles across the flat bottomed, bowl shaped space they could see the mountain slopes rising sharp blue-grey jagged edges from farm fields, all smooth greens and browns. Normally it was a view to be admired. But not today. Other things were on their collective mind.

It was usually not considered to be a very long drive to Hard's parent's home, measured either in time or distance. Now, this morning, it was a very long, a very silent, twenty minute drive.

As they passed the sprawling acres that adjoined Tinker's land, Tinker waved at Doc, J. C.'s employer, who was directing some sort of activity at one corner of his property.

Then they headed up onto *The Bench*. This was that area of Grandeville where the doctors, lawyers, and the more affluent businessmen lived. Right in the middle there was a twenty acre piece with only one house. This was a portion of the land that Hard's great grandfather had bought when he first arrived, long before the town was much of a town, and this part wasn't in town at all. It had taken three years for the local craftsmen to finish the great grandfather's house to the great grandfather's exacting demands.

The great grandfather was Alandale Fredrico Hardcastle, known as The First.

Hard was the Fourth.

House and property were still intact. Hard and his parents were quietly, sedately, politely, the richest family in the county, if not in most of the state.

The grounds surrounding the four-storied, many angled structure were, more or less, park-like.

Hard's grandfather, often called "Number Two" by family members, had pushed burnable shrubs and trees away from the house after seeing a large portion of early wooden Grandeville burn to the ground. Luckily the wind was blowing away from the Hardcastle property. But the grandfather had decided luck was to be utilized in whatever form it appeared. Now, Hard's father hired two grounds keepers to insure that his father's safety plans remained in effect.

Grandeville. The Hardcastle Residence.

The pickup entered the long driveway curving up to the Hardcastle residence. As they neared the front of the house, they could see J. C.'s old red van parked by the front entrance.

J. C. was standing next to it, waiting for them, all six foot, four inches of lean athleticism topped by brown-blond, sun streaked hair, male model face, wearing his usual ratty clothes. He had been helping Doc earlier and hadn't bothered to change.

As they disembarked, J. C. smiled at the four young women. "Hi, there." He knew Smoke and Chicken. He had met the other two for a brief moment a week ago.

Smoke nudged Chicken in the ribs. "He is pretty, don't you think?"

J. C. winked at Smoke.

Chicken smiled sweetly. "Most truly bespoken, Dark Sister. Fair youth do have most passing fair a'mien."

Tinker stepped around them, took J. C. by the arm and started for the front door, grumbling at Smoke as he passed. "All right, knock it off." J. C. was half a head taller than Tinker.

J. C. rang the door bell, and smiled at Chicken.

"What's going on?" asked Tinker.

"I'll let his mother tell you. Then you can decide for yourself. It doesn't make any sense at all, not for Hard it doesn't."

The door swung inward. Hard's mother peered out at them. In her mid-fifties, she was still an elegant person, of thirty.

"Oh, it is John and J. C." She looked past them and smiled warmly.

"And these must be the rest of John's young ladies. I have been, we have been, hearing all about them. You know how gossip flies in a small town like this. Do come in, and introduce us, won't you. I expect you have come to visit Alan."

She always called her only son, Alan. His father called him Freddy, sometimes "The Fourth," when he was in a joking mood. Everyone else called their son, "Hard," on almost all occasions. No one called him Alandale Frederico Hardcastle, the Fourth, except his parents on really formal occasions.

J. C. nodded. "Yes, we have. But first, could you tell Tinker exactly what you told me?"

She nodded and beckoned them into the house. "Of course. Come into the parlor. We can be more comfortable there than standing out here on the steps." She led the way.

The parlor was a comfortably furnished room, all soft overstuffed furniture. The outside wall was dominated by the fireplace and its flanking floor to ceiling windows. Once they were settled, and Tinker had made the required introductions,

Hard's mother smiled weakly at him from the depths of her wing chair as she explained, "There isn't really much to tell. Just a week ago, Alan went off to take a short hike. You know how he likes to hike. He said he would be back in time for dinner. But when he returned, Alan was a mess. His clothes were filthy, and heavily worn. And he couldn't explain how they got that way. It seemed to be as much a surprise to him as it was to me. In point of fact, he seemed somewhat dazed, more so than usual."

She shrugged her shoulders slightly to signify that both

Tinker and J. C. knew her son's mannerisms as well as she did.

"Then he went upstairs and changed his clothes, washed and joined his father and me for dinner. Two mornings ago, as I was doing the laundry, I found some rings in his jean pockets, the ones he had been wearing on his hike. When he returned from town I gave them to him. He took them and looked somewhat surprised that I had found them in his pocket. But then, as he examined the one with the large, round red stone, he stared at it, just stared at it, for the longest time, his eyes wide open, like he was seeing something else. Then he moaned and collapsed. I called his father in from the yard and we carried Alan up to his room. Then we called Doctor Shimp. He could find nothing wrong with him. And all the doctor can tell us now is that my Alan is just lying in his bed, dying. My only son is just lying there dying from something unknown."

Tears began to run down her cheeks.

"Alan is just lying in his bed and dying. And no-one knows what to do."

She blinked, leaned forward, and gently placed one hand on Tinker's arm. "John, maybe when you talk to him it will make a difference. J. C. did. Nothing happened."

Tinker patted her hand gently. "O. K., I'll have a try. May we go up now?"

She nodded. "Of course. You know where his room is, so you just go ahead. I think I will just stay here, if you don't mind." She turned her head away and stared out one of the windows.

Tinker stood and headed from the room and up the stairs, the wide main staircase, followed by the others. In the upper hall, he halted.

"You didn't get anything at all, J. C.?"

"Nope. Not a wiggle nor a twitch. His eyes are open, but just gazing into space. No reaction. Other than a blink every once in awhile."

J. C. waggled his hand in front of his eyes. "Couldn't even get him to blink at that."

They halted outside Hard's room.

Tinker took a deep breath, eased open the door, and called, "**HARD**? Care for some visitors?"

Silence.

J. C. shrugged his shoulders. "Go on in. You won't get an answer."

They stepped into the bedroom. It was, like all the rooms in this house, on the large size. The bed was king-sized. Large windows filled the wall on either side of the head end of the bed.

Several long, low dressers sat against one wall. Near the door a small chest sat on a low table. Under either window were placed two low tables holding the alarm clock, a radio, and a number of dog-eared books. A few of these had a number of slips of papers poking out.

Tinker stopped at the foot of the bed and stared at the pale face of one of his closest friends. The body lay absolutely motionless.

It was strange to see Hard this way, he was always full of energy and motion. His eyes were open wide, staring from some deep inner space.

Hard looked right through them. He was watching something only he could see.

"Oh, my," whispered Messenger, staring all round eyes at Tinker as he looked around the room.

"Where's these rings that his mother found?"

J. C. walked over to the chest, lifted the top and took out a small box, opened it and handed the box to Tinker. Inside were a number of rings. Tinker picked out the ring with the large red jewel and held it up in his finger tips. The gold glowed softly. The jewel seemed to pulsate in the bright sunlight.

Messenger gasped. "Magic!" She stepped closer, peering from the ring to Hard and back again.

Tinker's head snapped in her direction. "What?"

"What?" echoed J. C. "What did you say?"

Messenger pointed at Hard. "There are strands binding it to him. But they are weakening."

"Tinker?" asked J. C., staring at Messenger.

Smoke nudged J. C. out of the way with her shoulder and peered closely at the ring, then at Hard. "MindMate, may I peer into him?"

Tinker looked at Chicken. "What do you think, Princess?"

"No harm will she ever bring, Lord Love. She will be most cautious, tis true always."

"O. K." Tinker nodded. And looked at Smoke. "Go ahead. Take a look."

J. C. suddenly burst out. "What are you talking about? What is all this nonsense about magic and peering into him. What do you mean. What are you guys talking about?"

Tinker frowned at his friend. "Shhhh, J. C., be quiet. I will explain later. But for right now, just stand there and watch. Maybe we can find out what is killing him."

J. C. stared at Tinker, then he stepped around and stared at Smoke.

Smoke walked past him and stood next to the side of the bed and leaned over, close to Hard's head. She spoke softly. "He has been on a very strange journey."

Hard began to twist and turn, mumbling.

She turned, light flashing off the mirrored lens of her sunglasses. "Messenger, take that ring."

J. C. snatched it from Tinker's hands in one lightning move and clenched his fist. "No way, that is enough of this. Let's get out of here."

Smoke shoved her sunglasses up over her forehead as Fair Morn slipped up behind J. C., grabbed his upper arms and lifted him off the floor. J. C.'s feet dangled, not touching.

"**HEY!**" shouted J. C.

"**SMOKE! FAIR MORN!**" snapped Tinker. "**STOP IT!**"

Smoke stepped around Tinker and stood in front of the still dangling and very surprised J. C. and spoke to Tinker, "He is one of your best of friends and should be told. We can not stay hidden from your friends in this land forever." She pushed the sunglasses further back, nestling them in her thick black hair.

"Set him down," she said.

Fair Morn slowly lowered J. C. to the floor but retained her grasp on his arms.

Smoke stared into his eyes. "I am stronger and quicker than you are J. C. And she is even stronger. Messenger must have that ring. Look at my eyes."

J. C. gasped, and stared at her. "My god, I do not believe it."

Two orange gold eyes stared at him, the black pupils vertical slits in the bright sunlight streaming into the room. Then, for just a moment, he thought he saw staring at him the face of a gigantic creature covered in thick black fur. The face had a long dog-like snout and great protruding canines. But the eyes were the same. Then all he saw was Smoke, a very pretty young woman with very alien eyes.

She smiled at him. "I am MindMate to John Tinker. As are the Princess Chicken, Messenger, and Fair Morn. We mean no harm to your friend. Or to you. However, we must have that ring. Give it to Messenger, please."

Dazed by what he saw, or thought he saw, J. C. handed over the ring.

Messenger took it. "It is a powerful thing." She walked around to the side of the bed and pulled one of Hard's arms free of the blanket and slipped the ring on a limp finger.

Smoke stepped to her side and bent over.

Messenger whispered to her.

Then Smoke spoke to Hard. "Call her name, Hard, call her name!" She pushed at his mind, and repeated her instructions.

Smoke waited. And repeated the process.

Messenger quickly backed away.

Hard's face twitched. His eyes rolled, his face twitched. Then he whispered something. His tongue licked his lips. His head flopped from side to side.

"Again," demanded Smoke.

"Ramp."

"One more time. **LOUDER!**"

"**RAMP!**"

Messenger lunged, shoving Smoke away from the bed and against the wall. "Back, back, back!"

Chicken jumped toward the door.

Tinker shoved J. C. sideways against the chest and the wall.

Fair Morn leaped and snatched Messenger into a far corner.

A wisp of smoke was curling up from the bare wood floor at the foot of the bed. It was black. Dense, thick, black. Oily. It swirled and eddied, spinning upward into a heavy column that twisted around and around. The stuff was all soft billows, sucking in and out, defining something inside.

"What the hell is that?" demanded J. C.

"**CALL HER NAME!**" urged Smoke.

Hard's head snapped back as he screamed, "**RAAAAAAAAAAAMP!**" The smoke solidified and shimmered, and shifted, shape and form.

Then it quick dissipated, seeping into a tall individual, dressed in a bulky, thick, travel worn and badly stained black robe. The arms slowly rose and shook the sleeves back allowing slender hands to reach up and throw the hood back.

"I knew you could do it, pretty," she said, then stared at the figure on the bed, gasped, and ran to his side, throwing herself down next to him, kneeling at the side of the bed.

"Husband, what has happened, what has happened to you?"

Looking up, she glared at the others in the room. Slowly she rose to her feet, her face contorting with rage. Stark force gathered in the room, electrical crackling echoed from the walls.

"Husband?" J. C. stared at her.

She stared at them. "What have you done to him?" Her menace was total.

Smoke disappeared.

Ramp smiled in her direction. "You can't hide from me, mindshifter."

Smoke reappeared. And stated, "MindMate, this is Ramp, Hard's wife."

Messenger nodded and stated, "She is a powerful magician. Really really!"

J. C. stared from one to the other. Nothing he was seeing or hearing was making all that much sense. Not to him, it wasn't. Not at all. Not even a little bit.

Ramp pointed at Tinker. "For the evil deed done to my husband, you die."

Messenger's hand shot up her left sleeve.

Tinker's harsh whisper stopped her motion. "**NO!**" He was watching Hard's face.

Messenger pulled her hand back. "But, MyTinker?"

"Ramp, stop," rasped Hard.

Ramp turned. The crackling faded away.

Hard flickered a weak smile as he whispered harshly. "These people are my friends. She," he feebly indicated Smoke, "saved my life by making me bring you back." Tears were trickling down his cheeks.

Ramp slipped to his side again, kissed the tears away, and began to murmur to him.

Tinker turned and threw open the door to the hall, "Ah, perhaps it would be best if we all waited downstairs." And stepped to one side.

Chicken slipped into the hall.

Smoke grabbed J. C.'s arm and yanked him with her.

Fair Morn crowded after them.

Messenger stepped out, then Tinker pulled the door

closed, and followed the group downstairs.

"I'll tell his mother he has pulled out of it. And that he is not to be disturbed until he comes down. We can all wait out on the lawn."

As they clattered through the main hallway on the ground floor, Chicken herded everyone toward the front door, including J. C.

"My Lord," she said, "we will await thy pleasure in fair shady glen yonder." She pointed out toward a grassy patch almost encircled by large trees framed by the now open door.

"I will only be a little bit," said Tinker, entering the parlor. He had heard it, ever so faintly. A door closed upstairs. As he closed the parlor door, Hard's mother said, "I made some tea for everyone, John. Are you leaving already?"

He shook his head and smiled. "Ah, no, we're not. We are just going to sit outside on the grass for a while. I'll get a tray from the kitchen and carry everything outside."

He pointed toward the door. "Ummm, Hard is coming down. I think he'll want to talk with you. We will just be out there."

He hurried, before she had a chance to say anything, into the kitchen and carried tea pot, cups, and cookie platter, on a large serving tray, out the back door and around to where the rest had settled down. The curls of steam drifted upward from the spout of the tea pot.

The spot that Chicken had selected was large and mostly encircled by tall pine trees creating a wonderful sense of privacy. The grass was thick and well mown. Through one artfully arranged gap they could see the house across another large open space of recently cut grass.

Fair Morn eyed the cookies as Tinker arranged things, before sitting down. He cautioned her, with a light tap on the back of one of her hands. "Just take two. Smoke?"

"He is recovering rapidly."

"How do you know that?" demanded J. C.

Smoke turned to face him, she had her sunglasses back

on. "Because I am telepathic."

"Come on." J. C. snorted loudly.

"MindMate?"

Tinker sighed, and looked at the incredulous expression on J. C.'s face and said to Smoke, "Oh, well, you might as well. He wouldn't believe anything that I tell him. Go ahead, convince him."

Smoke looked inside, and said, "Amazing. There are few minds like this in any world."

"I'd be surprised if there were," replied Tinker, pouring the tea.

Chicken reached over and handed J. C. a cup of tea. "Sugar?" He took the cup and watched Smoke very carefully. And shook his head.

Messenger handed him a cookie. "Don't worry, she won't hurt you." She smiled at him. She still had her sunglasses on. "Really really!"

J. C. stared at them. "What are you people talking about?"

"He is writing a book," said Smoke. "The manuscript is kept on a computer disc labeled 'Keep Out'."

J. C. choked on cookie crumbs and hastily swallowed a mouthful of tea. "No one knows that, no one."

"We do, now," giggled Messenger.

"Kitten. Whish," cautioned Chicken.

Messenger ducked her head.

Fair Morn smiled gently at J. C.

"Ahhhhh, J. C.," said Tinker. "Don't pay too much attention to them. They tend to get a little rowdy."

He refilled his tea cup and grabbed another cookie, whacking Fair Morn's hand at the same time.

"Leave some. Hard and his wife might like a few."

Hard and Ramp were walking slowly across the front lawn toward them. She held one of his arms, steadying the still somewhat wobbly Hard.

"How can that be his wife," whispered J. C. as he stared

at them. "Tinker, drive me home. My mind's crumbling."

"No, it is not," stated Smoke. She looked over at Tinker who was beginning to look worried as he watched J. C. "For him," she explained, "it is just momentary disbelief. He will recover rapidly. Also."

"Oh, my," said Messenger. "She is very pretty. So is he. MyTinker, are all your friends so fine and handsome?"

She smiled at J. C.

"I don't think so," mumbled Tinker.

Messenger's hand flew to her mouth, her eyes rounded in surprise. She quickly leaned close to Tinker and whispered harshly. "She is not all there."

"What ?"

"Crazy, crazy, crazy," said J. C.

Her magic is bent, said Messenger inside Tinker's mind.

"Now what's going on?" He knew it was a rhetorical question, but he had to ask anyway.

As the pair met the group, Hard eased himself into a sitting position near Tinker. Ramp smoothly settled next to Hard.

"Hi, Tinker," said Hard, smiling at him. "Thanks." Then he nodded at J. C. "Hello, J. C. You catching the flu, you don't look so good?"

"Glad we could do something," said Tinker. "Hard, you know Chicken and Smoke. This is Messenger and Fair Morn."

"I am Ramp," said Ramp, by way of introducing herself.

"My wife," added Hard, slipping one arm inside one of her's. "My mother took it amazingly well. Although she did stare, just for a moment, at her clothes."

Ramp's robe was now spotless and new looking.

"What's wrong with her clothes?" whispered Messenger to Smoke.

"Not many people around here wear robes like that," answered Hard. "Actually, no-one does. More tea, Miss?" He reached for Messenger's cup, knocking his own over in the process.

Tinker laughed. "Fully recovered."

"I will take care of that, Husband," said Ramp. The spill faded away, the tea pot steamed as it refilled. The platter was reheaped with cookies.

Messenger yanked off her sunglasses to look more closely at Ramp, then at her hands. "It is your rings."

Ramp stared back at her and peered closely at Messenger's eyes and gasped.

"Ramp?" asked Hard.

"Husband, she is . . ."

Hard stared quickly from his wife to Messenger and back. "What?"

Ramp's voice fell to a low whisper. "I do not know."

J. C. stared to laugh. They all turned to stare at him.

"All right, all right," he said, waggling a cookie at them. "Now I understand. This is all some kind of a big joke at my expense. You guys must have been practicing long and hard. So I have been bambozzled."

"Bambozzled?" whispered Messenger to Smoke.

Smoke shrugged.

"Ahhhhhh," said Tinker, before anyone else could start talking. "This is going to be rather difficult for you to understand."

"And we haven't been fooling you," interjected Hard. "Or anything."

"Pon my word," stated Chicken firmly.

J .C. looked at Tinker, then at Hard. He frowned. "You want to explain that?"

Hard took Ramp's hand and said to her, "J. C. and Tinker are my best and long time friends. And these ladies are friends of Tinker's."

"More than friends," stated Messenger.

Hard looked at her. "What?"

"What, what?" replied Messenger.

"Husband," cautioned Ramp.

"What? OH!" He blushed. Then he smiled at them all,

and asked, "Do you have time?"

"For what?" asked Tinker, chuckling at his own 'what'.

"For me to tell you a story, at least as much as I remember. About how I came to be married, things like that there."

"Sure," said J. C. "Why not?" He was ready to be entertained.

Tinker nodded.

"No interruptions, then. O.K.?" Hard looked from one to the other.

"Right," said Tinker, stretching out, flat on the grass, his head cradled in Fair Morn's lap. She brushed the hair from his forehead.

Smoke sprawled flat and dropped her head on Tinker's stomach.

"OOOOF!"

"It all began about a week ago," said Hard.

"A week ago?" J. C. stared at Ramp. He knew she hadn't been in town a week ago or ever. His grapevine would have known. It was a small town, after all.

"J . C., please?"

"Sorry."

"Well," said Hard. "I decided to take a short hike, just for the afternoon, up on the ridge, the one behind Tinker's place and there I met . . . "

Hard told them of his encounter with Mirf, the hob-goblin, how he met Ramp, and everything that had happened that he could remember, until he returned. Most of his memories remained pretty vague.

But he remembered clearly that one event, the horror of seeing Ramp die.

They had been walking down the trail, well behind Mirf and the rest of the party. Hard had turned to look back up the slope. He pointed, and asked, "What's that?"

A small black dot was hurtling through the air,

following the path, singing a single high-pitched note.

Ramp looked, gasped and shoved Hard behind herself, spinning him around, and screamed, "**NO WARNING, NO WARNING. TOO LATE, TOO LATE.**"

As Hard spun around he heard it, that dull thump and Ramp's gasp.

She turned to look at him, a stricken expression on her face. A glistening wet splotch was creeping across the front of her dark robe.

Staring past Hard, she told their companion, "Mirf has powerful enemies. Run and warn the advance party."

Then she slowly sank to her knees, and whispered to Hard, "Hold me, Pretty, fore we part."

Hard dropped to the ground and wrapped her in his arms, moaning deep in his throat.

She gently pushed him back and smiled weakly, pointing at the stain on his clothes. "Don't worry about the mess, husband, it will all fade away. As will I."

He slumped. "Can't we do anything?"

She shook her head. "It was a magical thing. And there is nothing that I can do . . . now. Just hold me for these few short remaining moments."

Her voice grew stronger, more urgent. "You must tell your helper friends of this. They must know."

"There are no others here."

"Just listen to me and at the correct time do as I say!" She pushed at his chest and sat back, a last difficult movement.

"Don't," cried Hard.

"Yes, I must." She began to twist rings from her fingers and hand them to him. "Here. Put these in your pockets . . . don't tell Mirf . . . just remember . . ." And she instructed him in what and when and where to do the necessary thing.

He took the rings and shoved them deep into one trouser pocket without looking. The red stone flashed.

Ramp smiled one sly smile at him. "There pretty one . . . that is that. One kiss . . . " She leaned forward and gently brushed her lips over his.

He felt the tingle run over his body. And then the robe collapsed and became an empty heap.

He stood, turned away, and screamed.

And screamed.

And screamed.

Ramp clenched his arm tightly and poured a calm spell over him. And felt him relaxing as the painful memories were pushed away.

J. C. poured himself another cup of tea and sipped quietly and watched Hard's face.

The tea pot never seemed to empty. He ate another cookie from the never diminishing pile. "I don't believe it."

"We do," said Chicken.

Messenger leaned forward and gently reached out to place the tip of a finger on one of Ramp's rings. "Yes. Certainly Big Red."

Ramp jerked her hand away.

"I don't like this," grumbled Tinker.

"MindMate?" asked Smoke.

"It is Big Red again. He is up to something."

"Nay, Me'Lord, tis mere coincidence." Chicken shook her head.

"Humbug," stated J. C.

"Right," agreed Tinker.

Messenger looked at the lawn and began to part the closely clipped stems with her fingertips. "Where?"

Smoke reached over and jabbed her in the ribs with one fingertip.

"**OUCH**, Mom."

"O.K.," said Tinker, ignoring them, He sat up, looked at the rest of himself. *Well gang?*

Yes, they all replied.

"This will take a while, it is a long, long story. But I'll shorten it. And," he glanced over at J. C., "it will satisfy your curiosity about these four beauties."

He smiled at Hard and Ramp. "And by the way, we have already met Willawa and Ripple. They are both hale and hardy."

Hard and Ramp smiled at the news.

"You guys are all going bug-nuts," commented J. C.

"Listen, and judge for yourself," said Tinker. Then he told his story.

They sat near the destruction that had been the place of Dram, The Evil One. All of Tinker's companions on this quest sat nearby.

Smoke and Chicken joined him, Smoke sitting on one side, Chicken on the other. And then Smoke explained how among her folk, the Velvetmist, females would join with a male and begin building a new group. She and Chicken had talked and had decided to do this. And they had both felt that his love for them would allow this. And then, Smoke did it, joined their minds into a single multi-bodied being.

And in a different place, much, much later in time, he told how when he woke from a state of exhaustion, he had found that Smoke and Chicken had joined Messenger to them. Messenger's mind had been collapsing from a massive fear reaction to them. Her tribe had many, many tales that told of demons and monsters that consumed The Messengers. And Tinker, Smoke, and Chicken had fit her tales. Chicken had agreed that it was the only way to save her. So Smoke had worked faster than was normal and Messenger became them. But something had happened. In her haste Smoke had done something unknown. And it had altered Messenger in ways they were still learning about.

And then, not long after, Messenger had broken the magical bonds linking Fair Morn to Big Red because she had felt sorry for her. And this had transformed Fair Morn from a magical jest to an alive being. And, after much argument on the part of Tinker, Fair Morn had become them.

Then he told them of all the other beings they had met and a number of the things that they had done.

When he finished, Tinker stood and stretched and looked around at the silent audience.

Hard smiled.

J. C. looked fairly blank.

Ramp was staring at Smoke.

"What's the matter?" asked Tinker.

Ramp pointed at Smoke. "There have been rumors of her race, but no one has ever traveled there, and no one believed that it could be true. And you," she pointed at Tinker, "are Legend. The Chosen One."

"That's me all right." The corners of Tinker's mouth jerked wryly. "Hard, what do you think?"

"I am certainly glad we are friends."

"Crazy as bed bugs, one and all," said J. C. Then he smiled. "But that's all right, guys, I like you anyway."

Tinker glanced over at Smoke. "Where is Hard's mother?"

"In back of the house, weeding her garden."

"O. K., this place is private, we can't be seen by anyone from the street. It is time to convince J. C. of our truth, such as it is. Right? You do need convincing, don't you?"

J.C. nodded. "You betcha. But you don't really have to try, we're still friends." He took another cookie.

"Smoke, anyone out there at all, who might notice us?"

"No," she said, "but be careful, his mind is beginning to jitter."

Tinker looked over, frowning. "J. C., are you sure you are all right?"

"You guys are making me nervous." J. C. wiped one hand back over his hair.

"O.K., this will be painless, but I think it will make our point." He pointed. "Fair Morn, stand over there."

She rose and walked to the indicated spot.

"Show him," said Tinker.

"One?"

"What?" asked J. C.

"It's all right. Do it."

Her great wings began to open. And open. And open. She sighed. "The sun feels good, it is so nice and warm."

The great butterfly wings pumped slowly, gently, back and forth. The many colors reflected brilliant spots in the sunshine. Rainbow dots danced across the grass and the small group of watchers.

J. C. choked and twisted around to stare at Tinker. "In my tea. You put something in my tea."

Tinker glared at him. "You know better than that."

J. C. nodded. "Right. I do. But." He twisted back to stare at Fair Morn. And whispered, "That is not possible. It is just not biologically possible."

"MindMate," snapped Smoke. "Hard's mother is coming around the house, headed our way.

"**FOLD 'EM, FOLD 'EM,**" cried Tinker.

Fair Morn did, folding and folding and folding , and sat demurely next to J. C., gently bumping his shoulder with her own. "I used to be a magical jest, remember?"

"Oh, there you are, dears. May I get you some more tea and cookies?"

The platter emptied, the tea pot stopped steaming.

"Thanks, mother," said Hard as she gathered up the tray. Tears glistened in her eyes as she looked at her son. Then she turned and hurried back to the house.

J. C. was sagging heavily, his face quite pale.

Fair Morn wrapped an arm around his shoulders. And kissed his cheek. "But now I am a real person."

"How can you do that? Have wings? Put 'em up, put 'em down?"

Fair Morn shook her head. "Just the way I was made. Ever ask anyone how they wiggle their fingers?"

"SMOKE?" asked Tinker, carefully watching J. C.'s face.

"He is making a rapid adjustment. Really an unusual mind in there."

"Hard to believe, Tinker, hard to believe," mumbled J. C. as he stared up through his eyebrows at Tinker. Slowly he straightened up.

Fair Morn released him.

He winked at her. "You didn't have to let go."

"I think you need something stronger than tea," suggested Tinker.

"Right," said J. C., nodding agreement.

"Here," said Ramp, handing J. C. a small, dust-covered clay bottle. She had fetched it from somewhere. "It is a restorative."

J. C. took the jug, tipped it up, and took a big swallow. His eyes bugged out, his face flushed red, sweat erupted and ran in rivulets down his face. He gasped. "I'll say."

Tinker looked at his wristwatch and stood. "I've, we've, got to get back home. How about we all have dinner, later? At my place? O.K.?"

Hard looked at Ramp, who said, "Of course. Husband, did you not promise me?"

Hard blushed. "Sure. Seven?"

"Right," said Tinker. "J. C.?"

J. C. stood. "I'll be there." He started for his van, turned and waved goodbye to everyone. Then he walked away. He only wobbled a little.

The van drove slowly down the driveway. J. C. leaned sideways, heavily, one arm propped on top of the open window.

After saying goodbye to Hard's mother, thanking her for cookies and tea, Tinker and the four piled into their pickup and drove slowly down the driveway, waving gaily at Ramp and Hard. All four of them did, Tinker had both hands tightly gripping the wheel.

"I am not going anywhere. You guys are not going anywhere. We are staying at home!"

"My Lord, fret thee not." Chicken nibbled on his ear until an upraised shoulder stopped her.

"Right," said Tinker. He had already begun to worry. And they all knew it.

"Let's get some tacos," suggested Smoke.

"A little snack," added Fair Morn. "On the way home. Just to carry us to dinner." She nudged Smoke. "I will help cook dinner."

Grandeville. Tinker's place. Early Evening.

Dinner had ended.

Master Chen had ordered Chinese. One of his restaurant staff had brought the many course meal out to Tinker's house. It was a celebration for Hard's marriage. It had saved much work, cooking such a big meal for such a big group. Fair Morn thanked him.

Now they all sat around in the living room, pleasantly stuffed, very relaxed, sipping on some of Doc's premium liqueurs. J. C. had brought several bottles, saying that Doc was happy to hear that Hard had settled down, gotten married and all that.

"Tinker?" asked Hard.

"Umm?" Tinker was taking a sip and holding it in his mouth just to savor the taste.

"Ah, isn't it awfully crowded?"

Tinker swallowed. "We are going to start remodeling tomorrow. The contractors start then. I decided that it was faster to do it that way. However, we are going to do the painting and final details ourselves. And they want to plant a large vegetable garden behind the dojo and Messenger wants a large flower bed along the side of the rear deck."

"I forgot to tell you," said J. C. "There is a big slump out in the great depression just past your near pasture. What with all the excitement when you arrived and everything, it slipped my mind. Chen and I saw it just before you came back." He hesitated, then added, "The last time."

Tinker and Hard both looked over at J. C. Nothing ever slipped from J. C.'s mind.

He grinned back at them and shrugged his shoulder. "Well, I just didn't think it was all that important. Now, hearing the stories that I have heard, I guess that it is."

"What stories, Nephew?" asked Master Chen, looking over at Tinker.

"Ah, I'll tell you the rest tomorrow, after practice. You've already heard most of it anyway. After we are done checking out the, ah, slump. Oh, and I told the realtor that I would buy the place next door. The stuff from Macabre had better be there."

He pointed in the general direction of the place next door. "The Guard, Goose and Lady Chen can live there, if they want."

Lady Chen bowed her head to Master Chen. "Grandfather?"

Master Chen frowned. "You will be careful."

It wasn't a question, it was a command.

"Yesssss." Her final esses always came out slightly hissed.

Tinker grinned. "Right, they will all make great cowboys."

Lady Chen stood and bowed three times to Master Chen and then to Tinker. "Thisss humble one isss overwhelmed by your generosity, and your giftsss, Chosen One. When may we move?"

"Anytime. The owners had already moved to town before putting the place up for sale. They left everything behind, fully furnished."

Lady Chen smiled at Goose. "White Warrior, shall we inspect our new home?"

Goose leaped to his feet. "Indeed. Sire?"

"Good night, Goose," said Tinker.

Goose offered Lady Chen his arm. "My Lady, wouldst take small walk? The Guard will form noble escort."

"Asss you wish," answered Lady Chen, most demurely.

Chicken jumped up from the couch where she had been sitting on one side of Tinker and kissed Lady Chen and Goose on both cheeks and walked outside with them.

Those still remaining in the living room could hear Goose calling The Guard.

"Tinker?" Hard was blushing, a rather bright red.

"What ?"

"Isn't it illegal? Or something?"

"What?"

"Four of them."

Tinker suppressed his laughter. "I think I will form a corporation. They can all be stock holders and officers. Ahhhhh, and all living at headquarters. Here. But there is nothing illegal or wrong going on."

J. C. grinned. The rumor mill would go crazy. Chicken and Smoke had already raised more than a few eyebrows when escorted around town by Tinker.

J. C. cleared his throat. "Tinker, I will ask Shannon to get her husband to set up the corporation, papers, and all. After all, he relocated his company headquarters to the valley. He ought to know exactly what needs doing."

"Good idea. If he agrees, Morgan's presence will keep the nonsense to a minimum."

Tinker looked around the room. *Fair Morn?*

I am outside, One. I needed some exercise. And I am being very careful.

Chicken poked her head back through the outside, front porch door. "My Lord, We will with Our Own Brother Goose and Chen to new domicile walk. Ta, ta."

"Princess, I will walk with you, if I may." Master Chen rose and left with them.

J. C. stood. "Tinker, this has been a long, a very long, and mind-boggling day. I'll see you later. I need sleep, a whole lot of sleep."

"Night, J. C."

J. C. stopped and dropped one large hand on Hard's shoulder. "I'll get you a wedding gift if you will tell me what you want."

Hard nodded. "O.K. A couple days?"

"When ever. Night t'all." J. C. closed the door behind him.

Soon they could hear his van rattling down the driveway.

Messenger walked around, refilling their glasses, then sat next to Tinker, and whispered into his ear. "She isn't all there."

Looks all there to me. Although that bulky robe she wears makes it hard to tell.

Messenger giggled.

Ramp looked at Smoke, and asked. "Mistress Smoke, would you show me what you originally looked like?"

In the open space before them, she appeared. A great cat-like shape covered in thick light-absorbing, black fur. Her head was dropped low in order to allow her long ears to stand upright. She curled her lip, exposing rows of glistening white teeth. The canines, elongated, great daggers, curled down past her lower jaw. The prehensile long tail floated around and lightly caressed Ramp's cheek. Ramp sucked her breath in sharply.

The gigantic predator disappeared.

"I really miss my tail," said Smoke. "Of course, hands work pretty well." She threw an arm over Tinker's legs. She had been sitting on the floor against him all evening.

Messenger, sitting on the couch, half-turned and shoved an arm behind his back. Her other hand was idly playing with a button on his shirt.

"So, what are you going to do now?" Tinker's question was directed to Hard.

"Sit and relax. Why?"

Ramp nudged Hard with an elbow. "OH! I thought we would travel around, show Ramp my world, taken an extended honeymoon. Run the family business, things like that. Rest. How about you?"

"R and R, lots and lots of it. Started a new book. Got a lot of house to remodel. But mostly, rest, and peace, and quiet."

Messenger glanced quickly at Ramp, then at Tinker, and back to Ramp. Tinker didn't notice. Ramp did.

"Mistress Messenger?" asked Ramp.

"Why aren't you all there?"

"What?" Hard jerked around and frantically began searching his wife's form with his eyes.

"Messenger?" growled Tinker.

"It is all right," interjected Ramp. "She is just stating the obvious."

"What's obvious?" asked Tinker and Hard in unison.

"What?" repeated Hard, knocking his glass from the arm of the chair where he was sitting.

Smoke just watched.

A soft humming began to fill the room. Tinker leaped to his feet, spun, and glared at the far corner of the room where a great two-handed sword leaned in a dark shadow corner.

"FORGET IT," he yelled. He turned and shrugged his shoulders apologetically at Ramp. "We are not going." And dropped back onto the couch.

"I understand," said Ramp.

"We going somewhere?" asked Hard.

Ramp reached over and took one of his hands in her's, and held it very, very gently. "My husband, something, someone, interfered with my full return. We have to find a node and travel to Bahn Duhr Tohr, Willawa's domain, and visit my sister there. Ripple has the power to fix it. Else, my days are fewer than the fingers on your hands."

All the color drained from Hard's face. He swayed in his seat.

Smoke leaped up and over and held him by the shoulders.

Ramp placed her palm against his forehead.

Hard quivered. The color returned to his face. "In the morning," he mumbled. "We'll leave in the morning. It's still got to be up there, over the edge and down the back side."

He stood, pushing Smoke's hands away. "We have to leave, Tinker, ahhhhh, Ladies. Thanks for everything."

Tinker walked them out to their car, a low sporty two-seater.

"Be careful, O.K.?"

"Of course," said Hard. "I am always careful."

"Right." Tinker watched their car until the tail lights disappeared around the far bend, just before the long down grade past Doc's place, into town. Then he walked back and sat on the edge of the front porch and stared into the night.

She floated owl silent over the top of the house and settled lightly next to him. "One?" asked Fair Morn. Her wings made soft rustling sounds as they folded and folded and folded. She sat.

"I said we are not going anywhere."

"I know."

He looked at her, tears glistening in his eyes. "Then why do you think we are going to meet them, up there, on the ridge line, in the morning?"

Smoke knelt behind him and began to massage the tightness from the muscles in his neck and shoulders. She wrapped her arms around him, as he leaned back. "We will be all right."

Messenger joined them, sitting on his free side. "My Tinker, your fear for us pains us all. Please don't."

He looked at her. Tears were streaming down her cheeks.

"O.K., kitten, no more worries. We'll sleep late. And if they really need our help, I am sure they will let us know. After all, they can always give us a call before they leave Hard's house."

Fair Morn rose to her feet, her wings redeploying. "I

think I'll go next door, and see how things are going." She lifted into the air and drifted silently away.

Smoke ruffled his hair, "And I think I will go see how our land subsidence is doing. See whether Macabre really did it or not. I need the exercise."

She slipped silently into the darkness, eyes wide, pupils expanding to take in all available light, running lightly around the end of the house and out into the first pasture.

"That leaves just you and me, kitten," said Tinker.

"Oh boy," answered Messenger, slipping her hand inside his shirt.

Neither noticed the faint odor of flowers drifting softly on the night air.

Qailan the Observer lightly touched her beast as they blended into the shrubbery and wondered why the elseplace the unusual one was living in was so strange. It was really quite primitive.

Grandeville. Tinker's Place. Late At Night.

Smoke slipped into the bed, nestled up against Messenger's back, and kissed the back of her neck. "Salty."

Messenger mumbled, "Hi, mom."

"You are making waves," grumbled Tinker as the water bed roiled and gurgled.

"We just need to take the air bubbles out of it," said Smoke, heaving heavily, just to make waves and to make the bubbles gurgle.

"In the morning," said Tinker.

The water bed gave a gigantic lurch. Smoke stood up, stepped over them, and lay down next to Tinker.

"What are you doing?" he asked.

"No room on that side. You pushed her almost to the edge."

"You happy now?"

"As can be."

"Go to sleep."

"Sure." Smoke took a deep breath, exhaled slowly. And was sound asleep.

"Now," said Tinker. "Where were we?"

"You were about here."

"Here?"

"OH. Yes."

"What ?"

"Nothing . . . OH."

Tinker spun down into the green glow of Messenger's eyes, their minds blending, sharing sensations.

Dol Spar. Monetary Control Headquarters. Just Past Mid-day Meal.

"Billy be damned!"

Her fist crashed down upon the desk top. The wood thought of splitting, but it didn't.

"And other nautical expressions!"

"MIRF!"

"Sorry, General. But that is not our job."

"Some hob-goblin stayed behind, didn't it?"

Mirf grimaced, it wasn't a smile. "Yes, some hob-goblin stayed behind."

"You are the most qualified. And the most experienced."

Mirf flopped back into her chair, shoving her legs straight out.

The General admired her legs, even in trousers, even in uniform, she was someone to look at, someone to admire. And it was not just her form he checked. He looked into her face. Her eyes hadn't switched back. Hob-goblin eyes.

"Mirf. Please?"

"Raz Baz."

"I could make it an order."

"I could resign."

"It would still be an order."

"Order-schmorder."

She waggled her shoulders and threw her arms wide.

What happened under her blouse did distract the General. He sighed. Loudly.

"So, O.K.," grinned Mirf, well aware of what she was doing, of what he was watching. "I will do it. I don't know what. BUT. I will do it. Just for you."

"Take whatever you want."

"Such a deal I wouldn't wish on my enemies."

"Two turns vacation, after."

"Four."

"Three. A deal?"

"A deal."

"A deal is a deal. For three."

"All your's." She sat up.

"That one is settled, done."

"One can only hope."

"Things are stirring all over."

"How bad?"

"Many. Three agents gone, disappeared."

"Oi-vay. Free rein?"

"You have license to steal."

Mirf sat straighter and grinned. This time it was a broad smile. Hob-goblin delight.

The General winced. Then he folded his arms and leaned on them and the desk top.

"See Plans. It is already a twisted thing. We don't want it to snarl."

She jumped to her feet, saluted and turned, and grabbed the door knob. It twisted off in her hand.

With a loud hiss of breath, she slammed her hand through the door panel and jerked the handle on the other side. Stepping from the room, she twisted her head around, answered his silent question.

"Yas. Some hob-goblin stayed behind." And stomped down the hall.

The General told the orderly who ran up to stare at the damage and the rapidly departing young woman in the severe suit to get another door installed. RIGHT NOW!

And he growled into the outer office, "And whoever has those flowers can get rid of them right this instance."

Pac Lac Bac. Mid-Afternoon.

The owner of the hotel peered cautiously through the shattered doorway at the wreckage of what had been one of his best guest suites. He had told his wife that it been a very bad idea to rent anything to a pair of witches. Of course, he had added, he really had very little choice in the matter. All knew that it was very unhealthy to deny these folk whatever they asked for. And they did pay well.

From deep in all that wreckage, from one of the outer rooms someone groaned. The owner hesitated, and then hoping for the best, he carefully trod past the shattered remains of the furniture and things unknown.

In the living room he saw one of them, crumpled in a dark heap in one corner. It was the one that wore the grape and green robe. Kneeling in front of her he peered into her eyes, eyes that were just beginning to focus.

"May I be of assistance?"

Her eyes flickered from side to side and then settled on his face.

Sucking in a deep breath, he repeated his question.

"Food. And drink. Now!"

He hurried from the disaster of his rooms and once he regained the hall began to order his curious help to bring food, drink, and all the necessary accessories to those rooms.

Once all was in progress of being accomplished as ordered, he spun around and hurried back into the suite of rooms. And stopped and stared as he stood just inside the door.

Everything was as it had been. Perhaps even a little bit better.

"You may bring in the food and drink and put them here. We will sit on the balcony."

He hurried in that direction and watched that one help her dark companion out onto the balcony and to one of the chairs next to the small table.

Two servers rushed in, bearing large trays.

"Now go away," ordered that one. "We wish to be left alone for two days. Food and drink will be left at the appropriate time in the other room. Do not disturb us."

As the owner and the servers hurried away, the living room door closed itself. They heard the bolt slam shut. That door hadn't had a bolt before.

Grandeville. Tinker's Place. Late At Night.

Something cold touched their chests.

He felt Messenger jerk.

"EEEK."

"Brought you two something cold to drink. You always work up a thirst."

Tinker shifted to a sitting position and took the two bottles that Smoke pushed into his hands while Messenger squirmed around and up. Then he shoved one in her general direction. There was no moon, the bedroom was pitch black to his eyes.

"Thanks, Smoke."

A bottle gurgled on his other side. "Brought one for me too. Chicken and Fair Mom said they'd walk back from the other place in the morning. Master Chen is also staying over there to visit."

"Yum," said Messenger. "This is good."

"Canadian," said Tinker. "I can tell by the taste."

"I'll get three more," said Smoke, lurching from the bed, causing more waves. The bed gurgled at them.

"I like your home, our home," said Messenger.

"Me too."

Tinker leaned sideways.

She moved closer, gave him a kiss. And giggled.

"Smoke was right," she said. "Salty."

"Three more," announced Smoke.

"Thanks, again."

"Service with a smile." She pushed her face in front of his, nose touching nose. "See."

"Not much," said Tinker.

"Yes," said Messenger. In the pitch black of the night filled room, her eyes glowed soft green. She could see perfectly well. And they knew it. She grabbed two of the bottles and pushed one into Tinker's outstretched hand. It was no problem. To her the room was almost as bright as noon.

When they had finished, they set the bottles on the floor, under the overhanging ledge of the bed.

"Kitten," said Smoke. "I can just make you out. What are you doing?"

"Getting ready to pounce."

"OH NO, YOU DON'T," shouted Tinker. "You'll break the bladder."

"MindMate, the toilet is just down the hall."

"SMOKE. I was referring to the thing under us that is holding all the water that we are trying to sleep on top of."

"I know that."

He sighed. "Well, I gotta go down the hall anyway." He climbed over her and out of the bed and padded down the hall. They could hear him mumbling something to himself.

"Are we going to go, tomorrow?" Messenger's eyes watched Smoke.

"I don't think so."

"Hey," said Tinker, bumping into a warm body as he reentered the bed after his trip down the hall and back again. "You took my spot."

"I always sleep in the middle," answered Smoke.

"Wait'll the remodeling is done. No middle."

"For now til then, I get the middle."

"O.K., you done moving around? Ready to sleep?" He kicked the covers into shape.

"I suppose."

"You sure?"

"That tickles. I suppose." She wasn't ticklish.

"We can sleep late."

"Ahhhhh, ummm. We have a problem."

"What?"

"Bed's leaking."

"Oh my goodness," yelped Messenger, sitting up, then leaping from bed, yanking most of the covers with her. "It's wetter and wetter and wetter. Really really wet!"

There was a long, slow exhalation of breath. It was Tinker sighing.

"We can sleep in the living room, on the floor, sleeping bags and mats, and covers, and stuff." He rolled from the bed.

Then the hall light snapped on as he began to search for the sleeping bags, and mats, and covers, and the rest of the stuff in one of the hall closets.

Kragkoptar. Inside.

B'waas and Shlm, sitting, talking. About what was. Sitting and talking in the dark of the room.

"They are coming?"

"Believe so."

"Our sister had many daughters."

"As nasty a clutch of witches as could be, ever was."

"This problem is the magician."

"Last of the litter."

"Ramp?"

"Yes."

"Thought I remembered. She named R-names."

"She was being correct."

"Ranna."

"The first."

"Riz."

"Second. Dedid the Mad Magician."

"Rekel."

"Third. Prickly correct."

"Rbat."

"Fourth. She went far if one believes that tale."

"Snaggled."

"Yes."

"Ripple."

"Fifth. The worst of the lot. Rangle."

"Settled down."

"Mated Old Hanred."

"Advises The White Warrior."

"Yes. Now the Clan Head."

"Reptar."

"Sixth. Disappeared."

"A puff of smoke."

"Yes."

"Rumtah."

"Seventh. The lucky. Fought Tartook."

"Pieces everywhere. Almost as rangle as Ripple."

"Yes."

"Reep."

"Eighth. Somewhere."

"The Silent One."

"Yes."

"Rotak."

"Ninth.

"Raft."

"Tenth. Fast."

"No move see."

"R-Bar."

"Runt of the line."

"Startangled Grotz of Derry's Dung."

"Ramp."

"Twelveborn. Last."

"Magician. One of his."

"Wouldn't want that name-group anger flaring."

"Better help."

"Yes."

Grandeville. Tinker's Place. Early Morning.

Tiny Rosebud, the emissary of The Garden Gnomes, peered out from the forest, across the great open grass covered space, and stared at the house. That house was rather strange. It appeared as if it had sprouted, or grown, in some manner unknown. Or perhaps known only to the inhabitants, she supposed.

This was the correct elseplace. This she knew. It was the correct elseplace. So that structure must be the correct dwelling.

She started down the slope and out into the grass, headed for the house. The grass was tall, the Garden Gnomes were not. They were a tiny folk.

She slipped through the pasture, headed in a straight line toward her destination, only the tip of her tall, conical red hat poked up above the grass. Tiny Rosebud had an absolute sense of direction, as did all The Garden Gnomes, so there was no chance of her losing herself and her direction in the growth.

High overhead, circling, drifting, hunting an early breakfast, a hawk spotted the movement in the grass. He tucked in his wings and rocketed down, ready to snatch this large rodent. It would be the first of many that he would catch this day.

A Small Piece of Cultural Data.

Grandeville is a small, rather isolated, rural community of 8,000 population (more or less) tucked away in the mountainous corner of northeastern Oregon. It survives in a provincial unawareness of many things, being overly conscious of the ancestors who settled the place long after the westward migration brought California, Washington, Oregon, and Idaho into statehood.

The town sprawls down from "The Bench," a shallow bench along the edge of the next door mountain slope, to The Blue River, named after the color it has when the first snow melt surges from the canyon and out across the valley proper, always threatening to jump its banks and flood the surrounding farm land.

There are two newspapers published in town, a weekly and a daily (except for Sunday). The Daily, The *Grandeville News*, tends to ignore anything happening outside the edge of town. The weekly, *The Mountain View*, tends to ignore anything happening in Grandeville and prints whatever the publisher happens to feel like publishing.

Grandeville. Tinker's place. Early Morning.

Tiny Rosebud sat up and scolded the hawk. And told him that he should have known better. The hawk stood in the tall grass and apologized profusely while Tiny Rosebud waggled a finger at him. Then she waved the hawk away.

And while the hawk soared up and up and began to circle, once again searching for breakfast, Tiny Rosebud headed toward her goal.

The only mark of her passage was the one small patch of flattened grass.

Periodically she crossed over a rodent run. The hawk had explained that this was a favorite hunting area due to the large numbers of food sources running about.

As she pressed on, she noticed that this was not a cultivated field but one of wild grasses, native species that had reclaimed the field. And that these grasses were of a particularly tall variety.

Fair Morn and Chicken stepped into the living room and stared at the floor, at the tangled mass of sleeping bags, mats, covers, and stuff.

"Pears a'Us they did riot," observed Chicken.

"Did not," mumbled Tinker, yanking a blanket up and over his head.

Chicken and Fair Morn tip-toed around them and headed down the hall. In a moment, Chicken came back, knelt down and poked her head under the cover's. "Oh. Messenger."

She moved sideways. "Morning, Great Sister."

Smoke yawned and stretched, her arms reached out from under the pile, and grabbed Chicken by the waist.

"My Lord," said Chicken into Tinker's face. "Thee wert much too violent. Fair bed clothes be heaved int far corners."

He looked up into the upside down blue eyes, glittering happily at him. "I was not. The bed sprung a leak. Why are you batting those baby-blues at me like that?"

"Tis fair morn, Me'Lord."

Smoke yanked her forward, around and down.

Tinker sat up and looked at the clock on the wall. "It is only five-o-clock in the morning." He threw an arm over Chicken's waist and pinned her in place.

Fair Morn dropped on her knees behind him and ruffled his hair.

"You broke the bed"

"Stop that. I did not."

Messenger stood up, wrapped a blanket around herself toga fashion, and headed into the dining room and said back over her shoulder, "I'll make breakfast."

Smoke sat up. "I better help." She ran down the hall, calling back at them, "Shower first."

Fair Morn flopped into the vacated space, rolled onto her back and stared up at him.

"O.K.," he said. "Now what?"

Chicken looked up at him. She appeared perfectly innocent.

Fair Morn's face was blank.

Tinker decided this was all a very bad sign. Chicken couldn't look that innocent even if she was, especially when she was trying so hard to look that way.

"Sweet Prince, tis not be most proper do We but thusly query Thee?"

"Now what?" he repeated.

"Now what, spake he? Now what, spake we? It do be most Opportune as thee hast unloosed Our Verra Own belt, fumbled outrageously with Our Verra Own shirt, and even now do caress Our Verra Own soft stomach in most familiar a'manner."

Chicken craned her head around and peered at Fair Morn.

"And even as We do now watch, thee do be a'leaning pon us and do besetting that Fair Maid in fair state of dishabille. Now what, repeat We?"

"I figured to torture this innocent maid in order to get you to spill out your secret."

"My Lord," she gasped.

"Works that way in all the spy movies, Princess."

"Bad habits from horrid cinema be not thy forte."

Not horrid, interjected Smoke, speaking directly in their minds. She liked spy movies or any other movie that had lots of action.

Fair Morn wiggled and moaned dramatically. "Foul fiend."

"We will Ourself thee tell," said Chicken hastily. "Cease thy abuse of that Our Wing'd Sister!"

"Heh, heh, heh," responded Tinker.

"You really don't have to stop," whispered Fair Morn.

"O.K., speak!" demanded Tinker of Chicken.

"Me'Lord, Fair Prince, Terrible Warrior, Abuser of the Innocent, We did think to prepare ourselves for Great Journey with thy Noble Friend and his Magical Bride."

"**NO! NOPE! NO WAY! NO HOW!**"

"T'was but a'passing thought, Our Most Negative a'speakin' Prince."

"Just let it pass, Princess."

"He is your good friend," offered Fair Morn.

"Our good friend," corrected Chicken.

"Enough," stated Tinker bluntly.

"My Lord?"

"I will make you a deal, Royal Meddler."

"Be what manner of deal do this?" Chicken hitched

herself closer to him, suddenly very cautious.

Smoke came from the hall and Messenger drifted from the kitchen to listen in person. Smoke dripped water onto the floor.

"We stay home, right here. We don't stick our collective nose in their business. Ramp is very capable and Hard has previously undetected attributes."

"And?" prompted Chicken, ever more cautious.

"And, if they need help, we'll do it. But not until then. We have a house to expand and rebuild. I have a book to finish. There may be a fortune to manage, if Macabre really stuck all that treasure out in our meadow like he said he was going to do. O.K.?" He pinched her.

Chicken frowned. And twitched.

"One?" asked Fair Morn.

"Yassss?"

"How will they ask for help?"

"Beat's me. But, judging from the way we have been dragged into things before, I am really and truly confident that if the need should arise, we are going to get the message loud and clear, all right."

"Be thee certain pon this, Sweetling?" Chicken tickled him back.

"As certain as anything we have done to date."

"Ummmm," she said, trapping his arm.

He gave her a gentle squeeze. "When's breakfast?"

"Five minutes," announced Smoke, hurrying away.

Messenger began to set the table in the dining room.

Grandeville. Sharp Ridge. Early Morning.

"And if I remember correctly," Hard was saying as he stared around at the open space on either side of the trail.

"It was just here, where, and when, I first met Mirf. Down that way should be where node is located." He pointed over the edge toward the west.

Ramp was swinging his arm back and forth, enjoying

the walk.

The ridge wasn't exactly as Hard remembered it. The rock tower was missing. And the path didn't seem to meander quite the way it had. But on the backside there was a path pitching steeply downward.

Hard pointed toward the bottom hidden from sight by the trees and stated, "Down there should be the woods that Mirf and I walked through to reach the Gold and Silver Portals. The Keeper was down there. I had to give it something first. It liked my trail bar."

He patted his jacket, over a bulging pocket. "I brought several."

"Husband?"

Hard looked at her and explained, "The Super, New and Improved, Ever Lasting, Granola Trail Bar."

Ramp slipped her arms around him. "Hold me, Lovely."

"As used on Mt. Everest." He did. "What's wrong?"

"Nothing."

"Oh."

"We have to go to Bahn Duhr Tohr."

"I know, that is what you said."

"It was a good idea to tell your friend, John Tinker, of how we met. Otherwise he wouldn't have told us of his experiences. If he hadn't, we wouldn't have known where to find Ripple. Nor would we have known that he was The Chosen One of Legend."

"Well, I would never have guessed that he had been doing all those things out there. But it certainly explains why he puts up with all the gossip about living with Chicken and Smoke."

"And now he has Messenger and Fair Mom," added Ramp. Her lips brushed over his lightly. "Did I tell you that the ladies of my clan are most protective and jealous, and that you shouldn't try to emulate your friend."

"You did." He blushed. "And I wouldn't do that."

She pinched his side. "Let's get to the bottom of this

slope and see if The Keeper is still around."

"Sure," he said. He was caressing her hair.

"Let's go."

"What?" Hard looked surprised.

"All mine," said Ramp, stepping back and turning him in the correct direction in one smooth motion. "Down the slope, Husband."

They carefully stepped their way down the steep trail as it switched back and forth, down and down, into darkness, into dim wet forest.

Ramp watched Hard, carefully. This was no place for slipping and stumbling over small things under foot. Or not under foot.

Soon they could begin to see the meadow down below.

Hard stopped and stared around them.

"Beauty?"

"This isn't working." He pointed at the trees closest to them. "See?"

"The trees?"

"Yes."

"Look like trees to me."

Hard's foot slipped. He had been kicking idly at a stone on the path. He grabbed a small sapling to keep his balance. "That is the problem."

He watched the rock bounce down the hill and finally stop, wedging itself in a small thicket of brush.

"That is the problem?"

Hard scuffled his boot, digging a small foot hold in the path.

"Yes."

Ramp stepped close and brushed a few errant strands of hair from his forehead. "Why is there a problem with our surroundings looking like they do?"

"Because when I came this way before, with Mirf, the forest changed as we walked lower. It became a dark, dank, twisted thing, with eyes and things peering out at us."

"I see."

Hard's head snapped right and left. "Where?"

Ramp gave him a gentle shove forward. "Let's go look around in the meadow."

Hard started to respond, stopped, slid forward on another loose stone, stopped, and looked around. Then he began to walk, very carefully down the slope. To the meadow.

At the bottom, they paused and then walked out into the middle, the more or less center of it.

Hard wandered a bit and found the area where Mirf had torn up the turf. The hob-goblin's claw marks were still visible.

He pointed. "See, that is from Mirf."

Ramp sat on a fallen tree, the trunk a gray silver, the bark having fallen away long ago.

Hard came over and sat next to her.

"Sit and wait," said Ramp.

"I am," answered Hard.

She slipped an arm around his waist.

"And waiting," said Hard.

They did.

They waited.

A chipmunk cast a quick peek at them from a nearby pine. Forest birds dithered from tree to shrub and back again.

"Ho, hum," said Hard. He tugged her against his side.

"Do you smell flowers?" she asked.

"No."

She leaned her head on his shoulder.

"Awfully bulky robe."

"I must be properly dressed to travel in these lands we head toward."

"Inflexible custom, no doubt." He half turned toward her.

"As you know."

Suddenly she sat up, pushing his hand away, gently.

"It is here. Somewhere."

Hard looked here and there. "It what? Who?"

Loud grunting came from one side of the meadow. Slowly it approached them. Nothing was visible. The chipmunk bolted for shelter in another tree. The birds scattered, chattering loudly. At something.

"I think that sounds like The Keeper," said Hard.

A large round blob materialized, or rather, appeared.

It had been there all along.

Now it became visible.

"Last time," said Hard. "Mirf kicked it."

The mound twitched, began to change shape. A head appeared, and spoke to them. "That will not be necessary, thank you."

A second head appeared, it smiled at the first head, then at Hard and Ramp. It took a second look at Hard. "You again."

Then it winked at Ramp. "Pretty, pretty, pretty."

Hard kicked at it. It was too far away. His violent motion caused him to slip from the log and flop to the ground.

"You part hob-goblin?" asked the first head. The Keeper was now human appearing down to the waist.

"Course not," said Hard. He stood and brushed bits and pieces of leaves from his backside. "We need to use the node."

"Cost ya," said head one.

"Yah, cost ya," said head two.

"Shhhhhh," said one. Two stuck its tongue out at one and grimaced.

"I brought some trail bars," said Hard. He pulled them from his pocket. "One for each of you."

They grabbed for the bars. And missed. The legs weren't quite finished and Hard was standing just beyond reach.

Hard yanked his hands back. "Where's the way out?"

Both heads swiveled back and forth. "Around here someplace," said one.

"You want to try the Gold and Silver Portals again, I suppose," said two.

Ramp stepped up to Hard's side. "No. All we wish is a node. To take us to Bahn Duhr Tohr."

"That all?" asked one.

"Cost two trail bars," said two, its eyes squinted almost shut.

The arm on that side pointed. "There it is, over there."

A large pool of water shimmered in the sunlight. A large bubble floated to the surface and popped.

"Urp," said the pool.

"That is the node?" gasped Hard. "It just belched."

"Certainly," said head one. "It just isn't very well mannered."

The Keeper walked over to the edge of the pool on just finished feet. The arm on the other side pointed at the glistening surface.

"Right through there, two passages to Bahn Duhr Tohr."

"For two trail bars," said head two, smacking its lips.

Hard placed one trail bar in each hand.

Ramp took his right hand and tugged him to the edge of the pool.

The water sloshed back and forth.

"Give our regards to that nasty witch," cried both heads as Ramp and Hard stepped into the pool

Clear Bandler. Tripple. Plum Duff's Home. Early Morning.

She leaned forward and wiped the sweat from his brow.

"You are all mine, my dear $1.98."

He nodded and reached up, his fingers lightly stroking, his palms gently touching.

"Smooth, smooth."

"You always say that." She let her full weight press against his hands.

"OHHHH . . . that is nice."

"You always say that." He lowered her toward his chest. "Always say that."

They forgot everything but each other.

Much later, he gently tickled her ribs.

"Ummm?" She shoved her arms under her chin and peered into his eyes.

"Duff, don't worry."

"You are leaving."

"I don't know."

"I am coming with you. This time, I am coming with you."

"Maybe I am not going anywhere. Except over to Pratville for a show tomorrow."

"I feel it."

"Me too." He grinned.

"Not that. Ummmmmmmm. The Guild. I have been hearing things. Think they will return?"

"Probably not. They don't know how to move from here to there."

"I will pack. OHHHHHH. Later."

Two suitcases floated from the closet and drifted into the room and across the floor, skimming a few inches above the thick rug. They stopped next to the pair.

"Tell them to go away. I do not like being watched. Except by you."

He waggled his arm at them. "Back. We don't need you, yet."

The bags drifted back to the closet, jostling each other to be first through the opening.

"Close the door," she said.

The door slammed shut.

"OOF," she said.

Grandeville. Tinker's Place. Early Morning.

Tiny Rosebud, the Garden Gnome Emissary, strolled

through the tall meadow grass headed back toward the dwelling of the one to whom she was supposed to plead the Garden Gnome's case.

She had been visiting the three green houses of the nearest neighbor. She had admired the great variety of cacti and succulents being grown in them. She had avoided the gigantic caretaker as he went about his business. In fact, she had spent three days, mostly in the green houses, and had noted the others who also dwelled in the nearby sprawling residence.

Now, however, she was headed back to that other one's house to see whether he and his band had returned. And as she strolled through the tall meadow grass, having easily slipped through the fence, she kept checking the clear blue sky overhead for that hawk. She wasn't sure that he would remember what she had told him and she didn't want to be knocked over again.

As she approached the house, having carefully edged around the barn, telling the chickens to stay calm, Tiny Rosebud stopped and stared. That place was teeming with activity.

A great number of men were building, or rebuilding, the entire side of the house. And the flower bed was being redone and greatly enlarged. Glancing past the smaller building she could see that the vegetable plot was also being made larger.

Walking into that turmoil was no place for a small Garden Gnome, especially one as small as Tiny Rosebud. So she headed across the pasture for the forested slope. She would wait there until enough quiet had settled over that place. Then she would make her approach and make her plea.

Space. 20.08.00.09 ARX. In Ship's Notation.

The heavy set figure strode into the room, rolling from side to side. One arm was thrown around the waist of a young woman whose skin glistened soft burnished silver tones in the dim light.

"A small snack," she said.

He kissed her on the cheek. "I shall be happy to die in your arms."

Turning, she smiled and rubbed his stomach. "I was referring to your favorite."

"Fallen to second place. Now."

He enfolded her in his arms and smiled. It was a real smile, a rare thing. For him.

"Can't have your stomach growling at inopportune times."

"A much reduced stomach."

"Much healthier."

"I shall die from healthy."

"We monitor your vital signs always. There is no danger."

"Even?"

"Even."

"Is that kind of voyeurism necessary?"

"Of course. Wouldn't want you to expire in process."

"Better there than facing some low-life."

She rubbed against him, slowly, and suggested, "Let us have a snack."

"You'll warp my already warped mind."

Turning away, she tugged gently on one of his arms and led him to the table, already set with two places.

He settled into his chair.

Standing behind him, she massaged his thick shoulder and neck muscles.

"You are looking younger."

"In truth," he said through a mouth full of doughnut, "I do. In your hands I look like my old self. Speaking of which, how are those things we picked up from MacVey integrating."

"The computer spoke a strange dialect, but we can now speak to it. Those things were mainly data on the surrounding star clusters. There are at least three potential customers there."

He chuckled and rubbed his hands together.

"Good, good. Nothing like a little mayhem, chaos and carnage to make a man feel young again."

She sat next to him. "We need to talk."

He shoved the platter over. "Have a doughnut. About what?"

"Sensors are picking up strange disturbances. Our current heading is taking us in their general direction."

"Threatening?"

"Not yet."

"The new tool worked extremely well."

"Nearly created a black hole when it fired."

He beamed. "But it didn't. We could always change direction."

"A little." She bit a doughnut. "One of those customers is not far off the line."

"HO, ho, ho, ho, ho. A big job?"

"Half a continent, no more."

"Small thing. Let's do it. Just for fun." His eyes gleamed. He smiled. There was no warmth or humor in that look.

She wrapped her arm around his. "You mentioned something about Rampa Four?"

He surged to his feet, pulling her up with him. "We will need ample room."

She grinned. "Next, through that door. Ample with soft surfaces and soft and comfortable thick floor coverings."

A door slid open. Gentle golden light slipped out, soft music beckoned.

She nudged him that way, tugging his shirt loose as they walked.

Hissing softly, the door closed behind them.

The great spacecraft gently changed direction.

Grandeville. Tinker's place. Mid-Afternoon.

Tinker stepped back and arched his back, stretching and groaning.

Dropping the paint brush into the water-filled bucket, he turned and gazed around, at the room, and at a job well done. It had been a many week project, now successfully completed. That included the vegetable garden and the flower beds.

"**DONE**," he announced. "**IT IS DONE**," he called. "**LET'S GET SOMETHING TO EAT**."

"**SHOWER**," yelled a voice from one of the upper rooms.

"**FOOD!**" responded a voice from a lower, deeply recessed space on the main floor.

"Pounce," whispered a soft voice in his ear as she wrapped her arms around his waist and pressed herself against his back, and gasped, "OH . . . my."

"What ?"

"I stepped into your paint tray."

"Let go and do not move."

She released him.

He stepped away and turned to see. And began to laugh.

"It is not funny," she grumbled.

"Don't move. Stay there. We don't want brown footprints on the new floor."

A lithe figure clambered down a tall ladder and dropped lightly to the floor. She had blotches of light blue paint everywhere.

"Prithee, My Love, say what manner of jest do thee be a'playing enow?"

"It is not a jest," grumbled Tinker.

"How long do I have to stand like this?" asked Messenger. She seemed to be covered with green lines and swirls.

Tinker looked up just in time to see Fair Morn leap from one balcony to the next and slide down the ladder, facing outward. She walked over and stared down at the foot in the paint tray. Then she looked up and over at Tinker, who had draped one arm over Chicken's shoulders.

"One, why is she standing in the paint?"

"I am hungry," announced Smoke as she came from behind a curved section of wall, carrying paint bucket and brush. She obviously had been working with a light grey.

Fair Morn had a streak of rose across her cheek and two large patches of the same color on the front of her shirt. The shirt was one of Tinker's old ones.

"What did you do," he asked, pointing at the blotches.

"Bumped into the wall."

"My Lord, did We Ourself not say she do protrude most dramatically?"

His hand swung. "And how did this get so blue, so wet with blue?"

"We did Us bend forward for to peer most closely at some small defect. And thus did We plunge sweet anatomy in most full paint pot."

He kissed her on the cheek, on a clean spot, released her and turned to Messenger who was standing patiently, waiting, her toes wiggling up and down in the paint.

Smoke knelt, lifted the brown Messenger foot, and began to wipe the paint away with a handy rag.

A small Chinese gentleman strode into the room, looked at them, and stated, "Nephew, I will set the food outside, on the grass. Lunch time."

"Thanks, Chen. Shall we?" Tinker headed for the door, following Master Chen.

The rest trailed after him.

As they settled on the lawn and began to eat, two figures strolled around the far corner of the house.

"What ho, Sire," called one. "Be thee preparing costume party?"

"Nope," said Tinker. "Have some lunch."

The small Chinese woman with the speaker bowed to Master Chen and settled herself next to her companion who was heaping two plates with food and smiling at one and all.

"They do be most gaudy, Sire."

Tinker nodded. "That's what happens, Goose, when you use cheap help. BUT." He held up one hand, cutting off a series of protestations just starting. "They did a good job. The rooms are finished and beautiful. It has been a hard month's work, but we are done. In fact, we just finished. We'll clean up after lunch. Stay for dinner?"

"Who be a'cookin?"

"Master Chen."

"Delighted." Goose grinned broadly. His eyes darted downward.

"Sire, thy one hand tis blue."

Tinker hastily began to wipe his hand on the grass. Chicken winked broadly at her brother.

Messenger giggled.

Fair Morn heaped more food on her plate and on Smoke's.

"Why are each of them a different color, Great Master?" asked Lady Chen, glancing from the various painted ladies to Tinker.

"Separate color for various parts of the chamber. Good thing we used latex. The bodies will come clean fairly easily. We'll just save those clothes for later projects."

Lunch passed quickly. Everyone was hungry from having worked past their normal lunch time.

Master Chen popped out of the side kitchen door to warn them not to eat too much as dinner wasn't all that distant and he was preparing a special meal to celebrate the end of the remodeling project.

At this announcement, Goose's smile became even broader.

Tinker stood and headed back into the house and the newly remodeled bedroom complex.

It was mostly Smoke's design with bits and pieces added in from everyone else, the whole somehow twisted and turned into a pleasing and functional design.

Dumping his clothes into a hamper that fed through the wall into the laundry room, he took a quick shower and walked into the next room and sank into the spacious tub of steaming water. He sighed a very low sigh of contentment.

"AHHHHHHHHHHHHH!"

Behind him he heard the shower restart.

"Sweet prince, Our Verra Own true loverly, wouldst come and scrub away Our blues," called Chicken.

"O. K., O. K. ," grumbled Tinker as he lurched up from the tub and plodded over and into the cascading water jets, grabbing a bar of soap as he passed a storage shelf.

"Looks like most of it is coming off, all right."

"Me'thinks We do Ourself most wild Celt appear what with one blue and t'other au natural."

"How did you do that?"

"As did We once recently afore relate and thin thy shirt do sop through."

"You might start a new fad."

"MY LORD, never wouldst We these fair knobs wantonly display so."

"Just kidding. Turn around, let's see how much you got on the other side."

She turned.

"And how did you do that?"

"Me'Lord, We did step Ourself back for to gaze pon Our Own fair handiwork and wet wall did smack Us so."

"You guys are real hazards when you have a paint brush in hand."

"Wash Our hair, Prince Grumble. Please." She handed him back the shampoo bottle and took the bar of soap from his hand.

"O.K. Ready?"

"Indeed." In moments he had raised a mound of lather and was scrubbing gently but vigorously.

"Next?" It was Smoke.

"O.K. Rinse off, Princess, you're done."

Messenger came into the shower room and sat against the wall, grabbed a foot and yanked it around, to begin vigorously scrubbing the remains of the brown paint away.

"How does she do that," mumbled Tinker.

"Very flexible," answered Smoke, poking him in the side with the shampoo bottle she had just pulled from his hand.

He turned, took it back, and smiled. "Looks like you were more careful than these other guys."

"Of course." She poked her head under one of the jets of water, straightened up and waited, eyes tightly clenched shut.

As he soaped her hair, he heard Chicken walking out, then the splash of water as she dropped into the hot tub.

"MyTinker," asked Messenger, now standing and well coated with soap suds.

"Take a number," said Tinker.

She gazed around the spacious shower room. "Number?" Then she received the reference, a little mental nudge from Smoke.

"OH."

"O.K., Smoke, rinse it. Come on Kitten, let's get your hair."

"Me too." It was Fair Morn.

"Slow poke," observed Tinker.

"I was eating."

"Anything left?"

"Master Chen said he didn't want any leftovers left over."

"He say what's for dinner?"

"Chocolate cake," said Messenger, wobbling back and forth under the water jets.

"Oh, good." Fair Morn took the shampoo bottle from her hand and stepped back into a water jet.

Tinker finished scrubbing Messenger's hair and turned to Fair Morn.

"O.K., Tinkerbell, it is your turn."

She shoved the shampoo bottle at him and turned around. "I have different kinds of wings and I do not require magic dust."

"Right," said Tinker, pouring a glob of soap into his palm. He could hear the murmur of voices as Smoke and Messenger joined Chicken in the hot tub. As he worked up a good lather, he began to hum.

She leaned back and asked. "You enjoy your work?"

"Sure. A clean seraglio is a happy seraglio. Good thing you are so light."

"Why?"

"Keeps me from being knocked over. Keep your head bent forward, I don't want soap in my eyes."

Grandeville. The Hardcastle Residence. Early Morning.

Fredrico Alandale Hardcastle III threw open the front door to his home and started to step through. He didn't make it. In fact, he almost knocked down the startlingly handsome, that was how he saw her, startlingly handsome, young woman dressed in some sort of gold colored suit of a somewhat military cut.

"OH," he said, jumping quickly backward.

"Your pardon," she said. "Is this the house where Hard lives?"

"Yes," he said, turning and calling to his wife. "Dear, would you come here, please? There is a young woman here inquiring about Freddy. I am late enough as it is for my meeting with Charles."

As his wife walked down the wide central hall past the ornate, great staircase, he slipped past their visitor and hurried toward his car still parked in the driveway.

"Really very sorry to be rushing off like this," he called back over his shoulder, rushing off.

"Goodbye, Dear," called his wife.

She smiled at their visitor. "Won't you come inside, my

dear, and have some tea. I always have tea in the morning, maybe a cookie or two."

The young woman followed her down the hall and into a cozy room.

"There," said Hard's mother, shutting the door, pouring tea, handing a cup to her visitor, and then sitting down. "Are you a friend of Alan's? He has such interesting friends."

"More like an acquaintance," came the reply around a mouth full of cookie. "Is the boychick here?"

"Who?"

"Hard."

"Oh, no. More tea?" The tea cups were refilled.

"Oh, no?"

"Yes. Do have another cookie."

The visitor reached out and took another. "Thank you. Umm, will he be back? Soon?"

"Oh my, I can't really say."

"You can't?" The young woman was beginning to fidget slightly as Mrs. Hardcastle III smiled happily at her.

"No. He is on his honeymoon and I don't think they will return until they are ready. I suppose."

"Mazel tov. He got married?"

"Yes. Rather a surprise to his father and me. Pretty girl. If you'll tell me your name, I will be sure and tell them you dropped by for a visit. When they return."

"Mirf."

"My," she gasped. "People have such interesting names these days, don't they?"

"They are? They do?"

"Oh yes. John's ladies have names like yours, sort of. Chicken, John says she is a real Princess. Smoke. Messenger. And Fair Morn."

Mirf sat upright and stared at Hard's mother. "John's ladies are named Princess Chicken and Smoke?"

She nodded. "And Messenger and Fair Morn."

Mirf carefully set her tea cup on the table, leaned

forward and peered into her host's eyes.

Mrs. Hardcastle III thought that this young woman with the interesting name had the most peculiar looking eyes.

Mirf asked, carefully, slowly, "Is this John with the ladies named John Tinker?"

"Oh," she beamed. "Do you know him?"

Mirf jerked back, slamming into the chair. "OI VAY! The Chosen One is a friend of the boychick." She carefully didn't add that this seemed rather strange, this being such an isolated, backward, and primitive world.

Hard's mother gently patted her on the knee. "I am sorry, dear, but I don't understand."

"Does The . . . John Tinker live somewhere around here? Maybe he can tell me how to find Hard?"

"Not too far from here. Maybe twelves miles. And his wife."

Mirf stared at her. "John Tinker has a wife also?"

"Alan's wife. Ramp. She has another interesting name, don't you think?"

Mirf hurtled to her feet, one hand striking her forehead. "OI GAVALT! Oi, oi, oi. Ramp? She is alive? How? With him?" She hissed softly through her teeth.

"Perhaps you would like some more tea, dear? To calm you down? You really shouldn't get so excited, you know. It is bad for your health and for your blood pressure."

Mirf dropped back into her chair and took the offered cup. "Perhaps you could give me directions. I need to talk with him, John Tinker. It is most urgent that I do so."

"Well, Ms. Mirf," Mirf's knee was patted gently, once, "you just relax and finish your tea. Then I will drive you out to his house. I haven't seen it since he started rebuilding right after he came by and saved Allan's life."

Mirf's eyes rolled wildly. "What?"

So Hard's mother told her all that had happened, at least all that she knew of what had happened.

Mirf hastily set her cup down and rose to her feet. "May

we go now? Please?"

"Surely, my dear." Hard's mother stood and headed for a side door. "Come this way. My car is in the garage." She set her tea cup on the fireplace mantel as she passed by.

I Am Not Sure That I Like This!

Somewhere. Unknown. Unpleasant.

It was a shadow-filled, brooding landscape, all shades of darkness. Gray and black clouds menaced the rolling landscape below, enveloping the highest hills in soft wet embrace. The ground seemed to bubble up wet glistening between the vegetation, a quivering dough soft thing trying to reach up and ooze over their feet.

A narrow, muddy track worked its way down the shallow drainage between two dense grey-green growth covered slopes.

"Where are we?"

"Husband, I do not know."

"Oh, oh."

"Things are more wrong than I had suspected."

Hard stared at their surroundings. "More wrong than this place?"

Ramp took one of his hands. "This is only an indication. Someone, something, interfered with our passage to Bahn Duhr Tohr. We are being opposed by powerful forces."

He smiled. "That's O. K. You are a pretty powerful force all by yourself. Ripple certainly is, at least from what I remember."

"What do you remember?"

Hard turned and wrapped his arms around her. "You. I remember you, everything about you, magician-wife."

"And?" Her lips brushed lightly over his.

"Bits and pieces. Mirf. Ripple." He blushed.

"Hum," she said.

"Your sister is pushy, forward, and brazen." His blush deepened.

Ramp's smile grew wicked. "And she is pretty. And attractive. And, I think you messed around."

"A little," he mumbled. And frowned. "I think."

She patted him on the back pocket. "That's all right, dear. I understand. After all, she is a witch."

"Certainly is. Ummmm?"

"I think that we ought to follow this mucky trail. We will have plenty of time for ummm this evening. Let's see if we can find a node."

"Right," said Hard, releasing her, spinning around, and stumbling over some small thing. "Let's find a node and get out of here."

They headed down the track, trying to avoid the mud.

A Small Bit of Cultural Data.

The Kingdom of Bahn Duhr Tohr had been, until its most recent merging into a whole, a series of large and small kingdoms, each with a unique name and a unique color scheme. These color schemes were relegated to their Royalty and to their armies. It was very useful to combatants to be able to recognize friend from foe in the chaos of massed combat.

Many of the kingdoms, but not all, could trace their existence back into the dimly remembered past. Some even argued that they existed long before written records came into use. The kingdoms large and small, frequently merged, or broke apart, as the normal political intrigues and royal wheelings and dealings, created large kingdoms out of smaller ones, or as so often happened, smaller kingdoms out of larger.

But, in spite of the usual turmoil over boundaries and royal household alignments, all the kingdoms were dependent upon each other as no single one had all the resources necessary for true self-sufficiency.

The bonds between the rulers and the ruled were tight and mutually advantageous. Rulers who did not keep the needs of their folk foremost did not last long. Of course, the occasional battle with a neighbor was accepted as just part of life. Battles were, for the most part, short. This was due to their usual approach to warfare that assumed that most of the fighting would happen between the royalty of the houses in contention. The knights and lessor troops often suffered nothing worse than broken bones. Most of the time during the first melee and charge.

Bahn Duhr Tohr. The Royal City. Late Morning.

"Sweet Ebony Delight, what is agitating you so?" he asked, book nestled in his lap. He was reclining on the couch, pillows stuffed under his back, knees tucked up, supporting the massive tome.

The object of his question, normally sprawled across his lap when he was trying to read, was pacing around the room, dropping into a chair, getting up, walking about, only to plop down into another chair, and then to repeat the process again. Somewhere, overhead, a dull rumbling of thunder, or something like that, could be heard.

"Hum, hum, hum, hum, hum," came the response to his question.

"Midnight Hue Hummer, come hither, I am feeling neglected. And the sound that I hear overhead is, no doubt, frightening the local merchants and villagers." He dropped the volume on the floor. It made a heavy thump, and puffed dust into the air.

She looked over at her husband. In his place lay a green, scale-covered dragon smiling evilly at her. Its tongue flicked out. One talon beckoned at her. She walked over, tumbled into his lap.

"That really is an ugly looking worm, husband."

Hanred, himself again, smiled, slipped one hand around her waist. "It is that, my dusky handful." He tugged her blouse loose.

"Illusionist Mate, my skin is midnight moon pale."

"I was referring to your fuliginous being, Inky Morsel." He was loosening the row of buttons.

"Mate for life, are you trying to distract me?"

He slipped the silky material from her shoulders. "Did have something like that in mind. Ah, more or less."

"Your hands are besmeared from that ancient tome you were reading."

"I do seem to be leaving some fairly erotic marks on your hide."

"Hide?"

He started at her chest. And nodded sagely. "Definitely lop-sided. This one is firmer and larger, by some small measure, only apparent to my discerning eye and finely defined sense of touch, than its equally lovely neighbor."

She rolled forward. "Hanred . . . "

He jerked. It was a bad sign, her starting a sentence like that. It hardly ever happened.

"I am sure that a little soap and water, liberally and lovingly applied, will restore your pristine . . . "

She hissed at him, "I am not worried about your mauling, fiddling, or smudging."

"Good." One hand slipped up, cradled her neck and pulled her closer. He touched her lips with his own.

The ceiling grumbled. A dark cloud was forming against it.

"Well, why didn't you say so?" He released her and leaned back, his knees still up, holding, supporting her.

Her fingers wiggled the buttons on his shirt loose. "I am deeply bothered."

"Anything that I can do?" Now he was beginning to become worried. Anything that could bother her was something to be very much worried about.

"No." Her fingers idly rubbed back and forth across his ribs. "Unless one of those dusty tomes has an answer."

He grabbed her bare shoulders in a firm clasp and gave her a slight shake. Then he did it again. And smiled.

"Why are you staring at my chest. Nothing has changed."

"Jiggle dance," he said, giving her another slight shake. "However, all that aside, what question are we trying to answer?"

"I am uneasy about my sister."

"Which of the violent witch horde is it?"

"None. It is Ramp."

"Ahhhh, the magician who died?"

"She is alive."

"True?" He sat upright, his hands dropping away.

"I know it. I feel it."

"That comely youth was far more clever and devious than his appearance or manner ever suggested."

"I know not how the deed was done, but done it was. She is alive. And in deep trouble. And needs help."

"Tell me your question so I may delve into the mysteries."

"Two questions to answer. Where is she? What is the trouble?"

He handed her the blouse. "Cover yourself, brazen witch. And leave my ribs alone. There is a huge volume in the other room of arcane augury that may contain the very answer to the questions that you pose. If I can find it. It may take some digging."

She stood, slipped on her garment, and looked at the seething mass pressing against the ceiling. Two predatory eyes glowed red down at her.

"Go away, you aren't needed."

The clouds dissipated as Hanred started for the library, lugging the other volume with him. He paused by her side, kissed her on the cheek and patted her hip, and suggested, "Perhaps, Ripple, Advisor to the Queen, could whip up some small food stuff to sustain me in my labors."

She laughed. It was a most unusual thing to do. For a witch.

He strolled into the adjoining room, calling over his shoulder. "I will bathe afterwards, these things are dusty dirty."

Paradise. Bright and Sunny Mid-morning.

"She is beautiful," she said.

"Yes," he agreed.

They were standing side by side on a grassy knoll, admiring the sunset. His arm was thrown over her shoulders, her arm was around his waist. A young couple was strolling up the slope toward them, walking hand in hand. They smiled at each other a lot.

"A beautiful wife," he said.

"For an only son," his wife answered.

"I owe John," he said.

"Do you think he needs anything?" she asked.

He laughed. "No. He has everything he needs. He either finds it or steals it."

"What did he ever steal?"

"My wand. My creature."

"He didn't do that."

"She did. All part of the whole."

"I don't think you want to take them back, do you?"

He chuckled softly. "Of course not. But what can I give him?"

"Peace and quiet."

"I wasn't planning on bothering him."

She turned and tapped him sharply on the chest with one knuckle. "Can't lie to me. I can see from your expression."

He sighed. "You are lovely."

Her brows furrowed. "What are you up to now?"

He pointed up at the rapidly darkening sky. "Bad trouble, I feel it. Tangled and twisted."

"Fix it," she whispered. "Leave him be. He deserves to

be left alone. Find someone else."

His face fell as he gazed into her eyes. "We need a focal point."

"Leave him alone."

He sighed. An even longer, even sadder sigh than before.

Their son glanced at their faces, from his mother's to his father's. The color drained from his face. "Oh, no. Hello, Father."

The son's wife gasped and swung her arms around her mate's chest, clutching him tightly. "Husband?"

"I'll go," said the son.

"No," said his father. "We will wait. And watch. For a little while."

"Find another way," said the father's wife. "Neither our son nor John needs to go."

"Let's go inside," said the father. "I need to study what is happening. Maybe I am over-reacting."

He popped his hands together.

Once.

They disappeared.

The Six Lands. Warm and Pleasant Time. Afternoon.

The old man and the young man strode down the Main Way, enjoying the day and each other's company.

Running down the outer edge of the left hand sleeve on the jumper that the old man was wearing were two red strips. Between them, there was a gold stripe. In the past, it had been a green stripe. But that had been changed. This decoration signified to one and all, to everyone who lived in The Six Lands, that this gray-haired gentleman was a Grand Master. He was the first one to appear in three generations. He had high hopes for his grandson, the very one just now walking by his side.

They both walked with a spring in their steps, a spring that came from having taken many walks such as the one from which they were just returning, a spring noticeable in those folk who did. The old man's right leg obviously wasn't working as well as it once did. But it still had that spring in his step.

Suddenly, he stopped and stared into some middle distance only he could see, listening to something only he could hear. A single tear trickled down the weather-lined cheek. His grandson waited patiently, as was right and proper for a grandson to do. He stood, silently, and watched his grandfather carefully, only daring to speak when it was obvious that he might do so without interrupting something.

"Grandfather?"

The old man laughed. It was a merry, delighted laugh.

"Tears Trimblechin," he said formally. "Run ahead and bring me, from my closet, the black wooden box bound with silver bands. However, no matter what you may hear, do not open that box. It could mean your death." He smiled at the startled youth.

"And if we, if you, should survive our trip, why you just might become the next Grand Master in time, in time. **GO! RUN! HURRY!**"

Tears ran toward the home, pondering as he ran the strangeness of what he had just been told.

Grandeville. Tinker's place. Mid-Morning.

They jounced over and up the last part of the driveway and lurched to a halt in the wide parking space.

"There," announced Hard's mother, satisfaction and accomplishment ringing in her voice. "John's house. He must still be here. That is his truck."

Mirf slowly uncoiled her fingers, stiff from hard clenching, from the car door handle, sucked in a deep breath, and bolted from the automobile. Holding the car door open, she leaned down and spoke quickly to the driver. "No need to wait. I will ask John to help me get back to town."

"Oh." Hard's mother looked puzzled. Then she smiled.

"Oh, all right. I will just head back to town. Very pleased to meet you, Ms. Mirf."

"It's been vunderbar," said Mirf, slamming the door and hurrying to safety on the far side of Tinker's pickup.

The car lurched, stopped, the driver's window slid down. She called, "They really ought to be up by now! It is after eleven."

Mirf nodded and started for the front porch and door.

Clear Bander. Tripple. Morning.

The rain fell from the ceiling. He stretched and yawned, and said, "Warmer."

The petite figure standing next to him danced lightly away, and said, "Colder."

"Warmer," he said. "Don't splash, don't splash. That is ice cold."

"Colder," she said, her skin glowing red. He admired that skin.

"You had better turn it cold or we will never get started on this trip," she said. "**COLD.**" It was a demand. The ceiling obeyed.

"**ARRRRRRRGGGGG,**" he screamed, running for safety.

The two suitcases jostled out of his way. He grabbed a towel and frantically began to rub himself dry. He called for his clothes, his traveling clothes, and was shoving his wand up the left sleeve of his somewhat tattered, multicolored robe when his companion strode from the falling rain smiled happily at him.

"Breakfast." A table appeared at her command, places set, food hot and steaming.

The two suitcases jostled around his legs, floating inches above the floor. "Wait over there," he said, pointing.

Slowly they made their way to the indicated spot.

"I have already packed them," she said. "For traveling."

"Hey ho," called a disembodied voice. "May I enter?"

"It is Orotundy," said $1.98.

"Sneak peek," growled Plum Duff. Her clothes settled around her.

"**OUCH, OUCH, OUCH!** I was not peeking," screamed the voice.

"Enter," she said, nodding at the table. It set itself for one more guest.

A large, a very large, round man slid into the room. He was rubbing his backside and glaring at the small woman dressed in red clothes shading toward purple.

"Join us for breakfast?" she asked.

"Delighted," said Orotundy.

As they ate, he explained why he had come for a visit.

The Guild of Magicians was worried. Strange things were happening *out there* and life was turning hazardous to the innocent traveler especially if that innocent traveler happened to be a magician.

"Branpher went to Star's End for the Great Festival and something ate him. Others have had bad experiences as well. Well, maybe not as bad as that, but bad enough. Zinngle lost an arm. He grew it back soon enough, but still, it was most unpleasant. Prapson got lost inbetween, almost didn't make it out."

"Why are you here?" asked Duff.

Orotundy looked sideways.

$1. 98 nodded.

"We are not sure you should be going. Not the both of you, that is."

"Who is this we?" asked Duff. Her tone made their round guest nervous. He hastily took another helping of breakfast, just to calm his stomach.

"The Guild, the Guild!" Orotundy looked at $1.98 for assistance.

$1.98 smiled at him.

"We are going," stated Duff. "If he goes, I am going." The light in the room began to dim as something began to suck it away.

"Yes, yes, yes, yes, yes," agreed Orotundy. "Of course. I am just carrying the message, that is all." He took some more food. The room light returned to normal.

"OH," he said, sitting upright and plunging his arm into his chest. "I have something for you."

His arm pulled free. He handed her a ring with a brown jewel fastened with deep green d'metal.

Plum Duff gasped.

$1.98 recoiled.

Wind whistled through the room.

"TAKE IT, TAKE IT!" screamed Orotundy.

Duff snatched the ring from his trembling hand and jammed it on her left hand index finger.

Orotundy hastily scanned the table. The food was gone.

"Why are we given the Guild Master's ring?" asked Duff.

Orotundy cleared his throat, "Ahem, ahem. We, The Guild, talked about it, your trip, you see we knew $1.98 would go, and we thought that you would probably go with him, this time, so we thought, that is, The Guild thought, that it might help you two survive Out There, so we unfolded it, and now you have it." He sighed. "Wear it in health."

He jumped to his feet. "I have to go. Goodbye."

He stepped into nothing. His voice called back, "$1.98, do be careful, do be careful."

$1.98 rose to his feet and stared vaguely at the wall.

Duff stood and walked around the table and wrapped her arms around him.

"Ready?"

"Yes," he answered, picking her up, holding her in his arms.

"We are not traveling anywhere, this way," she said.

He kissed her. "I know." And set her down.

They followed the suitcases out and around the corner. And.

Then.

They walked.

Into.

Out.

There.

Pac Lac Bac.

Two weeks of days had passed since the spell cast.

Both were healed. And waiting.

Of course, neither of them was waiting very well. Witches did not wait well. Their normal impatience crackled hazard if waiting went on too long. And too long for a witch was not very long at all.

Turintor walked back out and onto the balcony and stared out over the railing at nothing in particular. She was considering some small bit of mayhem to cast out upon the folk of this small town, folk that didn't mind waiting, just to create a bit of distraction. She frowned, just a little. Once she had heard a tale told of a witch that had extreme patience, a patience that could last for hours and hours, days even.

She shrugged. Such a tell tale had to be a child tell thing.

Her silent companion joined her. She was idly chewing on the silver tip of a long black wand. The wand was hissing softly.

"I feel the need to be elsewhere. The spell werk will find us in all ways," Turintor suggested. Her eyes glanced sideways.

Her companion nodded. And slipped the wand up her left sleeve.

"I seem to remember a small village located in Snark's Fen. What was that name? It had several spell shops."

Turintor stared down at the town below the balcony. "Dawla!"

She turned back to her companion. "Shall we?"

Grandeville. Tinker's Place. Mid-Morning.

Tinker was sprawled on the couch in his pajamas, robe loosely tied at the waist. As far as he was concerned, it was early morning, this morning. They had decided to celebrate and christen the new addition/revision to the house. Last night. They did. And now they had just crept into mid-morning's bright light.

Smoke was in the dining room setting out dishes for breakfast.

Master Chen had gone to town early and would return late, so his note had said. He had set out all the ingredients for waffles and other things before leaving.

Chicken, wearing a pair of Tinker's pajamas, was draped over the same couch. And Tinker.

Faint running water sounds came from their quarters, echoing down the long hall into the living room. Messenger was showering.

Fair Morn entered the room, tugging on a pajama top, water still glistening on her skin.

Tinker glared at her. "If you guys keep grabbing my pajamas, I will have to buy them by the dozen."

Smoke walked from the dining room, stopped and ruffled his hair. "They are most comfortable." She was wearing a pair of them also.

"They are," said Fair Morn, buttoning the lower button of her top. "But maybe a little snug."

From outside they heard the dull thump of a car door closing.

"Just what we need," grumbled Tinker. "Visitors."

Smoke reached out with her mind, and smiled. "Hard's mother."

Suddenly she stiffened, her minds shouting warnings to them all. She spun and ran toward the kitchen, intending to come from behind this creature. Fair Morn charged back down the hall toward their quarters.

Someone knocked on the front door as Chicken sprang

to her feet and leaped for the wall where her sword hung.

"Come in," called Tinker, wondering what was going on now. He wasn't quite ready to leave the comfort of the couch.

The door opened and she stepped in.

Chicken hurtled herself between Tinker and their visitor.

"HALT!" The blade whipped back and forth in the space between them.

Their visitor smiled at her, at the slim figure wearing baggy, loose pajamas, large fuzzy slippers on her feet, flicking a gleaming weapon back and forth, and glaring at her.

"Which one are you?"

Tinker reached out and patted Chicken on the hip. "You wanna move over a bit so I can see?" He sat up.

Chicken side-stepped, just a little.

The woman held out her hands. "See? No weapons."

Smoke crashed through the front door, slamming it back against the wall. Everyone jerked.

"Now what's going on?" asked Tinker.

Fair Morn stepped into the room, pointing a large, ugly black device. "Do not move, even a little bit," she ordered. One finger flicked a lever on the weapon's side. It made a soft 'pop'.

Smoke leaped sideways.

"Don't fire that thing in here," said Tinker. He was calm, he was very calm. Last night's celebration had burned away all the energy he might have used to get excited with. "You will take out the entire outside wall."

Their visitor's eyes jumped from person to person. She couldn't see Smoke but knew she was off to her side somewhere.

A young woman stepped from the dining room. She had a large towel wrapped around her hips, the ends tucked in. In one hand she held a long, slender black rod. "MyTinker?"

Tinker grabbed the coffee carafe from the floor next to the couch and refilled his cup. "I don't know. What started all this? Excitement."

The woman rolled her eyes at Messenger. "Nice build."

"She is not what she appears to be," explained Smoke, now poised to attack, from this person's rear.

"She isn't? May I sit down?" The woman stared at Messenger.

Tinker waved a hand. "Sure. Take that chair."

She sat as Smoke edged around her, stepping into view.

Their visitor's eyes carefully watched the four women, tightly focused upon her every movement, as they settled themselves.

"You know me?" asked Tinker. "Who are you?"

"I am Mirf."

"You?" Chicken stared at her.

"Oh, my," gasped Messenger. "Certainly doesn't resemble anything like the one in the story."

"Ho Ha," said Mirf. "So the boychick remembered. And he told you."

"Only some of it," said Tinker. "You are a hob-goblin?"

"Wrong! I was. But what you see is really me. Before. And after."

"Changed," said Smoke. "Not what she appears to be."

Tinker stared harder and noticed that she really had strange eyes.

"So I didn't get rid of all of it. Bad luck." Mirf shrugged. "So who's to complain. I am mostly me. I look like me, not that meshuggener hob-goblin."

"Smoke?"

Mirf could feel the mental caress.

"She feels me, MindMate. Most unusual."

"Hob-goblin residue," explained Mirf.

"Means no harm," continued Smoke.

"Good," said Tinker. "You guys want to de-arm? This morning I am not ready for a war in the living room."

Chicken hung her sword back in its place.

Messenger stuck the wand into her hair, which was

bundled on top of her head, her hair partially wrapped in a towel.

Fair Morn took her weapon back to their quarters.

"You want some coffee?" Tinker asked Mirf. "You wanna get some more clothes on, kitten?" he asked Messenger.

"Oh," Messenger blushed. And hurried away.

"Nice bod," commented Mirf. She smiled at Messenger's back.

"Beauty's a flower," she added. And said to Tinker, "Twelfth Night. Willy S."

Chicken and Smoke sat on either side of Tinker.

He just stared at Mirf. "That's Chicken, that's Smoke." And nodded as the others returned. "Fair Morn and Messenger. Fair Morn is the taller one. You wanna talk to us, Mirf?"

Mirf nodded. She did.

A Small Bit of Cultural Data.

The Faan witch clan is unique. Of all of the witch clans scattered across the universe of universes, they are the only one that does not maintain a clan house. And, unlike all the other clans, the members of the Faan are all and only generationally linked. The magic of the Faan flows down through the female members, much the same as all the other witch clans. However, among the Faan it is from mother to daughter.

The Faan clan, unlike the other clans, are trained almost exclusively by their female relatives, mainly by their mother and their aunts. But if a sister has learned some new and unique twist, it may be shared, sister to sister. It is due to this multi-generational sharing and training that has made the Faan noted throughout the witch clans as being the most powerful clan and to be avoided if at all possible. And some few understand that at some point in the long ago long ago, in their mating with their chosen mates-for-life, from other witch lines, that something unusual happened that twisted and transformed their genetic material.

The result of this event was that, at times, their offspring are born with new and unique abilities. This tends to explain why the Faan do not maintain a clan house. Members of their clan, most often, prefer to wander and to study and collect magic and magic spells. And other things.

Bahn Duhr Tohr. The Royal City. Late Afternoon.

Hanred staggered from the library clenching a gigantic tome with both arms. He was dusty, he was dirty, he was smudged. He was smiling.

"Sweet Darkness," he laughed. "Clean off that table. This thing is wrenching my arms from their sockets. But it is what you were looking for. I think."

Ripple cleared the table and jumped back as he heaved the volume up and onto the table top and dropped it heavily. Dust eddied in all directions. The table creaked loudly, the ancient wood ready to crumble.

"You are filthy."

"I am that. And successful." He wrapped his arms around her. "And what is my reward, Dusky Delight?"

She grinned wickedly. "I will fill the tub. And scrub your back."

He yanked her against himself.

"Husband, are you leaving handprints on my backside?"

Hanred craned his neck. "Seems to be so." He dropped his hands. "Step back." She did.

"There. That is prints fore and aft."

Her teeth chewed on the corner of her mouth. "It seems that peering inside your great book must wait awhile."

"Reward for a reward," he said. "And then."

"And then?"

"Why," he laughed. "Another reward for another reward."

She reached out and began to unbutton his shirt. "Let's

get you out of these filthy clothes."

"My idea exactly, Midnight Confection." His arms weaved through hers, his fingers deftly opening her blouse.

"Tub," she said.

"Tub," he agreed.

They disappeared.

From that room came the sounds of a great splash.

"Ahhhhhhhh," sighed Hanred.

"Hum, hum, hum, hum," responded Ripple.

Crandle. The Remains of Azat.

"HO. Ho, ho, ho, ho, ho, ho, ho."

It was laughter. It wasn't laughter. The stocky figure smiled through the visor of his helmet at the rubble and smoke surrounding him. The ruins stretched to the far horizons and beyond.

A woman, glistening soft burnished silver, stood by his side.

"No reasoning with them, was there?"

He shoved the visor up and beamed at her. "Folks like that never understand, Gyre my own. But, it is another pestilence removed. I am hungry. I am thirsty. And I crave you."

She kissed him on both cheeks. Ship reacted instantly.

They were back on their vessel.

He glanced at the wall display map. "We are heading right for the heart of it, aren't we?"

"Yes. The center of the disturbance."

"How long?" His arm encircled her waist.

"Not long. Portal-part will leap us there quickly." Her arm snaked around and pinched him through a small gap where he was slipping off the armor. "But not too quickly."

An Unnamed Place. Dark of Night.

The disturbance looked out and frowned. This was starting to become more complicated than first planned.

Angry eyes peered into the red glow of the well and saw that she was firmly enmeshed on the dark path. A short struggle, then she would die. All these other stirrings would happen too late.

He hurried the spell. And felt the dark pouring into the mixture. Deep crimson flickered across the room. In the soft glow the book spines writhed and quivered as the power pulled free.

Soon, he thought to himself, soon it would be over. And she would be dead. Then he could turn his attention to the rest of them.

Somewhere. Unknown. Unpleasant. Early Evening.

Candle light filled the tent with golden glow. Her skin tones answered in kind. He sighed.

"A heavy sigh," she said.

"A happy, unbelieving sigh," he answered.

"What do you not believe, my pretty?"

"That you are really my wife. That a beautiful magician of wondrous powers is my wife. That I was so lucky as to find you the way I did. And that . . . "

She pressed her fingers over his lips. "Shhhhh. I am real, am I not?"

He nodded.

"That is all that matters. You are handsome. I am lucky."

Gently removing her hand, he said, "You really do not believe me, do you?"

"Husband always tell their wives that they are beautiful."

"I thought that we had this conversation once before and that I convinced you that time?"

"Not totally."

"I'll prove it to you."

Her look was cautious, her tone careful. "How?"

"I will ask Tinker?"

She sat up, pushing him away. "Husband, the women of my clan do not parade themselves for anyone but their mates."

"Tinker's ladies," he hastily corrected.

"The same. He sees what they see."

"He wouldn't have to."

"I will talk with the Princess Chicken when we return. Not you."

"O.K. But."

"What?"

"If she, or they, tell you what I am sure they will, then will you believe me?"

She grabbed him and pushed him over. "Of course. Just for you, Husband."

Later she told him that they were stuck.

Hard's eyes popped wide. "I didn't think that was possible."

"I am not referring to what you are doing to me, what we are doing. We are stuck in this world. It is a trap. There is no node. We have to wait for rescue. So. . . "

"So," he said, his forehead touching her's.

"So, we must be on our honeymoon. Now, what else do your folk do when they do this thing you call honeymoon?"

Stumpf. Just Past Lunch Time.

He stood upon the last of the mountain peaks, the last of The Nine Peaks. He had done it, climbed them all, in one season. He grunted to himself, unslung the great cudgle hanging from his belt, and wacked off a small piece of the peak. This chunk of rock was added to the other eight pieces in one pocket.

No one had ever climbed all of the Nine in one season. He had worked and saved and planned this event for four cycles after returning home. Worked hard and long. And he had grown some more, much to his surprise. Now he was a head taller than everyone he met. He was a good third bulkier, also.

His twice grandfather had blamed all this on his twice grandmother's lineage, saying that there was always something suspect about that line. There had always been vague rumors of large folk way back then.

Of course, he hadn't believed the rumors or his twice grandfather's stories. But, now, here he was. Big, and standing on the tip of Drapf, the last of the peaks. No one ever used its formal name in proper company as Drapf was a particularly graphic, lewd, and coarse swear word. Many of the things in this world carried such labels, including the name for the world itself.

This linguistic peculiarity spoke volumes for the general outlook of the inhabitants. They were not a very optimistic race. Every word ending in '-pf' was coarse and vulgar.

"BY DUMPF," he said. "What will I do after this?" He grumbled a little bit more, standing, staring out into the hot, arid landscape that was the planet Stumpf.

A voice spoke to him and told him.

"HUMPF," he said, almost smiling. "I suppose that I should get down, travel some, and dress properly."

He wondered whether he would survive or not. Then he shrugged his shoulders, such matters were best left to folk that worried.

Grandeville. Tinker's place, Mid-Morning.

"So, what are we supposed to do," asked Tinker. He was surrounded as he sat slumped comfortably on the couch.

Chicken sat on one side of him, her legs tucked up and under.

Messenger had returned, grabbing another pair of his pajamas, and sat snuggling against his other side.

Smoke and Fair Morn sat on the floor on either side of his legs.

"The boychick's wife is the focus of powerful forces.

These forces are disrupting a large segment of the universes. It, they, them, whatever, have to be stopped."

"**NO!**"

"Bubee, you are The Chosen One, not me."

"No," stated Tinker. "My hero days, such as they were, are over, done with."

Mirf stared at him. This was going to be much more difficult than she had assumed or expected. "Nothing is more depressing than the conviction that one is not a hero. George Moore," she mumbled. Then smiled at him.

Everyone winced.

"I will give you anything you want." She swung her arms wide. "Anything. How's that for openers? A universe of universes to select from. I am authorized to do whatever you wish."

"Anything?" asked Tinker, looking at her.

"If it is there, it is your's."

"Peace and quiet," replied Tinker, snapping a quick smile at Mirf. On and off.

"Meshuggener. This elseplace produces nothing but meshuggeners," she grumbled. And stood up.

"Final offer." And inhaled, deeply.

"Oi," she sighed. "What I have to do to make a living. And such a living and such an offer as I have never made or done before."

Her fingers began to pluck the fastenings loose down the front of her blouse.

"Take me." And mumbled, "What's one more, more or less?"

"Oh," cried Messenger. "She is pretty. Really really. And she has strange eyes also."

"**NO, NO, NO!** Mirf, stop that! Messenger, knock it off!" He sighed and frowned at Messenger. "You promised."

He lightly kicked Smoke. "You all promised. No more additions."

"She made the offer," whispered Messenger.

Mirf stood in front of them, legs wide, hands on hips, blouse open to her belt buckle.

"SO! It's a deal? You get one slightly hob-goblined, but luscious morsel, me, and I get services rendered by you, ho ha, a pun if there ever was one."

"**NO!**"

"I'm gorgeous."

"**NO!**"

"I'm willing."

"**NO, NO!**"

"I'm a failure." Mirf crashed back into her chair.

Smoke leaned forward and handed her a cup. "Have some coffee."

Somewhere. Unknown. Unpleasant. Sometime After Breakfast.

They were sitting outside the tent.

Breakfast was over.

They were just sitting there, on the soft rug, sipping coffee, looking out at the view, such as it was. Dank, dreary, low sagging clouds, heavy marching shadows. They sat on the edge of a small clearing, looking down and out at the overgrown valley floor.

The muddy track they had followed wandered down into the growth, and disappeared, swallowed alive by gray-green-black tangled undergrowth.

"Not exactly my idea of a place to honeymoon," grumbled Hard.

"This honeymoon thing is similar, in certain of its customs, to those of my clan, lovely one. Place doesn't matter." Her eyes glittered with happiness.

He smiled. "Perhaps we might see what your customs are like?"

"As the children of many an elseplace are wont to say," she said, untying the top bow fastening her blouse. "I'll show you mine, if you'll show me your's."

Her eyes rolled wildly. Without a sound, she collapsed.

"**RAMP!**" He leaped to her side. Crouching, bending over, he gently patted her cheek. He didn't know what else to do.

Grandeville. Tinker's place. Getting Close to Lunch Time.

"Knock, knock," said a voice.

He stepped through the open front door into the living room, looked at the tableau, and grinned.

"Another one? Really, Tinker, you are going to injure yourself."

"Who's this big meshuggener with the pretty face?" grumbled Mirf, looking around at the speaker.

"Mirf, this is J. C. Smith, a close friend of mine. And Hard's. J. C., this is Chief First Inspector Mirf, Monetary Control."

"Wow, I.R.S.," said J. C. "That is quite a uniform you don't have on." He was admiring the decolletage.

"Wow, yourself," grumbled Mirf.

"She," said Tinker pointedly, "is not mine, our's."

"My, my, a free agent." J. C. smiled. "Going to be in town long?"

"Passing through," suggested Tinker.

"I could use an assistant." Mirf smiled at J. C.

He winced.

Then he leaned forward and stared at her eyes.

"Tinker?" It was a long, drawn out word.

"Yah, I know. This is, this was, Hard's hob-goblin."

"I am nobody's hob-goblin," she snapped.

"Oh, boy." J. C. dropped into the chair, pushed forward by Smoke as she stepped from the dining room and announced, "Breakfast. Let's eat."

Mirf leaped to her feet. "Vunderbar. What is it?"

"Waffles, bacon, sausage, scrambled eggs, toast and coffee," called Messenger.

"I was hungry," explained Smoke.

"Sounds good to me," said Fair Morn, slipping into the dining room.

Tinker followed them, one arm around Chicken, beckoning for J. C . to follow. Tinker whispered in her ear, "I don't like this."

Bahn Duhr Tohr. The Royal City. Much Later in the Afternoon.

"AHHHHHHHHHHHHH."

She yanked herself from his embrace, hurtling herself from the tub, water flying in all directions. Scrambling to her feet, she ordered on her clothes, and ran into the adjacent room.

Hanred charged after her. "Ripple, what is it? Surely I wasn't being too rough?"

Dense clouds swirled across the room, half filling the space overhead, tendrils just brushing the tops of their heads. Angry red eyes glowed from the darkness. The mouth yawned wide, flames crackled and belched from deep inside. Thunder grumbled, the walls shook.

"Quickly," she said. "Show me what you found." She pointed at the tome lying on the table.

Hanred pushed her aside and threw open the book. Dust billowed over them. Rapidly flopping the heavy pages over, he found the spot, and nodded.

"Here it is. At least, from the title, it sounds correct. Very old, very arcane. Can you understand what it says?" He stepped out of her way. Puddles formed around his feet.

Ripple leaned over the page, one finger tracing across the sentences. The writing was ancient, the letters strangely shaped, but her training in the arcane languages had been wider ranging than most.

"Yes." She held out one hand. "Something to write upon and with."

He ran to the library and back again and shoved them at her. She snatched them and rapidly wrote out a list.

"My clever own love, can we find these things? Now?"

Hanred grabbed the list, scanned it, and smiled. "Of course. Ready yourself, Darkness. It will be but a short moment." He started for the outside door.

"One moment," she said.

"Yes?"

"You aren't dressed for the streets. You aren't dressed at all." She jabbed a finger at him.

He was dressed, clothed in the proper royal garments. Blowing her a kiss, he dashed through the door, gold pieces jingling in his pocket.

Space. 20.25.49.89. AIT. In Ship's Notation.

"Where are we heading?"

"Straight into the heart of the chaos."

"Sounds good to me."

Macabre's fingers lightly stroked the small bumps down her spine. He was sitting up in a welter of heavily brocaded blankets. Gyre nestled in his lap. His other hand reached out and snatched a doughnut from a tray that had just floated from a wall slot.

"What kind did we get?" he asked, prior to taking a big bite.

"Your favorite." Gyre leaned back against his legs, just now raised and bent to form a support for her. He handed her the confection and grabbed another.

"In my old age, I am a contented man."

"Not so old."

"Easy for you to say. You are older than I am."

"Only ship self. I was just created."

"Born," he corrected.

"Made," she corrected.

He laughed. "That also." One finger traced feather-touch circles over her skin. Goosebumps raised and faded away as he did.

"Looks like silver. Tastes like silver. Feels like silky soft skin."

"I could have Med Section change it."

"Never! Silver is just fine. We all agree on that."

"All?"

"The Vipers. The Sparkling Tigers. Me. Especially me."

She took his hand and gently nibbled on the tip of the extended finger. "Then I will stay as I am."

"Good." Macabre took another doughnut. This one was heavily dusted with powdered sugar. "The best of all possible worlds. John was really surprised wasn't he? Just before we eliminated Dram, when you appeared."

"He was. Would you like more than one?"

"I have already had two." He licked his fingers clean. "But three would be fine." And grabbed another doughnut.

"Female forms."

"Ah."

"I could have as many sisters as you would wish. Med Section could produce them as easily at it produced me."

His free hand pulled her forward. He kissed her. "No. You are it."

Her eyes closed.

"What?"

"The Monetary Control is involved. One of them just traveled to that backward world on the far edge."

"John's elseplace?"

Her eyes opened. "Yes. Past tense. The signal came the long way around."

He beamed. "Life is getting interesting. Very interesting. Why are they involved? Monetary Control."

"The disturbances."

"I have always steered clear of that crowd. They never give up. Look what happened to that pair of scum, Ko Lett and The Harken Ryder. Terminated."

"Time for subtlety."

"Long time since I had to be subtle."

"Hone your skills."

"Another good idea."

He carefully set the doughnuts safely to one side and wrapped his hands around her waist.

Bahn Duhr Tohr. The Royal City. Gathering Dusk.

The door banged open.

Hanred charged in, a large sack clenched in one hand. "Got it all."

Ripple was bent over the great volume, her arms plunged elbow deep into another place through one of the pages. Blue glow bathed her from waist to forehead. Strange odors, and colors, drifted in the air.

He handed her the first ingredient, naming it. Then the next three. Blue puffed green. Black flames erupted, coating her. Everything made of cloth, touched by the flame, dissolved.

"CAREFUL!"

"I am always careful, husband."

He handed her the rest of the materials.

She reached deeper, speaking to something.

Suddenly she jumped back. The tome snapped shut. The table top split, the legs exploding into kindling. The concussion blew the volume into sections and threw her across the room. Hanred didn't feel a thing.

He gasped and ran to the sprawled form. She lay still, a broken rag doll, limbs akimbo, eyes open, blank, staring.

"Always careful," whispered Hanred, gently scooping her up, carrying the limp witch to their bedroom, tears blurring his vision.

Somewhere. Unknown. Unpleasant. Mid-Morning.

The sky split open.

A figure tumbled down, spun, and landed on her feet, just at the edge of the carpet.

"Dim dim dim dim!" she snarled. A belt of some red woven material clenched the baggy dark smock around her narrow waist. Equally baggy trousers draped over black, calf length boots.

"What are you?" She glared at Hard. "And if she is dead, you are on your way to ugly horror."

"I am Hard," screamed Hard, leaping, to his feet, fists clenched. "That is my wife. Go away."

He stepped menacingly toward her, this short person with the bad manners, the very bad manners.

She jumped at him, grabbed one of his wrists in an iron clasp, leaned over, and waggled a finger at Ramp.

The sky tore open and sucked them upward.

"**WHOA** . . . ," shouted Hard.

Grandeville. Tinker's place. Lunch Time.

"So, big stud, what are you staring at?"

Mirf sat across the table from J. C. holding a piece of toast in one hand and began slathering it with jelly with her knife. Her blouse had opened further. She jabbed across the table with the knife. "You there, the one with the hob-goblin appetite. Take a deep breath."

Fair Morn looked startled, puzzled, but she did as requested.

"There you go, cute stuff," said Mirf addressing J. C. "Stare at those for a while."

She leaned slightly and nudged Smoke with her elbow and asked loudly. "Doesn't this guy have some chickee he can shtoop?"

Tinker choked on his coffee and slumped lower in his chair. "You gonna be around long, Mirf?"

"Whada ya say, ogle-eyes? Think I ought to, you will pardon the expression, hang around for awhile?"

Mirf rolled her eyes at J. C.

He suppressed a smile. One corner of his mouth was twitching violently. "You really were that hob-goblin that dragged Hard around?"

"Bingo-rooney!" She gestured with her toast. "That was me all right, like I said once upon a time."

Then she stared down. A great glob of jelly was

creeping over bare flesh.

"Such a klutz," she murmured, popping the rest of the toast into her mouth, yanking her blouse away from the offending smear, and vigorously wiping away the sticky presence with a napkin. Much to J. C.'s amusement and delight.

"Need any help?" he asked.

Tinker leaned sideways and murmured to Chicken, "Let's run away from home."

Outside, somewhere, there was a brilliant flash of light, a loud ripping noise.

"Now what?" asked Tinker. He didn't expect to get an answer.

"Rain?" said Mirf, nibbling on the corner of a waffle delicately.

The front door banged open and slammed into the wall. A tall woman charged through the living room and then into the dining room. She wore a black shirt with an ornate pattern woven over the front panel, a black vest, a long flowing black skirt, and black sandals.

"Which one of this group is The Chosen One?" she demanded, frowning darkly at them all.

"He is," said Mirf, pointing with her waffle.

"You must come with me," she demanded, now glaring in his direction.

"I quit," stated Tinker. He stared at her face. She looked vaguely familiar. And rather surprised at his response.

"Good luck, shikseh," said Mirf. "I already tried. Persuasion. Gold. Everything. Even my voluptuous beautiful bod, to do with as he wished. No sale." Her eyes traveled up and down this stranger. "Sooooooooo? What do you have to offer?"

"Death!" she snapped.

Messenger's hand flashed up and down. The wand erupted. The flame-blast hurtled the stranger into the living room. Something exploded. Pieces of cloth, bits of wood, and stuffing blew from the living room, into the dining room and over everything directly in front of the doorway. Glass tinkled.

"Damn," said Tinker. "That was the couch. And the windows."

"I'm sorry," whispered Messenger, staring at the gray billows surging from the black filled living room.

"Ho boy," hissed Mirf, twisting in her chair, peering at the mess.

"What the hell is that thing?" asked J. C., surging up, half-standing, wondering which way to run, staring at the long black stick held by Messenger.

"Worry thyself not, Our kitten." Chicken patted Messenger's arm. "T'was most correct a'thing to do."

"I'm gonna punch Big Red in the mouth the next time I see him," grumbled Tinker. "This must be all his fault."

"One?" Fair Morn cast him a sideways glance.

"It really is all his fault," explained Tinker. "If he hadn't got me into it in the first place, all this wouldn't be happening now. Good thing we don't live in town."

A very angry woman stomped out of the smoke. Her skirt hung in tatters. On her right arm she still worn a sleeve. Around her neck, the collar, still buttoned. The rest, blouse and vest, was gone.

"Not too bad," commented Mirf. "On the small size, but nicely formed. What do you think, J. C.?"

"DON'T!" shouted Tinker.

Messenger's hand jerked, the wand waggled, her eyes remained focused upon this person who had threatened Tinker.

"Who are you?" he asked.

All watched her carefully, amazed that she had survived the blast.

"May I sit?" she grumbled.

Smoke shoved a chair under her.

"Nice legs," observed J. C., winking at Mirf.

"OHHHHHHHH!" gasped Gyre, sweat pouring from her face and body.

She peered into Macabre's eyes. "Just now. Black forces. Powerful black forces. Widely scattered. Sensors picked up the flashes."

Under his hands, he could feel her relaxing. "You felt it?"

"Yes. I shall revise the circuits."

"Where?"

She smiled. "Just at the end of you."

"Ahem. What worlds?"

"Umpkennel."

"Never heard of that one."

"Data banks say it is a small and isolated piece of mud in the five six sector."

"Strange. The other's?"

"Bahn Duhr Tohr. Earth."

"Change heading."

"Did. Earth?"

"Yes. Do you read minds also?"

"No, there are no circuits that are capable of that. But your manner of operating is plain. To me."

"How long?"

"We have time. Two days, as measured on John Tinker's elseplace." She wiggled slightly.

Far Corner. A Rather Sunny Day.

Abadoda nodded to herself and thought that the name of this elseplace was quite appropriate.

The relocation to their new home was done and it was a wonderfully isolated corner of the universe of universes. Few folk wandered through this elseplace which pleased the local folk greatly.

She strolled down a long hall in their new dwellings and into the small room to peer into the newly placed viewing well.

She sniffed at the air carefully and then waved one hand over the still surface. And stared down into the depths.

That strange organism was looking to become loose in the universe of universes again and appeared to be somehow involved in a great disturbance. And that awful witch clan appeared to be swirling around them as well.

She nodded to herself and thought that this would take careful watching and careful thought. She swirled the water in the well and headed back down the hall.

Bahn Duhr Tohr. The Royal City. Early Evening.

Plaster dust, ceiling fragments, and three figures rained down through the glowering cloud.

The smallest figure landed on her feet.

Hard tripped on pieces of splintered wood and managed to create a large cloud of dust when one boot tromped on top of a severed portion of the tome of arcane knowledge before he fell and crashed into the rest.

"Oh." It was the faintest of gasps.

"**RAMP!**" Hard crawled through the debris to cradle her limp form in his arms.

The short woman slashed a vicious cut with a blue wand at a taloned arm extending down from the swirling cloud overhead. It was trying to grab her.

"Don't you dare touch me, cretin."

A door thudded open. A great dragon eased its sinuous form through. It hissed at them and spoke. "What is all this? Dinner?"

The short woman ran over, stood on her tiptoes and kissed it on the tip of its snout. "Uglier every day, Hanred."

Hard's head snapped up. "Hanred?"

The dragon disappeared. "It is I."

Hanred hurried over to stand and stare down at Ramp's face. "Ummmmm, barely alive. But alive, none the less. Into that room, over there. Hurry."

He helped Hard support Ramp and then aimed them in

the correct direction.

The short woman ran into a different room, calling gaily, "Ripple?"

Grandeville. Tinker's place. Lunch Time.

She stared at Messenger and asked haughtily, "Are you going to fire that thing again?"

"Probably not," answered Tinker. "Sorta depends upon what you do."

"Me. Nothing."

He turned his head and stared at the billowing smoke. "What a mess."

"Oh, that." She snapped her fingers. The smoke and debris was sucked away. The windows made whole. A new couch created.

"Who are you." He sat up and refilled his coffee cup.

"Me?" She beckoned with one finger. A food platter slid over to her. An empty plate settled in front of her. Heaping her dish, she took a small taste.

"Tickle, tickle, tickle. What do you call it?"

"Scrambled eggs with cottage cheese and green chilies," explained Messenger.

"I am Reptar, Ripple's sister. She threw me here."

"The witch?" asked Tinker.

"Dark Advisor to the most Noble Queen Willawa and King Toucan?" asked Chicken.

"Haven't heard about that Toucan fellow. But I had been traveling . . . in other parts."

J. C. was staring at her. "You are really a witch?"

She nodded. "Oh yesss." Then she looked more carefully at him.

"Hum, hum, hum, hum. My, you are a pretty."

Mirf glared at her. And snatched another helping as the platter hurried by. "Drinble."

"Watch your mouth, fatty," snarled Reptar, taking a bite from a square thing. She missed the dark expression that flashed across Mirf's face.

"Waffles," stated Messenger. "Whole wheat and peanuts."

Reptar's eyes fastened on J. C.'s face. "You have the look of a youth still unmated. Are you?"

"HEY!" shouted Tinker. "Can we get down to business? Why are you here?"

Reptar's head snapped around. "This IS business." She spit the answer out.

Messenger's wand crackled loudly.

The witch flinched.

Mirf stood up, walked around the table and stopped next to Fair Morn. "Make room." She pushed a chair into the space, and sat. Next to J. C., directly across the table from the witch, and stared at her.

"So why are you here?" It was an impatient question. Tinker was now sitting straight and getting more than a little irritated. From the living room something began to hum loudly.

"Gentle, My Lord," cautioned Chicken.

"Ripple threw me here. To gain your help."

"To do what?"

"Powerful, and terrible forces, are attempting to kill our youngest sister before she births."

"Kill? Rampeleh?" asked Mirf, startled by this piece of news. "Birth?"

Reptar's head swivelled toward Mirf. "Shut your mouth."

In one fluid motion, Mirf surged to her feet, leaned over the table, as her right arm shot out. Her fingers clamped around the witch's throat. She dragged Reptar across the table, and smiled as ugly a smile as anyone at the table had ever seen.

"Urk," was all Reptar had time to say.

Holding Reptar up by the neck, her arms dangling, her spine bowed, Mirf hissed at the witch, face glaring into face. "If you move or try to move, I will squeeze this egg from its stem."

The witch's face was red, her eyes beginning to bulge.

"From you, I want no more smart mouth. I had enough trouble from that Ripple."

Reptar's face was shading to blue. Her eyes were rolling wildly.

"So, sweety, to me be pleasant." Mirf grimaced, her eyes seemed to glow. "Or I'll start by ripping off various of your appendages. Understand?" Mirf dropped her.

The witch sprawled loosely, gasping loudly amid the wreckage of breakfast.

Mirf sat and looked at Tinker. "So, what do you think, Chosen One?"

She placed one palm on top of Reptar's head and shoved her off the far side of the table. Along with plates, serving platters, and various of the food stuffs.

Then Mirf smiled sweetly. She thought it was sweetly. No-one else did. "And just for you, I will clean up this mess not counting that shiksa."

She stood and tapped J. C. on a shoulder. "You can help."

"Yes, ma'am," he gulped.

"For me, it's Mirf. Never a ma'am."

Smoke picked up the limp witch, still gasping violently for breath, and carried her into the living room.

The rest followed, leaving Mirf and J. C. to clean up the dining room.

Kragkoptar. Inside.

B'waas and Shlm, sitting in the dark, talking. About what they knew.

"Chaos."

"Terrible pain."

"Three tumbled."

"The clan is strong."

"Ripple."

"Spell burned."

"Ramp."

"Incomplete."

"The twins."

"Speak it softly, danger lies unsighted."

"The twins."

"Alive."

"Reptar."

"Near breath stopped."

"Dark vengeance will burn throughout the lineage."

"Yes."

"They will come falling upon us."

"They are blood of our blood."

"He . . . "

"Sssssshhhhhhh . . ."

"You know?"

"Yes."

Grimble's Gate. Dark Past Midnight.

He was angry. The knowledge had flown to him. Now he was on his way. It would be a long and convoluted journey to make. He might not arrive in time. Thus was his anger grown larger.

Wind, and other things, whirled around him as he stomped across the grass covered plain. Ahead of him everything fled. Behind him, all was torn and blasted, debris raining down, marking his passage.

His passing was also marked by the long line of deep depressions stretching back into the darkness.

Grandeville. Tinker's Place. Just Past Lunch Time.

They were scattered around the living room. Smoke had laid Reptar on the new couch and was sitting by her head. She stroked the hair from the witch's forehead. Reptar seemed to be recovering.

"Nice looking couch," said Tinker.

Reptar struggled into a sitting position. "I made it."

"Thanks."

"It is comfortable," said Smoke. "Longer and nicer than the other one."

"Now what?" asked Tinker.

Messenger looked at Smoke who shrugged her shoulders.

Fair Morn looked at Tinker.

He looked at Reptar.

Chicken came from the hall door and handed Reptar the top from one pair of Tinker's pajamas.

"Here, cover your charms. Our Lord needs not distractions."

"Piffle," said Tinker.

Reptar took the garment and put it on. She looked at them. "Is this your tribal costume?"

Messenger giggled.

"No," said Smoke. "Just a comfortable thing for lounging in."

"Getting to be one," suggested Tinker.

"Ripple said that you are to come," commanded Reptar.

"I, we, do not work for Ripple," stated Tinker.

"Why didn't Ripple come herself?" asked Fair Morn. "She worked the spell to throw you here."

"We are not going," growled Tinker.

"My Lord?" Chicken looked at him.

"The deal was that **IF** Ramp asked for help we would go. She isn't asking."

She nodded. "Most true, My Lord."

"So, we are not going." He looked at Reptar. "How are you going to get home?"

"My sister will . . " The flash dazzled their eyes. Thunder rolled. Reptar was gone.

"She took the pajama top," cried Messenger.

Chicken sat on the arm of Tinker's chair, leaned against him and ruffled his hair.

"STOP THAT."

"Sweet Prince, shall we go a'town enow?"

"What for?"

"For to purchase thee additional tribal costume?"

"Oh boy," said Messenger, jumping to her feet. "Shopping."

"One?" asked Fair Morn.

"What?"

"Can we buy different sizes? Please? This one is overly snug." She plucked at her pajama top with her thumb and forefinger.

"Sure. Let's buy you guys your own pajamas. In appropriate sizes. While you are there you can explain to the clerk why you are wearing men's. Instead of lady's."

Chicken started for the door. "We do wear as We do chose. Tis nay concern of coin squeezing a'merchant."

"Where are you going, Princess?"

"For to shop, My Lord."

"Not in my pajamas, you're not."

"Oh?" said Chicken.

"It would be unseemly."

"Indeed?"

"True."

Chicken began to take off her top. "We will Us hurry."

"J . C. is still here."

Chicken ran for the hall.

Messenger tittered and followed. So did everyone else.

In minutes everyone was changed and ready to go. They clattered out through the kitchen.

"We are going to town, J. C., to buy pajamas," explained Tinker, leaning from the kitchen archway into the dining room. "See you later."

"Just about done," said J. C.

"Clean as new." Mirf waved her arm. "Where's that witch?"

"Went home." said Tinker.

"Vunderbar. We will wait here. The big stud can show me around. But I must leave, soon."

"We won't be long," said Tinker.

J. C. walked out to the truck with him. "I have never seen anything like that before. Ever."

J. C. glanced over his shoulder at the house.

Tinker laughed. "Believe us now?"

J. C. nodded and laughed. "Tinker, I believe, I believe. It is just a little hard, but I do."

"Ah, J .C., just a few things to know."

"What?"

"Don't touch that sword leaning in the corner of the living room, or the big ugly weapon in our new quarters. Lethal, deadly."

"O. K. That's it?"

"Sure. You are in good hands."

Tinker laughed at J.C.'s expression and jumped into the truck, started it, and headed for town with an excited to be going shopping crew.

Bahn Duhr Tohr. The Royal City. Evening.

"Sister, sister," cried the short woman, standing by the side of the bed, gently stroking one limp arm. "I am back."

"I will recover," came the faint reply.

"Glad to hear that," said Hanred, entering the bedroom. He sat on the edge of the bed and gently took one of her hands in his.

"Ramp?" asked Ripple, looking at her sister.

"Got her. And something else. It acted like it was her mate."

"R-Bar, don't be crude," hissed Ripple.

"He was going to attack me." R-Bar smiled at the thought.

The air crackled faintly.

"He is Ramp protected," explained Ripple. "You could

have been injured."

"Hum, hum, hum, hum!" said R-Bar.

A rasping voice called wildly from the central room. "RIPPLE!"

"In here," answered R-Bar.

The tall woman staggered into the room and stood clenching the door jamb.

"You disappeared," gasped R-Bar.

"I have returned."

"Rather strange costume, even for you," observed R-Bar.

"One of The Chosen One's cohort gave it to me, Runt."

"What did you do?" asked Ripple.

"I almost died, sister. Why didn't you tell me that there was powerful magic involved?"

Ripple struggled to sit up. Hanred quickly stuffed several pillows behind her back.

"What powerful magic? He now has powerful magic?"

Reptar shrugged off the pajama top. "I almost went far. Twice."

She arched her neck. Dark smudges glared against the pale skin. Small red blotches, with sharply demarked red lines radiating from them, sprinkled her torso.

"Must have been quite a brawl," observed Hanred.

"One of his tried to blast me into nowhere. Then a creature calling itself Mirf almost twisted my head off."

"MIRF?" said Ripple and Hanred.

"That hob-goblin," hissed Ripple.

"No," replied Reptar. "It was a woman."

"Husband, stop staring like that. Sister, clothe yourself."

Reptar put the pajama top on and leaned against the wall.

R-Bar stared at her. "What is wrong with you?"

"I am near far, small sister. I haven't the strength to recreate my cloth."

She began to slide down the wall. "Help me."

Hanred leaped from the bed and caught her in his arms. "UMP! Almost as heavy as you, Dusky Armful."

"Put her in the empty bedroom. And do not spent a lot of time tucking her in."

Hanred winked lewdly at Ripple and staggered away with his burden.

R-Bar sat on the bed. "Will they live?"

"Reptar is mostly exhausted, strangely injured. Ramp is in great danger. Hanred will assist. But you will have to do it. The book is marked."

"Right away." R-Bar jumped down and ran into the central room calling gaily, "Oh, Hanred . . . "

Grandeville. Tinker's place. Early Afternoon.

"So, it's a nice place," said Mirf.

"Certainly is," agreed J .C.

They had wandered the house and were getting close to finishing their tour of the surrounding lands. Both felt that this house of Tinker's was an interesting, if not more than a little strange, architectural design.

"So, cutie, tell me about yourself, a little."

"What's to know?" asked J. C. "Cutie."

"How about John Tinker, and them, for starters?"

"Wal, anything for the Little Lady," drawled John Wayne.

Mirf looked at him from the corners of her eyes, but didn't say anything.

So he told her.

J. C. had come to the area about eight years ago to work for Doc, Dr. Kappa Heckmann, an anthropologist, as his research assistant and chef. Doc had persuaded J .C. to leave his career of forever student, to stop burying himself in graduate studies, to stop gathering degrees in everything he bumped into and to start living in the real world. J . C.'s involvement in college had started at a younger than normal age when a distant uncle had learned of his nephew's unique gifts. He told J. C. that he would pay for his education as long as J. C. stuck to it, not realizing what this would turn into. But the uncle had been as good as his word. And given J. C.'s mental gifts he had found that he could have a rip roaring good time being a student. Then Doc had appeared. And then, there he was, living in rural Grandeville. Not long after he had arrived, while visiting the local outdoor supply store, Leonard's, he had heard Tinker and Hard discussing the merits of this and that equipment, walked over to talk, and and from then on they were the fastest of friends.

J. C. laughed. "And everything was as normal for us as normal can get, given that this is Grandeville, a very quiet, rural part of the world."

He explained to Mirf how Tinker had suddenly disappeared, had seemed to being fleeing from something in Grandeville, stayed away for about a year, and had then returned. And shortly thereafter, he was living with Smoke and Chicken. Tinker hadn't explained and no one had asked. And then he had returned with Messenger and Fair Morn.

J. C. nudged Mirf's shoulder. "But now we know, don't we? Don't answer, it was a rhetorical question."

While walking in the pasture, Mirf had buttoned her blouse, casting a sideways glance at J. C. as she did. He just walked along, now telling her about the pasture and the slump that was the Great Depression, and headed them back toward the house.

As they entered the kitchen, he asked, "Want some coffee, Mirf?"

"Sure."

J. C. fixed the coffee maker and leaned back against the countertop while it worked. "There are probably some cookies over there." He pointed at one of the kitchen cabinets.

Mirf opened one and peered inside.

"It is the green can."

Mirf took the lid off and reached in. Then she handed the can to J. C. "Look pretty good."

"Thanks." J. C. took a few. And observed, "Must have been made by Messenger. Oat meal with raisons. She said that she liked this kind the best."

"Boychick?"

"What?"

"Come with me."

"Where?"

"I need help."

"Didn't look like that to me."

"That witch let her mouth get in her way."

"I don't know anything about witches. Or hob-goblins for that matter." He smiled at her.

"So who's a hob-goblin?" Her eyes glittered. "Eh, maybe a bad question? So, I'll make you a deal."

J. C. grinned. "Same deal as the one you offered Tinker?"

Mirf grinned back. "Does that mean I've got a lech here?"

"Not really." J. C. shrugged.

"Good. Wouldn't want you to think I was easy."

"Somehow I wouldn't believe that of you."

"Ho Ha, an expert, are you?"

"Here and there."

"So boychick, what do you know?"

J. C. told her. He listed all the degrees he had collected and all the subjects he had studied before Doc had convinced him to become Doc's assistant.

"My, my, my," said Mirf. "Who could tell." She ate another cookie.

"Yah, I know," mumbled J. C. around his cookie.

"Pretty is pretty. Don't knock it."

He handed her a cup and picked up the pot. "Here, hold still, I'll pour." He poured. "What would I do, if I came with you?"

"Keep me company. Help me. Things like that there."

"Like what?" He watched her face intently.

She sucked in a deep breath and kissed him on one cheek, and said, "With me, who knows? I play it as it comes. But, I've been making a list." She tapped her forehead. "Ever since The Chosen One refused."

J. C. didn't say anything. He just sipped his coffee and looked at her, face blank, eyes recording everything.

"It's an adventure, bubeleh, a chance to see new worlds. Maybe make a fortune even. Or two."

She rubbed her thumb and forefinger together. Her eyes appraised him.

"It's dangerous, isn't it?" he asked.

"To you, no lies. Yes." All brusque business.

"How dangerous?"

"We might die. Horribly."

"Not much of an offer. Horrible death."

"For me, it'sa a job." Mirf smiled at him. Somehow, this time, it was a real smile.

"And you like it."

"You betcha, boychick. I love it. You might love it. Who knows, it could become yet another career."

J. C. laughed. "What would I need to bring?"

"Just you, big boy. We will pick up anything else we need as we go along."

"And how long might that be?" He refilled his coffee cup and took another cookie.

"As one of your famous folk suggested, time is relative. For here, one, two, three days, maybe. For you, who knows. Long as it takes."

"Ummmm."

"Do it, J. C ."

"Why?"

"I like you. We will make a good team. And you know where the trail is that Hard used. Right?"

"Sure do."

"Well?" She nudged him with an elbow, and stated, "Adventures are for the adventurous. R.H. Davis."

J . C. grinned at her." "You are manipulative, Mirf."

"Of course." She grinned back.

"Have to go home, get some better clothes, sturdy boots."

"You got any for me?"

"Wellll, I just might at that. Let's go." He set his cup on the counter top.

"Ho Boy." Mirf spun and slammed him on the shoulder with one hand, rocking him sideways. "Let's give a go."

"In a minute, I need to leave a note for Tinker."

J. C. rubbed his shoulder and went looking for paper and pencil.

And then they rattled down the driveway and the road to Doc's in J. C.'s old van.

The Six Lands. Late Afternoon.

They stepped around and out. And walked out from behind the tree trunk. The suit cases jostled along behind them.

"Where are we?" she asked.

"The turn was to The Six Lands."

"How much further?"

"The road is over there. That way is the village." He pointed. "We should find the place about half-way."

"Why are we here?"

"To meet a man. You will like him."

"How do you know that?"

"Because."

"Why?"

He smiled.

She stepped closer. "Tell me."

"He is short like you." He laughed and wrapped his arms around her. "You met him once before."

"If we were at home."

"I know. Shall we go?"

"Let go."

"Maybe I won't. For a little while."

"Does your short friend have an extra room?"

"I don't know. I have never visited his home before."

"Let's go find out."

He kissed her forehead and released her. "It is not very far."

"Too far," she said, tugging him into motion.

Grandeville. Tinker's Place. Getting On Towards Dinner Time.

They piled from the truck.

Arms crowded with packages, eyes gleaming, they banged and pushed against each other on the way back into the house. Inside, Tinker flopped on the couch, and sighed.

"What a day, so far."

Smoke opened her package and held up the top for him to admire.

"Not too bad," said Tinker. "For black."

"Black is a good color. Comfortable. Coffee, MindMate?"

"Sure. Thanks."

Chicken passed Smoke going the other way, walked slowly into the living room, a piece of paper held in one hand. She sat next to him.

"John Love?"

"What? What's that? Why so quiet?"

"My Lord, J. C. did himself run off with the strange Mirf."

"You've got to be kidding."

"Nay jest, Our Prince. This note does say he do be about to see all that we did speak upon and that he do now be her assistant."

Tinker mumbled something under his breath. They all felt his mood darkening.

Smoke came back and handed him a full cup and two cookies. "J. C. should be all right."

"Loud Mirf do pear most capable."

"I'm sure that you are right, Princess."

"Surprise," cried Messenger, bouncing forward. She and Fair Mom held out what they had bought.

"We got you some new sets of pajamas," said Fair Morn.

"Six pair," giggled Messenger.

"All for your own," said Smoke.

"Me'thinks," said Chicken. "That thee dost need view these pretties of our's."

"On the flesh," laughed Messenger.

"As it were," said Smoke.

Fair Morn stepped behind the couch and began to change.

He reached into Smoke to watch her through Smoke's eyes.

"No peeking," said Fair Morn.

He stopped before Smoke blocked him out.

Messenger ran down the hall followed by Smoke and Chicken.

Fair Morn stepped around and stood, facing him, watching his face. "One?"

"My goodness," said Tinker.

Messenger popped back into the room. "See." Her pajamas were a light green.

"Black is better," said Smoke, standing behind her.

"EEEK," said Messenger.

Smoke had pinched her.

"Nice yellow," said Tinker as Chicken slipped into the room.

She gave him a short bow. "We all do well, Fair Prince?"

"I'll say. Guess I'll just have to put on one of my presents."

"Goodie," said Messenger, hurtling a package at him.

He caught it, stood, and started for their quarters, and yawned, "But I think that I am ready for a nap."

Grandeville. Tinker's Place. A Little Closer To Dinner Time.

"Umm?"

"Thee hast entwined thyself in soft covers." She knelt and yanked. He rolled, unwinding.

"Huh? Hey . . . "

"Thee did spin in Sweet Orpheus arms. We do Us require some fair warmth and comfort, do We not?"

"Sure, Princess." He kicked everything into some semblance of order.

She yanked up an edge and flopped down next to him.

Tinker mumbled and yanked the covers over his head.

"Me'Lord?" asked Chicken as she felt his fingers run up her chest.

"Do you know the fact of three?" he asked.

"No."

"Three buttons, no more."

"Thee jests."

"I wouldn't do that."

"That does tickle."

"Button three. And one bow."

"My Lord! We have been undone."

"Right."

Stumpf. Morning. Warming Up.

"So, where are we?"

"A good question. Too bad I don't have a good answer. I don't know. But, it's ugly."

"Not very assuring." J. C. twisted his head and looked at their surroundings. Behind them was the shallow cave from which they had just stepped.

It was a stark, hot, dry environment they had entered. Jagged rock everywhere. Little vegetation. Colors all red, brown, yellow.

Soaring cliffs defined the narrow defile they were facing. Overhead, the sky had a brown red cast to it.

They were both dressed in heavy jeans, thick shirts, good jackets, sturdy boots. J. C. shucked off his jacket, tied the arms around his waist, rolled up his shirt sleeves, and unbuttoned the front of his shirt. Mirf followed suit.

She pointed.

"That way, J. C." And started down the slight dusty path as it twisted back and forth. Small dust puffs slowly drifted away from their foot prints.

J. C. followed her. "How come you don't know where we are?"

"Some nogoodnik has jiggered around with the node. Let me tell you something else, bubee, that takes some real nasty to do that. Worried?"

"Nope."

"Why not?"

"Confidence in your knowledge and skills, Chief Inspector."

She whirled around. "You're pulling my leg, right?"

He looked down at her legs. "No. You are standing on them." He looked up. "You got Hard back home, didn't you? Right?"

"Right."

"You got yourself back, right?"

"You betcha, bubee."

"So, I am confident."

Mirf stepped closer to him, reached up and lightly patted him on the side of the face. "I am beginning to like you, J. C."

He reached over and did the same thing. "Well, under all the off-putting mannerisms, you are not too bad yourself. What do you think we will find at the other end of this gorge?"

"No idea. Let's go find out." Mirf spun and started along the path again. "We need to find another node."

They didn't exactly hurry, not in this heat, but they didn't dawdle either.

In a deep rock shadow Naplar the Observer watched the pair walking away and into the heat. He poked his beast to remind it to remain silent. And followed them.

Grandeville. Tinker's place. Inching Toward Dinner Time.

"SweetLove, be thee awake?"

"Ummmmmmm?" He rolled toward her.

"Me'Love?"

"Ummmmm?" He reached out.

"Thee does Us a'tickle."

"Uh, huh. Gets to be a pointy rascal, doesn't it?"

"Cease and desist."

"How come it is so quiet in here?"

"To town they did all go."

"Again? Chen come back?"

"Nay, they did travel in most fair chariot."

His eyes popped wide. "Who's driving?"

"Messenger. She does contain all thy motor memories and skills."

He exhaled slowly. "She doesn't have a driver's license. Now what's going on?"

"We did council, we did."

"And." He held her gently.

"They do intend great quantity of food stuffs for to purchase."

"For what?"

"Travel, My Lord."

"WHAT?" He sat up flinging covers and quilts in all directions.

"You can't be serious. Look!" He tapped her with his finger tip. "Scar. Scar. Scar. How many more? The next one could be the last one. Goes for all of you. Me too, for that matter."

He jabbed a finger his side. "What do you think that is, a tattoo?" His frown darkened. "We can't keep doing things like that, someone might die." He stared into nowhere.

Chicken lurched at him, knocking him backward, wrapping her arms and legs around him. "We do understand, really and truly, We do. But, My Lord, Ramp's Hard, and now thy friend J. C., do be gone."

"Ramp's Hard?" He frowned up into sparkling blue eyes.

"Tis most true," she said, kissing the tip of his nose.

"Well, Chicken's Tinker ain't going anywhere."

"Thee did promise solemn make."

"We get a message from Ramp?"

"Nay."

"Then?" He rolled them over.

"Tis most mighty distraction."

"Uh . . . huh."

"We do but prepare."

"Oh . . . kay."

"OH . . . aye . . ."

Paradise. Evening Blending Into Late Evening.

They were sitting in the living room watching the fire as it crackled in the fireplace. His wife smiled at him.

Big Red smiled back and looked at everyone: his wife, his son, his daughter-in-law. "So far, everything seems to be moving along in the correct direction or directions. John will remain unbothered by me."

Dancing-All-The-Day slipped her arm around his waist. "Good, they deserve to be left alone." Then she looked pointedly at her son.

"And that means banish any thoughts you might have of running off, getting involved," stated Big Red staring at his son, nodding at his wife.

Their son smiled, said good night, and left the room, his arm around his wife's shoulders.

After the door closed silently behind them, Dancing-All-The-Day asked, "Will it stay this way?"

Big Red ducked his head. "Hard to say. This is getting to be a very complicated business, this confusion. Magical forces, good and bad, as well as other forces are jumping all over the universes. Right now all I can do is watch. And wait for the most opportune moment to act. If there is one."

Diawi Fitable. Bright. Sunny.

The folk of the small village of Grou Pep fled their central gathering space and hurtled down each of the four ways that led from that space.

The cause of all that terror and fear was a woman who stood calmly facing the large warrior not too far from her.

His armor and leather garb were grey in color and heavily battle scarred. This was in stark contrast to her forest green almost black unsoiled robes, apparently untouched by the normal wear and tear of long distance travel.

The robe flared widely and seemed to float just above the paved surface of the central gathering space. She clenched a short golden staff in one hand.

He held a very large and battle notched sword in his right hand.

"Sooooo," she purred with the whisper of warning from deep inside the hood of her robe. "You would tempt death?"

"Brazkar has seen death in many forms and in many elseplaces." He waggled the long blade at her. "I require food and lodgings. You stand in my way. None do that!"

"You would steal from the innocent, Brazker the almost dead?"

"I would know the name of the female corpse you are about to become."

Her staff soft crackled. Something soft shadow dark seemed to step from her and toward Brazkar. "This one," she softly said, "is Lady Nighttouch."

His weapon hacked at the dark shadow thing surging around him.

She turned away as the body crumbled into a heap.

"Come!" She headed for the East Way followed by shadow darkness.

Stumpf. Mid-Morning.

It had been a hot and dusty and long, two-hour hike to the end of the narrow defile.

J. C. had jerked his shirt completely loose. It now hung flopping over his hips. Their surroundings reminded him of numerous trips he had taken into the California desert on various activities with Doc.

"At least there is no humidity. Makes the heat bearable," he observed.

"Rag bag," answered Mirf, debating silently to herself about whether she ought to shuck her shirt all together. She glanced over at J. C.

"Boychick, are you easily distracted?"

"No. Why?"

"Just curious." She grinned at him.

"I'd keep it on if I were you. This looks like prime sun-burn country to me."

"Rim dimble." Mirf began to roll down her sleeves and button her shirt.

J. C. grinned back. Then he stopped walking and pointed. "Looks like more of the same."

They looked out over the country spreading before them. The defile behind them was no more than a crack in the face of what appeared to be ever upward reaching mountain range of rock stacked upon rock. The plain in front of them appeared to be mostly dust and rocks, dry and barren, everything all soft reds, oranges, brown-rust. The only feature that broke the desolation was the broad path that bent along the edge of the rock barrier from which they had stepped.

"You see any signs of water?" he asked.

Mirf squinted into the harsh light, first one way then the other.

"That way." She pointed, then tapped the side of her nose. "The hobgoblin part smells water."

"Pretty handy."

"Handy-schmandy."

"Grump."

"You betcha, boychick."

"So how far is it?"

"Not too far." She started off. Toward the water.

They walked in silence. Mostly silence. Mirf was mumbling to herself.

J. C. paid no apparent attention to the noise. Actually he was, but he was also watching their surroundings and wondering where they were, where they had come to, and whether anything lived in this most stark of stark places.

High above them, standing on an outcrop of reddish rock, one of the living things stared down at the road and the beings who were headed along it, walking toward The Barren Wastes.

From this high up, they were just specks in motion. They didn't look like demons, but with the unknown it paid to be somewhat cautious. So it would be best to stay high and follow them from some distance. Especially as these small creatures were headed toward the camping space.

He stared at his surrounding and sniffed loudly. No flowers grew this high up.

The Six Lands. Warm and Pleasant. Late Afternoon.

The grandfather took the box from his grandson and eased the silver bands from it, handing them to the grandson. Then he carefully removed the top and took out the cloth wrapped object inside, pushing the empty box at his grandson. The grandson took it, carefully watching everything that happened, noting every action, every detail, It was the mark of a Teller of Tales.

His grandfather smiled gently at him, recognizing the reason for that intensity of gaze. Slowly he unwound the cloth revealing the dagger and its sheath and its belt.

"It is beautiful, is it not?"

Tears nodded. And gathered in the cloth shoved in direction.

His grandfather fastened the belt around his waist and patted the dagger. "Only I may handle this blade, Tears, only I. This is my weaponkin."

Tears stared at it, his eyes growing rounder and rounder. "This is from your Tale? It is real?"

The grandfather ruffled Tear's hair. "Oh yes, it is real."

"I thought you just made it all up."

"Yes. Who would believe otherwise. Come, we have to get ready, we have a new Tale to see."

We . . . We do?"

The grandfather laughed. "Indeed, we do." He pointed into the distance, to one side of the woods.

Tears looked.

Two figures were walking toward them. One was normal size, the other a giant.

Tears gasped. And blushed. He should have noticed. And stepped closer to his grandfather's side.

His grandfather threw a protecting arm around his shoulders. "Do not be afraid. They are friends. I recognize the big one. And I think I recognize the other as well."

Tears watched them approach. "Really?"

"Oh yes, really. Your adventure is about to begin. You are about to see a new Tale, one of wonder and amazement." And laughed, a very delighted laugh.

Bahn Duhr Tohr. The Royal City. Late Evening.

"Little Shadow, this is not my kind of business."

"Just hold the book steady so I can read it. And stop looking so nervous ."

Hanred stood in the middle of the debris, holding the great book open, flat against his stomach, pages facing out, peering apprehension and lots of worry over the top at the short young woman dressed in black.

R-Bar stood facing him, intently reading the inscription, staring over the top of the large kettle that floated in the space between them. She was humming happily, flinging this and that into the kettle as the directions specified, saying the appropriate words at the appropriate time.

The glow from the kettle shifted from yellow to red to

green to blue.

"And one to go!" she gurgled happily, pitching the last item in and dancing backward.

Hanred leaped away shouting, **"CAREFUL! CAREFUL!"**

The kettle began to vibrate faster and faster. Something oozed into the air, a presence more than a form. Suddenly it split into pieces, darting in three directions at once.

Hanred dropped the book, adding a gout of dust to the already dust haze laden air in the room, and charged into Ripple's room.

She was sprawled half out of the bed, legs still tangled in the covers. She gave him an upside down grimace.

He crashed to his knees next to her, throwing his arms around her.

"Either help me back into the bed,' she grumbled. "Or drag me all the way to the floor."

Failing her legs, she tumbled out, knocking him over, spilling over him as she sprawled. Hanred wound up on the bottom.

"Are you all right?" It was his question, but she asked it.

"Yes I am. But I am weighted down by ample amounts of Dusky beauty."

"I take that as a compliment," she said, wiggling into a more comfortable position.

"Witchy Delight, you sound much improved."

"I am. It was a powerful but unpleasant cure. She did well. Help me up, then check on the others."

Ripple sat up and patted his stomach.

"Let R-Bar clean up the mess in there." She wobbled to her feet and crawled into the bed talking to him over her shoulder, "See to Reptar. But, I expect you not to dawdle at your labors."

Hanred stood. And pinched her.

"OUCH!"

"Definitely much improved," he said, gently pressing and tucking the covers around her, brushing the hair from her face, kissing her forehead. Then he spun on his heels and hurried from the room.

"Hum, hum, hum, hum," murmured Ripple to herself.

He found Reptar sitting up, breathing heavily through her mouth, the pajama top sweat plastered to her.

Hanred hurried away and quickly returned carrying a bowl of cool water, towels and clothes. He gently loosened and removed the soggy garment and sponged the glistening skin.

"Hum, hum, hum, hum," she whispered, rolling her eyes at him. It was a vocal mannerism that all the sisters of the Faan clan shared. The flush rapidly faded from her skin.

"You seem to be recovering nicely."

"I am. Ripple is very adept."

"R-Bar did it."

Two arms fastened around his waist while someone rubbed against his back, and stated, "I expect to be rewarded handsomely."

Hanred pried the arms loose, twisted around and in one deft motion shoved the sopping cloth down the front of her baggy upper garment.

R-Bar leaped backwards, yanked her belt loose, and tugged her dripping smock forward. The cloth splashed onto the floor.

"Dim, dim, dim, dim!" she snarled.

Reptar laughed.

R-Bar scooped up the soggy thing and hurtled it at her sister's face. The towel stopped in mid-air and dropped to the floor.

Hanred hastily backed from the room. "I will go see how Ramp is doing. Ladies."

Reptar frowned at him.

R-Bar stuck out her tongue. "Don't be so nasty," she snarled. Witches didn't like being called ladies.

"I know," he said as he kicked his way through the mess

in both rooms, Hanred spoke loudly over his shoulder. "Ripple said for you to clean this up, R-Bar."

"Dim, dim, dim, dim!" growled back her answer.

Bahn Duhr Tohr. The Royal City. Mid-Morning.

Ramp was sitting on the small couch, Hard next to her. She was leaning against him with one of his arms over her shoulders. They were both dressed in comfortable, loose-fitting clothes.

"Looking much improved," said Hanred, nodding at them.

"Alive," replied Ramp.

"Thanks, Han," said Hard.

"Ripple's spell. R-Bar did it."

"R-Bar?" asked Hard.

"The short one that wears that red belt, a bit of daring, is R-Bar."

"Oh," said Hard. "Her. She growls."

R-Bar poked her head into the room, glared at Hard, saw that Ramp was recuperating, and grinned wickedly at Hanred, "Oh, Hanred . . . "

A purple-green plant with waving limbs and grey flowers whose petals puckered open and closed turned toward her. "Yes?"

"Dim, dim, dim, dim!" growled R-Bar. "You know I hate those things. GAK!" She jerked back and spoke to him from around the doorjamb.

"I could really use some help. Please?"

Hanred turned back to Hard and Ramp, himself again.

"She," he explained, "is the only one that says please. Rest and recover, Magician. You have worried us much, all of us."

He walked into the other room, grinning. "And what is my reward if I should decide to help you clean up this mess?"

"I will think of something," replied R-Bar gaily.

Grandeville. Tinker's Place. Late Afternoon.

Tinker's eyes opened. All he could see was the wall, painted a cool blue. He was lying on his side. Someone was pushing against his back. Slipping sideways, he rolled flat, then over. Somehow he had twisted completely around in the bed.

"We are back," intoned Fair Morn, poking his stomach gently with one fingertip.

"I can tell," mumbled Tinker.

"You can't sleep all day."

"Why not? I need the rest. What's going on?"

"Oh, nothing."

"Oh, oh." Tinker threw back the covers back and sat up, then rearranged himself properly in the bed.

Fair Morn wrapped her arms around him, leaned against him, her head on his shoulder.

"Let go"

She nibbled on his shoulder. "Say please."

"Let me go. Please."

She held him tighter. "Nope."

"Watch that squeeze, I have to breathe. What is going on?"

"A surprise." She released her arm. Just a little.

"Yes?"

"Yep." She leaned back.

He didn't have a choice. He fell onto her.

HELP!

The only answer he received was giggles and laughter.

"I give up."

Bravo, My Lord. It was Chicken.

"Maybe I will become a hermit."

"Grumble, grumble, grumble," cooed Fair Morn, throwing a leg over one of his.

"You guys are all getting goofy," he said. *Smoke?*

What?

Will you please come in here and pry this winged thing off of me? Please?

Busy.

Everyone is busy, right?

Most true, Sweet Prince.

"Me too," breathed Fair Morn next to his cheek. "I am not a thing."

"Right," said Tinker. "Busy, busy."

"As a bee."

"As an overgrown moth."

She relaxed, but didn't let go, merely rolling and pushing him so she could sprawl lazily over him.

"Comfy?"

"Yes, One. You?"

"Sure." He managed to yank one arm free. "We gonna lay around like this all day? I am hungry?"

Her eyes glittered.

"Didn't you get anything to eat in town?"

She nodded. "We ate some of those flat things inside the bread. At the little house by the large road."

"How many burgers was it?"

"Only four."

"A snack," he said, tugging her face closer to his, brushing her lips lightly with his. "Yum, yum. Onions."

"I like onions."

"You like anything edible."

"I like you," she said, nibbling lightly on the side of his neck.

"Moths can't be carnivores." He shoved her over and gave her a little nip. And then another.

My Lord, leave off thy gnawing of Our winged sister. A proper meal does thee await on fair grass.

The Six Lands. Late Afternoon.

"She is very nice." said Tears.

"I think so," said $1.98, smiling at everyone.

"Thank you, Tears," replied Plum Duff. "But that does not mean that you are coming with us."

They were sitting in the middle of the field having a picnic, ordered up by Duff, and discussing where to go from here. Duff had brought in a soft green pastel colored rug, pillows, and a number of dishes and food containers with beverages appropriate for the meal.

The grandfather stated firmly that Tears must come along.

$1.98 munched on something tasty, waggled it at the grandfather.

"Sorrowful, are you really coming with us?"

"Absolutely. I realize that given my age I might not return to The Six Lands. But," he held up one hand to stifle comments. smiling brightly at his visitors. "When I go on a trip to tell tales, The Tale, I might not return either. Not due to fearful hazards but due to natural processes. So, I put it to you and Duff this way. Is it any different what kind of trip it might be if I do not return?"

He laughed softly. "I concede the point that it might make a difference to my survivors. However, there still will be a mighty tale to be recorded and to be retold. Tears is the next one. My sons have neither the interest, nor, as it happens to turn out, the raw talent to do so. So. We are going."

Refilling his cup and Duff's, Sorrowful gently smiled at her, then at $1.98. "Hopefully with you."

"Seems that we have company," said $1.98.

Duff patted his knee. "Yes, Dear." Then she looked into Tear's face, her expression stern, glacial. "You will do exactly as you are told, exactly as we say."

Tears realized that this was not a debatable point. He glanced at his grandfather.

Sorrowful threw one arm around Tear's shoulders and hugged him tight. "Of course. He will stay by my side. And I will tell him how to keep out of trouble."

Sorrowful laughed at $1.98's expression. "I know, I did not, before. But Duff is correct. Age will keep me from doing impulsive things. So and so. Now I must go home, dress appropriately for the trip, and say my goodbyes."

He stood, Tear's jumping to his feet to stand by his side.

$1.98 rose to his feet. Duff waved away the picnic.

Sorrowful linked his arm through one of her's. "I have extra rooms and it will be something for my wife and sons to meet you and $1.98. My eldest son can get enough mats together to make a large enough sleeping place. Shall we?"

"Of course," said Duff.

Tear's peered around his grandfather at her as they started to walk down the path. She winked back at him.

$1.98 followed them, the suitcases trailing at his heels.

The brown jewel on her finger flashed in the sunlight. The d'metal seemed to glow green fire.

Tears made mental notes of these details. They were the things that made tales great. And made the Teller of Tales great.

Grandeville. Tinker's Place. Well, It Is Kinna Dinner Time.

They sat on the grass, in the shade of one of the fruit trees, at the edge of the front lawn. A light breeze drifted up the slope from the valley, gently ruffling their hair. A large cloth covered the grass. Platters of food were artfully scattered on its center.

"My Lord, be this not most pleasant?"

Tinker nodded at Chicken. "Very nice. Ummm?"

"Yes?"

"You guys didn't go to town dressed that way, did you?"

Messenger violently shook her head. "Oh, no!"

"We changed our clothes after returning," said Smoke.

Chicken sat on her knees, legs tucked under. "We do in most fair tribal garb ourselves. To be same as thee and she."

"Might start a new fad," said Tinker. "Pajamas as leisure wear."

Messenger crawled over and sat by his free side. "They are very comfortable," she said, refilling his glass.

"Yep," he replied as he slowly let his gaze wander from one face to the next. Four happy expressions looked back. "You guys ready to tell me, now?"

"We are that, My Lord." Chicken nodded.

"O.K.?" He sipped from his glass.

"We do into village quaint betake ourselves, rather they do this as full well thee know, to food stuffs in some quantity buy."

"And?"

"We do pack everything as might be required. Food, gear, everything."

Smoke smiled at him. "Everything is ready."

"Funny food," added Messenger.

"Funny food?" asked Tinker. "What kind of food is funny?"

"Desiccated," replied Fair Morn.

"One do naught but pour water pon it," explained Chicken.

"And we can carry great quantities," added Fair Morn. "Because it is light." She winked at him. "Like me."

"So we bought large amounts," said Smoke. And indicated Fair Morn. "She is not desiccated."

Tinker hunched his shoulders up around his neck as he lowered his head. "And you-all figure that we are going somewhere, don't you?"

Chicken reached over and touched his arm. "Oh, My Lord, glower not so darkly pon us. Tis only that we do feel it a'coming, we do. All."

"And we are going well prepared," stated Smoke. "This time." She refilled her plate and Fair Morn's.

"Oh, yes," added Messenger, pressing against his side, grabbing one of his hands in her's. "Really really prepared!"

"And this time," added Smoke in a low, flat tone of voice, her eyes seeming to glow an orange gold predatory light. "We are not getting any more scars, none of us."

"That is right," stated Fair Morn. "And we are not

taking any chances, either."

"Oh, really?" said Tinker.

"My Lord, our Verra own true love, we do, most heavily, so discuss this matter and we do decide!"

"That we are going to kill it, whatever it is, if it looks bothersome," added Smoke.

"FIRST," snapped Messenger, her cheeks flushing red.

"Regardless," said Fair Morn, reaching for a platter, just to add a little bit more to her dish.

"Ahhhhh," said Tinker. "You ladies sound like you are getting awfully mean."

"We are," they chorused.

"But we are not going anywhere," stated Tinker.

"Not yet," they said, crowding around him. "But we are ready."

"OOOOOF," he said. They all hugged him at the same time.

Then they stood up and carried him into the house. They would finish the picnic, later, inside.

On the back ridge, twilight began flowing down the slope. They had started their lunch that late in the day. The lunch had been kinna dinner.

Three Trees Town. A Warm Sunny Day.

Ransapal, the Sluba mage that lived in the small town, sat at an outside table of the only inn in the town. His companion for the past several seasons sat across from him waiting patiently for the Server to bring their noonday meal. Town folk occupied the other three tables, enjoying their meals and the lovely day. And after the passage of the past several seasons the town folk had finally, and mostly, become accustomed to Ransapal's visitor. Of course, some did not. They usually sat in another room.

The folk had finally stopped wondering and speculating about him and her. After all, she lived in his house and accompanied him everywhere. But as far as anyone knew, that pair had never even touched each other. And the folk wondered about that also. And they thought that his behavior was rather strange as he, Ransapal, had laughed and enjoyed the company of one or another of the local young lasses. Before she had come into their town.

The Server hurried up to their table, set their plates, their food, and hurried hastily back inside the inn. He had never become comfortable with that mage's visitor.

She began to eat as soon as Ransapal served out the food. Her gold rod lay alongside her plate. "This is different," she said, soft whisper quiet. It was her normal tone of voice, the usual speaking voice of the Divineal of Thantala.

Ransapal poured, filling their mugs from the steaming blue container, and nodded. "I ordered a special meal."

"Why would you do that?"

"For special occasions."

"So?"

"We are finished." He took a sip from his mug. "You now know everything that I know about that which you wished to study. And you have three volumes of notes and data."

"True?"

He nodded. "Most true."

She paused and set down her eating utensil. "Then this one will have to do something."

He blanched, and sat back in his chair, stared across the table at her, and cast every protection spell that he knew over himself, and hoped that she would not harm any of the local folk. It was too bad, in a way. Some of the local folk that had run away had been returning from Gnarly Knoll, having decided that it was safe to do so.

She took a sip from her mug and spoke soft voice to him, "Ransapal, this one owes personal debt for lodging in your dwelling, for eating your meals, and for all the knowledge you did import."

She waggled one hand to cut off his comment. "This

Ransapal has been well mannered, most cautious, and," she cleared her throat, "most kind." She stood, flowing up in one smooth motion. "Walk with me. Back to your home."

And soon, all to soon as far as he was concerned, they stood in his rear garden area, out of sight from anyone who might wander down the narrow lane. Out of sight from his somewhat distant neighbors who might happen to stare over this way.

Turning to face him she reached up, tugged her hood back, and smiled at him.

He gasped, knowing he was about to die. And stared at her. Masses of jet black hair framed a face of soft beauty. Pale grey eyes watched him from a very serious face. "Is this one so ugly?"

He grabbed his mug and took a long pull. They had carried their mugs and their jug with them. After several swallows he managed to gasp, "NO! Not at all." And gestured wildly, splashing a few of his flowering shrubs. "In never has it been told that any did ever see the true face of one of The Divineal." He cleared his throat several times. "Ever!" He blanched. She was getting ready to kill him.

"Are you ill? Was our meal unclean?"

Violently he shook his head. "No! Shock! Surprise!" His hand shook as he refilled his mug. "None else."

She reached up and touched a small mark on her forehead just between and slightly higher than her eyebrows. "Put here by The Lady of Death. The Broken Circle." Dropping her hand, she leaned forward, and whispered gentle soft, "Stand still, Ransapal. Be quiet as death."

She flowed toward him as he jerked. Stepping lightly across the space separating them she reached out and softly set her fingertip on his forehead in the same place she had touched on her face, and took it away, leaving a small black mark.

"Long seasons past this one stated debt of The Order and now of this one. What does this Ransapal ask for?" She waited, pale grey eyes watching his every twitch. "Any thing?"

He stared at her. "What form of magic are you that touches a mage so surely with no fear of magical harm or explosion?"

Her head tilted slightly to one side. "Death may touch anything, magical or otherwise." She waited. "Ask."

He cleared his throat. "My needs are few. My life here is comfortable. And unbothered." He shook his head. "I do not know what to ask."

"Then this one will ask instead."

He jerked. "What?"

She slipped close, very close, almost touching him. "Kiss this one, Lady Fairdeath, Divineal of Thantala, Ransapal, mage of the Sulba guild." She waited, patient as death itself.

Resigned to his fate, he leaned forward, and very, very carefully, very gently did as she had asked. And much to his surprise he didn't die.

Bahn Duhr Tohr. The Royal City. Late Afternoon.

The room was clean and repaired, the furniture restored. Hanred was on the couch, back propped up with pillows, half sitting, half lying, legs outstretched.

Ripple sprawled across his lap, her fingers idly playing with the buttons on his shirt.

R-Bar sat with his feet in her lap.

Reptar was in one of the large chairs, her legs tucked under, wearing her regular clothes.

On the other couch sat Hard. Ramp was stretched out, eyes closed, her head in his lap, her hands crossed over one of his.

"Dark Morsel, I gather that you are fully recovered from your labors and from your medicine."

Ripple slipped her hand inside his shirt. "You may thank the child."

R-Bar sat upright, throwing her shoulders back. "Sister, I am not a child!"

Hanred leaned sideways and peered at R-Bar's smock.

"She is correct."

R-Bar winked at him, her tongue caressing her lips. "I am older than Ramp."

"MY, my." Hanred wiggled his toes.

"Derry's Dung is nice this time of year," suggested Ripple to her youngest witch sister. "For Derry's Dung."

"Dim, dim, dim, dim," snarled R-Bar.

"Find your own," snarled back Ripple.

Reptar smiled at them. "I found the most gorgeous, unmated one, even prettier and larger than Ramp's." And sat up straighter.

R-Bar stared at her, eyes glittering. "Where?"

"At The Chosen One's abode."

Ramp's eyes popped open. Hard leaned over and whispered, "She must mean J. C."

"Shhhhh," said Ramp.

"Speak tell," commanded R-Bar, watching her sister intently.

"Nothing to tell. I wasn't there long enough to know."

"Oh," grinned R-Bar. "Too bad."

Smoke, oily dense smoke, began to seep upward from the floor, oozing into the space between the couches. It formed a thick cloud that billowed gently.

"May I enter?" asked the cloud.

"Don't play games," snapped Ripple.

The cloud disappeared with a loud 'POP.'

A tall woman stood smiling at them. She wore black trousers draped over glistening black boots. Her blouse was tucked in. Over this she wore a long coat that reached to the backs of her knees. Her clothes were made from some dark material that shed no light. Her black hair was an ornate design of coils and braids. She was taller than Hard.

"Hayou, Rumtah," greeted R-Bar.

"Hayou, Runt." She nodded at her shortest, youngest witch sister, who nodded back.

"Hayou," said Reptar.

Rumtah jerked her head around, her hair flying. "Reptar, you are looking unsettled."

"She hasn't been well," said Hanred.

"You are Ripple's?" asked Rumtah, staring at him.

"All mine," stated Ripple. "Forever."

Hanred smiled.

Rumtah turned, a fluid, smooth motion, seemingly boneless.

"Greetings to you, Ramp Magician, and greetings to you, Ramp protected one."

It was the proper and formal witch salutation to a member of the clan after a long absence.

"I'm Hard," said Hard.

"Really?"

"His name," explained Ramp.

"Ripple's call said that you are in danger, youngest sister. Why is this so? How can this be?"

"She is in a birthing way," answered Ripple, swinging her feet to the floor as she turned and sat up, using Hanred for a backrest. He grunted softly.

"Of little," said Rumtah, waving one hand. A gesture of dismissal.

Ripple pointed upward. Dark clouds swirled low over their heads, pouring down and around them until they were surrounded, encased in a shell of darkness.

"Twins," said Ripple.

Reptar hissed loudly. R-Bar covered her mouth with one hand, her eyes going wide as she stared at Ramp.

"Twins?" rasped Rumtah.

"Twins," restated Ripple.

A rod of green fire snapped into Rumtah's hand. "No wonder you called."

She glanced at her sisters, then back at Ripple. "Difficult times."

"What will they be?" whispered R-Bar.

"Magicians," said Ramp.

R-Bar leaped straight up, her feet landing on the couch cushion, a dark creature twined around her ankles, growling loudly. "Who dares cause the trouble? To you?"

Ripple waved one hand, thunder rumbled loudly around them. "That we have to find out. First!"

"Then we kill it," stated R-Bar happily. The creature at her feet chattered its teeth in agreement.

Stumpf. Late Afternoon.

"Just ahead, bubeleh."

"What?"

"Water. Must be a spring."

Mirf was correct.

Just ahead, bubbling from a crack in the rock face, spilling liquid delight into a shallow basin carved long ago, ran a small stream of water.

"Ladies, first," said J. C.

"Don't be a smart mouth," said Mirf, plunging her face into the pool.

J. C. stepped forward and gave her a shove, his hand on her back, Then he leaped backwards as she reared up, snarling, and spinning around.

J. C. was a safe distance removed, grinning.

"**BOYCHICK!**"

"Girlchick?"

"**WHAT DO YOU THINK YOU ARE DOING?**"

"Admiring the view."

Mirf's shirt was plastered to her torso. She was wet to the waist, dripping puddles onto the dust dry ground.

"**RAZ BAZ.**"

"May I have a drink?"

"Sure," said Mirf sweetly.

"Stand over there, please." J. C. pointed.

Mirf, grumbling to herself, walked to the indicated spot. And waited.

J. C. bent over to take a drink.

In one smooth motion, Mirf leaped and hit him, hip level, shoving him in, She jumped back.

J. C. didn't move. Head, shoulders remained under the water. A few bubbles burst on the surface. He still didn't move.

"Oi, yoi, yoi!" She leaped forward, grabbed the back of his belt and heaved.

J. C. lurched upright, whirled around, and wrapped his arms around her, shouting, "**SURPRISE!**"

Water poured from him, from them both.

"Messhuggener! Let me go."

"Not yet."

"I am stronger than I look."

"I know that."

"Let me go."

"First things first."

Mirf hissed. "What might that be?"

"Stop being such a hard case."

"I am a hard case."

He tightened his arms. "Doesn't feel all that hard to me. Soft. Warm. Wet."

"Boychick?"

"Yes?"

"So, O.K. It'sa deal."

"Sure?"

"A deal's a deal."

J. C. dropped his arms.

Mirf didn't move away.

"Well," asked J. C.

"You are really something else," said Mirf.

"That's me."

"Don't be such a hard case, J. C."

"It's a deal. Mirf."

She stepped back. "I need another drink."

J. C. stepped sideways, made a grand sweeping gesture with one arm. "Ta dum."

Mirf bent over and took a drink.

And after a while she straightened up and said, "Let's go."

They headed down the path.

Behind them, something heavy dropped to the path with a dull 'THUMP.' Dust billowed in soft waves over everything, including them.

"**BY DUMPF**, small folk."

Mirf whirled around in a low crouch, fingers arched into claws.

J. C. turned around, looked up into the glowering face. "Certainly grow them big around here, don't they?"

Mirf gurgled.

"What is the name of this place?" asked J. C. He pointed at their surroundings.

"**STUMPF, BY DUMPF.**" One great arm gestured dramatically at everything.

The gigantic figure hung the immense wooden club it had been clenching in one hand onto his belt, a jewel set into the small end flashed golden light against his side.

"You are Mountain, aren't you?" asked J. C.

The glowering face bent lower, taking a closer look at J. C.'s face. "You do not look like demons. How do you know my name?"

"I am a friend of John Tinker's. Pleased to meet you. Call me J. C."

"**BY ALL THE ROCKS AND STONES,** John Tinker." Mountain straightened up and peered around. It was also a very dramatic gesture. "Did the portal leave you here?"

"Nope," said J. C. "We came by node."

"Why are you here? And how do I know that you are what you say you are?" The great cudgel was back in his hand.

IJ.C. looked him over. *That cudgel doesn't really look all that large when he holds it.* Then he told Mountain various things about Mountain's adventures with John Tinker.

When he finished, J. C. stepped aside. "This is Mirf. We are traveling together."

"Hungry?" asked Mountain.

"You betcha," said Mirf.

"My camp is that way." Mountain pointed in the direction that they had been walking. This was another very dramatic gesture.

J. C. smiled to himself. He was just as Tinker had described.

"We will follow you."

Mountain clumped past them and down the path, making large dust puffs as he stomped along.

And they followed, staying back, allowing the air to clear before they walked after the gigantic form lumbering ahead.

"J. C.?" whispered Mirf.

"Yes?" he whispered back.

"How did you know who he was?"

"I remembered."

"Vat?"

"Everything."

"Explain."

"I remembered everything that Tinker told me and that Hard told me, about their adventures. So when I heard the name of this place and saw that jewel, I knew who it was."

"Remembered?"

"Like I said."

"Everything?"

"Told you about that."

"Hum bug."

"Your choice."

"To do what?"

"To believe or not to believe."

"Shakespeare, you are not. Believe me, I know. He was shorter."

J. C. laughed.

"With less hair," added Mirf.

Medium Pieces

Grandeville. Tinker's Place. Early Morning.

It was moving.

The morning air was moving.

Across the grass meadow.

Bright light streamed down from the skylights into the open space common to all the bedrooms.

The cool breeze drifted through the open windows into one of the bedrooms.

Tinker's eyes popped open.

Someone sat up and peered into his face. Great, golden eyes.

"Morn . . ," he mumbled.

"MindMate." She bent down and nibbled lightly along his chest.

He shoved.

She resisted.

So he shoved again.

"Smoke?"

"If moths can nibble, then so may carnivores."

"I don't want to be nibbled."

She sat up and licked her lips, her eyes fully focused upon his face. A predator's stare.

He sighed. He didn't like that stare.

She watched him.

"What?"

"Our minds have agreed," she stated.

He nodded. He knew. "Right. We will leave right after breakfast."

Snatching the covers away, she pounced, arms and legs wrapping around him.

"OOOOF!"

"Gotcha!"

"Smoke?"

"MindMate?"

"Is it really necessary to pounce, to do that, so early in the morning?"

"I thought so."

He pinched her.

"Eek."

"Not very convincing." So he did it again.

"Eeeeeeek!"

"Much better."

"My Lord?" Chicken dropped to her knees next to the bed and peered sparkling blue eyes at his face. And frowned darkly. "What do be thee a'doing to Our Dark Sister?"

"Not much."

"Morning, morning, morning," bubbled Messenger as she leaned on Smoke's back and ruffled her hair with one hand. "Warm Day, Mom."

"Messenger," growled Tinker. "You are a lot of weight."

She peered over Smoke's shoulder at him. "I am not a lot of weight."

"The two of you are."

Smoke sat up, thrusting Messenger backward.

"Much better," said Tinker. "Who's making breakfast?"

"Master Chen," answered Chicken.

"Who said to tell you that it is time to eat," added Messenger. "Now. Really really!"

"Right. Let's go eat. Shall we?" He looked pointedly at Smoke who was sitting on his legs.

Loud thumping sounds, heavy duty splashing sounds came from the shower room, echoed across the open space and into his bedroom through the open door.

I could use some help.

"I will , I will, I will!" sang Messenger. She turned and ran from the room and through the corner of the common space and into the shower room.

"OH, NO!"

"She do once again forget herself for to shed fair pajamas." Chicken smiled, stood, and banged Smoke's shoulder with her hip as she stepped past, headed for the dining room.

Smoke's eyes seemed to expand and glow as she shrugged off her pajama top and leaned forward.

In the dining room Chicken told Chen that the rest would be along in a short while.

Chen shrugged and sat down at the large dining room table and ate breakfast with Chicken. She poured coffee into his cup.

Grandeville. Tinker's place. Sometime Later in the Morning.

Chicken and Chen were sipping from their coffee cups and admiring the view through the dining room window when Messenger and Fair Morn joined them.

"I hung my pajamas on the outside line. Would you please bring them in when they are dry, Master Chen."

"Of course," said Chen, standing and pulling out chairs for them.

Then he hurried into the kitchen to bring out their breakfast.

"Oh, yum, yum, Belgium Waffles," said Messenger. "I am hungry." She nodded violently. "Really really!"

"Thee two did dally most long. Are thee not besodden?"

"Princess Sister, she scrubbed my wings. I thought that

it might be a good idea before we start. Who knows when we will have another opportunity until we return. And they get itchy being closed for long periods of time."

"OH!" Messenger's hand flew to her mouth, her face blushing a bright red.

"Kitten?" asked Chicken.

"Oh dear," whispered Messenger.

"What did thee do?"

"Well, I didn't see Smoke, or MyTinker . . ."

"So you looked," said Fair Morn, looking at the empty platter sitting on the table.

"Yes." It was an almost inaudible answer. "Mom's going to be so unhappy."

"Kitten!" snapped Chicken. "Thee knows thou ought not privacy so to violate."

"I forgot," mum bled Messenger as she looked down and poked at the tablecloth with a fingertip.

Chen bustled in, set a large platter on the table. It was brimming with waffles. "Many, many, many," he said, winking at Fair Morn.

He handed a long black cylinder to Chicken. "Give this to the slothful one when he finally wakes up."

"Oh he is awake," chirped Messenger. She blushed again.

Kitten! snapped Chicken.

OUCH!

Fair Morn took two waffles.

Tiny Rosebud stepped from the tall wild grass onto a neatly mown domesticated variety and saw the two gardens.

One was vegetable, the other was ornamental.

Feeling just a little bit hungry, she had eaten several kinds of berries inside the forest, now she headed for the vegetable patch.

Wandering from variety to variety she touched the soil, tickled a few earthworms, and convinced several plants to hurry up. After enjoying her repast, she ordered the weeds to relocate and reorganized the tomato plants.

Then she walked around the back of the building to visit the flowers in the rather usual garden that ran alongside the deck that stretched the length of this side of the house.

"What be this thing?" asked Chicken.

"It was sticking in the front lawn. It appears to be the kind of thing he might understand."

Chicken handed the black cylinder to Messenger.

"Magic," she said, gently taking the long cylinder. She stared at it, running one finger slowly up and down its length.

"It is a message from Ramp, asking us to come." Messenger stared at Chicken. "How did he know?"

"Ask him. LATER. Eat. Now."

Messenger carefully laid the device on the table and did, grabbing the last waffle out from under Fair Morn's reaching fingers.

"I'll make some oatmeal," said Fair Morn.

"Waffles, waffles," said Chen, setting another load down in front of them. He winked at Fair Morn again and sat next to Chicken. "When did he buy a new couch?"

"He did not to thee speak?" Chen shook his head.

So, while Fair Morn attacked the waffles, and Messenger grabbed a few survivors before they were all consumed, Chicken told Chen of their visitors.

And then Tinker joined them at the dining room table.

"And you are going again?" asked Chen.

"We are," said Tinker, answering Chen's question, taking a seat, looking at the empty platters, and then at Fair Morn. "You eat it all?"

"Nephew, there is more," stated Chen.

"Here," said Smoke setting down a full platter on the table. She had taken it from one of the ovens. Then she looked sharply at Messenger, who blushed.

Tinker didn't notice. He was spreading sour cream and sprinkling strawberries across his waffle.

When he looked up, he asked, "What's that thing?"

Messenger pushed it across the table. "A message from Ramp. Asking you, us, to come to Bahn Duhr Tohr."

Tinker stared at her, fork and arm hanging in the air. "What?" Slowly his arm settled to the table top. "When did that get here?"

"I found it sticking in the front lawn, Nephew, early this morning. Eat!" Chen reached over and tapped Tinker's forearm with a fingertip.

"Huh? Oh. . . forgot." Tinker chewed on the forkful, looking very thoughtful and far away.

"My Lord?" Chicken's brows wrinkled as she stared at him.

"I, we, decided we were going this morning. Did we really make that decision? Smoke?"

"We did. But I think that you felt its presence and purpose which then triggered your memory of the promise that you made. To go if called. No manipulation required."

"Well," said Tinker, standing, leaning forward, lightly slapping Fair Morn's hand and taking the last waffle. "I know you guys are ready. Am I?"

Smoke made a quick trip to the kitchen and returned setting yet another filled platter on the table, this time well out of Fair Morn's reach.

Chicken stood and walked behind him and rested her hands on his shoulders. "We do feel thee be most ready. Enow."

He leaned his head back. "Yah, me too. Packs are packed. What else?"

"Mere change of attire, fetch weapons, Me'Love."

He shoved the last piece of waffle from his plate into his mouth, took a final sip of coffee, and swallowed hastily. "Let's do it."

As they left the table, Smoke held Messenger back. "We need to talk, kitten."

Fair Morn stood, leaned, and yanked the platter over.

"Now what is going on?" whispered Tinker to Chicken as they stepped into the Chamber, the name they called the large open space, and headed for their bedrooms.

"Pay thee no mind, Love. T'was but some minor lapse."

"Oh. Ummmm?"

"My Lord?"

"You have any idea where my clothes are?"

Chicken laughed. "Sweet Prince, thy dark garb We had made most clean and do hung with Our Verra Own garments."

"So that's where they went."

"Indeed! Thee did fret so mightily, thus did We, thy Verra Own Queen, make for to minimize foul irritation."

He followed her around and into her bedroom.

Chicken opened her closet and pointed. "Just so."

The clothes hung, deep shadow material reflecting no light. Below them a pair of dark boots, equally shadow dark.

"Bad memories and good." Tinker removed his belongings, turned and dropped everything on her bed. Along with his pajama top.

Chicken stepped around him and leaned against his chest.

"Not now dear," he said. "I have a headache." And laughed at her expression.

She rubbed slowly against him and smiled a very slow smile. "Truly?" And wrapped her arms around him and held him tight.

"What's the matter, Princess?"

"We would stay, we all would, if thee so wish, promise solemn or no."

"Tempting, tempting, my very own fairy tale Princess. But no. I think, I feel, that we should go. I can't explain why, but . . . we must."

"Tis for thy friend."

"Yes. And his wife. I didn't realize how much he meant to me until I thought that he was dying. Goes for J. C. too."

"OH NO!" It was Messenger. She had just bounded into the room.

"What's up, kitten?" Tinker looked puzzled over one of Chicken's shoulders at Messenger's expression.

"Don't tell, mom," she whispered, stepping close.

Chicken half turned. "What?" she whispered back

"This makes twice in the same morning." Messenger was blushing violently.

"What?" Tinker was already lost by the conversation.

"Hist!" snapped Chicken, stepping away from him, hastily waving Messenger from the room. "Do go see to thy own gear and write most solemn a'note for Mine Own Brother, the Noble Goose, in the English language of this land. Go now."

"What exactly was that all about?" Tinker had his black shirt on and was just slipping the trousers from their hanger.

"Sweet Prince, tis just our kitten."

"Now what?"

Chicken stepped close and began to button his shirt.

"Oh, oh." He sighed. "So . . .?"

"Sweet Prince, she did peek. A lapse."

Tinker lifted her chin until he could look into her eyes. "At what?"

"Thee and Great Smoke."

"When?" He laughed. "OH, I see."

"Indeed?"

"Certainly explains all that blushing. But . . .?"

"What?"

"Just a moment ago, what was that all about?"

"Me'thinks young kitten did think we wert similarly engaged, if thee wouldst pardon some slight pun."

"Pun?"

"Engaged, My Lord."

Tinker started to laugh, holding her close, shifting slightly from side to side.

"Love?"

"Exactly," he said. "Love you all, as is."

He smiled broadly and realized it was certainly true, in spite of all their differences. Or maybe because of them. It was becoming harder and harder to tell. Did he love his hand or foot less? They were separate. They were fused.

John Love, we do plan most cautious be.

What me, worry?

It lurks, just there.

Can't be helped.

We do know, We do.

They both felt the others waiting.

"Get dressed Slim, adventure awaits."

Chicken spun away, yanking her traveling clothes from the closet, snatching her boots from a rack.

And when all were ready, they reassembled.

In the living room.

And waited for him.

Tinker took the giant sword from the corner, his fingers sliding gently over the golden jewel set in the hilt, feeling the weaponkin vibrating under his hand.

"Guess that we are ready."

Chicken snatched her blade from the wall and popped it into its scabbard .

"My Lord?"

"Right. Let's go. We have a node to find."

Outside, on the rear deck, Chen stood and waited.

"Nephew, take my dragon with you."

"Nope, she and Goose get to sit this one out."

Chen nodded, one brief nod.

Smoke handed Tinker his pack while Messenger helped Chicken slip her's on.

"See you later, Chen," said Tinker. He headed out across the back meadows, up toward the upper fence line, where the trail headed for the higher ridge. The rest followed after him. It was a ragged group.

Messenger spun around and ran back to Chen. She kissed him on the cheek. "Bye, bye. We will be careful. Really really!" She ran to catch up with the others all ready stepping into the lower edge of the forest, turning back one last time to wave gaily.

Tiny Rosebud was standing deep inside one of the large shrubs, carefully straightening out a tangle of limbs, when she heard all the clatter and commotion up on the rear deck. She peered out just in time to see them heading out across the pasture and up into the wooden slope.

Well, she thought, there was no way she would be able to catch up with them. It had been hard enough to track them to their residence. So, she though, she would just stay here and wait for them to return. They were too hard to follow. And there was lots of food and plenty of water here.

Although maybe she ought to follow them. She would have to think about doing that for some time.

Grandeville, Backside of Sharp Ridge.

"Somewhere around here, what do you think, gang?" Tinker stood and stared around the clearing.

Messenger pointed. "Over there, MyTinker. That pool is the node thingee."

They all walked over and looked at it.

"MyTinker?"

"What?"

"I think that I saw that funny little statue in our flower garden again."

"You did?"

"Yep. But it was in a different spot than the last time I saw it. But it wasn't there when we planted everything."

"Have to talk to J. C., see if it is some sort of a joke."

They stared at the pool again.

"Really?" asked Tinker as he pointed at the pool. "This is a node?"

"Magic," stated Messenger, nodding violently. "Really really!"

The sharp snap of a lever clicking spun them all around.

Fair Morn was aiming her weapon toward the center of the meadow. "Something is coming. I can see the grass flattening."

"Don't fire. Yet." Tinker stared at Smoke. "Where did you get that thing?" She held a large handgun in one hand. Now he noticed that she wore a shoulder holster on her left side.

"Master Chen."

"Chen?"

She smiled at him. "He said it would knock down almost anything."

"You really think you need that thing?"

She shrugged. "Perhaps not. But as we told you, this time we, your loves, are taking no chances." Her trigger finger tightened. Taking up the slack.

"Hold it, hold it!" snapped Tinker.

"I think that it is The Gate Keeper," whispered Messenger. "The one that Hard spoke about."

Chicken fished two granola bars from a side pocket and held them in front of herself using her left hand. She was keeping her right hand free and ready.

They all could see the grass flattening toward them. What ever it was that was approaching them, it was coming in a straight line.

It grunted.

A great lump, taller than Tinker appeared. It had two heads which stared at them. Oozing appendages, it lurched on newly created feet and walked over, waggling both arms.

"My, my," said one head, the left.

"They look stern," said the right.

The left arm made a grab for the granola bars. Chicken kicked the lump in that side as she leaped away.

"OUCH!" cried both heads.

"Another hob-goblin infected one," suggested the left.

"Ahhhh, fellows?" said Tinker.

"I am The Gate Keeper," they stated.

"Um, we need passage."

"For five?" asked the left.

"Costly," suggested the right. The lump sidled toward Chicken. She tossed the bars to Messenger.

"Oh, oh," said the right.

"She is a nasty," said the left, pointing with the arm on that side toward Chicken.

"Oooooooo," said the right.

Messenger walked up and placed one bar in each of the Gate Keeper's hands. "Passage, please?"

"Where you going?" mumbled the left, shoving the bar into its mouth. The bar went in sideways, making each cheek poke out past the sides of its head.

"Yes, where?" asked the right, dribbling crumbs and pieces of wrapping as it munched noisily.

"Bahn Duhr Tohr."

"Must be a nice place," grunted the left.

"Everyone is going there. Recently," added the right, spitting out the remainder of the wrapper.

"Ahem," interjected Tinker.

Messenger poked the Gate Keeper gently on its swelling belly with one finger. "We need passage."

"Any more bars?" whispered the right, bending away so that the left couldn't hear.

"No fair," gurgled the left. The bar was visibly making a leisurely journey down its throat.

Chicken walked up behind Messenger and slipped two more bars into Messenger's left hand which she held slightly behind herself. Then Chicken stepped away, left hand clenching the top of her scabbard, watching the Gate Keeper carefully.

"Weeeell," said the left.

"You have it," said the right. "Just step into the pool and you will be there. For five."

Fair Morn stepped over and eyed the water suspiciously. "One, this pool just belched."

"Yuck, yuck, yuck," said Messenger staring over at the water.

"What?" asked Tinker.

"It is just ill-mannered," said the left, eyeing the granola bars Messenger now held in plain sight.

"That is all," agreed the right. "We didn't create it, you know."

"Here," said Messenger, handing the bars to The Gate Keeper and walking quickly over to join the rest of her group now standing around the small pool staring at it.

"We join hands and jump together," said Tinker.

They did.

There was no splash.

"Urp," said the pool.

Far Corner. Early Evening.

The Phylota of Anaza had relocated to this elseplace. It had been carefully selected. It was far from the usual paths used by folk doing wander, especially the magical folks doing wander.

Here, in this elseplace, after carefully studying the

desired property, and after purchasing it through five layers of middle buying and selling parties, they felt that they would be unobserved and left in the isolation that they felt was necessary for the sorcerer phylota to live and work in peace.

The newly created viewing well had just been recently activated after days, and nights, of ceremony and enchantment. And now, several days later, the trio peered in at the image.

Hatopa, the Three Rank Sorcerer, pointed. "He has come into the elseplaces yet again. As was said in The Ancient Book of Songs."

"Most true." Abadoba, The Three Rank Sorceress, nodded. "But there are more. One, two, three, four. A very strange being."

Netanoda, Elixa, The Clan Head, reached out and swirled away the image. "We must be ever so careful else the Wood With know this. So far, no spell has discerned the intent of that feyal folk. We must be even more sorcerer cautious. That creature is the hinge of our future. The Ancient Book of Songs is unclear as to our why. But it is clear as the liquid in the viewing well that it is so."

She turned for the only door to this special chamber. "Come, let us assemble all together and pool our collective sense on this matter."

Dawla of Snark's Fen. Midday.

They faded in next to the ornate fountain in the village park.

Passing folk paid no attention. It was a frequent occurrence. Witches came and went. Leaving behind gold coins. The local economy did quite well from their visits. Everyone knew that it was the presence of the three spell shops that attracted them to this elseplace.

It was also a very unusual thing to have more than one witch Clan House in any elseplace. But the village of Snark's

Fen had three. It was even more unusual that witch clans in that close a proximity to each other did not irritate each other to the point of death and destruction.

But, for some reason, not understood by the non-magical folk of Snark's Fen, the three clans maintained a proper, if somewhat uneasy, relationship with each other.

Turintor headed them down a carefully groomed path toward the edge of the park, seeking an inn. Her silent companion walked by her side. They both felt the presence of the other witches, local and visiting.

It felt to Turintor much like A Foregather, a great magical fair of days where witches came to learn spells, buy scrolls, and other things, and if they were lucky, even find their's, a mate-for-life. Not often. But it happened, it did. Warlocks came to a Foregather as well.

After acquiring rooms at the *Spell Inn,* the pair headed down the street outside their front door. And soon came to a store labeled, *Pinel Spell Works*

The pair entered the small public room and stopped to look about. Two walls were covered with small pigeon-holes, each containing a spell scroll.

A tall thin witch dressed in the usual black robe came close, but not too close, and nodded at them. She introduced herself with the most formal of modes of address utilized between witches.

"I am Pinel witch Tapa spell caster. What do you seek?" She waited.

"Potri witch Turintor. My companion does not speak. Yet! We seek aid."

"Um." Tapa nodded. "Perhaps we might talk some over an appropriate beverage?" She gestured. A table and three chairs appeared. On the table top sat three steaming mugs.

"Most kind." Turintor sat and waited until the others had taken their places. "I will explain what we seek. It will take some time."

"I have that time." Tapa sipped at her mug. And listened intently as Turintor began her tale.

Grandeville. Tinker's place. Late Evening.

As the moon rose over the far side of the valley mountain ridges, two figures appeared and started walking across the meadow toward the house.

"Looks different."

"We are in the correct spot."

"Gyre, in the light from that small satellite, you are even more beautiful." He threw his arm around her shoulders and pulled her close.

"Unusual behavior for you."

"Backward behavior for a backward place."

"Danger!" she hissed, quickly stepping away.

In a flash he held weapons in both hands, eyes darting in all directions. He was standing some distance from her. "I don't see anything. Call The Vipers."

She spoke very softly. "Just there in the shadows between the two structures. See? Two green, glowing eyes."

"They are not moving," he said.

Something white drifted ghost quiet toward them.

"Be that you, Macabre?"

"Prince Goose," whispered Gyre.

"Prince Goose?" asked Macabre.

"Indeed. And My Lady Chen."

"Of course," laughed Macabre. "Of the green eyes."

The eyes blinked and she stepped from the shadows and bowed. "Your pardon, Honored Guestsss."

Macabre laughed. "Ho, ho, ho, ho, ho, ho, ho, ho. Better cautious than deceased." His weapons slid into their holsters.

They joined Goose, Chen now standing by his side.

"A pleasure to see you again. Has John spent his wealth yet?"

"Nay, tis unearthed still."

"Perhaps, in the day, I could offer some small aid?"

Goose shook his head. "T'would be most misspent."

"Why?"

"They do be gone."

"What?" Macabre looked at Gyre.

She nodded. "Yes. Ship sensors indicate that they are not here. I should have checked first."

"No, no, my dear, we had no need for that. But where did they go, Goose?"

"Bahn Duhr Tohr said partin' note."

"A planet of archaic cultures and multiple kingdoms, the main and largest and most powerful of which is also named Bahn Duhr Tohr," stated Gyre, quoting from Ship data banks. "This kingdom, a collection of kingdoms, is ruled by The White Warrior and her consort, Tinker's Queen's Brother, called Toucan, now King to Willawa, the Queen. From here it will take 7.24 days, as measured by this world's chronology."

"Might we not discuss thisss inside?" asked Lady Chen. "Master Chen isss making coffee."

Macabre's eyes gleamed in the moonlight. "Do you think he might make some doughnuts? Gyre has never seen or tasted them, ah, straight from the hands of a master baker."

Chen smiled at Macabre. "Asss you wish."

"A rare treat should never be overlooked. Or something like that. Beside, I feel, deep down inside, an hour here or there is not going to matter very much before this is matter is resolved."

"And what matter be that?" Goose stared at Macabre.

"Inside, shall we?" Macabre hastened toward the kitchen door.

It was open, light streamed forth, a yellow shaft crossing the nightdark. Master Chen held it open and waited for them to enter.

"Master Chen," said Macabre by way of greetings.

"Would you make some doughnuts for us, especially for Gyre?"

Chen nodded, one short nod, his eyes taking in all the details of this pretty woman who appeared to be made of silver.

"Grandfather," said Lady Chen, bowing deeply. "Thisss isss Gyre. She hasss not been a guest with usss before."

"Very pretty," answered Master Chen. "Macabre, will you take Prince Goose and this worthless creature of a Niece with you and catch up with John and his ladies?"

"I will," stated Macabre. As he spoke Gyre readied ship.

"Good," said Master Chen, shooing them all from his kitchen. "It will take about an hour." He handed a tray of cups to Lady Chen, the coffee pot to Goose.

Macabre rubbed his hands together happily as he followed them and Gyre into the living room. Where they sat and listened to Goose.

"And that note do be all we now do know," finished Goose, having told Macabre and Gyre all he knew about what had happened since they had last seen each other.

Macabre then related what he had seen and had been doing and observing.

Gyre passed him the last doughnut.

He almost looked sad as he bit into it.

"Prince, Lady, I think that this will be extremely hazardous. Stay home."

Goose violently shook his head. "Nay, t'would be most unseemly."

"And Grandfather hasss ordered me to go," added Lady Chen, looking demure and meek. "It isss my duty to obey."

"Then," Macabre's hands banged together. A soft puff of powdered sugar erupted. "That's that. You two ready?"

"I must pack," answered Goose.

"No need for that, Prince," stated Gyre. "I, Ship, can provide anything you might wish."

Goose smiled. "Then I do be most ready." He stood and offered Lady Chen his hand. "My Lady?"

She looked over at Master Chen, who nodded.

Macabre leaped to his feet, thanking Master Chen profusely for the treat. Then he nodded at Gyre.

The four of them disappeared.

Master Chen gathered up the cups, dishes, and tray, and carried everything into the kitchen, snapping off the lights as he went.

Then he went to bed.

After loading everything into the dish washer.

The Six Lands. Early Evening.

After the evening meal, they sat outside in comfortable cloth chairs. $1.98 sat on the ground next to Duff. It felt strange to be in a world where everything was undersized.

"Are you really a magician?" It was Sorrowful's oldest son. He didn't sound like he believed it, even though this person was very large and his father had said it was so.

"I am," said $1.98 brushing his sleeves back to his elbows.

"Careful, dear," cautioned Duff, knowing his rather unfortunate habit of letting his magic get away.

$1.98 opened his fist. A small iridescent creature flew slowly up and over and perched upon Tear's shoulder, chirping softly into his ear.

"Well done," whispered Duff.

Tears slowly moved his hand up, one finger extended.

The creature hopped onto the offered perch and said, "Hello, Tears. How are you?" Then it disappeared.

Sorrowful tried to stifle his yawn. Duff caught it. "Come dear, it is time for night rest. We leave early in the dawnlight?" She looked at Sorrowful.

"Yes, yes, we do. Early. Sound and comfortable sleep." He stood and beckoned. "This way."

$1.98 and Duff followed him to the spare room, the one his wife and sons had rearranged. Several large mats, large for the folk of Sorrowful's world, had been pushed together and covered with soft blankets.

Sorrowful slid the door closed as he left.

$1.98 sprawled across the makeshift bed and stared up at the ceiling. Their traveling bags huddled together in a corner.

"Duff?"

She sat facing him, leaned forward and placed her forehead on his chest. "Dear?"

"It hasn't been a half day since we left home. I am hardly ready to sleep all night."

She sat back and pitched her jacket over the traveling bags.

"And I have eaten two meals close together," he added. "Just to be polite."

She patted his stomach, telling his robe and wand to disappear.

They did.

She gave him another pat and rubbed a gentle rhythm. "Just have to work it off, Dear."

He touched her blouse. It faded to nothing, followed by her traveling breaches, Soft gray cloud wrapped itself along the contours of her body. Duff leaped to her feet and glared at him.

"$1.98, get this goo-gark off me!"

"Hold still," he said.

She was cursing and dancing from foot to foot.

He said something.

The gray stuff disappeared.

The light in the room took on a distinct green cast.

He sat up and held out his arms. She slipped into them, and said, "My magician, you are a real hazard. I will worry about the clothes, the food, the lights, and all those other mundane things. You will fight the demons and monsters."

"Slight miscue," he mumbled, lying back, taking her with him. "You may fix the light."

Duff smiled. The light faded to a soft golden glow. "I always liked that color," she said, throwing one leg across his. "We can take a nap later."

"Smooth, smooth," he said as his hands lightly flowed over her.

"You always say that," she sighed.

The light dimmed to nothing.

Space, 09.09.00.63. DXA. In Ship's Notation.

"Welcome to Ship, once again, Prince and Lady," said Macabre as he led them from the portal chamber and along one of the many corridors toward a lounge.

After they had settled into comfortable chairs, Macabre beamed at Goose. "Your rooms are just down the corridor. Follow the guide lights. We will have plenty of time to sit and talk before we arrive at Bahn Duhr Tohr."

"Aye, Lord, tis so. T'will most pleasant to Mine Brother Toucan again be a'visitin'."

"Spit it out, Prince. I see something else in your face."

Goose grinned. "Indeed. What think you of a'visitin' most Great Red Magician afore we do Bahn Duhr Tohr a'go?"

Macabre thumped the arm of his chair with one hand. "Should have been my first thought. I must be getting too old for this business. Yes, let us pay a visit to that master manipulator and see what we might pry loose, information wise, from him."

"10 point 405 earth days," announced Gyre. They all felt the great interstellar vessel shift.

"That long?" asked Macabre.

"I could portal jump," said Gyre, placing one hand gently upon his shoulder.

He reached up and covered it with one of his own. "Bit chancey."

"2 point 336 days."

"Into the fray, Lord," said Goose, smiling broadly.

"You are correct, Prince. Into the fray it is. Jump it is."

"And devil take the hindmost." Goose held one of Chen's hands.

"Full defense, Gyre." Macabre bounced to his feet, rubbing his hands together. "Come, we have things to do."

He spun around, then back and gave his guests a courtly bow. "I will leave you to your own devices. Tell ship whatever you might wish, it will be prepared." He stepped through a door which had just hissed open and stomped away.

"Ho, ho, ho, ho, ho, ho, ho." Gyre kept pace at his side.

Chen and Goose followed the guide lights down a different grey metal corridor.

Then they stood in their rooms.

"What need we?" Goose looked around the room.

Chen hissed softly as her long fingers released his and carefully placed his scabbard on the table. Long fingernails deftly unfastened the buttons on his shirt, then the fastenings on her blouse. "My Master and Lord, thisss great machine will only require a small amount of time to prepare all we may ask of it. Silver Gyre said it will take two daysss before we reach our destination."

He felt the tips of her claws slide gently over his back, heard the soft sound of cloth falling. "Dragon Mine, get to the point get."

"Asss you command." Her eyes glowed emerald fire. She gently pushed him back toward the bed.

"Lusty wench."

"Impaler of fair maidensss."

"Indeed."

Ramna Dir. A Warm Sunny Day.

She stood in the middle of the large meadow at the intersection of the two roads and listened to a solitary bird sing in one of the tall trees surrounding the green opening. Mounted on a stout post next to the intersection were four sign boards telling all who happened to pass this way the name and direction of the four nearest towns.

Lady Lastgift flowed in the direction of the town that she would visit.

Another bird joined the first one in singing into the silence and the warmth of the meadow. Their joined song had nothing to do with the bodies lying in a wide circle around the intersection.

The robbers whose camp was tucked into the forest not too far from this same intersection had thought to rob and assault the single traveler as she had stopped to get directions from the signs.

It was a very isolated elseplace.

The Six Lands. Early Morning.

They gathered outside in the early light.

Sorrowful made his farewells to his wife and sons. The eldest had brought the other son from his stead to see his father and nephew away. Sorrowful folded the letter and pushed it into his wife's hands.

"For you it should only be two or three days." He smiled gently. "I shall miss you greatly. I will take care of Tears. And he shall take care of me. Sons, a Great Tale calls. We go to hear. Come, Tears."

He turned away from his family and said softly, "Which way?"

$1.98 pointed across the clearing. "You are ready?"

"Yes. Let us proceed. Before I find that I cannot."

Sorrowful pushed Tears gently into motion.

Duff slipped up to Tears' side and linked her arm through one of his, saying, "Come Tears, walk with me. $1.98

will lead the way."

They walked across the meadow, their luggage jostling along behind them. Sorrowful and Tears each wore a small travel pack on their backs.

Just between two trees the small group halted.

"Tears," said $1.98. "Take my hand. It is here where we step through." He reached down and took the small hand in his.

"This way," said $1.98. They took one step. Into elsewhere.

Duff nudged Sorrowful in the correct direction and took his hand.

The luggage followed. There never was a problem for them.

Space. 09.28.34.10. ATH. In Ship's Notation.

Goose sprawled loosely upon the couch.

Chen sat upright, legs tucked underneath, next to him.

Macabre slouched in a large chair with Gyre standing just behind his right shoulder, her left hand resting lightly on his shoulder.

"We are almost there," said Macabre.

"49 minutes, 31 seconds, on the tone," announced Ship from a ceiling speaker. "BEEP."

"Your gear is waiting by the outside door," said Gyre. "But we shouldn't require any of that on Paradise."

"Indeed not," agreed Goose. "The Mighty Wizard may produce objects at whim."

Chen spoke softly, "Mighty Warriorsss, we must presss him, in very subtle waysss, for answersss to our questionsss. That one isss not free with hisss information."

"Subtle ways," mumbled Macabre, stroking his chin and looking from face to face. "Not exactly my strong point."

"Nor mine," said Goose. He sat up and threw an arm around Chen's shoulders. "Me'thinks tis a skill certain fair dragons do in abundance have."

"Gyre?" asked Macabre.

"It is not a well developed circuit."

"We need to fix that."

"I will carefully study this person."

Macabre beamed and rubbed his hands together. "Ho, ho, ho, ho. And he hasn't met you before. Ho, ho, ho, ho."

They all felt the great vessel shudder.

"Down and in place," stated Gyre.

"T'was fast," said Goose.

"We were pulled," explained Gyre.

"Big Red?"

Gyre nodded.

"Shall we?" asked Macabre.

They followed him to the exterior door.

"Subtle and devious," said Macabre. "Wonderful. Especially the devious part." He punched the door release.

Paradise. Warm and Pleasant Mid-Day.

The grass was green, the sky blue, the breeze soft, warm and pleasant.

They gathered at the bottom of the exit ramp and looked around. The ridge where they stood, surrounded by forested slopes, was covered in thick grass. Not a structure was in sight.

Gyre shone burnished silver in the sunlight.

"Very interesting," said a disembodied voice.

Macabre's weapon snapped its muzzle toward the spot.

"Would you shoot at me?" Big Red stood there and smiled at them.

Macabre laughed and holstered the ugly, black thing. "Merely a reflex, Big Red."

Big Red beamed at them. He was a thickly structured person and dressed, as always, in clothes of various shades of red. Soft maroon pants, light red shirt, rosy red jacket, red cap with one red feather poking out at a jaunty angle.

"Prince Goose, Lady Chen, welcome to Paradise. Macabre, welcome. And . . . .?"

"Big Red, this is Gyre."

"Gyre . . . ship?"

She stared at him. "I am Ship. I am also Gyre, the individual standing before you. I am also Macabre's."

Big Red strode over to them. "Welcome, one and all." He held out his hand and shook one of her's.

"Amazing." He obviously was inspecting her closely, finding her a treat. "Not magic, not magic."

Macabre threw an arm around her shoulders, a protective gesture. "She can explain better than I can."

Big Red clapped his hands together.

Just once.

Now they stood on a broad lawn facing a large Tudor-style house.

And three waiting people.

Big Red laughed lazily. "Everyone knows most everyone." He turned to Gyre. "Gyre, may I present my wife, Dancing-All-The-Day, my son, Silly-All-The-Day, and his wife, Treena. This is Gyre." Then he made shooing motions with his hands. "Let's go inside and get comfortable, and talk."

Inside, he led them down a hall into a large living room, all wood panels and open beamed ceiling, and waved his arms in broad gestures. "Make yourselves comfortable. Food? Drink? Ahhhh, red wine?"

"Splendid." Macabre bowed.

"T'will rare treat be," answered Goose.

Chen handed him one of the goblets which materialized on the table in front of them.

Silly raised his. "Prince Goose, it is good to see you again."

Silly and Treena had joined Goose and Chen across the room from the others.

"Fare thee well?" asked Goose.

"Oh yes." His wife nudged him gently as Macabre, Big Red, and Gyre plunged into an animated conversation on the other side of the room while Dancing-All-The-Day went off on an activity of her own.

Silly leaned forward and spoke softly. "Prince, I, we," he looked at his wife, who whispered a low, "Yes."

"We owe you a great deal, a great debt," continued Silly.

"Nay, nay."

"Yes, we do," stated Silly firmly, broaching no discussion.

Goose conceded the point.

"So then. I want to come with you this time."

"Nay."

"I must."

"I will that not do."

Chen gently tugged Goose back. He was beginning to lean forward. "My Great Warrior, may thisss humble wife speak?"

"My Lady . . ."

"Silly," said Chen. "The Noble Prince cannot take you with usss asss we have no idea of what we will face. Hisss Lord, felt such great hazard asss to leave usss at home and thusss out of danger. Macabre and Hisss Lady are looking for John Tinker because they have seen signsss of thisss danger, and wish to aid him if he wasss planning some involvement in thisss thing. We cannot take you into such a situation. It would not be proper. You are not a warrior. You are just a young man who feelsss an obligation."

Silly blushed and began to interject.

Chen placed one finger against his lips before he could. "If you must help usss, use your influence with your Great Father. He cannot stand and watch without giving usss aid."

Her eyes released Silly's and shifted to Treena's.

"Dutiful wife, I plead with you and your husband to do thisss. Gyre saw immense forcesss gathering. The Magical One must help."

Treena recoiled from the intensity of Chen's stare.

Chen blinked.

Treena relaxed.

Silly cleared his throat. "I will see what I can do." He whispered to them, "I could always steal another wand."

Goose giggled. "Sweet Messenger be lethal a'plenty with the one already shoved up her left sleeve. She doth need no other. In truth, I know not what aid we must have. But, I know Mine Lord will."

Goose raised his goblet. It had refilled itself. "A toast to success. And thy happiness, sweet youth."

Treena took a small sip as did Chen.

Goose emptied his glass and watched it refill. "Praps, we might keep some such thing?" He winked broadly at Chen.

Silly took a swallow from his own glass. "Oh, he might just do that."

Goose smiled. "T'were mere jest. But tis most fair a thought, me'boy."

Macabre looked past Big Red, over at the animated conversation on the other side of the room, and asked, "Wizard, what caused John to leave home? The Prince only knew a few details, something to do with a friend's wife."

"Ramp," stated Gyre.

"Yes." Big Red nodded. "One of my students, a very talented one, talent runs in her clan. Mostly witches though, some sort of strange genetic thing. A disturbance almost eliminated her not long after her husband impregnated her. But it was outwitted. Somehow. They are now visiting her sister Ripple, the meanest of the lot. That clan draws tight when danger threatens. All manner of forces are getting involved. It is confusing even for me. A very great danger is building and building."

"Ho," said Macabre. "Hum," said Macabre.

"Even for you," stated Big Red.

"A fact of life."

Big Red laughed. "I suppose it is, for you." His eyes angled sideways. "And for Gyre," he added hastily.

"We seek information," said she. Suddenly Gyre twitched, her eyes popped wide, and rolled wildly. Then she gasped softly.

"Gyre?" asked Macabre.

"I have loaded ship's data banks," said Big Red.

She smiled at him, then at Macabre. "He did. Those things are scattered all over the universes of universes. It will be hard to chose."

"What?" demanded Macabre.

"Who to kill First."

"White Warrior, it isss very bad." Chen's acute hearing had heard everything being said on the other side of the room. Her eye's flickered green fire, dragon nature pushing toward the surface.

"Dragon, release me," commanded Goose. "Thee be a'crushin' Mine own leg."

Chen looked down. Her fingers were clenched tightly on his thigh. They sprang open.

"OH. A thousand, thousand pardonsss." She bowed her head. "Do with me asss you wish."

Goose took her hand and slowly stroked his finger over it. "Mine very own pleasure." He giggled.

Treena blushed.

Silly burst in. "Don't beat her, Prince, I didn't realize."

Treena jabbed him in the ribs.

Chen looked up and smiled, and said, "We will be leaving shortly. Sweet youth with lovely wife, speak to your father in private."

Macabre lurched to his feet, and called. "Goose, we must leave. Now!"

Silly hastily twisted a ring from one finger and shoved it into Goose's palm, bending his fingers over it, saying quickly. "Take this, take this. Say nothing."

"What be this?"

"A . . . um, guardian." Silly rose to his feet and said loudly. "Goose, Chen, come again and stay longer. Promise?"

Goose laughed. "Did it ever be so possible, we will that do."

Chen bowed. "May it come to passss. Perhaps you might come and visit usss. It might be easier?"

Silly nodded. "Now that he might do."

Macabre was waving his hands. "Outside, outside."

Goose patted Silly on the shoulder and bowed to Treena. "Fare thee well, Noble Sir and Lady. Till we do meet again." Chen tugged at Goose.

They headed outside and joined Macabre and Gyre. She took them back.

Inside.

Ship.

Ship began to accelerate toward the nearest target.

A Rocky Place. Neither Day Nor Night.

"Where are we?" asked Duff.

"It appears to be a cavern," answered $1.98.

They were surrounded by rock. The opening disappeared in two directions, slowly twisting away. Soft light illuminated gray dimness. The stone was mostly gray with white patches.

"Nice light," she said.

"Thank you," he replied. "This is the wrong place."

"$1.98," hissed Duff.

"Something interfered."

"Just like your tale, Grandfather," said Tears.

"I am afraid that it is so," said Sorrowful. "Your adventure has started. See all, hear all." He touched the hilt of his dagger and felt the slight vibration.

"You are to do whatever you are told to do," he said to Tears. "By anyone. Do not hesitate."

"I will," said Tears, his eyes wide with excitement, nervously licking his lips.

"Let's go this way," said $1.98.

"Carefully," added Duff. A short white wand appeared in her hand. A delicate electric crackling filled the silence.

$1.98 winced at the sound and stepped to one side so he wasn't walking directly in front of her.

As they walked, he pointed at the floor ahead of them. "It has a slight up rise. Perhaps it leads out. I want to reach John Tinker."

"Maybe this is the correct place," suggested Sorrowful.

"Doesn't feel right," said $1.98.

"Where is John Tinker?" asked Duff.

$1.98 mumbled something.

"Dear?"

Tears stepped to the other side of Sorrowful.

"I don't know," said $1.98. "I used a generalized spell to seek the correct time and the correct place."

Duff hissed.

$1.98 threw his hood over his head.

"We can ask the inhabitants where we are," explained Sorrowful to Tears, who was beginning to look around at the encircling rock and trying to not look worried.

"I was older, by quite a bit, than you are when I was called," explained Sorrowful to Tears. "And I really was not sure whether I would ever see house and hold again. Every time."

Tears began to relax. "This reminds me of The Tale Of The Small Worm."

"Exactly," said Sorrowful, smiling at his grandson's skill at selecting an appropriate tale for occasion.

The tunnel suddenly ended. A narrow ladder thrust up

and through a circular opening high overhead.

"I will go first," said $1.98. He started to climb. Just before disappearing into the ceiling he called down. "I will let you know when to come ahead." Then he disappeared up.

The luggage jostled closer to the trio.

Duff sat on one of the bags.

Sorrowful looked around wondering why anyone would come down here. Then he examined the ladder and how it was built. He was just pointing out some of the fine details in its construction to Tears when a sharp crackling blast echoed from the hole overhead followed by a gout of dust and smoke.

Duff clambered up the ladder calling back at them, "Stay here, stay here!"

Eight rungs above the opening and she was standing in total darkness except for the faint light streaming up from below. Commanding blue light, she kept climbing.

It was a narrow shaft that eventually left her standing on a rubble strewn floor. Dust was still eddying in the faint air currents.

Her light brightened until she could see the entire chamber. On the far left wall she saw a massive blasted splotch with a great crack running from floor to ceiling.

Walking over to it, she saw that some of this damage was new, no doubt caused by $1.98. Bouncing golden balls of light ahead of her, she called, "$1.98?"

"Duff, I am in here." His voice echoed from a side tunnel. The crack had cut across it. "In here."

She stepped into the square shaft and sent a few spheres ahead.

Bright flashes of red glittered brightly in the yellow light.

$1.98 was standing in front of them.

"What are those things?"

"Red jewels. I think." He kicked at a small mound at his

feet, scattering them to his left. "Watch what they do.

The glittering jewels twitched and jittered and crept back together, making their heap again.

Duff reached down and picked one of them up. Holding it in her palm she peered closely at it. "It doesn't seem to have any feet. And it is warm."

$1.98 stepped to her side. "I wonder what they are?"

"Magical beasts, perhaps," suggested Sorrowful. He had grown tired of waiting and had come up to see what there was to see. Tears stood by his side. The luggage came trailing right behind them.

$1.98 tapped the jewel in the palm of Duff's hand on its top with one fingertip. "Can you tell? I couldn't."

Duff tapped it with a short, silver wand. The jewel squeaked at her.

"DUFF!" snapped $1.98, whipping a long black wand from his sleeve. The air crackled around them.

She flinched. "What?"

"They are coming at you."

She looked down. The mound she had picked the jewel from was beginning to flow up the side of her leg, apparently headed for the one she held in her hand.

"They seem harmless," she said.

Glittering jewels flowed higher.

"Let's see what they do. And put that thing away, Dear."

$1.98 shoved the wand back into his sleeve.

"And tell me," she said. "What did you do to cause that much damage?"

"I saw something leaping toward me." He pointed. "And most of that crack was already here."

"What did you see?" asked Sorrowful.

"Strange."

"OH!" gasped Duff. She pulled the neck of her blouse out and peeked inside. "They, ahhhhhh, tickle."

The jewels had slipped up her side and were flowing steadily upward, over her rib cage, having slipped under her blouse where there was a small opening just at the belt line.

They all could see the faint red glow spreading widely as the creatures headed for her shoulder.

"Looks erotic to me," commented Sorrowful.

The jewels began to slip out from her under her collar and over her shoulder and down her arm toward the one she was holding.

Sweat glistened on Duff's face, she was breathing heavily. "Uhhhhhhh, these things are dangerous." She sighed as the last of the red glitter trailed over her shoulder. She looked at $1.98. "You would not believe what they did." Her hand was now a cluster of glittering crimson lights.

"Duff?" $1.98 was frowning deeply.

"Perfectly all right, Dear. Out there they are quite safe." She winked at him. "I'll tell you about the other part, later." She wiped her face with her free sleeve.

"What are you going to do with them?" asked Tears.

"Leave them be," answered $1.98. "We have to go the other way. This tunnel is clogged with them. And now I don't think we want to try and wade through them."

"It would be ecstasy death," said Duff. She bent over and watched the cluster flow onto the floor.

When the last of them was off, she peered closely at her arm and hand. "No marks, no pain. Strange creatures."

$1.98 gestured. "Shall we go that way?"

Stumpf. Evening.

Mirf and J. C. were to share one blanket, one of Mountain's blankets. And one of Mountain's pads. The gigantic man was mumbling and grumbling about folk who traveled unprepared as he fixed and prepared a meal.

Later, after they had eaten, they lay side by side looking up into the darkness.

The high rock walls blocked away most of the night sky. A few bright specks, bright stars glistened red through the atmosphere of Stumpf. None of this elseplace's moons were in the sky.

Mountain was fast asleep. They were slowly drifting that way.

"Mirf?"

"What?"

"How come Mountain speaks English?"

"He doesn't. And before you ask, the node did it. Happens every time. It is the why the many times and places can interact and visit and trade. And it is why there is a Monetary Control to insure that the trade is honest and the many forms of currency are not debased."

"O. K."

"That is it? Just O. K .?"

"Sure."

Mirf hissed softly to herself, then nudged J. C. gently with an elbow. "You mind if I get closer? I am cold."

"Nope."

"You may put an arm around me if you wish. But."

"What?"

"Don't start fondling things."

"Good night Mirf." He took deep breath, exhaled slowly, and eased into sleep.

"Raz baz," mumbled Mirf, loosening her belt and tugging the blanket in.

A Rocky Place. Afternoon.

Well past the crack, walking steadily through the tunnel, they finally saw a faint light. The tunnel had been empty since leaving the red jewels. They had not run into other inhabitants, saw no more of the sparkling creatures, and saw no indication that anything had come this way.

"Looks like natural light to me," said Sorrowful.

"Yes," said $1.98.

Duff extinguished their light glow as they silently, carefully approached the brightness.

It was a cave with a broad open mouth. The tunnel they exited from was one of many that ended along the vast back wall.

Sorrowful carefully scratched a small mark next to the mouth of the tunnel from which they had just stepped. Just in case.

Sorrowful and Tears waited while Duff slipped on soft toes toward the front, $1.98 just behind her and to one side, his right hand hovering near his left sleeve.

She was holding a white wand.

The luggage waited next to Tears, who gently stroked one of the bags on the side.

"A real adventure," he whispered.

"Indeed it is," replied Sorrowful. "I wonder where we are."

"No one around," called $1.98, waving one arm, beckoning them forward.

But there was, in a manner of speaking.

A large town sprawled not far from the base of the slope they looked down, out onto an immense plain. A well worn path meandered from the base of the talus slope of the cave into the forested space between town and slope.

"Looks like they come up here frequently," commented $1.98.

"Well Dear, shall we find out where we are?" Duff nudged $1.98 with her elbow.

Down the talus they all slipped until they jolted to a stop at the bottom, at the beginning of the path. Tears and Sorrowful had rattled down, the luggage gliding serenely with them, halting next to $1.98.

"Sorrowful, you and Tears go ahead of us. They might not like magicians here," said $1.98.

"Come, Tears, you are about to meet your first elseplace of strangers. Let us see what these town folk are like. It is most often quite interesting."

Sorrowful and Tears started down the path, each filled with wonder. Sorrowful from experience, Tears from excitement.

As they walked into the town, Tears gasped, "Giants."

Everyone they passed was as large as $1.98.

"You will find," began Sorrowful, "that in most places the inhabitants are larger than our own folk. $1.98 and these are, more or less, the usual size. We are rather small."

"Duff is not."

"An exception to the rule." People stared at them, then went about their, business.

Soon they passed a store, and then another. The road they walked along appeared to be the main street. It was rather narrow and twisted, but all in all, a straight main street.

They slipped past three men in animated conversation.

Sorrowful smiled.

Tears looked puzzled.

"How will we ever find out anything? We don't speak their language?"

"Tears, a Tale Teller does not mush his words together." Sorrowful frowned. "Oh my, oh my indeed. I forgot." Sorrowful waved Duff and $1.98 to join with them.

"What is the matter?" Duff's eyes darted about trying to locate the trouble.

Sorrowful explained, " . . . and so you see, while we are able to speak with the folk of the elseplaces, Tears cannot."

"No problem," said $1.98, shaking back his sleeves.

Duff stepped in front of him. "I will do it, Dear."

"Will it hurt?" asked Tears, trying not to look as afraid as he felt.

"You will never feel a thing," said Duff. $1. 98 winced. She tapped Tears on the forehead with a small red wand and caught him as he fell.

"You carry him, Dear."

$1.98 cradled Tears in his arms. "Let's find an inn."

Sorrowful looked from magician to magician.

Duff took one of Sorrowful's hands in hers. "He will be all right. It is just a deep sleep."

"He will probably have a headache," said $1.98.

"No, he will not," corrected Duff.

"This town is called Bebarrah," said Sorrowful. "At least, that is what I thought I heard."

Duff shook her head. "Never heard of it. Dear?"

$1.98 shook his head also. He was much more widely traveled than any of them, but he had never heard of this elseplace either.

"I could consult," he suggested.

"Once we have a room," countered Duff.

Sorrowful pointed. "That place with the bright orange sign. Does that sound like a good place? The Cavern of Delight."

Duff shrugged her shoulders.

$1.98 headed for the door.

"The Cavern of Delight it is," said Sorrowful, hastening in front of him and yanking open the door.

As they stepped in, a large person dressed in gray and orange patterned material greeted them.

"Welcome to our guests. Welcome to Bebarrah. Welcome to The Cavern of Delight. How may we serve you?"

"We require two sleeping rooms, bathing facilities, and food," said Sorrowful.

"The finest in the zoona, gentle elder. This way." With a grand sweep of a massive arm, she urged them through another door and led them up a grand staircase and into a sitting room with adjoining bedrooms.

"Facilities straight across," she said. Whipping a folded paper from an ample pocket, she flopped it open and handed it to Sorrowful.

"See pick," she said.

Sorrowful took the sheet and selected several items from the list.

Retrieving the paper, she refolded it and slipped it back into her pocket and held out one hand. "Bla chop."

Sorrowful looked at $1.98 who reached out and dropped four glittering gold coins into her palm.

"Kind kind welcome." She beamed and left them to their own devices.

Duff perched on one of the couches. "Set Tears here, Dear. Then consult."

$1.98 gently laid Tears down and sat on the floor saying something complicated in a sing-song voice. Vague shapes floated around him and muttered. He waved one hand and looked at Duff.

"Bebarrah, a town catering to visitors seeking a certain rare enjoyment at The Cavern of Delight, a large grotto on the hillside above the town. It is reported that if a visitor is well-favored they will experience a transforming, ah, zeedar. It doesn't translate. Some visitors disappear, some go mad, most have nothing happen to them. It is a kind of mystical event."

"Interesting," said Sorrowful.

"What do they call those red jewels," asked Duff.

"They were not mentioned," answered $1.98.

She grinned at him. "Those things must be responsible for the zeedar."

$1.98 gazed into her eyes. "Some go mad."

"I can understand that."

"What?" asked Tears.

"How's your head," asked $1.98.

"I feel fine. Where are we?"

"In an inn called The Cavern of Delight," said Sorrowful. "We ordered something to eat."

The outer door thumped, Sorrowful opened it. The large woman entered and set an equally large, covered tray on a small table at one side of the room. Then she left.

"Smells good," said Tears, sitting up.

"Shall we eat?" asked Sorrowful.

"I will serve," announced Duff, walking over to the tray and lifting the lid.

She did.

Stumpf. Morning.

The sun was fairly high above the rock rim by the time they roused themselves from sleep.

Mountain thought this pair were more civilized than most of the small folk that he had met, they knew how to sleep. He stretched and sat up.

J. C. opened his eyes and was surprised. He had slept soundly. Mountain's pad had been very comfortable.

Mirf was wrapped around him. Carefully, gently, he eased her away and rolled her onto her back and sat up and looked around.

It had been almost dark by the time they had arrived at Mountain's camping spot. This was the first time he could take a good look. They were in a narrow canyon on a high bench bordering a gravel filled arroyo. He could feel the heat beginning to beat down, bouncing from the rock walls. It reminded him of the California desert, from the many times that Doc had dragged him out there on archaeological expeditions.

Turning, he looked at Mirf, brushed the hair away from her face.

Her eyes popped open.

"Morning," said J. C. "Sleep well?"

She smiled, a soft gentle smile. It made the most amazing transformation in her, from stern official into very pretty woman. "I did. What's for breakfast?" And sat up.

"Flat terbat," announced Mountain, yanking dark orange slabs of something from a sack and handing each of them a chunk.

Mirf turned the thing around and around in her hands.

"Like this," said Mountain, snapping off a piece and popping it into his mouth and chewing. The terbat made crunching noises.

"Sounds like a bowl of puffed rice," said J. C. He was struggling with his piece of breakfast. It didn't want to break.

"BY DUMPF, here," grumbled Mountain. He took the food from J. C., set it on a rock, and struck with the side of his clenched fist, shattering the food into fragments.

Mirf smashed her's with a rock. "Dim dizzle."

"Not bad," said J. C., crackling loudly. He whispered to Mirf, "If you like processed cardboard."

"Food's food," crunched Mirf.

Mountain finished packing his camp as his two guests crackled their way through breakfast. As soon as the noise stopped, he stood and swung his pack onto his back and started to walk down the trail.

"This way, we go this way."

"Where are we going?" asked Mirf and J. C. at the same time.

J. C. laughed.

Mirf frowned.

"Home," announced Mountain pointing at a place just ahead. The path branched. One arm of the path disappeared into a narrow split in the rock. The other arm followed the arroyo, staying on the high bench. He turned into the narrow place. Mountain just fit.

An hour later, they stepped out.

Into a scene of glaring rock surfaces and sun glare. Radiant heat banged into them from the blazing white sand and rock.

J. C. could feel the skin on his face drying out.

"The Barren Wastes," announced Mountain pointing dramatically out over the space in front of them. He led them a short distance to a rock overhang and deep shadow. Here another spring bubbled into a rock basin. The overflow disappeared a few yards out into the rock strewn wasteland.

"Drink," commanded Mountain.

J. C. stepped aside to let Mirf go first.

"We are going through that?" asked J. C.

"We are," said Mountain.

"Not during the day?"

"Of course."

"Think again," said J. C. "It is night or not at all. If we try to cross there now, we will be fried in no time."

"HUMPF. I have crossed many times. During the day."

Mirf finished drinking and turned toward their gigantic guide.

"We are not human camels. He and I would die."

Mountain frowned at her. "What kind of thing is a camel?"

J. C. explained, pointing out all the similarities between camels and Mountain's folk that he could think of using all the examples he had heard from Tinker.

Mountain sat with a thud. Dust puffed out around him. "Demons are said to lurk in the night on The Barren Wastes. They eat people." He rolled his eyes at Mirf.

Mirf hissed. "Biz bosh."

"Exactly," agreed J. C. "Biz bosh." He pointed at the crack. "We'll go back the way we came, you can go ahead."

"**ROCK ROLLING NO!** I will go with you small folk. I have been called." The last sentence was a pronouncement. Punctuated by a large fist thumping on a hollow resounding chest.

"Really?"

Mirf yanked J. C. backward. "Take a drink, boychick." She looked at Mountain. "What's on the other side?" Even in shadow, sweat trickled down her face.

"Home. I live just there." Mountain pointed straight across.

"Will you be able to find your way across in the dark?"

"The Great Two will light our way. And, **BY DUMPF**, I know the way."

"Then," suggested J. C. "Let's sit and rest until dark."

"Vunderbar," said Mirf, sitting and leaning against the rock face.

They sat and dozed the day away. Waking and drinking, frequently.

Ramna Dir. A Small Village. Late At Night.

She stood, still as still, and waited for The Seer to speak.

The temple was small, stone, circular with a domed ceiling. Tendrils of smoke drifted upward from the central alter bowl and wandered into the night through the small opening directly above the soft glowing fire.

Con'da'la'an, The Seer, one of the few remaining True Eyes of Godan, stood, eyes closed, and waited for the words to come.

"Offspring," she rasped. And swayed from side to side, just a little. "Powerful. Unusual."

She jerked as her eyes flew wide. She turned and faced the other. "What are you?"

"This one is called Lady Lastgift."

"You were not called."

"This one was sent."

"I would see to whom I speak."

"Few would dare peer Death in the face."

Con'da'la'an nodded. "Few have seen all that I have seen." She waggled one hand loosely.

In a single fluid motion the hood was swept back and pale green eyes looked at The Seer.

"Death has a very fair countenance," observed

Con'da'la'an. "Is this my time?"

"This one would ask the True Eye of Godan for the rest of her vision."

The Seer nodded. And told her.

Bahn Duhr Tohr. The Royal City. Afternoon. Between Courtly Duties.

It had been two days and Ripple had been called to The Queen's presence.

"Sweet Queen, Noble King." Ripple had brought Hanred with her. They were in the private quarters of The Royals.

"Dark Witch, Honest Advisor, We have need of information that only you can provide."

"As always, ready," said Hanred.

"Just tell me," said Ripple. Overhead began to darken.

"We do hear strange things be occurring in thy quarters. Pray tell us of these matters."

Ripple frowned. "It is the business of my clan."

"And of Our's as well," stated The Queen. "For We are acquainted with that Noble Youth as are you. We would know, for We fear that there may be some threat to this, Our Kingdom, and We must be well prepared for all eventualities."

Hanred nudged his wife. "Tell her, Dark Loveliness."

The Queen patted the space next to her. "Sit and tell."

Ripple did.

And Toucan, The King, and Hanred listened carefully. It was a short narration.

"So that is why I have called some of my sisters here."

Toucan stood. "We offer our aid. This thing must be most evil." He laid one hand on his Queen's shoulder. "And we have had experience in this, we have."

Willawa, The White Warrior, Queen of Bahn Duhr Tohr, kingdoms great and small, reached up and covered his hand with one of her's.

"We will raise the mightiest army ever seen," said the Queen.

Ripple shook her head. "We, my sisters and I, know not yet what makes this threat to Ramp. A great assembly of fierce warriors with idle hands poses a greater and more eminent threat to the kingdom."

Toucan laughed. "True. Yet games and feasts a'plenty for two hands of days would be no threat."

"Indeed." Willawa smiled. "We think it is time for a Grand Fest. It is time to make the court worry about who is rising and who is falling in this Our favor. We think a great contest for heros and the massed clashing of armored, mounted arms will put all in fine fettle for war. If you, Dark One, feel such a need."

"A clever idea," said Hanred.

"It will take time," said Ripple. "Before we know."

"We will so proclaim The Fest this day at an audience. Lords and Princes will come running from every corner of the kingdom. In two days they will begin arriving, the last in nine days. From that last arrival will begin The Royal Games. So it will be a major celebration. The merchants will sing."

"Indeed, indeed," agreed Toucan. "Fair coinage will flow heavily."

"And the Royal Coffers will swell some small amount as well." Willawa nodded at Ripple.

"I ask a favor, My Queen."

"Ask, it is your's."

"I, we, must leave this fair kingdom and visit my, our, Aunts."

"Be thee gone long?" asked Toucan.

"I can not answer. We will not know until after we get there."

"We will miss you greatly," said The Queen.

"Sweet Queen, my youngest sister will stay here. She is a powerful magician."

"A magician?"

"Happens in the best of clans," said Hanred. "**OUCH!**"

Ripple had jabbed him with one finger. "The youngest and the last is always a magician." She waved one hand and they appeared. "My Queen, this is my sister Ramp and her husband Hard." They had appeared in the center of the room.

"Welcome to you both," said Willawa. "And most welcome to you, Noble and Sweet Hard. Husband, this is the one of which We bespoke." She smiled at Hard.

"Indeed," said Toucan, smiling at his queen.

Hard blushed.

Ramp looked at him, and said softly, "Her also? Husband, you were very busy in my absence when you were traveling."

"Hum, hum, hum," said Ripple, realizing that Ramp knew about her and Hard in the elseplaces when Hard had no memory of his wife.

"Nasty, nasty," said Hanred softly in his wife's ear. He could tell what she was thinking from her expression.

Ripple spoke so only Hanred could hear. "It was before I met you."

"Good. For I like that boy."

"Will you act in Ripple's stead while she travels?" asked Willawa.

"I will, Queen," answered Ramp.

"Good," said Ripple.

She and Hanred disappeared.

Bahn Duhr Tohr. The Royal City. Later.

The room they entered was large, dusty, dim, and smelled of being long locked up.

Willawa swung open the blinds of the two-story windows flooding the opposite wall with sunlight.

She gestured at the wall and the great design covering it.

"That, My King, is The Great Map of all of Bahn Duhr Tohr. All that is what you reign over."

Toucan looked at the map. It sparkled rainbow colors in patches of odd shapes and forms. The rivers were deep blue edged with silver. The rocky reaches etched in black and gold.

Willawa slipped one of her arms under one of his. "Each fiefdom, every Lord and Prince, wears the colors shown here. This is the registry, the statement of sovereignty, of holdings, great and small, Every army will be so colored."

The blazing white of Willawa's reignplace attracted his eye.

Toucan pulled her toward the map and pointed at a gray section nestling in a narrow edge not far from the Royal City. "Sweet Queen, what Lords wears so dour a suit?"

She smiled at him. "That is The Always Empty. Our legends tell us of a great and vicious battle that emptied that land. None, ever since, have desired to live there."

"None?"

"Three kings ago, a younger Prince anxious to improve his lot convinced his father, the then King, to take that land. The young Prince took a small force and many messengers and rode to that place. The first messenger returned saying that a road two armies wide passed deep into that place. A second messenger, mostly mad, and dying, told of sudden death, horrible and swift. None but he returned. None have entered that place since. We have no need."

"Indeed," said Toucan, turning her around and wrapping his arms about her. "This room is most private, is it not?"

"Oh yes, very private." Her fingers tugged at his shirt.

"Indeed? T'will be no Court business here?"

"My King," she said, pushing him toward the divan. "This is court business."

"Indeed."

Stumpf. The Barren Wastes.

They had hiked for a few hours when J. C. noticed it. The horizon was suddenly brightening. Two large moons sailed into the night sky. The three travelers and everything else now cast shadows.

"Now we will hurry," said Mountain lengthening his stride.

Hurrying behind him, sweating heavily, came J. C. and Mirf. Even at night the Barren Wastes radiated large amounts of heat. No cooling breeze blew out here.

"Ho boy," said Mirf. She rolled up her sleeves, tugged her shirt loose and unbuttoned it.

An hour later, J .C. yanked his shirt off and tied it around his waist. The temperature was still rising.

"Boychick," said Mirf. "This is no time for you to get excited." She yanked off her shirt and tied the arms around her waist. "Nor is this the place for modesty."

He didn't turn his head. He was putting all his energies and thoughts into following Mountain.

And the temperature rose higher.

The bottoms of his feet were beginning to sting. So he asked her, "How's your feet?"

"Hot as hell," rasped Mirf. "If you'll pardon the expression."

"Half way," bellowed Mountain from far up ahead.

They trudged on.

And on.

And on.

The moons had set. The temperature was dropping, just a little bit.

Mirf and J. C. were staggering and lurching after Mountain who was steadily getting further and further ahead of them. It seemed to them that the sun had suddenly hurtled itself into the sky, drenching them in a ruby glow.

"Boychick," wheezed Mirf. "It's been nice to know you.

And believe me, bubee, I am sorry."

J. C. shoved the coins in his mouth from cheek to cheek with his tongue, trying to get enough moisture to answer. "For what?" he croaked.

"Talking you into this."

"I volunteered."

Mirf stumbled closer and grabbed his shirt tail, using it as a guide.

"Hang on," rasped J. C.

"Dumbkopf, I am," snarled Mirf.

From a distance they heard Mountain yelling something. It sounded like "soon."

Bahn Duhr Tohr. The Royal City. Evening.

"We are ready," said Reptar.

R-Bar grinned wickedly. "Are you coming with us, Hanred?"

"He is coming with me," stated Ripple.

"Hum, hum, hum," answered R-Bar.

"Stop fussing," said Rumtah.

"Are any others joining us there?" asked Reptar.

"The call is out and spreading," said Ripple. "Husband, you may stay here if you wish."

Hanred slipped an arm around her waist. "Dark Light of my life, I couldn't do that. And think of this, you wicked lovelies. Even among all that witchery, some illusions may be required or needed. And I am the best."

Ripple looked at him and without looking anywhere else said, "R-Bar, take us."

The short witch carved open the air with a glittering silver wand.

Stumpf. Mountain's Home. Mid-Morning.

J. C. slowly became aware of the interesting realization

that he stood in a dim but cool room.

He had one arm tightly wrapped around a wooden pillar. It was the only thing that was keeping him from falling over. His other arm was wrapped around Mirf who was sagging heavily against him.

She felt gritty from the light covering of the dust acquired in The Barren Wastes. One of her arms was swung over his back and around his neck. Her head hung limply on her chest.

Somewhere in the room, someone was banging around doing something.

"**BY ALL THE ROCKS AND STONES**," boomed Mountain. "I greatly thought I was going to loose you small folk to the Burning Demons of The Barren Wastes."

"Mirf?" croaked J. C. It was his third try. And first successful attempt at speaking.

Her head slowly rose until she could see his face. Something deep in those strange looking eyes flickered.

"J . . . C . . .?"

He tried to smile. His lips split. They were dry and parched. He could taste blood as he licked them.

"That's me," he wheezed.

"Hard . . . case . . ." She pulled herself upright, still leaning heavily against him.

He clenched his new found friend, the pillar, tighter.

Mountain stomped around and stood in front of them, bent over and held a large spoon in front of J. C.'s face. Something thick, surged back and forth but stayed in the bowl.

"Drink."

J. C. took a sip. Then a mouthful. Then the rest, Sweat burst from his body. He felt better.

Mountain dipped the spoon into a container and shoved it under Mirf's nose.

"Drink!"

She did. Same reaction. "Let's not do that again," she

rasped.

J. C. found that he could now stand without holding onto the post. He still held Mirf who had, somehow, turned and was leaning against his chest, her arms wrapped around his waist.

"I owe you a bunch, J. C."

"Forget it."

"A debt is a debt."

"Hum bug."

"Debt is better than death. English proverb, 1659."

"Mirf?"

"Mountain must have a really monstrous bed," she whispered. "You want to put it to me?"

"Lovely offer. Crudely put. All I could possibly do now is collapse."

"Me too," she said sagging against him.

"Rain check?" he asked, brushing her hair from her forehead.

"Maybe. Think he has a tub?"

"Mountain," asked J. C. "Do you have a tub?"

"I do. And I already filled it for you. Through there." He pointed.

Mirf lurched upright, stepped back and trapped one of J. C.'s hands. "Come on, boychick. You can join me. I will need help getting the rest of my clothes off."

"Oh boy," said J. C.

"Wise guy," snarled Mirf, yanking him into motion.

"Not too long in there," cautioned Mountain. "You require food and drink, **BY DUMPF.**"

"Raz baz," replied Mirf.

The tub was outside, fed constantly by a mildly warm spring, and set mostly into the ground.

J. C. shoved her in, clothes and all and toppled in after her.

"No comment," she said.

He reached down and began to take off her boots. "Just soak," he ordered.

After wringing out her socks and setting them to dry next to her boots he began to yank off her trousers.

"No messing around, boychick."

J. C. grinned. "Wouldn't think of it."

"To me, you couldn't sell a used car."

"There," he dumped her clothes next to the tub. "Virtue intact."

She tickled him with her toes while he was struggling out of his clothes. "You're no help," he said.

"Did you ask?"

"Didn't think of it."

"Ho Ha!"

J. C. leaned back and sank down until his chin was just touching the surface of the water. "I didn't think we would make it out of there alive."

"Me neither. Thanks," she said. She blinked her eyes. "I mean it."

They soaked.

"Out! **BY DOUBLE-DUMPF, OUT.**" Mountain threw down towels. "You need to eat and drink."

"And rest," added Mirf.

"Recharge our batteries," said J. C.

Mountain dropped to his knees and peered at him. "Do what?"

Mirf saw J. C.'s smile starting. "Don't."

J. C. ducked his head. "It is just an expression. Where I live, it means I need to rest and relax."

Mountain stood and announced firmly. "And eat and drink."

"That too," agreed J. C. He clambered from the tub and swung one of the towels around and around and up and over one of his shoulders. "Toga party. Lots of towel there."

Mountain picked up their clothes and took them

somewhere.

Mirf heaved herself from the tub and stood looking at him. "So what do you think? I think I lost twenty pounds. At least."

"My, my, my."

She grabbed the other towel.

"John Tinker missed a good deal," said J. C.

"Way it goes. Let's go eat and drink."

"About time," grumbled a loud voice from inside the building.

"That guy has a lot of Mirf," laughed J. C.

Inside they found their host sitting on the floor, his back against a wall. Scattered in front of him were a dozen pieces of bright cloth upon which sat many dishes of food and strangely shaped containers of various kinds of beverages. He pointed. "There. And there. I have few guests, my manners are unused. Drink. First."

J. C. sat and peered into the large cup handed to him. "More of that goop?"

"No. Ducmer. A restorative."

"Ahhhhhhh, Ducmer." J. C. took a large swallow. "Not too bad. It has a certain authority, a subtle tickle to the palate."

Mountain looked at him. "Are you really from John Tinker's elseplace? You speak differently."

Mirf drained her cup, and nudged J. C. with an elbow. "Let's eat."

Mountain waited until each of them had started, then he began.

It was a long meal, one with many kinds of food, one with many selected beverages. But, finally, Mirf and J. C. convinced Mountain that there was no way they could eat anything else.

"HUMPF. You will miss this and this and this." He uncovered a number of additional dishes.

"Go right ahead," said J. C.

"It's all right by me," added Mirf.

So, Mountain did.

When all the dishes were empty and all the containers drained, Mountain heaved himself to his feet. "Next room," he announced.

They followed him.

He pointed to a couch-like piece of furniture and waited while they got settled in it.

"You must have one last drink. It is a **STUMPFING** custom."

"Sure," said J. C.

Mirf nodded.

Mountain poured and handed each of them a cup and sat in a chair.

"**STUMPF BY DUMPF!**" He took a long swallow, his face flushed red. "**RAR-RUMPF.**"

J. C. took a tentative sip. "**WOWEE!** Kickapoo Joy Juice."

"NO. Fempor."

Mirf took a swallow. "**HO BOY**, what a jolt."

"You make this stuff yourself?" asked J. C. taking another swallow. It wasn't too bad this time. He thought that most of his taste buds had been numbed.

"Family recipe," said Mountain, refilling their cups. "Traditional end to such a meal."

"Tradition," sang Mirf, snapping her fingers and swaying from side to side. She set her cup on the floor. Mountain reached over and refilled it. She held it steady for him.

"Local ingredients, I suppose," asked J. C.

"Of course, the finest Arech and Pfum."

"Doubt I could find Arech and Pfum back home," whispered J. C. into Mirf's ear. He stood and wobbled from side to side. "Bed? Where . . . is . . . the . . . bed?" He knew his body was shutting down and wanted to get to the bed before it did. Small amounts of alcohol did it to him every time.

"Next room." Mountain pointed.

J. C. grunted and grinned a very lopsided grin.

Mountain had made a very dramatic gesture and J. C. was feeling very amused. By everything. Somebody took his hand and gently hauled him away.

"Come on, I'll get you there."

She did.

In the nick of time.

J. C. was toppling as they reached the guest bed. Luckily, it was built low to the floor.

Grabbing his ankles she heaved the slack body all the way into the bed. Then she stepped over him, tossed her towel aside, yanked his away and lay down, tugging the blanket over them, mumbling to herself, "Rest and relaxation."

Krandal's Dirt Bag. A Rather Pleasant Day.

The folk in the central space of this rather oddly named town, stopped their several endeavors, stared at their visitor, gasped, and ran in as many directions as there were streets exiting from the central space.

The cause of all this excitement on the part of the inhabitants of Krandal's Dirt Bag stood and looked around the central space.

This pair had just arrived, had just suddenly appeared in the central space. Actually, one of the pair looked around. The other just stood, still as still can be.

He, the one looking around, was dressed in the soft purple edged in green robe that identified him as being of the Sluba mage Guild.

She, the one who stood so still, was wearing a robe of a forest green color so dark as to be almost black. The hood of her robe hid her face so thoroughly that anyone who would dare to peer that way would only see darkness looking out. She held a short gold staff in one hand.

He watched the last person hurtling away and started in the same direction. "I believe that there is a small inn just down this street."

"This one will follow," came the soft whisper from his companion.

Ransapal nodded. And walked down the chosen street. And hoped that their sudden appearance had not frightened the locals to the point of panic and an ill conceived attack.

Kragkoptar. Inside.

B'Wass and Shlem sitting, talking. About what was. Sitting and talking in the dark of the room.

"They are here."

"Yes."

"We will have to see them."

"Yes."

Kragkoptar. Outside. Grey and Cold.

They were standing at the base of a small knoll.

Ripple pointed up at the large structure seeping over the upper surface, sections sprawling over the edge, down the slope.

"They live in there."

"Dim, dim, dim," snarled R-Bar. "Trick maze."

Rumtah rubbed the green wand idly over her cheek, up and down, her eyes carefully watching up there. "Hum, hum, hum."

"Let us in," said Ripple softly, speaking to The Aunts.

"You may enter," said a voice.

"Yes," said another.

Kragkoptar. Inside.

They all stood in a large room floored with black shining stone.

Two great, black clad forms sat overflowing their chairs,

sitting side by side. Their faces were obscured by deep shadow. Their hands lay loosely clenched in laps obscured by other deep shadows

The vast chamber was dimly lit. Black draped itself from high corners and far reaches, just contained. Waiting.

Ripple stepped forward. "This is mine, Hanred."

"Old Hanred," said B'Wass. "The Master Illusionist."

"Yes," said Shlm.

"You haven't met my sisters," said Ripple.

"We were present."

"At all birthings."

"The runt is R-Bar," said Ripple.

"Startangled. Grotz of Derry's Dung."

"Yes."

"The taller is Rumteh," said Ripple.

"The lucky. Fought Tartook."

"Pieces everywhere."

"And she is Reptar," Ripple nodded.

"Sixth. Disappeared."

"Back."

"The clan must gather," stated Ripple.

"Great danger," said B'Wass.

"Yes," said Shlm.

"Will you help?" asked Ripple.

"Yes," said B'Wass.

"It is our clan," added Shlm. She placed her arms on the sides of her chair. Her joints creaked loudly. It had been a long time since she had last moved. Dark forces instantly gathered swirled angrily in the high corners of the room.

R-Bar hissed. Her beast snarled by her side.

Someone was walking from out there into the room.

She had the broad shoulders of an athlete. Her stride was hard, military. She wore a long robe of heavy black material, knee length black boots, highly polished, black gloves of fine leather. Her hair was tied back into a thick pony tail. A jet velvet hat completed her costume.

"Hayou, Ripple," she said. "I received your call. Hayou, Aunts." She folded her arms over her chest. "Hum, hum, hum, hum." And peered at the others standing nearby. "That thing is ugly," she said to R-Bar.

"Still wearing flashy clothes," she said to Reptar. "Whose is that?" She indicated Hanred.

"My mate for life," snapped Ripple. The air crackled around her. "Hanred, this is Rekel."

He eyed this sister carefully.

She ignored him. And glared at Ripple. "What do you want? Why are we here?"

"A great thing threatens Ramp and her unbirthed."

"She found one?"

"She did."

"Unbirthed?"

"Twins."

Keening, twisted forms swirled around Rekel. "Who? Or what?" Her eyes glittered.

Shlm shifted in her chair. The air cleared.

B'Wass said. "There are many rooms here. Settle. Eat. We will talk."

The room cleared. The sisters were sent to their rooms. To rest.

"Our sister's offspring are strong."

"Yes."

"Pretty nice room," said Hanred, giving it a quick check. It was a habit he had retained from his traveling days.

"I want to be held," stated Ripple, stepping in front of him.

He grabbed her. "A wonderful idea."

She hissed.

"Husbands like to squeeze their wives," he said, one hand dropping down as he loosened his grip, tugging her blouse free. His finger's lightly stroked the small of her back.

"Hum, hum, hum," hummed Ripple, tilting her head back, arching her neck.

His lips stroked the hollow where neck joined shoulder.

"Rekel is a pain," she said. "Always has been." She nudged him. "Witch bother."

He smiled at her. "She does seem to have a rather sharp manner." Unfastening the last button, he slipped her blouse back and off her shoulders.

"Placid or angry, a delight to my eyes you are, Dark Witchy Delight."

"If I may interject some small observation."

"Of course."

She stared down past the end of her nose. "Your hands seem to take a certain delight as well." She sighed. "As gentle as they are."

"**DIM, DIM, DIM!**" snarled R-Bar, thrusting into the room. "I will not room share with that Rekel." She threw her hands over her eyes. "Pardon, pardon, pardon. I will leave." She shimmered and began to fade.

"**STAY!**" commanded Ripple.

R-Bar shimmered back in.

Hanred stepped to one side as Ripple waggled one hand. Her blouse was back in place. "Take your hands down, little one."

R-Bar cracked her fingers, peeked out through the open space, and dropped her hands. "I didn't realize you were, ah, oh, dim, dim, dim, doing things."

"We were not doing . . . things!" snarled Ripple.

"Yet," amended Hanred.

"Come here," demanded Ripple.

R-Bar stepped cautiously forward and stopped, not yet decided upon what to do or whether she ought to make a run for it.

"Husband," said Ripple sweetly.

He cringed inwardly.

R-Bar's eyes darted from face to face.

"Dear," cooed Ripple.

Now Hanred was really worried, it was getting worse and worse. Witches sounding sweet, or cooing pleasantly, were right on the edge of doing vile.

R-Bar began wrapping protection over herself.

"Yes?"

"This child is always teasing you with her charms, is she not? So . . . you may fondle her if you wish."

"I may?" stuttered Hanred.

R-Bar backed up, her eyes watching him carefully. "You wouldn't?"

"**GRAB HER!**" snapped Ripple.

R-Bar crashed back against the wall, arms crossed over her chest. "**STAY AWAY!**"

Ripple started laughing, real laughter. It was a most strange thing for a witch to do. "You are safe, Runt. I was just teasing. Come here, sit next to me."

Ripple sat on the lounge.

R-Bar stared at her.

Hanred opened a cabinet and handed beverages around, and sat on the other side of the short witch as she sat next to her sister.

"It might have been fun." He grinned at her.

"I really didn't mean to interrupt."

Hanred slipped a comradely arm around R-Bar's shoulders.

"Husband," cautioned Ripple.

"That was rangle," grumbled R-Bar, looking at her.

"I was Rekel bothered," replied Ripple.

"Really? Me too."

"That sister witch is like a narn spell."

R-Bar nodded. "Exactly."

"A little snack, perhaps," leered Hanred. A thing of grasping tentacles and sucking mouths drooled at the petite witch.

Eyes twinkling, she threw her arms around the thing. "Why not?"

"Not me," said Hanred. He waved one hand and pointed at the small table that had appeared in the center of the room covered with dishes of foodstuffs.

Ripple had just waved it in.

"Hum," said Ripple, rapping her sister on the shoulder. "That is mine."

R-Bar let go, jumped to her feet and began piling things on the platters, handing one to each of the others.

As they ate, R-Bar asked in small voice. "Where will I find mine?"

"Unexpectedly, in a strange place, most likely," answered Ripple.

"He is a'driv. Ramp's is a'driv. Hum, hum, hum."

"Little one, listen. We are sister witches, all. Save one, of course. Each mate, if found, is a'driv. Such pulls us. But your find enfolds."

"May I stay?"

Ripple hissed.

"Please?"

"My hearts melts," sighed Hanred, grinning broadly at Ripple.

"You just want to see what is under all that baggy clothing," snapped Ripple.

"Merely for comparative purposes and learned curiosity." Hanred winked at R-Bar.

R-Bar beamed happily back at him. It was not exactly proper witch behavior.

In another room, some small conversation.

"You feel used."

"Near far."

"Where," hissed Rumtah.

"Ripple threw me at The Chosen One. His urh-witch

stabbed a wandbolt. She is young and unpracticed."

Rumtah shook her head. "No such thing."

"The Legend has one."

"You mis-saw."

Reptar yanked off her vest and ripped open her blouse. "Read these magic stains."

Rumtah sucked in her breath and stepped closer to her sister, bending forward to peer closer at the strange marks. Her fingers flowed lightly cross Reptar's skin.

"You almost joined Rbat far?"

"Spell fixed by R-Bar."

"She is becoming adept."

"Growing."

Rumtah straightened up, her hand gently fondling her sister. "These magic marks will keep you weak."

"I require dark."

"Yes," said Rumtah, clamping one hand over her sister's mouth as she plunged a short green wand into her chest. She drove the startled witch to the floor and held her until all her limbs had gone limp.

Rumtah looked into the empty starting eyes. "Hum, hum, hum." Then she began to strip her sister's clothes off, dropping them into an untidy pile to one side.

Rekel thrust into the room, and gasped. "What have you done?"

Rumtah leaped to her feet, struck her once in the forehead with the flat of one hand, and shoved the collapsing figure into a corner. Then she lifted the limp Reptar onto a bed and began to peel away her skin.

Hanred sat in the gigantic bed, his back against several pillows.

Ripple was nestled in his lap.

R-Bar sat next to them trying to look innocent.

"Stop trying," said Ripple.

They were all wearing bed clothes of soft dark material.

Hanred patted his wife's hip. "Dark Delight, you will have to behave with the young one in the bed."

"Hanred," grumbled R-Bar at his comment.

"She is no child," stated Ripple.

"Obviously," agreed Hanred, rolling his eyes at R-Bar.

R-Bar grinned wickedly and leaned against him.

"Hum," said Ripple.

"Genocidal fiend!" gurgled Rekel as she fell into their room, lurching, crashing into their bed.

R-Bar leaped to her feet, her creature snarling, snapping its teeth.

Ripple rolled around and lifted Rekel's head up by the hair and stared into her unfocused eyes. She let go.

"I will need some help. Drag her to a sitting position"

Hanred rolled Rekel over, pushed her up and wrapped his arms around her, tugging her backward. "**OOG!** She is a heavy one."

R-Bar leaped from the bed, changing back into her regular clothes.

Ripple patted Rekel's cheek, none too gently. "Wake up, wake up," she hissed.

Rekel's eyes fluttered and focused. "Rumtah," she gasped.

"Speak!" demanded Ripple. Overhead, dark clouds swirled and gathered. Angry red eyes glared down at them. The air crackled.

Rekel, gasping and choking, told them what she had seen.

Ripple banged her back against the headboard. "Do nothing hag." She reached up and yanked a golden wand in. It glittered with energy.

She hurtled herself and Hanred out.

Rumtah was sprawled in a great-chair, legs akimbo, arms dangling.

Her face, clothes, and body, were sweat streaked, wet

stained dark red. She could barely hold her head up to acknowledge Ripple and Hanred.

"Hayou, sister," she rasped.

"Dim, dim, dim!" snarled R-Bar, arriving behind them. Reptar's nude body lay on the bed.

"Why?" hissed Ripple, the golden wand ready to erupt.

"What?" mumbled Rumtah. She rolled her head so she could see who was speaking. "What why?"

Ripple strode to the bed and slid her palm over Reptar's body.

"Hum, hum, hum, hum, hum."

"De'done?" mumbled Reptar.

"De'done," answered Rumtah, jerking her head up.

R-Bar walked over and poked Reptar with one finger, "Really de'done?"

Reptar nodded as she sank back into deep sleep. Dragging a blanket over her sister, R-Bar gently tucked her in.

Ripple looked at Rumtah, sound asleep in the great-chair, and yanked Hanred back to their room. After explaining what really had happened to Reptar, she threw Rekel back to her room.

"Let's get some rest," said Hanred, leading her back to bed in their room. "Too much excitement for me." Snuggling under the covers, he cradled her in his arms, as she ordered. "Dim, lights," said Ripple.

The bed gave a great heave as R-Bar dropped in. "I'll do it."

Ripple pushed closer to Hanred.

"Hum," she said.

When Hanred opened his eyes, he was lying on his side. Someone was pressing against his back, arms around his waist. He could see Ripple. She was lying on her back, staring at the ceiling.

"Pretty rangle," said a soft voice from up there.

Hanred tried to turn to take a look, but the person

behind him was in the way.

"Black Wonder love, where is R-Bar?"

"Under the covers somewhere."

"Ah," he said.

She rolled onto her side and looked at him. "Ah?"

He cleared his throat. "Then it must be she."

"You are nice and comfortable," said R-Bar, letting go, rolling over, and looking up. She frowned. "Why are you up there?"

Hanred rolled onto his back, now that he could, and looked.

A woman was lying on the ceiling, facing down. He felt a twist of vertigo. For a moment he felt as if he was looking down not up.

She wore a high-necked black blouse under a black sweater. A long, heavily pleated skirt covered mid-calf black suede boots. A jagged scar marked one cheek.

"Because there is no room in the bed?" She smiled.

"We could make room," offered Hanred smiling up at her.

"Up there is Ranna," explained Ripple. "Down here is Hanred. Mine."

Ranna dropped lower. "Hum, hum, hum." She stared at Hanred and slowly licked her lips. "When is my turn?"

The air crackled. R-Bar leaped from the bed, hastily getting out of the way.

"Not our's!" stated Ripple. "Mine."

"I didn't want to room with that Rekel," explained R-Bar.

"Who would," laughed Ranna, tilting around until her feet touched the floor. She sat on the edge of the bed. "I thought that maybe you were starting a new custom," she said to Ripple.

The air settled down.

"The eldest should know better."

"You have always been the most creative."

"Your arrival has solved a problem."

"What?"

Ripple chewed at one corner of her mouth. "R-Bar can be with you, in your room."

"Hum, hum, hum," said Ranna.

"Tak prat!" stated R-Bar loudly.

"Where did that child learn to curse so coarsely?"

"She has been around."

"I am not a child," snapped R-Bar.

"I will take her off your hands." Ranna stood up and winked lewdly at Ripple. "You have other matters." She twisted away, taking R-Bar with her.

"What other matters?" asked Hanred as Ripple swivelled around to lean back against his legs which he had quickly yanked up. Her fingers played with the buttons on his top and tickled his ribs.

"I believe, that some time ago, before we were interrupted by the runt, that you were having your way with me."

"Me?" He had already loosened the three ties of her garment.

She leaned forward so he could slip it free.

"Yes," she sighed, sliding into his arms.

"Ummm," said Hanred, his hand crabbing sideways across the blanket She looked up. He was staring at something over her shoulder.

He was staring at a black patch of air that was shimmering and reshaping itself in the middle of the room. A slight figure wearing a dark, hooded robe stood at the foot of the bed and stared at them. Her eyes were deep pools of night in the darkness of her enfolding hood. She floated just above the floor.

Hanred shoved Ripple's top into her hand and whispered, "Visitor."

"**TAK PRAT!**" exploded Ripple. The room seemed to shudder, a thick jet cloud smiled hungrily down at everything from overhead. Lightning flashed in its depths.

She whirled around.

"Angry words, sister" sighed the shadows, near whisper breath.

"Oh, Reep. I didn't know it was you."

The room resettled itself.

Reep hadn't moved. She stood and looked at them, still as still. Her voice, breeze soft, whispered, "You called. I came."

"Come sister," said Ripple gently. "Sit by us."

Reep drifted wraith silent over and sat on the edge of the bed, tucking her hands into her sleeves.

"This is mine, Hanred," explained Ripple soft voiced. "Hanred, this is Reep. The Silent One."

"Hayou, Reep," said Hanred.

"Old Hanred, are you?" whispered the shadows.

His eyes flew wide in surprise. "You know of me?"

"In many places, The Master Illusionist is known." Her eyes never blinked.

She stood and dissolved away.

Ripple turned and grabbed him in a tight embrace. "She likes you."

"Such staring eyes."

"Those eyes speak death."

"She is very strange. And frightening."

Ripple frowned. "You were frightened? I have never seen you frightened."

Hanred took one of her hands in his after she released him and clasped it between both of his. "That sister ought to frighten anyone with any sense at all."

Ripple leaned closer. "I will tell you a secret."

"Good," he said. "I like secrets." He tossed her top to one side.

"When we were growing and training, learning and

studying, only I and one other could control her wild strange. She would listen to us. The rest would retreat, every witchy one."

"And the other one?" He brushed her hair back from her forehead.

"Guess."

He grinned. "R-Bar."

"Hum, hum," she said, her lower lip pushing out, pouting.

He wrapped her in his arms and brushed that lip with his. "Lovely pout."

"How did you guess?"

"I think it is R-Bar's liveliness. She has a sparkle. It seemed to me that the one would enjoy the other, somehow."

"I always thought that it was because Reep knew she was so different and R-Bar was the runt."

Hanred shoved a pillow behind her back.

"I locked the room, this time," she said, tickling his stomach.

Krandal's Dirt Bag. A Rather Pleasant Day.

The pair strolled along one of the many narrow streets of this rather strangely named town. Actually he strolled. She appeared to flow or glide by his side.

His soft purple robe cast a faint glow on his companion's dark forest green almost black robe.

Her robe seemed to absorb it.

The inhabitants they met ducked their heads and looked away. It wasn't the mage. It was his companion.

"Not too far," he explained, "to where lives Banna witch Tza, a dealer in knowledge, dark and other." He wobbled his head. "If she hasn't relocated."

Then he explained that the Banna witch Clan specialized in knowledge of the very Dark and of the Other which was never named. Long many ago the Banna witch Clan had scattered across the elseplaces and had delved into areas of knowledge most wished to remain unknown. None knew the location of their Clan House nor how many members there actually were in the Banna witch Clan.

Before she could ask, he said, "She will speak with us. Long times past I did a favor for Tza."

"This Sluba mage Ransapal is more than one would think."

He halted and indicated a narrow-fronted shop with a single door painted a soft green trimmed in deep blue. "There."

And headed that way.

Stumpf. Mountain's Home. Morning.

"BY DUMPF!"

CRASH!

Two pair of eyes flew open. One pair blue, one pair something else.

"BY DOUBLE-DUMPF!"

CRASH!
CRASH!
CRASH!
CRASH!

Mirf sat up and stared toward the other room.
J. C. sat up and stared at Mirf. He smiled.
She looked at him and snarled. "What are you gaping at?"

"Body like a valkyrie, mouth like a lumberjack."

"If you were a gentleman, you would keep your eyes closed." She dragged the blanket up to her neck.

"If you were a lady, you wouldn't be in bed with me."

"We were just sleeping together, in the literal sense," she hissed.

Mountain stomped into the room, something mangled dangling from his hand.

"Bright day." He wiped his hand on his pant leg. He was dressed all in black. The material reflected no light. "Pesting rockrails. Food is ready. I am ready." He tossed the thing out the window and stomped back into the other room.

"Looks like we ought to get ready," said J. C. "Da da, ta da daah, da da, ta da daah!"

"Music in the morning, such a treat," said Mirf. It wasn't a compliment. It didn't sound like a compliment.

"Wagner," said J. C. "From the Ring Cycle."

"Poofkins."

"Ride of the Valkyries," laughed J. C.

"I know the music, dumbkopf," snapped Mirf. "And you sing off-key."

"Oh, anguish." He looked dramatically wounded. "Oh, agony. Oh, wounded pride." He sniffled, stiffling a smile.

"Oh, meshuggener ding dong," laughed Mirf. "Where's my clothes?"

Mountain leaned in the window. "Clean and dry." He dropped two piles of clothes and boots on the bed. "Time to eat." And backed away.

Mirf sorted through the piles, found her belongings, moved to the edge of the bed away from J. C. and began to dress.

He grabbed his stuff. He finished first.

"TA DAH." He spun around, arms wide.

Mirf was just tucking in her shirt and fastening the last button.

"Need some help?" He grinned at her.

"Let's eat breakfast, helpful."

"Good idea," he said, sweeping one arm grandly at the door.

"Ladies first."

Mirf gurgled as she walked past.

As the last item was eaten, Mirf said, "We have to find a node big enough to schlep this guy through."

"How?" asked J. C.

Mirf tapped the side of her nose. "The nose knows. I will find it. There is one nearby."

"**BY DUMPF. WHERE?**" Mountain looked dramatically from side to side. He didn't see anything. They were eating outside.

Mirf slowly turned her head from side to side, sniffing loudly.

She pointed.

"**MUMPFING MUD!**" Mountain rose and stared in the indicated direction. "That way?"

"You got it, bubee." Mirf stuffed one last piece of something into her mouth. "Shall we go?" she mumbled.

"Might as well," answered J. C. He shoved a couple of bread-like things into his shirt.

"**BY DUMPF**, you lead." Mountain pointed at Mirf, then swung his pack onto his back.

They followed her along a winding trail that took them into an area of craters and fractured rock. Some of the openings had standing water in them, some were empty, some were filled with mud that popped and gurgled. Everything steamed, sending strong odors into the air.

"Nice place," observed J. C.

"**RARE RUMPFING BEAUTY**," agreed Mountain.

Mirf stopped them at the edge of a vast pool of crystaline water, light flashing brightly from its surface.

They could see the bottom, way down there. It was soft, grey-green ooze that shifted slowly as an occasional bubble floated up.

"The node," announced Mirf.

"This thing?" J. C. stared at the bottom of the pool. **"BY DUMPF!"**

"We'll just hold hands and jump in."

"How does this thing know where we want to go? Huh?" J. C. backed up.

"Bahn Duhr Tohr." Mirf grinned at him. "There! I just told it."

He stared at her. "That's it?"

"You betcha."

She grabbed his hand. "Let's go."

Mountain stepped up behind them, crouched, gathered them into his arms and jumped.

"RAR RUMPF!"

Bahn Duhr Tohr. Somewhere.

They stepped from the hollow in the high rock spire,

"Oooops," said J. C.

Mirf and Mountain both grumbled.

Two vast armies filled the plain before them. One was dressed entirely in red, the other in green. They crashed and banged into each other, their mounts rearing and kicking. Swords flashed in the sunlight. Armor glittered from arms and bodies.

Then someone noticed them. The din began to fade in waves across the battlefield. The ranks opened and two armor clad figures jangled toward them.

"Put me down," hissed Mirf.

Mountain bent over and set them both down and snatched the great club from his belt, slipping his pack off with the other arm. **"BY DUMPF**, there are many."

The two figures halted their creatures in front of the trio. One snapped his visor up.

"What manner of thing is this?" He pointed his weapon

up at Mountain.

"He is just a little large. Who are you?" J. C. smiled up at them.

Mirf hissed.

The other threw his visor up. "Fear not, Fair Lady, neither my men nor I would bring harm to you."

"Nor me nor mine," snapped the other, glaring at the one in red. He was wearing green. He smiled at Mirf. "I am Lord Rahn of Bihn Mahd Qahn."

"And I," said the other, "am Prince Wahd of Dahn Bihr Nahn." He bowed in his saddle. "And at your service," he added hastily.

Lord Rahn looked at J. C. "And who are you?"

"I am J. C. That is Mirf. He is Mountain. Where are we?"

Lord Rahn and Prince Wahd stared at him.

"Know not what kingdom this is?" asked Prince Wahd.

"Nope."

"These strangers are bewitched," said Lord Rahn.

"Seems so," agreed Prince Wahd, drawing his sword. "Do you think they are a threat to The Kingdom?"

"**HEY THERE!**" shouted J. C., just to get their attention. "Before you two yahoos get too excited, you want to tell us where we are?"

Prince Wahd banged his visor back into place.

"WE!" he pronounced, "now stand on the frontier of Bahn Duhr Tohr." And growled at them, "Explain that yahoo curse!"

"**BINGO**," snapped Mirf.

Lord Rahn stared at her. "This is a very strange oath, Fair Lady."

"We demand an audience with Queen Willawa and King Toucan!" stated J. C., crossing his arms over his chest. "We have come to aid Ripple's sister." And smiled up at the pai and explained, "Yahoos are sorta dumb."

Prince Wahd shoved his visor back up and stared down

at J. C., frowning darkly. "You profess to not know where you are, yet you demand to see our Queen and our King, and name them by their very names? And you dare to call us unlettered?"

"You got it, schmuck," snapped Mirf.

J. C. cringed.

"So," shrugged Mirf, "they don't understand." She fished around in her shirt pocket and flashed a small golden disc at them and waggled it at them. "Monetary Control. We wish to visit with The Kingdom's Treasurer."

Prince Wahd and Lord Rahn went pale-faced.

"Of course," gushed the Prince.

"In my carriage," offered the Lord.

"Delighted," said Mirf, grabbing J. C.'s arm. "Where is it?"

Lord Rahn gave a piercing whistle. The ranks behind them parted and a carriage thundered through, pulled by a matched pair of beasts.

"I will walk," grumbled Mountain.

Mirf swung open the carriage door. "Hop in, boychick. We ride in style." She stuffed the disc back into her pocket.

He did.

The carriage jolted after the Prince and the Lord.

Mountain and the two great armies followed.

Mirf grabbed J. C., shoving him sideways onto the seat and kissed him. "Just a little thank you," she said to her startled traveling companion.

"For what, Fair Lady?"

"Lady-schmady," snapped Mirf. "For saving my life, dumbkopf."

"Those blokes wouldn't 'uve 'urt you, ducks."

"Not here. Back there, in the desert."

"Oh, there."

"Yas. There."

"Just doing my job," he said, sliding one arm around

her. "Chief First Inspector Mirf, Monetary Control."

"We had better sit up."

"Think so?"

"Yes." She did. "Wave to any people we pass, they'll love it."

J. C. waved gaily.

There were only two armies to see him flailing his arm out the window of the carriage.

It was a long and dusty ride before they approached the vast city built of white stone.

"Bahn Duhr Tohr!" announced Prince Wahd.

The two armies stopped outside the city gates and began to set up their camps as the carriage rattled deep inside, toward the castle.

Up a broad avenue and finally into a great open courtyard they clattered, to be greeted by a figure in a flowing pure white gown, one arm resting lightly on her husband's arm.

The Prince and the Lord leaped from their mounts, knelt and proclaimed in unison. "Hale Great Queen. Hale Great King. At your service."

The Queen greeted them, held a hushed conversation, and ordered servants to take them to their quarters and to see to their animals, gear and servants.

"So," said Mirf, "that's the King and Queen. Let's go." She threw open the door and stepped down followed by J. C.

"You are from Monetary Control?" asked the Queen.

"I am," said Mirf. "But that is not why I am here, I was just calming down those two."

The Queen laughed. "Then why are you here? And what is that?"

Mountain had just walked into the courtyard.

"That's Mountain," said J. C. "I am J. C. This is Mirf."

The King stepped forward. "Have you grown?"

"**BY DUMPF**, Prince, I have."

"King," corrected the Queen.

Toucan smiled happily up at Mountain. "You are here most welcome. And these your friends. And I will order the kitchen a great meal to prepare." He beckoned to a waiting servant. "You did hear what I just did say?"

"Yes, Your Majesty. At once, Your Majesty." The servant dashed across the courtyard.

The Queen stepped to the King's side. "You know this large . . . man?"

"Indeed I do. An old companion of great adventures. But I know not this pair."

"Friends of John Tinker's," explained Mountain, starting toward the kitchen part of the castle. His nose had picked up cooking odors.

"Indeed?" said Toucan.

"Indeed," answered J. C. "If you would tell Hard that I am here, I am sure he will want to see us."

Willawa's eyes snapped from the departing Mountain to J. C. "You know the comely youth called Hard?"

"For many years."

High overhead a window banged open and someone leaned way out.

"**HEY, J. C! WHAT ARE YOU DOING HERE?**"

An arm yanked him back inside.

"Shall we go inside?" The Queen led them into the castle.

"My King," she whispered. "You have very unusual friends."

"Indeed?"

She smiled. "Indeed."

They sat in the Advisor's quarters.

Mountain had to stay downstairs in the Great Hall.

Ramp greeted J. C. warmly.

Hard clapped him on the back.

"Never thought to see you here, buddy."

J .C. smiled. "Me neither. I got talked into it."

"Didn't take much talking," mumbled Mirf.

"Wowee," whispered Hard to J. C., jabbing his friend in the ribs with an elbow. "Where'd you find her?"

"Tell you later." They settled themselves in chairs and on the couches.

Ramp looked at J. C. "Why have you come?"

"She'll explain."

Mirf did. As much as she had been told or knew.

"Ripple spoke true," said Toucan. "The armies will be needed."

Mirf was looking unhappy.

"Lady?" asked Willawa.

"That witch is not going to be happy to see me," said Mirf.

"Why not?" asked Hard.

"We met before. When I was a hob-goblin."

Hard leaped to his feet. "**YOU!**" And glared at her. "You are that Mirf?"

"That's me, boychick."

Ramp stared at her.

"Easy, Rampeleh, easy," cautioned Mirf.

"Yes," stated Ramp. "It is you."

Willawa glared at Mirf. "You are that foul mannered hob-goblin?" Her eyes darted toward one wall. A large war club hung there.

"Oi vay," hissed Mirf. "Were! Not am!"

Ramp laid a gentle restraining hand on the Queen's arm. "Not her fault. It was the hob-goblin nature."

Mirf relaxed and exhaled.

"There are still traces," observed Ramp.

Mirf shrugged her shoulders. "So I had a little bad luck." She looked around. "Where is that witch anyway? And her sister?"

"Traveling," answered Ramp. "Which sister?"

"Which sister?"

"I am the twelveth, and last, of the daughters."

"Reptar." Mirf sank low in her chair. "Eleven of them, eleven. Ho boy, am I ever in trouble."

"Ten," corrected Ramp. "Rbat went far. They will not hurt you."

J. C. explained what had happened at Tinker's house.

"Here," said Ramp, extending her hand, palm up. A ring appeared. "Wear this, Mirf, always."

Mirf picked it up and stared at it. "What is it?"

"Protection. Where do you journey from here?"

"Not a clue." Mirf slipped the ring on one of her fingers.

"Maybe Ripple will have an idea," suggested Hard.

"We must wait and see," said Ramp.

"Many days have already passed," said Willawa.

"And many great armies do a'gather in," added Toucan.

"You may have the suite next to this one," said Willawa, rising to her feet. "Duty beckons us."

Toucan laughed. "Indeed."

They left.

"Come on," said Hard to J. C. "Let me show you around."

"I think I shall retire to our rooms and think," said Mirf.

They scattered leaving Ramp alone.

"Ripple," she whispered. "Ripple."

Kragkoptar. Inside.

They sat.

Scattered around the great room.

Facing the Aunts.

Rumtah and Reptar sat side by side.

R-Bar sat on the floor leaning back against Hanred's outstretched legs. She had one arm back behind herself, trying to tickle him. He was ignoring her. So was Ripple, ignoring her sister

Ranna sat near Ripple.

Rekel sat off to one side, by herself.

In a far corner stood Reep, obscured by the deep shadows, great staring eyes watching, watching.

Ripple spoke, to the Aunts, to her sisters. "We are agreed. All will seek some trace of this thing that threatens our sister."

"Our clan," said B'waas.

"Yes," agreed Shlm.

"The Aunts will be our focus and connection. Rumteh and Reptar wish to travel together. Rekel, Ranna, and Reep prefer their own company. R-Bar will be with me, for awhile. I must speak with Ramp before I do anything else."

Ripple looked from face to face finding agreement, smoldering malevolence. She nodded.

They left.

Each in her own fashion.

Far Corner. Very Late Evening.

"Which clan?"

"Faan."

"You are sure?"

"I checked our records. Twice!"

"The worst of the worst."

Abadoda nodded. "Most true."

"Most strange."

"That clan is hunting in all directions. And crackle great irritation."

"And the one of our future is entangled in this?"

"Also most true."

"Fetch the old book of Great Spells. It is time to begin building a multiwrap."

"Who?"

"The most skilled. And begin to amass supplies. But

gently. We do not wish to alarm the local folk."

Dawla of Snark's Fen. Dark Night.

Tapa nodded and handed the scroll to Turintor, saying, "Never before have I tried such a thing. The user may be injured or sent far."

"Understood." Turintor took the scroll. Her companion nodded.

"One comment more."

"Yesssssss?"

"The spell is strange, witch strange. Nothing may occur."

Turintor shrugged. "Of no matter. We," she indicated the silent witch, "are satisfied. The search we make is necessary."

"Yessssss," agreed Tapa. She hesitated. Then leaned forward. "If you are successful . . . "

"Yesssssss?"

"The thing responsible for this quatarna," she sucked in her breath.

Turintor nodded. The term was similar to her clan dialect. It meant a crime so vile to the witches that the cause must be removed forever.

"We, the Pinl clan will aid the Potri clan in clan pact to do this, if you find the answer."

Turintor stared at her. Most witch clans did not pact. It usually violated witch independence in deed and thought.

"Most true," stated Tapa.

"Agreed," replied Turintor. Her companion nodded.

"We are done?"

"Done." Turintor stood.

Her companion flowed to her feet and gently touched Tapa in the center of the forehead with her thumb and bowed her head.

The pair left the shop to rest and to gather the necessary

ingredients for the spell.

Tapa retired to her lodgings and sent a call to her clan members, telling all of this strangeness she had just heard and of the clan commitment.

Bahn Duhr Tohr. The Royal City. Night.

The dark shape slipped shadow quiet into the room, fast as night. It stood and stared at the pair in the bed.

"Hello, Raft." It was Ramp, speaking softly so as not to waken Hard.

"I heard Ripple's call."

She was instantly standing by Ramp's side, then sitting on the bed. Her gaze floated across Ramp, noting Hard, nodding her agreement, then back to Ramp, sucking in a fast breath. "Twins. You are birthing twins, Magician." Nodding her head again, she smiled. "Worlds will quake at this."

She sat next to Hard, frowned and leaned closer. "Hum, hum, hum." The air crackled faintly. She jerked back, hissing. "Rap, rap, rap."

Hard opened one eye and blinked. For a moment he thought he saw someone sitting there. Now he wasn't sure he had. From the other room came a dull thump.

"Just Ripple returning," said Ramp. "Go back to sleep." Hard did.

Hanred flopped back into a chair making a sighing noise.

"Softly, husband," cautioned Ripple. "Else you will waken them."

R-Bar dropped lightly to the floor, gurgling happily to be away from the Aunts. Someone tostled her hair in passing.

Raft stood in front of Ripple. "I just arrived. What are we to do? I visited Ramp, saw her condition."

"We gathered at the Aunts. All are looking for a trace."

"Hum, hum, hum."

"Hayou, Raft," said R-Bar smoothing her hair back in

place. "Why come you so late?"

Raft stood next to her and threw one arm over R-Bar's shoulders. "I was a long, long way off and out."

Hanred stared at this sister. He didn't see her move from here to there. Somehow she just changed position.

"And you are Ripple's," said Raft, sitting next to him.

"Hanred," said Hanred.

"Show me something," she said, standing in front of him.

A soft terslug snapped a tentacle at her.

"Very nice," Raft whispered in his ear. Hanred turned his head and smiled at her.

"Husband?" cautioned Ripple.

"What?" He sat on the other side of Raft, she had been talking to an illusion.

Raft stood next to R-Bar and spoke to Ripple. "I heard that Old Hanred was the best. Now I know." She kissed Ripple, then R-Bar, then Hanred on the cheek.

"Just there," said Ripple.

"Of course," said Raft. She was gone.

"Never in all my travels," said Hanred. "Never have I ever seen anything or anyone move that fast."

"She has a special gift," said Ripple.

"Ohhh, Hanred," sang R-Bar merrily. "Would you tuck me into bed? And kiss me goodnight? Please?"

The terslug wrapped a tentacle around her waist and dragged her closer to its mult-toothed maw.

R-Bar gurgled, deep in her throat.

"Husband, put that child to bed. And give her one kiss. But no more. And nothing else."

"I am not a child," growled R-Bar, taking the terslug to her room.

Ramp slipped into the room.

"We didn't mean to wake you."

"It was Raft, staring at me. The sisters are well?"

"All that I saw. Riz and Rotak didn't show. Neither did Raft, until now. But I can talk to her in the morning."

"Where's Hanred?"

"Tucking R-Bar in. Go back to sleep. We can all get together in the morning."

"We have some other visitors."

"I will see them in the morning." Ripple went. To her bedroom.

R-Bar gurgled merrily.

Hanred gently tucked her in.

"Hanred?"

"What?"

"You don't think that I am a child, do you?"

"No. You are a very attractive young lady and a very adept witch."

"I wish to be kissed like one."

"Ahhhhhh?"

"Ripple said that it was all right, just one. And she didn't specify how."

"A very witchy thought process."

"Kiss me."

He did.

"Hum, hum, hum," she said when they finished.

"My, my," he said.

"Let's do it again."

"ONE!" said a stern voice, taking Hanred away.

"Now," said Ripple. "Give us a kiss."

"With pleasure," said Hanred.

They wound up on the couch.

"Hum, hum, hum," said Ripple. "Maybe I will let you kiss her goodnight all the time."

"Take us to bed, Ebony Wonder."

She did.

Raft wacked R-Bar on top of the head with an open hand.

"OUCH!"

"Shame on you."

R-Bar sat up, rubbing the top of her head. "For what?"

Raft watched her from the foot of the bed.

"For slipping that little spell on Ripple's."

R-Bar scowled. "Don't tell her." Her eyes darted around the room. "Think she will detect it?"

Raft sat next to her, her arm around R-Bar's waist. "I'll never tell."

They whispered and giggled into each other's ears. For most of the night. And finally fell asleep in each other's arms, snuggling under the blankets, having swapped a number of spells and incantations.

Ripple's eyes popped open. "That little sneak."

Hanred woke with a start. "What?"

"Oh, nothing. Just something that I just remembered."

"Oh." He wrapped his arms around her. "Go to sleep."

She did.

Bahn Duhr Tohr. Somewhere.

They stepped up from the slight depression in the open plain.

Fair Morn fired and two acres of plants, animals, and top soil disappeared, silently disappeared. Weapons leaped into other hands.

"I saw something rear up," explained Fair Morn.

The grass on either side of them came up to their chests.

"There are a number of them around us," said Smoke. "All harmless."

Everyone relaxed.

Something to their left raised up, stared at them, grass stems protruding from its slowly chewing jaws. It blinked and dropped back down."

"My Lord, we do take nay chance this trip," explained Chicken. "As we did thee tell a'home."

"If this is Bahn Duhr Tohr, we are way outside the city," observed Tinker .

"MindMate, a large army is approaching. From over there. They are very relaxed, going to some kind of party or festival."

Tinker looked around. There was no place to hide.

"O.K., gang, we might as wait for them right here. Put the weapons away. And don't attack anyone unless I say so, all right?"

"Indeed, Me Lord, we do be but thy Verra Own most humble and obedient fair maidens." Chicken smiled sweetly.

"We will behave," said Messenger, stuffing her wand up her left sleeve.

"As long as they behave." Fair Morn snapped her weapon back into the long holster strapped to her right thigh.

"That rise." Smoke pointed.

And soon, the first riders appeared. Then the rest of the army.

Armor, clothing, banners, all shades of powder blue. Four long lines of warriors, wagons rattling and banging at various points in the lines. Laughter and gay chatter drifted over the grass to the waiting group.

Then the first pair reigned to a halt, stared at them, and then slowly approached. Behind them, all fell into silent watching.

"**HELLO**!" called Tinker.

Smoke and Fair Morn stepped away to his right, Chicken and Messenger to his left.

"Remember what I said," he hissed at them.

Yes, Boss, they all answered in unison.

The riders halted and stared down at them. Tinker decided this pair must be brothers. They looked very much alike.

"We are a bit lost. Can you tell us the way to Bahn Duhr Tohr?"

They continued to stare at Tinker, then noticed the others. Both smiled broadly.

One said, "That is a most pleasing body that you have with you, Stranger. Do you trade?"

Chicken glared at the speaker, her left hand tilting the hilt of her sword forward. "Churlish youth, My Lord do but ask of you directions. So speak you now to that question, properly!"

"Brother," laughed the older of the pair. "You asked of the body and the body has answered you."

The younger nudged his mount forward toward Chicken. "A fine body to spit such fire."

Tinker stepped forward, his weaponkin beginning to hum. He could feel it vibrating against his back.

"Hold, My Lord, for this callow child do need not thy hard lesson a'learn, yet do require such tutoring as We do feel befits his station." She smiled at Tinker, then looked at the older and grinned.

In one motion, Fair Morn stepped over, reached up, grabbed the younger by the wrist and yanked him from the saddle and slammed him to the ground. His armor clanged loudly.

Chicken knelt on his chest, whipped a long dagger from her boot and slipped it easily between his chest plate and helmet. "Will you speak to us, enow?"

"Yes," he gasped.

His brother was spinning his mount in circles. The rest of the women had disappeared.

"O.K.," snapped Tinker. "Princess, let him go. Smoke, enough of that."

Chicken leaped to her feet.

Smoke reappeared as did Messenger.

The older urged his animal forward and watched his brother remount, rubbing his neck. He had removed his helmet. He stared at this suddenly reappearing group. "Who are you?"

"I am John Tinker."

"And we do be his Ladies," snapped Chicken, glaring at the younger one, daring him to say anything, anything at all.

"I am Prince Ahn. You have already met Prince Pahn, my younger, and, somewhat, impulsive brother. And as for the first question, Bahn Duhr Tohr lies in the direction we are headed for all are called by The Queen to the greatest festival of arms ever held. Will you ride with us?" He laughed easily. "My brother will gladly loan you his carriage ."

"Sure," answered Tinker. "It will save a lot of walking."

"You are most welcome and kind, Prince Ahn. We do thank you." Chicken made a courtly bow.

Prince Ahn smiled at her and Fair Morn. "It is my pleasure to do so."

He beckoned a rider forward, issued instruction, and in a few moments, an ornate carriage banged through the tall grass.

He laughed. "Climb in, Sir and Ladies." He laughed again and waited until his brother had ridden to the front of the line, and said, "It was good to see Pahn smash the grass. He has much to learn if he expects to rule."

As soon as they were aboard, the carriage swung to the front of the line, just behind the two Princes.

It was some time later, much further down the road, when Prince Pahn drifted back and leaned from his saddle to peer in a window of the carriage, and said, "Fair Yellow Lady, please accept my humblest of apologies."

Chicken smiled warmly at him. "Fair spoken, Noble Prince, do you be harmed?"

He laughed. "Only my pride was damaged. But my ribs were bruised."

He smiled at Fair Morn. "May I never meet you in combat." He laughed again as he headed back to rejoin his brother.

"Whew," sighed Tinker.

"Whew?" asked Messenger.

"Meaning that I am certainly glad that he didn't decide that we were to be permanent enemies of his. We don't need an army chasing us right now, do we?"

"Oh, no," agreed Messenger. "But he was being rude."

"And I didn't throw him down really hard," said Fair Morn. "Beside, I could have shot him."

Tinker sighed and slouched deeper in his seat. Chicken leaned against one side, Messenger got the other.

"We will this time no chances take, My Lord," said Chicken sternly. She nudged his ribs gently.

"A whole army?"

"Piffle, Our Love."

He laughed. "Right. Piffle."

"Piffle," agreed Messenger, tugging his arm up and over her shoulders.

"One," asked Fair Mom. "What do you do when you piffle?"

"Trade places with Chicken and I'll show you."

"My Lord," gasped Chicken. "The image in thy mind do be most crude."

"Well," laughed Tinker. "It was just a thought."

It was three days later when the carriage, the Princes, and their aides clattered into the great Courtyard. The army busied itself making camp. Outside the city walls.

Everyone was well acquainted, now.

Chicken had bested Prince Pahn, four out of five, and Prince Ahn, two out of three, in sword practice. Both now saw her in a much diferent light than when they had first met.

Pahn flirted with Messenger and gave Fair Morn wide birth.

Both treated Smoke with deference. She hadn't said or done anything.

As far as the Princes could figure it, Tinker must be a

Royal from one of the furthest away, stranger parts of The Kingdoms, traveling with warrior trained Ladies of his court.

Willawa and Toucan greeted their new guests in the Courtyard as they dismounted.

"Welcome Prince Ahn. Welcome Prince Pahn." The Queen smiled warmly and then turned to greet the rest of their party as they spilled from the carriage.

"Highness," shouted Toucan, running over to greet them. "How come thee to be here?"

Willawa bowed low, very courtly. "Most welcome to you, Lord John Tinker, Chosen One, Queen Chicken, Mighty Smoke."

The two Princes turned as they heard these royal greetings and stared at their guests, their mouths falling open. They hastily dropped to one knee, worried by the worst breach of court etiquette they could ever imagine.

"Toucan," whispered Tinker. "What is their problem?"

"Me'thinks, Highness, judging by most white, pale faces, those Noble Princes do be a'feared they did fail in some duty most royal to thee and thine. All here do know of The Chosen One of Legend, and did not mine own most lovely Queen not most low bow make and so name thee thus."

"I'll never get used to this," said Tinker. He turned and raised his voice and addressed the stunned pair. "Rise Princes. We are very grateful for the use of your carriage. It was a great favor to us."

The Princes jumped to their feet and were quickly ushered away by several attentive servants who were following quickly whispered instructions from the Queen.

"I didn't think we would ever visit here again," said Tinker to Willawa.

"Lord Tinker, this has been a time for visitors. But who are these additional two Ladies with you?"

"Oh, right, you haven't met them before. Messenger, Fair Morn, this is Willawa, The White Warrior, Queen of Bahn

Duhr Tohr. And her King, Toucan, the brother of Chicken and Goose."

Willawa smiled at them. "Come, we will show you to your quarters. Baths will be ready by the time we get there."

"Oh boy!" Messenger beamed at the Queen.

Willawa laughed. And led them inside the castle.

Chicken linked her arm through Toucan's.

At the door to their suite Willawa halted as she threw it open, allowing them to proceed. "Will you join us later, Lord Tinker, in our quarters?" she asked.

"Sure," replied Tinker. "Um, yes, Your Majesty."

"A servant will come in, oh, two hours."

"We'll be ready."

Loud splashing noises echoed through the open door indicated that someone had already found the bath.

It's me. EEEEEK!

Smoke had joined Messenger.

"This Kingdom does produce a liqueur most extraordinaire, Highness," said Toucan as he smiled and left with his Queen.

"My Lord," said Chicken, leaning against him, arms wrapped around his waist. "Fine bath be most monsterous pool."

"Yes?"

A splash signaled Fair Morn's entry.

"There be two."

"Must be some bathroom."

She unwound herself and pulled him into the main room and then in a different direction away from the loud splashing. "Two rooms."

"Ah, ha."

"My Lord?"

"Flash of insight."

In the room, he stared at the tub. It was set flush with the floor and resembled a very large hot tub.

"Room for a mob." He sat down and yanked off his boots and socks. A small cloud of dust rose from them.

Someone discretely cleared their throat. "My Lord, My Lady, if you will leave your clothes just there, they will be cleaned and returned as fast as possible. I have laid out other clothes in your chambers. The Queen said you had your own hand maidens traveling with you?"

Hand maidens? It was Smoke.

"Correct," said Chicken. "Just leave their attire with our own."

"Certainly. Should you need anything at all, just pull that cord." The woman left.

Chicken draped her clothes on the indicated spot, carefully placed her sword and other weapons on the stone bench and eased slowly into the steaming water. She was faster than he was.

"Most wonderful."

"Oh, yes. Hot!"

"Wouldst scrub Our back, Noble King?"

"You betcha." He found a large sponge-like object which began to foam as he began to rub.

Chicken hummed softly.

Messenger was gently massaging the long wing muscles running down Fair Morn's back as she sprawled face down on one of the couches.

"Hand maidens?" she asked Smoke.

Smoke looked at her, then said, "Young girls who take care of people's hands."

"Really?" Then Messenger saw the joke in Smoke's mind. "Oh, mom." She patted Fair Morn's shoulder. "How's that?"

"Not bad, for a hand maiden."

"I don't know how to be a hand maiden."

Be thyself, Our kitten. It was Chicken.

Messenger looked at the large bed. *The servants have laid*

out all our clothes.

      Many thanks. But hurry not.

A Few More Pieces

Bahn Duhr Tohr. The Royal City. Afternoon. The Royal Chambers.

"Highness." Toucan handed Tinker a goblet of green glass filled with a lightly tinged liquid.

He looked at Chicken. "Sister Queen?"

"Indeed, Brother King." She accepted a filled goblet from Toucan.

Willawa raised her's. "Hale and Hearty . . ."

"Ummmmm?" interrupted Tinker.

"What Lord Tinker?"

"They need glasses also."

Toucan nodded, set his glass down and poured and handed Smoke, Messenger and Fair Morn a filled goblet.

"Thanks," said Tinker.

"Most gracious," said Willawa.

She will understand not what we be, MY Lord.

"Personal bodyguards," said Tinker. "Extremely loyal."

"Most clever. I was told what happened to the Prince Brothers who accompanied you here. Who would suspect such beauty to hide such strength? And then be so surprised?"

"A number of our Lords." Toucan smiled at his Queen.

Tinker stepped back and held his goblet high, and looked into Willawa's eyes. "To great strength hidden in great beauty."

They drank. Willawa gave Tinker a brief nod.

Nicely bespoke, OurLove. T'was most Lordly done. Chicken winked at him.

Waving them to seat themselves, Willawa said, "Will

you have meals with us? We am sure The King is anxious to speak with his sister, your Queen. And We wish to learn of why you have come visiting Us, just now."

Oh boy.

Kitten. Smoke gave Messenger a stern look.

Sorry, Mom.

"Of course." Tinker smiled. "We would be delighted."

"The Princes spoke to us of a strange disturbance in Fahr Tohr Fahr Green, the place where they first met you. They had never seen such a thing before."

"Well." Tinker immediately knew what she was referring to. "We, ahhhhh, had a little accident."

Willawa cocked her head to one side and stared at him. "To speak of such destruction so off-handedly tells Us that tales of immense power may well be true."

How can I explain Macabre's weapon to a feudal Queen?

Magic, MyTinker. Tell her it was magic.

Right. Thanks.

Messenger suppressed her smile, especially after she was given another very stern look by Smoke.

"It was a magical device. We were, um, trying out a new spell."

"Will you show Us this thing?"

In our rooms, One.

"It is in our quarters." He blanched, remembering that he had left his weaponkin leaning casually against the wall.

"Lord?" Willawa jerked her head.

Tinker had leaped to his feet.

"Dangerous things. We left dangerous things in our rooms. I better go there and put them away. Now!"

"Have no fear. None would dare enter without Our, or your, permission. None would dare touch that which is not their's to touch. Unless so ordered."

As Tinker started to sit, Willawa patted the space on the

couch next to herself. "Shall we relax and talk?"

He sat next to her and caught the infinitesimal nod of Chicken's head as she moved away, slipping an arm through Toucan's, taking him over to the great, multi-paned windows. She began to have an animated conversation with him.

"How shall I address you, Lord?"

"Tinker. Everyone calls me Tinker."

"Then I am Willawa."

"Willawa it is, then."

"Tell me why you have come to Our Kingdom, Tinker."

"Looking for some friends."

Oh, my.

What?

MindMate, our kitten saw as I looked inside the Queen that Willawa knows your friend Hard. Her thought bled through as I looked. Smoke rolled her eyes. *He was very friendly with her.*

Tinker could hear Messenger's mental giggles.

What?

Tell you later. Otherwise you will get too distracted. Smoke smiled at him, a slight faint smile.

"Friends?"

"His full name is Alandale Fredrico Hardcastle IV. His friends call him Hard. His wife is Ramp."

"Oh, yes. Our Dark Advisor's sister and the comely youth. They are your friends?"

"Yes. Are they here?"

"No. They left."

His face fell. She half-turned, laid one hand on his thigh.

Steady on, My Lord.

Will you guys cut it out?

"Perhaps I could talk with Ripple?"

Willawa shook her head. "She and Hanred left two prior."

Damn. "Anyone say where they were going?"

"Both sisters said that they would let us know. That is the reason for The Great Festival of Arms. We propose to mass the mightiest army this Our Kingdom has ever called together. Ripple told us of a mighty but unknown foe and we propose to aid the sisters in their battle."

"Ah, Willawa?"

"Tinker?"

"Would it be all right if we stayed here until someone sends word as to where they are? Or what kind of help they might need?"

"Certainly. For it is a treat for Us to talk with someone who is not trying some subtle manipulation for position or favor in the court structure."

Tinker stood. "I think I need some time to think."

She touched his hand. "You will join us for the meal?"

"You bet."

Chicken kissed Toucan on one cheek. *Coming, My Lord.*

Messenger slipped an arm through one of Smoke's as she stood. *Oh, my. Oh, my.*

Now what?

They all made their goodbyes and were guided back through the corridors by a silent servant.

She drank too much, One. Fair Morn slipped an arm under Messenger's free one.

Closing the door to their suite behind him, Tinker leaned back against it. "I'll have to caution Toucan about his bar-tending."

Fair Morn and Smoke dumped the giggling Messenger into one of the beds.

"You better take a nap," he said to Messenger. "And while she does, we need to figure out what we are going to do next."

They stepped into the main, central room.

Chicken plopped into a chair, kicked off her shoes, and

propped her legs in another chair. "Tis conundrum. Nay, tis mystery."

He sat down and admired her calves. "Right. Ramp sent a message and then bugs out before we get here. And her sister is gone as well."

"Sweet Prince, it do seem a'Us, it do, that some strange business do be a'whirling around and about. We do like it not." She frowned darkly at the rug.

Smoke propped her chin on top of his head and dropped her arms over his shoulders. "Nor do I. This smells of . . . bad, evil, sinister, destruction."

"Definitely not good, huh?"

Smoke slipped one hand inside his shirt. "We are not taking any chances. Whatever hunts Ramp must be killed instantly."

Zap its butt. Messenger giggled from the other room.

Smoke reached out and put her to sleep.

"Have to find it first, Tiger."

"I was solid black."

"Body and soul," said Tinker.

Fair Morn stood, her wings unfolding. She began to flap them back and forth. "Ahhhhh, it has been days." The wind tostled everyone's hair.

"A little gentler, please." Tinker pushed the hair from his eyes.

Smoke suddenly tightened her arms.

"WHAT?"

"J. C. and Mirf."

"What about them?"

"They were here. I just found it in the Queen's memory. They left with Hard and Ramp." She had been gently probing, seeking clues for all the agitation among Ramp's sisters.

"Damn it." He joined Chicken in glaring at the floor covering.

"Everyone has passed through here, going somewhere,

and we have to sit and wait. Maybe we ought to go home. I'd rather kill time there than here."

Chicken swung her legs down and banged her feet to the floor, leaned forward and grinned at him. "But, Sweet My Lord, do we all be a'home thee would have nay opportunity for to fair treasures of sumptuous Queen ogle."

"Sumptuous?" He looked up.

"Well formed," offered Smoke.

"Stacked," suggested Fair Morn. "A slang term in your native language."

"What's with you guys? Every time we get near some good looking girl, ah, woman, er, female, ummmmm, you know what I mean, you start this kind of nonsense."

"Lecherous thoughts do leak into our minds?" Chicken smiled at him.

"Humbug. All the more reason to go home. I've got enough to lech at as it is. One, two, three, and four." His finger jabbed wildly.

"Sulk not, Our Prince."

"I am not sulking," he sulked.

Smoke tickled his ribs.

Fair Morn folded and folded and folded her wings, walked over, leaned, and kissed his ear.

"**STOP THAT!** O.K., we will stay."

Messenger hiccuped.

Tinker grinned at Chicken, and stared pointedly at her chest.

"Pretty nice treasures, all right."

She stuck out her tongue and stomped away. Out into the corridor.

Fair Morn went with her.

That left him with Smoke.

Chicken winked at Fair Morn as they swung the door closed.

And the predator caught its prey. In a manner of

speaking.

"So, now that you have dragged me down to the floor and have slobbered all over my chest, you big oaf, what do you want?"

Her great golden eyes peered into his. Smoke was sprawling on him and alongside him.

"I am not a big oaf. I am merely giving you a few kisses. And I didn't exactly drag you down here."

"O.K. I concede the last point."

"And you have been being very familiar with certain portions of my anatomy. Just now."

"Oh, well, way it goes. You guys are always making remarks, so I just thought that I would fulfill your prophesies."

"And certain male animal inclinations." She gave him another kiss.

"Certainly attractive for a predator." He tickled her.

"I am not ticklish," she said, squirming, just for the fun of it.

The dark clad figure dropped lightly to her feet not far away from where they lay. She was snarling. "Dim, dim, dim, dim!" And stopped and stared at them.

Smoke sprang to her feet, bounded to one side, her pupils snapping wide, eyes focusing upon this stranger who had suddenly appeared.

And tugged her gown shut.

As Tinker stood, R-Bar stepped close, tugged down her smock, and handed him his shirt. Her eyes were at the level of his chin. She waited while he slipped the shirt on, pushing his arms through the sleeves. Then she stepped closer and set her arms on his shoulders.

She smiled brightly up at him. "Hum, hum, hum. You may send the servant away, pretty." She waved her arm in the general direction of Smoke.

"My Lord," said Chicken stepping from one of the adjacent rooms. And stared at R-Bar.

"Hast thee now taken to molestation of children?"

She and Fair Morn had just returned, entering through a side door. They had sat and talked quietly, carefully providing privacy for the mutual maulings in the main room.

R-Bar spun away and snapped at her. "I am not a child."

"Forsooth." Chicken pointed at the witch's blouse. "Tis most obvious enow. You are a very pretty, young lady, ne'child endowed."

R-Bar turned back to Tinker and grumbled, "And I am no Lady either." Everyone knew that one didn't call witches lady.

"MY LORD? Hum, hum, hum? From what far flung kingdom do you hale? You are certainly not the typical pale, Royal creeper that is usually seen in the court. Hum, hum, hum." She stepped closer and ran a finger up and down his chest.

"One in each room? A very robust Lord you are. You may send those wenches away." R-Bar waved one hand and made pushing motions at Smoke and Chicken. From another door came a soft metallic snap as a lever was pushed forward.

Tinker looked over the top of R-Bar's head and to that side. "You can't fire that thing in here."

"I set it to a very narrow beam."

"None-the-less, you do not want to fire that thing in here."

"She might not," mumbled Messenger, yawning widely as she pushed past Fair Morn. "But I can." She waggled a long wand at them.

"Easy does it," said Tinker as R-Bar whipped around and hissed loudly at them. Dark was seeping out and around her feet.

"She is a witch," said Smoke.

"Really?" Tinker took another look at R-Bar.

R-Bar was staring intently at Messenger, who was stifling another yawn. "It cannot be," gasped R-Bar. She shook her head. "NO!" she gasped.

Messenger looked at Tinker. "What?"

"An urh-witch," gasped R-Bar, looking frightened and desperate at the same time. The air around her was making crackling noises. Dark was spreading wider and wider.

"Ahem, shorty." Tinker reached out and turned R-Bar gently around. "You wanna calm down. We certainly mean you no harm. Maybe we could all sit down and see what's going on? This time. Why you are here? Stuff like that there?"

R-Bar held his gaze for a long time. Then she nodded. The air calmed down. "I am not short!"

Smoke shooed everyone else from the room. *We will be in this other room. Be careful, MindMate, Messenger said she is powerful.*

Tinker sat on one of the couches and patted the seat next to him.

"How about you sit down?" He began to button his shirt.

R-Bar cautiously settled next to him, eyeing him suspiciously, fingering an ivory wand.

"Now, who are you? My name is John Tinker. We are just visiting here for awhile. And don't mind them." He nodded toward the other room. "They are just being a little nervous."

"I am R-Bar. And a witch, as she said. Is the dark haired one your Ka-beast?" She watched his face carefully. "Largest one I have ever seen."

"Nope, whatever that is. Not my line of work. How come you dropped in on us?"

"I was staying in these rooms. Before we left." She hitched closer to him and smiled. "All the beds are big and comfortable." She nudged him. She was trying to decide whether she had found her's or not.

"I know. But I don't really think that there is room for one more."

"Send them to the servant's quarters, strange lord."

She is pretty.

Go back to sleep.

"**OUCH!**"

"What was that?" R-Bar stared at the door to the room where the rest had gone.

"I think someone just got pinched."

R-Bar was now sitting against him, leaning slightly. "Do you have something against witches?" She frowned. Found males did not reject witches.

"Nope. Of course I don't really have much experience or acquaintance with them either."

"I could send your wenches away for you."

"I don't think they would like that."

"Oh, no matter," said R-Bar gaily. "I can always bring them back when you feel the need for a little variety." She thought that it was a very generous offer.

"**NO!**"

"I don't think that I like that no." She began to frown.

"Way it goes, as they say."

"You are mine! I found you." She slipped an arm around his waist. She had decided that he was nice. Very comfortable. Relaxing. Strangely calm feeling.

"Kiddo, you'll have to stand in line. They got here first."

"R-Bar, what are you doing?"

Another young woman was standing there.

"Hayou, Raft. Look what I found." R-Bar sat back and beamed at her sister.

"Very nice. Your's?"

"He has four females to play with."

"Get rid of them," snapped Raft. Witches normally did not share.

"**HOLD IT!** I will decide what I will do, Ladies."

They both glared at Tinker. He glared back.

R-Bar snapped at him, "That is not nice, calling us names."

Raft nodded. "Pak tak ladies!" she snapped.

The air ripped open. Hanred stumbled forward. "Rough landing." He stared at the tableau, then smiled.

"John Tinker, it is you is it not? The Chosen One? Where are your Ladies? Oh! Hayou, R-Bar, Hayou, Raft."

Ripple stepped out and stared at her younger sisters. "What have you two been getting up to, now?" They were both wearing very startled expressions on their faces. And a look that she recognized as witch intent.

R-Bar slipped sideways, making more and more space between herself and Tinker, and stared at him. "You? Are that One?"

Tinker sighed. "Yep. That's me."

She twisted out.

Ripple yanked her back. "Explain, Runt." She could tell that her youngest witch sister definitely had been up to something.

R-Bar looked everywhere but at Ripple. "I thought that I had found," she mumbled.

Ripple laughed, a very soft not-witch laugh and threw both her arms around R-Bar and held her until R-Bar began to laugh as well.

Raft stood in front of Tinker and stared at him. "You?"

"That's me," said Tinker, deciding to agree to whatever was going on. Somehow it felt safer to do that.

"John Tinker, are your Ladies here as well?"

Ripple looked around the room. Hanred smiled happily. Everyone was relaxing. At least as much as witches ever relaxed.

"Aye," said Chicken, entering the room followed by Smoke, the ornate bodice on her gown had been laced and retied.

"Princess," acknowledged Ripple.

"Shape changer," said Hanred. "Very nice. Um, your gown." He smiled at Smoke.

Fair Morn walked in.

Chicken introduced her. "This do be Our Own Sister, Fair Morn. And Our Sister, Messenger."

Three witches gasped as one as Messenger followed Fair Morn into the room. Raft stood in the furthest corner of the room.

Hanred admired the new pair. And looked at Tinker. And, silently mouthed, "Four?"

"You," hissed Ripple at Messenger, the air crackling around her.

"Me?" Messenger looked at Tinker. "What did I do?" She rubbed her eyes.

Tinker stood, walked over and threw his arm around her shoulders, tugging her against his side. "This is Ripple, the witch and Hanred, the Master Illusionist, and two of Ripple's witch sisters. You met the short one a moment ago."

"You magic'd Reptar." Ripple glared at Messenger.

"I am not short," growled R-Bar.

"She threatened MyTinker!" snapped Messenger at Ripple.

"What?" It was Hanred staring at Ripple.

"I did not," hissed R-Bar.

"Hum, hum, hum, hum," said Ripple. "I see." She looked carefully at Messenger. "And you are very protective."

Messenger nodded, her right hand resting just below her left sleeve, arms loosely crossed. Her eyes watched Ripple's every move.

Ripple was watching her equally carefully. "Yesssss." She exhaled the word very softly. "We tend to be that way."

Then she looked at R-Bar and Raft, who now stood next to Hanred. "Perhaps Reptar learned something?" she said pointedly to her two sisters. The air settled down and went quiet.

"Hum," said R-Bar.

"Hum," repeated Raft.

The two young sisters threw arms around each others shoulders and nudged each other, eyes focused on Tinker.

"My, my," said Hanred, his eyes slowly looking over Fair Morn and Messenger again. "My, my, my." He looked at Tinker, his eyes twinkling. "And they all get along?"

Tinker nodded. "Far as I can tell." Then he spoke to Ripple. "Perhaps we can sit and talk about where everyone went?"

Ripple beckoned a chair over and sat. "Yes."

Tinker explained what they knew and why they were here in Bahn Duhr Tohr. Ripple told him of the gathering and scattering of her sisters. R-Bar and Raft sat quietly and listened to everything, their eyes moving from face to face as the conversation ebbed and flowed.

"So, Chosen one, where do you go from here?"

"Tinker."

Ripple looked at him. "I do not know that elseplace."

Hanred shook his head. He had never heard of it either.

"Call me, Tinker," said Tinker. "I don't know. Maybe we should follow Ramp and Hard. Or go home. Right now, I don't see any real reason for us to do anything. We came because we thought that they needed help. But it certainly doesn't appear that they do."

"You could come with us to Fremter's Scabbard," offered R-Bar, sitting very straight, shoulders back, smiling slyly at Tinker.

She is pretty, offered Messenger.

Most well treasured, My Lord, observed Chicken.

Smoke gave a mental shrug.

Fair Morn didn't do anything. Then she winked. *Short. Like Messenger.*

Knock it off, said Tinker.

"What do you think," he asked Ripple and Hanred.

Ripple glanced at her youngest witch sister. "Hum, hum, hum, hum." And frowned.

R-Bar tried to look bothered. She failed.

"Once I traveled through part of that place." Hanred frowned. "A difficult folk. Unpredictable." He winked at the two young witches. "While those two are quite capable, it might be wise to have a wider range of, ah, talents in the search party. Whatever it is we face, we are racing the woman's calender."

Slipping one arm around Ripple's waist, he asked, "What say you, Midnight Delight?"

Ripple stared at R-Bar and Raft for a long time. They began to fidget and to look worried. Then she nodded. "Tinker, your urh-witch may knock them about if it is required. These two are high spirited and will take some control."

Shall we? asked Tinker. *Go with them?*

Smoke gave him a slow, predatory wink.

Messenger smiled.

Fair Morn shrugged slightly.

Princess?

Me'thinks this smallest one, this nubile wench-witch does but lust after thy body, Mine Prince.

Pounce, offered Smoke.

We will stay, said Tinker. *I, we, do not need to be running around with someone like that. You guys are bad enough.*

"We to Fremter's Scabbard will go," announced Chicken, chewing on one corner of her lower lip.

Tinker sighed. And nodded. And mumbled, mostly to himself, "Snooked again."

Messenger grinned. "Oh, Boy."

"We can take you," said R-Bar. She twisted out.

Raft nodded. "Be right back." And was gone.

Ripple beckoned in Willawa and The King.

"Dark Advisor," said The Queen. "It is good to have you at our side once again."

Smoke tugged Messenger with her, out of the room. "We'll start packing."

"You are leaving us?" Willawa looked at Tinker.

"We are going to someplace called Fremter's Scabbard. The witches think that this is a good place to check for clues as to what is after Ramp."

"We can send an army," offered Willawa.

"Or two," added Toucan. "They do be a'piling up." He smiled at his Queen.

"Ah, I don't think we need one. Not yet. Do we?" He looked at Hanred. So did Ripple.

Hanred shook his head. "Not on Fremtar's Scabbard."

"Send Raft to me if you have such a need," said Ripple. "She travels the fastest of all."

Chicken kissed Toucan on the cheek and stepped to Tinker's side.

"My Lord, we need change err we do leave."

Tinker smiled. "Well, thanks for everything, Willawa, Toucan. It looks like we're off."

"My Queen, may we talk?" Ripple looked at Willawa.

"Our quarters," said Willawa.

Ripple, Hanred, Willawa, and Toucan were gone.

Chicken and Tinker stepped into the adjoining bedroom to change.

Raft looked in and waited. In the main room. She was ready.

R-Bar landed lightly on her feet. And called, "READY?"

Fair Morn strode from the adjoining room, trailing clothes, pack and weapon. "Almost."

"You are magic made, true?" Raft looked at her. She could feel traces.

"I was."

"By whom?"

"Big Red."

Both witches sucked in their breath. And leaped away. Making space.

Messenger popped through the door. "Have you been there before?" She hefted her pack into place.

"No! Not!" they said, edging away from her, carefully keeping distance from Messenger and Fair Morn.

"Sweet My Lord," said Chicken, nuzzling his ear. "Be we here or a'home, plain waiting t'would most irksome be. Thus did we speak so."

"It's O.K., sweetie." Tinker was being his Bogart best, his hands sliding over her back and ribs. "We better finish getting dressed or one of those witches are liable to pop in to see what is keeping us."

"They do both be most young like sweet Messenger and of youthful spirits be'filled."

"Right," he said, buttoning his shirt, grumbling softly.

"We will chances none take," she answered the expression on his face as she fastened her scabbard in place, popping the sword up and down.

"Right." He flapped the great dark sword in place and grabbed his pack. "Let's go."

In the other room, he looked at R-Bar. "You gonna have any trouble moving us around?"

R-Bar and Raft pulled them all away.

Fringloe's Tar. Late Afternoon.

They tumbled from the doorway, a very mixed group. J. C., Mirf, Ramp, Hard, and Mountain.

All the buildings were gray, badly weathered wood. Green things grew in all the cracks and crevices on all visible surfaces. A low fog shrouded the roof tops. The taller structures pushed up into the soft cotton billows and disappeared. The light was soft and diffused.

There were no shadows.

"Ho Boy, some place this is." Mirf looked around and frowned.

"Fringloe's Tar," said Ramp. "It is a place where we may find some hint of what is causing the problem."

"So what's the problem?" Mirf had decided it was better to leave with Ramp and Hard than stay around Bahn Duhr Tohr and meet up with Ripple who would probably be somewhat unhappy about what had happened to Reptar. Witches were impulsive. And, she wasn't a hob-goblin anymore. Mostly. It was definitely safer coming here.

"**DUMPFING DAMP.**" Mountain observed the fog and wet, his brows wrinkling.

"The problem?" Hard looked at Mirf. "Do we have a problem?"

"NO. You do?" Mirf's eyes rolled.

"What?"

Ramp quickly told Mirf, J. C. and Mountain about the twins.

"Worse than worse," mumbled Mirf.

They had been walking down the street during this conversation and now stood at an intersection.

"So, Rampeleh, why are we here?"

"Mirf, we must find a person called Will Begood. He may be able to tell us something. Will hears things from many times and elseplaces, but he lives here."

The few folk on the street they passed stared wide-eyed up at Mountain. They hardly paid any attention to the rest of the small group.

"Which way?" asked Hard.

"That way." Ramp pointed and threw her hood up over her head, and walked around the corner, her arm firmly linked through one of Hard's. "I felt him this way."

Mirf slipped her arm under one of J. C.'s. "Let's go, big guy."

"Sure," said J. C.

Mountain followed them.

Twenty blocks later they stopped next to a low, long building. Lights shown in all the windows, all soft glow flickering. They could hear muffled sounds of laughter and singing coming from within.

"He is in here." Ramp indicated the building.

"I will wait outside. **TOO TUMPFING TINY.**"

"Shouldn't take too long," said J. C. "Be back in a bit." He opened the door and stepped inside, Mirf at his side.

Ramp and Hard walked in behind them.

"Do you know this Will?" Hard stumbled into the room. He had caught his toe on the threshold.

The large room was crowded, the air foggy with smoke which appeared to be coming from a number of fire-pits running down the center of the room.

"Any idea which one of these guys is the right one?" J. C. glanced over at Ramp.

She shook her head. "I can't separate him from the rest, but he is in here."

Mirf hissed. "So O.K." She sucked in a deep breath and bellowed into the din. "**SHUT UP!**"

All eyes snapped in their direction, all jaws snapped shut.

"Well, that bellow certainly got all their attention," observed J. C., slipping his arm free. He wanted room to move, just in case.

"**WILL BEGOOD!**" Mirf lowered her voice. "Will Begood, we wish to speak to Will Begood."

No one moved. No one spoke.

Mirf mumbled something to herself, then to J. C. "Boychick, do something."

"Who," said J. C. and Hard.

"Just what I need, twin owls," grumbled Mirf. "Your pardon, Rampeleh."

A rather large, red-faced man pushed through the

crowd and stepped out into the open space to glare at them. "You want to speak to Will Begood? Why?"

"You him?" snapped Mirf.

"May yes, may no."

"Maybe I will just break your arm," growled Mirf, stepping forward.

"Mirf!" cautioned Ramp.

J . C. tugged Mirf back.

"J. C." she snarled, shrugging off his arm.

"I don't think we want to start a bar brawl just now," he said. "Do we?"

"Raz baz."

Ramp stepped forward. "I wish to speak with Will Begood."

"Strangers, raft diddle." Someone in the crowd tossed a clay pot. It missed Ramp.

The next one hit Hard on the shoulder. "OUCH!"

As the third sailed through the air, Ramp thrust her hand out.

The pot curved back and cracked into the forehead of its previous owner, dropping him to the floor. He twitched a little, and lay still.

The mob surged forward. They didn't notice the large eyes peering through the window from the outside, wondering why it was taking so long.

Before the crowd could bang into the protection Ramp had thrown around Hard and the others, a large piece of the roof and ceiling was ripped upward.

"STOP, BY DUMPF!"

They did. A little too late.

Mirf had jumped in front of Ramp and struck the closest person in the chest, breaking three ribs and knocking him sideways into the wall where he slumped moaning loudly to the floor.

"So which one of you dumbkopfs is Will Begood?"

snarled Mirf at the mob gaping up at Mountain peering in through the hole he had made.

Fremter's Scabbard. Mid-Afternoon.

They came down at the edge of town.

The town was long and narrow. One side of the town towered high above the other side. The town occupied a series of terraces, the last and lowest bordered with a wide wooden street with a single waist high wall on the sea side. Beyond the wall, the sea stretched to the horizon. Somewhere down below the edge they could hear the surge and crash of waves.

Long, slow swells rolled across the face of the sea toward the town. Far down the street, a pier jutted out, numbers of some kind of sea-faring vessel were clustered in tight masses all around the structure.

"Fremter's Scabbard," stated R-Bar.

They were all here. Tinker didn't have to look, he knew. He felt complete. It was a comfort.

Chicken looked to the flat, far horizon. "My Lord, tis most pleasant to be near great ocean." She could smell the salt in the air.

"Let's go to town."

R-Bar nodded at them.

Raft waved at them from the third terrace above them.

"She will follow us," explained R-Bar, urging them onward.

They hiked up the narrow path and onto the wooden street. Rugged looking individuals were walking here and there. Faces and hands were weather beaten and weather worn.

As they passed the first group, and then the next and the next, all the men cast appraising glances at all the women.

R-Bar walked closer to Tinker.

A large, heavily muscled bystander lurched from his slumping stare against the sea fence and grabbed Smoke, pulling her against his chest with one arm while he fondled her with the other hand, his fingers jumping to tug at the buttons of her shirt.

"Ten for this un, perch-fella," he shouted, grinning broadly.

Smoke's forearm swung around, her elbow cracking into the back edge of his jaw. Twisting, she grabbed him and pitched him up and over the railing into the water below. And quickly checked for more attackers.

Two of his companions ran down the deck, circled wide around the small group, leaned over, and threw a long rope down to him. There were coils of rope placed at intervals all along the sea fence.

"Keep walking, gang," mumbled Tinker, starting everyone walking again.

They passed a small clump of men, who eyed them carefully, having seen the action further down the street.

"A fine school," said one to Tinker.

"One mack snapper there," suggested another.

They all laughed.

The next group Tinker and company passed were sitting, loose limbed on a long bench, drinking from a number of green containers.

They weren't really sure what had happened way down there. They eyed the group. And grinned at them.

"Perch-fella, perch-fella," called one. "Eight plus two for the little'un." He waved currency in his hand.

"Fair piece for trolling," laughed another, digging an elbow into the ribs of yet another.

"Black snapper is not so tasty as sunlight. Ten plus three." One jabbed his thumb at Chicken.

"Fast and slack," gurgled someone, emptying a container. "Snap bap."

As soon as they had some empty space around them, Tinker halted the group. "O. K., R-Bar, I think you had better tell us about this place. I don't like what I think those guys think that we are."

"Chosen One . . . "

"Tinker."

"Hum, hum. Tinker. This is a water denizen gathering town, filled with men. From far over there." R-Bar pointed at the far horizon.

"That is where the main community is. The men live over here for long periods of time, catch until an assigned quota is met, then return to their homes. Hum, hum. There are no women here. Hum, hum, hum. Most of the time."

"Except for a certain kind," grumbled Tinker.

R-Bar nodded. Once.

"Nice place."

"To find out what we need to find out, it is. Halfway down there is the main gather of this elseplace. That is where we might get our information."

"And how," demanded Tinker, "do we do that without starting a riot?"

R-Bar slipped close and looked up at his face. "I could send them all back to Bahn Duhr Tohr." She grinned. And poked his shirt with a finger.

"Sneaky little devil, aren't you?"

"Not so little." She inhaled deeply.

"Don't think about it. Let's go."

They all headed for halfway down. He sighed heavily. And wondered, why? Why is it always me?

Far down the walkway, he walked. Mumbling to himself about witches, especially short ones.

Tinker received many stares. Everyone recognized a killing sword when they saw one up close. He and it were all they saw. Smoke worked on that.

R-Bar looked unhappy at her, squirmed, and found Smoke's hold on her arm stronger than she would have thought was possible. The young witch could see everyone. It was just that the inhabitants couldn't see them, except for Tinker, of course. The rest had to be nimble of foot to avoid unseeing collisions.

R-Bar wasn't sure whether she ought to magic this female or not.

Tinker smiled at R-Bar and whispered, "Curses, foiled again."

And then Tinker was leaning against the sea fence, looking across the walkway at their destination.

"Now what?"

"We go in and listen," said R-Bar.

From inside came loud, happy noises, bangs and crashes.

Tinker grimaced. "Oh really? It already sounds like quite a party. If we go in there, it will be a riot. I doubt any of you guys are ready to be mauled by randy fishermen, just on the off-chance we might find something out."

Raft stood by his side. "I will go with you. They can wait here, silent and unseen."

"I wanted to go." R-Bar's lower lip pushed out. She glared at her sister.

"Fine." Tinker rolled his eyes at her. "Just suck in your stomach, stick out your chest, and I'll sell you to the highest bidder."

"Dim, dim, dim!" snarled the short witch, deciding that he wasn't nice after all.

"Don't growl at me, rover." He leaned over and kissed her on the forehead. "You are too cute for those guys anyway. Smoke, any problem?"

"No."

"You are as rangle as Ripple." R-Bar glared up at him.

"I take that as a compliment. Let's go, Raft." Tinker walked across the street, opened the door, and stepped into the din. And never saw Raft pass by.

"And I am not a Rover," snarled R-Bar at his back,

wondering what kind of a creature a rover was. And why he would call her that.

The crowd gave him just enough room to maneuver. Someone shoved a mug into his hand. So he took it and a drink. His stomach glowed, his eyes watered.

"Hum," said someone in his ear, who wasn't there.

Slowly, Tinker worked his way through the crowd. Everyone was mostly talking about life here, life at sea, and life at home. A few talked about a new perch-fella and the school that swam around him.

But he didn't hear anything else.

"Far back corner." Soft lips caressed the side of his face.

Tinker let his eyes slowly drift until he was looking into the dark, far back corner. A small group sat huddled around a table upon which sat some small thing emitting a soft yellow glow.

Wandering aimlessly, taking the slightest of sips from his mug, Tinker finally stood as close as he thought he ought to get. Close enough to hear the low conversations.

The men were playing a game with dozens of short sticks and talking at the same time.

"I'd say, Ter'wil paid in."

"Rat smack. There is no catch in there."

"Drag rear, Ter'wil did do."

"Nin, nin."

"Hee ho, if not, how does Ter'wil entostle in place with? 20 plus 8 catch, eeee?"

"How?"

"Ter'wil did say Hag Rambo paid in?"

"What catch?"

"Ter'wil to Hag Rambo green rar?"

All the listeners sucked in their breath through clenched teeth.

Then they wiggled their fingers and looked frightened. Tinker drifted toward the outside door.

Smoke, we need to find someone named Ter'wil.

And felt Raft pass by, lightly running gentle fingers across his cheek.

Tinker walked down the street.

Alone.

Apparently alone.

They were following by three men who were weaving from here to there. Smoke said that the image in their minds was of the person called Ter'wil and someone he had with him. They were going for a visit. She thought the someone was a female.

As the three were starting up one of the several staircases to Ter'wil's door, they sat down and fell asleep. Smoke winked at Tinker.

Tinker checked the street and started up the stairs.

Smoke suddenly bolted up a different one between the structures.

"**MURDER!**" she shouted, pointing.

Tinker ran toward that door. It was locked. As he waggled the knob, the door was blown outward, pitching him backward and down the stairs.

"**MY LORD!**" screamed Chicken, running toward him, sword flashing free.

Fair Morn charged the doorway, weapon in hand.

Messenger patted his cheek. "MyTinker?"

R-Bar peered around Chicken at him.

Spectators began to congregate. Some speculated on the explosion. Some speculated on the catch. Some began to get up a collection of money, trying to get a consensus as to which one would be the best value. Some asked where did they come from?

Smoke came down the stairs, dragging someone protesting loudly. She had him by the collar. He was making hard, banging sounds on the stairs.

The bystanders commented among themselves about

this black clad one and the person thumping downward.

"MindMate, this." She lifted the man to his feet. "This is Hag Rambo, who just demolished Ter'wil and the woman with him." And stepped away.

Tinker rose to his feet, gingerly touching the large lump on the side of his head.

R-Bar knocked his arm aside and said something. The pain and the swelling disappeared. Raft watched from across the street, standing against the railing.

Then the catch was gone. Everyone looked at everyone else.

Then at the shattered structure.

Then at Tinker.

Then they hurried away, wondering but not asking. Something that strange was best left alone.

"O. K., Hag Rambo, I need some answers."

The heavyset figure glared at Tinker. One eye was swollen shut.

"Urn mum."

"What did you buy from Ter'wil?"

"Um mum."

"Smoke, help."

She stepped in front of Hag Rambo. Whatever he saw threatened to buckle his knees and drained the blood from his face as he cleared his throat. "I caught the green rar," he whispered.

"What is that?"

Hag Rambo fainted.

"Now what are we going to do?"

"It looked like a kind of green fist, or glove." Smoke frowned. "The other one, Ter'wil, fished it up in a box, from the sea."

Raft hissed. She stood next to the crumpled figure and began lightly kicking him in the side.

"What?" asked R-Bar.

"I have heard of the Green Hand of the Demon Egof. Egof was broken and scattered, never to be found." Raft kicked Hag Rambo again. A little harder.

"Hum, hum, hum?" said R-Bar, staring at Hag Rambo.

"What is the Demon Egof?" asked Tinker.

Raft looked at Tinker. "The tales say powerful enough to steal unprotected children. Like our sisters yet unbirthed."

"DIM, DIM, DIM!" R-Bar booted Hag Rambo in the side of his chest.

Tinker shoved her aside. Then Raft. "We need to make him talk, not kill him. He must know who he sold it to and where we can find that person."

Smoke and Fair Mom lifted the inert body upright.

R-Bar, looking unhappy, woke up Hag Rambo, and took away his pain.

Tinker leaned forward. "Who did you sell the green hand to? I want to know?"

Hag Rambo's eyes darted wildly from face to face. He gasped. "Frap."

"Where does he live?"

"Two lane."

"Where's that?"

Hag Rambo pointed at the far horizon. And died. The thing had snapped from nowhere and back again. Taking his heart with it.

R-Bar twisted them away.

The thing snapped back, passing through the now empty air.

They stood on a crowded waterfront. Piers jutted wooden tentacles into the sea. Here the beach was wide with a gently sloping gray sand. Tall wooden buildings lurched into the sky, each leaning in a different direction. The tilt was slight but noticeable.

"What was that?" demanded Tinker.

"Do Dart, Tink."

"For the heart," added Raft, standing by his side.

Something snapped.

Everyone jerked.

Witches hissed.

Fair Morn was cradling her weapon in her arms. She had just reset the focus, snapping a lever to new setting.

The thing popped from nowhere. And exploded.

Raft congratulated her sister. "Very rangle."

R-Bar blushed, slightly. "First time." It wasn't much of a blush. Witches really didn't blush much.

"O.K., Shorty. Now what?"

"We have to find Frap," said R-Bar. She grumbled at him, and hissed, "I am not short."

"Two Lane is the next one back," said Smoke, shaking her head. "It is hard. Too many minds."

"Stop," said Tinker. Smoke did.

"And the Mag Wra," said R-Bar.

"What is that?" Tinker looked at her.

"The person that released the Do Dart. He will be angry now."

"And healing." Raft beamed at R-Bar.

"First we find Frap. Let's go." Tinker started them in the direction indicated by Smoke.

So they headed one block back. Here, in this town of odd angles and lines, they caused little disturbance. Some people glanced sharply at Tinker. Some smiled appreciatively at the school around him. But none approached them, or made loud comments. Most just walked past, intent upon their own business. It was a busy place, filled with busy people. They saw many strange visitors, coming and going.

"Which way, now?"

It was an intersection with people walking in all directions, some talking with others, some gesturing and explaining whatever, business or otherwise.

Raft and R-Bar held a whispered conversation. Raft nodded and pointed left. They went that way.

Three blocks later, they stood and stared at a shattered structure, partially burned, windows and doors blown away. Flame scars coated the outer walls above every opening.

"Here?"

Smoke probed the minds of the men standing, searching in the wreckage.

"Yes. They all think of the person Frap who lived here?" She indicated the burned out structure.

"Past tense?"

"Yes." Smoke turned her head and looked across the street.

Three stories up, on the facing wall, was an ugly stain. Person shaped.

"Oh, my!" gasped Messenger.

"Now what?"

R-Bar hissed softly. Raft had gone and returned.

"The Mag Wra lives in that building." Raft indicated the building with the ugly splotch that had been Frap.

Messenger stared at the building and grabbed one of Tinker's arms. "Ugly, ugly, ugly. Oozing from cracks and cranies."

R-Bar stared at Messenger. "Urh-witch, you can see it?"

Messenger nodded.

A short dark wand jumped into R-Bar's hand. She ran for the entry door. Raft was over there, waiting for her, something bronze glittered in her hand. They plunged into the structure.

Messenger released Tinker and whipped the long wand from her sleeve. "We have to help them." And ran for the building, Fair Morn right behind her, the space cannon cradled in her arms.

"Smoke, Princess, wait right here, please." Tinker reached up and swung down the great black sword. Then he ran into the building.

The street crowd, upon seeing the sword swinging down, scattered in all directions. The word spread rapidly. No-one was going to get close to this area for some time. A killing agent was on the loose.

They found a great lump sitting in a chair behind a table. They were the fourth floor. The right hand of the man was swaddled in cloth heavily stained by leaking body fluids.

"Spell blaze back." R-Bar indicated the bandaged hand and smiled.

He cringed. All knew that smiling witches were one step from doing mayhem.

Raft opened the closet at the far end of the room. "Hum, hum, hum," she sang.

She stood between Tinker and her sister, a twisted, gnarled green hand made of translucent stone held in one hand. It was part of a forearm. The arm and wrist were made of something else.

"Who wanted this?" Raft hissed, standing next to the Mag Wra, waggling the thing in front of his face.

"Speak, beast." R-Bar leaned over the table, glaring, hissing in his face.

"**WATCH IT!**" yelled Tinker as something on the table moved.

She spun away, something tearing. Ripping cloth. "DIM, DIM, DIM!" Parts of the table exploded as her wand erupted.

The weaponkin whirled in a great overhead cut, through the table, through a mound of mouldering stuff on the table, and the something that had lunged at R-Bar, fangs flashing.

Raft screamed from the far corner. "**SISTER!**" Her wand flashed, part of the wall blew into the street.

Tinker danced sideways.

The Mag Wra managed a broken smile. And sagged to one side.

R-Bar leaped into the table debris and kicked pieces in all directions. "Dim, dim, dim!"

Tinker yanked her back, throwing one arm around her. **"HOLD IT, HOLD IT!"** Then he saw that a sizable piece of her blouse was still clenched in the fangs of the thing he had decapitated.

She gurgled soft deep in her throat. Then he realized that he had missed when he had grabbed her around the waist. He jerked his hand away. And decided that was the problem with short people.

Raft banged the sagging Mag Wra on the side of his head with her wand. "Speak or die. Horribly." She smiled happily. And shoved him up right.

He gurgled. The sound came from deep inside his chest.

"NO," howled R-Bar.

The Mag Wra split open and died.

Messenger and Fair Morn charged into the room. They had been searching the lower floors.

"Oh, yuck!" Messenger stared at the remains in the chair.

"She is very pretty," added Messenger looking at R-Bar.

Fair Morn agreed. "Certainly is."

"Always has been well endowed." Raft was standing between Messenger and Tinker, handing the green arm to Messenger.

"Right," said Tinker. "Definitely not a child." He glared at Messenger. "And don't you even think it."

Messenger hastily shoved the arm back at Raft. "Horrid. Dark. Evil."

"Her?" He pointed at R-Bar.

R-Bar growled.

"That is," replied Messenger, pointing at the arm Raft held.

Fair Morn looked over Messenger's head at the object. "Looks like an arm."

Raft gave it to Tinker.

"Part of a statue," suggested Tinker.

"The Demon Egof," said R-Bar quietly. And growled at Messenger. "I am not horrid or evil."

"It reeks," moaned Messenger. "Ugly!"

Tinker spoke to her, "See anything else?"

"Broken. The strands hang in tatters. Someone, something, shattered the forces around it."

She whispered to him. "It wants to be together. Someone, out there, wants it to be together." Tears began to leak from Messenger's eyes and pour down her face. "**OOOOOOHHHHH**, MyTinker, we can't let that happen. Never, never." She quivered. "Never never!"

SMOKE.

Got her.

Messenger stopped shaking. She smiled, a very weak smile. "I am all right, now."

R-Bar yanked a brown sack from the debris on the floor and tossed it to her sister. "In there."

Raft grabbed the arm and shoved it into the sack and pulled the drawstring tight.

My Lord, be thee coming down soon?

On our way, Princess. "Let's get out of here and make some plans." He started for the door.

"One moment." R-Bar was rummaging through the shambles of the room. She stuffed a small volume into a patch pocket on her trousers, stepped in front of Tinker, stood on her tip-toes, threw her arms around his neck, and kissed him.

"Hum, hum, hum," she sang after finally pulling away from him. "Hum, hum, hum."

"Bug, bug, bug!" grumbled Tinker. "Let's go. Before the cops arrive."

He ran down the stairs.

"My Lord?" Chicken glanced over at him. "What wert

thee a'doing up there? Me'thinks thee hast said pon occassion many, here We do quote thee, four be a'plenty, and if mine innocent eyes deceive me not, thee has fair unrobed that witch."

"You know what we were doing as well as I do. And I wasn't doing that."

Smoke walked over to R-Bar and yanked her tattered blouse further open. R-Bar's eyes flew wide.

"SMOKE!"

"I am checking for fang marks, MindMate. That thing looked poisonous to me." One finger poked R-Bar gently. "See here. A red inflamed scratch."

Raft opened a small jar and gently stroked the ointment on the wound. "Reclothe, show off." She recapped the jar and put the container somewhere.

R-Bar's blouse remnants shimmered and rewove themselves.

"Whither go we?" asked Chicken.

"Right," agreed Tinker. "Whither? Any ideas?" He looked at R-Bar.

She nodded. "Perhaps. Let's go down to the next intersection."

They stood and waited for Raft to return. She was searching for something.

R-Bar stood with the dingy sack tucked under one am.

They watched the foot traffic going by, watching them.

R-Bar nudged Tinker and grinned. "I am pretty, am I not?"

He looked at her, his mouth dropped open. "Beautiful," he rasped.

He bugged his eyes out and said, "Luscious. Gorgeous."

His voice dropped to a harsh whisper. "Un believeable."

Finally it rose to a carnival barker's chant. "Hormone ripping!"

As the litany roared on and on, Smoke stepped next to the goggle-eyed witch who was staring open-mouthed at Tinker and ruffled her hair. "Good question, short stuff."

"Ladies, let's have a little more self confidence, shall we?" said Tinker, finally ending. He dragged in a deep breath.

"You want to ask that question again," said Smoke sotto voce to R-Bar.

"What did I do?" she asked Smoke as she frowned at Tinker. "I am not a Lady!"

"Chicken can explain. Go ask her." Smoke nudged R-Bar in the correct direction.

Tinker glared at Smoke. "And I do not care what female dominated bands of predatory telepathic carnivores do, or think, either. Especially think."

"That is redundant," stated Smoke, standing in front of him, poking a finger inside his shirt.

"What is?"

"Predatory carnivores." She curled her lips back from her teeth. And stepped back.

"You win."

"What?" Raft stood next to them.

"Never mind." He looked at her. "You are pretty also. Before you ask."

"Hum, hum, hum." Raft pressed herself against his side and looked up and into his eyes.

"Tabby cats," stated Tinker. "Drunk on cat-nip."

R-Bar hurried over and tugged Raft away.

Chicken stifled her laugh.

"Ha, ha." Tinker glared at her.

Chicken stopped smiling, walked over and slipped an arm through his, pulling him from the group.

Messenger followed. "My Lord, do not so dour be. These witches be naught but young ladies full of spirit."

"Like smiling pit bulls."

Messenger bumped against his other side. "They are

much nicer than that sister Ripple."

"O.K., you are right. So what?"

"Naught, Fair Prince. Fret thee not."

He sighed. "You are all up to something. I can feel it. And whatever it is, the answer is no. **NO!** No, no, no, no, no, no, no, nope!"

"Very negative," observed Smoke, walking over.

"Rah . . . ther," drawled Chicken. "Frightfully so."

Suddenly Tinker yanked her further to one side and leaned close, and whispered, "Princess, she did that deliberately?"

"Who? What? My Lord?"

"That kid witch. She let her blouse get torn open deliberately like some heroine in a romance, a bodice- ripping novel."

"Forsooth, Mine Prince, she do be most novel and struggled naught when thee do fondle her so."

"I did not fondle her. Not deliberately. She was going to attack him. Again. So I grabbed her around the waist and missed."

Chicken leaned against him. "Love of us all, do pray tell?" And suppressed her smile.

"What?"

"What spake she to thee when in thy manly grip thy hand did mold her womanly charms?"

He sighed. "Why all the ribald prodding, Princess? What are you up to? What are you guys up to?"

"Fair evasive an answer, LoveLord."

"She laughed. At least that is what I think she did. Events were getting gory in a hurry up there. But that is it. She laughed. Satisfied?"

"Oh, aye, Me'Lord. She hath smooth skin?"

"Stop it. That is quite enough. Go feel her for yourself. She will probably rip your hand off at the wrist."

Raft peered past Chicken's head. "Lord? R-Bar says that

we should to go to Dule Lairdont, next. Will you come with us?"

"What kind of place is it?"

"Hot and steamy," giggled a voice in his ear.

Raft stood next to Fair Morn and winked at Tinker.

R-Bar walked over and joined the group.

"Please? I won't tease you again." R-Bar looked at him, waiting for denial.

"O.K., kiddo, we'll go." He laughed, cutting of her protest. "I know, you are not a child."

R-Bar turned them out.

Apol Repar Yiens. Late Afternoon.

Rumtah and Reptar watched the figure dangling from the tree.

They were on the elseplace called Apol Repar Yiens. After drifting in and out of a number of small villages, they had arrived here, to the village called K'Amtarq, and paid a visit to a certain individual who was known to deal in unspeakable things. Folk in the other villages had been very willing to talk to the pair of witches. Mainly because of the expressions that the folk saw on the faces of the witches.

And after considerable debate with the man they had heard so much about, the two sisters had dragged one Dir Potsal by name, from his hut and hung him from a large tree where he now dangled, his feet clear of the ground.

Dir Potsal wore voluminous robes of many pockets.

Reptar was cutting the bottoms open, one pocket at a time. "It would be faster if you would just tell us what we want, dik dir." Another shred of costume fell away.

Rumtah's eyes glittered in the soft light inside the thick forest. "Perhaps if I poke this thing a little, it will speak." Her wand glowed brightly.

Dir Potsal's eyes rolled wildly. "Take all my possessions, black ones, everything. Even the gold buried behind my humble hut. Please, please, please!"

Reptar tossed another artifact of Apol Repar Yien's culture onto the growing pile. "Hum, hum, hum. Nothing of value here, nothing with a tale to tell. Poke him." She blocked his vocal cords as he started to scream. "But keep him alive."

Rumtah slipped her wand slowly out. "Shall we hear what our singer has to song us with?"

Reptar tossed two more objects on the pile and released him.

"Please, please, please! What, what, what?"

Reptar waggled an object under his nose and spoke to Rumtah. "I don't see how this sewer could work with all these things in all those pockets."

Rumtah snatched the thing from her sister's hand and threw it deep into the forest. "That is disgusting, ugly. Speak to me, brak food."

"Mercy, Dark Fen. I am grievously wounded, I require care and aid. Mercy!"

Rumtah slowly stroked his cheek with her wand and let it wander just below one of his eyes.

"What?" squeaked Dir Potsal.

"Sing-song," said Rumtah.

"I received a message," whispered Dir Potsal. And he told Reptar which pocket.

Removing a generous amount of cloth from that layer, she unfolded the pocket and caught the small message stone. "Hum, hum, hum. A large sum in advance for a certain artifact of foul interest. Who did you sell it to? Who received it?"

"It will kill me," he hissed.

"Slower than I?" Rumtah smiled, poking his side with her wand.

"Cease. Desist. Better to die swiftly." Dir Potsal told Reptar which pocket.

As she ripped it free, a green object tumbled to the ground.

Reptar picked it up. "A foot, part of a clothed leg." She ran one finger over the clawed toes. "Why would so much be paid for so little?"

Tears tumbled down Dir Potsal's cheeks as he whispered the carefully guarded secret. "Daemond Erchef, the foot of the duoded beast."

Reptar looked at Rumtah. "I never heard of this thing."

Rumtah wrapped the object in a piece of Dir Potsal's many layers. "We will keep it. This thing has a dire feel to it. The Aunts may know." Turning to Dir Potsal, she smiled. "Someone will find you sooner or later."

She and Reptar slipped out in a soft gust of dark.

Clausis Rep't. Late At Night.

Clausis Rep't, the merchant city, stretched and sprawled in every direction from the port. At the ground-level, vast, cavernous warehouses. Above these were piled the houses, offices, shops, restaurants, all the paraphernalia of living the good life.

Rekel had started just inside the door of a warehouse bearing a label-plate marked 20DAB-PXT20095. She was now well past halfway and getting more and more irritated. Behind her lay the wildly scattered contents of boxes and crates. What ever it was, she hadn't found it. Yet.

She kicked the inert figure in the side, none too gently. Still. No reaction. Rekel was getting tired of dragging this one along with her from place to place as she searched. But this merchant was supposed to know.

Somewhere, something dark, growled. Rekel nodded.

Chewing on her lower lip, the witch looked at the person on the floor. The spell hadn't been all that powerful. She decided that this was of pretend and that it was time to change that.

Digging her fingers into the mass of long dark hair brushed to a glistening shine, she hauled the woman across the aisle and propped her against an, as of yet, unopened crate. Then she bent over and slapped her across the face.

"Nuff pretense, merchant. It is time to tell." No reaction.

"Hum, hum, hum." Rekel took a small thing from somewhere, all legs and claws, yanked open the neck of the merchant's smock and dropped it inside.

The merchant's eyes flew open, her back arched, as she frantically tried to remove the creature.

The witch crouched in front of the merchant and watched.

"OH . . . OH . . . OH!"

"Pretty nice?" Rekel took a short wand and stabbed downward, killing the ran-dell. "Speak to me, funny eyes." The merchant had one brown eye and one yellow eye.

"**WITCH!**"

"That I am. Now tell me something that I do not know."

The merchant pressed her lips into a thin line.

"For one who makes their living trading, that is not a smart thing to do."

The strange eyes glared at her.

Rekel stood and said something.

The long, dark hair braided itself into a single strand, looped around her neck, tied a knot at one end and coiled upward, lifting the merchant until she stood on her toes, the knot anchored to the crate wall by a hook which had just extruded itself from the wood. Her arms hung loosely at her sides. Now they didn't seem to work. She had to stand on her toes to keep from being strangled.

"Hum, hum, hum."

The air crackled softly as something began to take shape between them.

The merchant gasped. "NO!"

"YES!" Rekel smiled at her. "I think you will talk. If you do not go mad. First."

"**NO!**"

"No?"

The thing edged closer, mouth puckering. The merchant tried to nod her head. "Yes, yes, yes! Take that thing away."

The witch waved an arm. The thing vanished. She stepped close to her victim and spoke softly. "Here is an interesting fact for you, collector of things. I have never seen what that would do. People always do what I want them to, first. You ready to talk?"

"What do you want to know?"

The merchant's expression relaxed. Deal making and trading were her way of life. And now this witch appeared to be ready to deal. And the merchant felt that she had better.

"I already know that you deal in things that the underground underground will not touch." Rekel then explained how she had come by that information.

The merchant cleared her throat. "You did that?"

Rekel nodded. "All by myself. Legs getting tired?"

"You couldn't have."

The witch reached somewhere. "I thought that there might be a few doubts, here and there, so I brought a souvenir. Recognize this ring?" She shoved it close to her captive's face. "And the fat little finger wearing it?"

The merchant tried to turn her face away. "Yes."

Rekel put it away. "So much for doubts. Those persons, including the one now not wearing this ring, or wiggling that finger, told me of a recent purchase and rumors of a potential buyer. I want that thing and I want that name. Speak."

The merchant blinked sweat from her eyes and tried to ease the pain in her feet. "What do I receive in return?"

The witch stepped closer, face almost touching face, and began to slowly rip the front of her captive's smock open.

The merchant tried to peer down, but couldn't. Her eyes darted wildly. "**DON'T!**"

The witch stepped back and held up a small creature, a very dead small creature. "Just removing this. They start to decay rapidly after death." She dropped it on the floor. It made a wet sound. "Life is a fair exchange," suggested Rekel, running a palm over smooth skin.

"What object?" gasped the merchant.

"Hum, hum. Good question, merchant. I do not know. I think that it has to be the vilest sort of something, something for great evil, a powerful object. One that is worth a fortune or two. What do have along those lines? And you may hurry, if you wish. I think your legs are getting close to the collapsing point."

"Let me down."

Rekel stepped back.

And watched.

And watched.

And folded her arms.

And waited. But not to well.

"Crate 9-l. Hurry."

The witch strolled casually away, humming to herself.

It took some time to find the right crate. It was small and almost hidden. She opened the box and removed a leather case. "Hum, hum, hum."

And strolled back.

Rekel waved one hand. The hook oozed downward allowing the merchant to ease the pressure on her throat. "This it?"

"Yes," rasped the merchant.

"Making progress." Rekel held the leather case in front of the almost closed eyes. "You are positive that this is it?"

"Ye . . . yes."

"Hum, hum, hum." Rekel opened the case and lifted out the object. The jewels glittered in the light filtering in through high dirt encrusted, one of these days to be washed, windows.

"This is a piece of something. It looks like a belt on a statue."

"It is."

"What? What is it from?"

"I, ummmm, do not feel well." The merchant slumped to one side, the braid tightening around her neck, holding her upright.

Rekel lifted her head by the chin. "You could feel worse. Tell me?" And wobbled the head back and forth. "Much worse."

"It is said to be a piece of a monster. Certain never to be named individuals spread the word that vast sums were available for any and all fragments, regardless of size."

Rekel turned the piece over and over, touching and caressing it. She looked up, eyes glittering. "I feel a certain power here. How does one test it to know that it is the correct thing?"

The merchant sucked in her breath. "I dare not."

"Oh?" The witch stepped closer.

"Please . . . "

"Test it!"

"Please. . ." Tears mingled with sweat, eyes pleaded. "I will give you anything, anything at all."

The witch's hand slid over the merchant's shoulder.

"Ahhhhhhhhh . . . no . . . no . . . nooooooooooooo."

Rekel lifted the merchant's head again and waggled it back and forth. "You are still alive, you know."

"I was told," sobbed the merchant. "To . . . to hold it close and say to it. I want power. I didn't try it. I was afraid. Leave me alone. Leave me alone."

"Hum." Rekel thrust the object against her prisoner. "Say the words."

The strange eyes stared into the witch face and saw only cold, dark, unfeeling pain staring back.

"I . . ." began the merchant.

The jewels began to glow.

". . . want . . ."

The air crackled.

Her flesh began to steam.

" . . . pow . . ."

Rekel yanked the object away and slammed her free hand against the merchant's jaw, stopping her from completing the sentence. Then she thrust the fragment back into the leather pouch and wrapped it tighter and tighter with incantations and spells.

The merchant's clothes hung loosely from a much reduced body. She had just lost a considerable amount of weight.

Rekel released the braid. The merchant tumbled to the floor with a thump to sit sprawling loose-limbed.

"It would have eaten you alive if you had finished that sentence."

"Leave me alone," came the whispered reply. "Leave me alone, leave me alone, leave me alone!" Tears poured from the hanging head, fingers plucked at tattered clothes trying to pull them closed.

In the absolute silence, the merchant painfully lifted her head and looked down the long aisle of destruction to the far door.

She was alone.

Eryth Globe. Early Evening.

Ranna leaned out over the balcony railing feeling the round smoothness cutting across her pelvis. The breeze ruffled her hair, rustled her clothes.

The people walking the streets of Eryth Globe far below were tiny specks. A very, very long way to fall, she thought. Her left hand was clenching the horizontal railing that ran along the top of the balcony wall. Her right hand was clutched around the neck of a man arched backward over that same railing.

His feet were just lightly touching the balcony floor. He was dressed in very bright colors. He was a tall, handsome person who didn't seem to be all that bothered by his precarious position.

"Ranna, my love," he croaked. "It must have been something that I said as I did not have time to do anything else."

"Pretty piece, I do not have the patience of my sisters, what little that they have of it."

"Surely you didn't invite them here?"

"Sweet thing, I am about to part company with you unless you give me those dark relics you purchased from that slime dealer, Fa Dimt."

"A long drop."

She heaved him over the edge.

He fell, cursing and swearing.

For eight long stories.

And was jerked to a halt.

Ranna had fastened a magic strand around one of his ankles and anchored it firmly to the balcony railing.

"Love toy," she called. "I have your crystal in my pocket. There will be no wings for you tonight."

"Nasty, nasty," he yelled back up at her.

She began to pluck small shreds loose from the tightly woven strand. As each popped, he jerked lower.

"In the golden green tril."

She laughed. "Don't go away." And walked back into the living room. Swinging open the doors of the magical storage device, she saw them. Two fragments of something, tightly bound in a spell. The intricate design she recognized as his handiwork. Whatever these things were, they had to be treated with respect.

Taking them, she dropped them into a place, and walked back outside and looked over the edge.

He waggled the fingers of one hand at her. "Up. I really would like to come up."

The strand contracted and reeled him in.

Standing, facing her, he smiled. "You are the most beautiful, and nasty, thing I have ever seen."

Brushing her lips over his, she sighed, "I am not a thing, pretty pretty. And I have to leave."

She backed away, halfway across the living room she reached into a pocket and flipped the crystal in a high arc toward him.

By the time his fingers closed over it, she was gone.

He shrugged one shoulder. It was probably safer not to have those things around.

Dule Lairdont. Mid-Afternoon.

Tinker wiped the sweat from his brow.

They had just arrived. It was hot here .

"Well shorty, you were certainly correct." He waved a hand at her. "Ah, ah. Yes, you are. In this crowd, you are short."

"Dim, dim, dim." R-Bar frowned at him. She was having trouble deciding whether he was nice or not.

Raft, standing near but not too close to Messenger, laughed softly.

"She is shorter, just a little," stated Messenger. "Why is she growling like that?"

"My Lord, tis heat excessive for irritating."

"Right." He was rolling up his sleeves and unbuttoning his shirt. "Where do we go?"

He winked at R-Bar. "But not too short."

R-Bar pointed. "Across the square. That tower where Raft is standing."

They headed across to the indicated tower. They were the only people outside at this time of day. There was no one to notice them.

"Ahhhh." Each one sighed as they passed through the tower door to the inside. It was cool, pleasant, and explained why no one was outside.

They walked down the long entry hall and stepped into the bright central core that was open to the roof. A vast square shaft filled with light reflected down and down, balcony after balcony to the ground floor.

"Oh my," said Messenger, staring up at the many levels.

"Which?" asked Tinker.

R-Bar pointed up. Four levels up, Raft looked over the railing wall at them and waved.

Tinker looked around the opening. "Don't tell me that this place has air conditioning but no elevator."

She shrugged a shoulder. And twisted everyone up.

"OOOOF." It was Smoke. They had come a little too close to a wall.

Raft waited at the far corner of the balcony.

Tinker started to walk that way. "Who or what are we visiting here?"

"The witch-witch, Palos and Qat, lives here. They are connected in low ways to many fingers of the unspeakable. From them we may learn much."

"Friends of your's?"

R-Bar hunched up her shoulders. "No, not friends. We just know each other. I, um, studied with them. For a short while."

"MindMate, there is a place that I cannot see. Just there." Smoke pointed across the open shaft, diagonally.

Raft stood there, waiting for them.

"Billows and billows," gasped Messenger. "Black, twisted cloud." Soft crackling came from her left sleeve. Blue-green fire slithered tentacles across her forearm.

"Whoa there, kitten. Hold on."

"STOP," cried Messenger, halting them all in the tracks. She whipped the wand from her sleeve and quickly tapped everyone.

Except R-Bar, who had twitched away as the wand passed by her face. For one quick moment they were covered in a bright glow, then nothing.

Shoving the wand back into her sleeve, Messenger smiled apologetically. "A protection, MyTinker. Her friends are dangerous."

"We are safe," stated R-Bar, firmly.

"Certainly hope so." The sword on Tinker's back was starting to hum.

As they walked up to Raft, Fair Morn's fingers fiddled with levers and knobs on the weapon strapped to her thigh. She was setting it to maximum width, maximum penetration, maximum power.

Tension leaped between their minds.

"Relax," said Tinker, pulling them into the central calm created by Smoke.

Raft nodded to R-Bar and placed one hand on her sister's shoulder. "The door is opening."

"Let's go in." R-Bar stepped into the hole.

They followed.

And stepped into a very ordinary appearing room. And met a very ordinary looking couple, a man and woman who were standing in the middle of the room, holding hands.

"He is Qat, she is Palos," said R-Bar, making the introductions. "This is The Chosen One of Legend. He/they are with me and my sister, Raft."

"R-Bar," said Qat.

"One of our best students," stated Palos.

The two pair of eyes flowed over the group, seeking, finding, learning.

"Ar-protected. You had no need," said Qat.

"We are learners," said Palos.

"Teachers." They both spoke in unison.

Palos waved chairs into place.

"We are seeking information," said R-Bar once everyone had been seated and it was the appropriate time to start. She carefully explained why.

Palos nodded when the witch had finished and looked sad. "Word had come. But we disbelieved."

Qat nodded. "Such an attack would rip too many fabrics, turn too much loose."

"The clan intends to put an end to it," stated R-Bar. "Tell us what you know. Please?"

Some silent communication passed between Qat and Palos.

"What we have to tell is but the merest of rumors. The vaguest of the vague."

Qat leaned forward. "Things are dying for such speaking, even so."

Raft hissed. From the far corner of the room.

Messenger sat upright, hands crossed over her lap, carefully watching Qat and Palos. Her right hand was tucked up her left sleeve, holding the wand.

"In a place unknown lives a thing, a person, more or less, who wishes a great disturbance to rip the fabric of the many." Qat leaned even further forward. "We have no sense of place nor do we have a name of this person, this you must believe. We speak only of that which we have heard."

"There once was a demon," continued Palos. "This demon's power was so mighty that the creature was struck into many parts. This, eh, person, of which we hear, is reaching out, asking for, and acquiring the pieces, to put it back together. This loathsome beast, once rebuilt, is meant to stop your sister from birthing."

Qat smiled at their ex-student. "Magician Ramp is said to deliver a great force. This force would have the power to seal away the evil, evil being of whom we speak. Thus and thus, the rending of the good delivers the evil."

R-Bar was snarling to herself, "Dim, dim, dim, dim, dim!" The air was crackling around her.

Raft stood behind her and began to massage her shoulders and whispered, "Gently, gently."

"Not much help," said Tinker.

Palos frowned at him.

Qat smiled.

"Chosen One," he said. "This little dark one will take you into the heart of the disturbance. Of that we are certain. Between you all, it will come to an end. Of that we are certain."

"Leave now," commanded Palos.

As they all stood and turned toward the door, she put a restraining hand on R-Bar, holding her back until the others had stepped outside. Then she spun R-Bar around, and kissed her on the forehead.

As the witch collapsed, Palos sank her fangs into the soft flesh, released her and threw the limp body out the door.

"MY LORD!" Chicken screamed as her blade whirled through the air.

He spun in her direction, his weaponkin singing wildly. The wall was blank.

Raft rolled her sister onto her back and felt for the pulse in her neck. Wet stains were spreading across one side of her blouse.

"Blow a hole in that damn wall," snarled Tinker.

Fair Morn whipped her weapon up and around and waved them away with her left arm. "Move back."

"**NO!**" R-Bar sat up. "**DON'T!** Please. I am all right." Dark light flared in her eyes and quickly faded.

Raft stared at her, chewing her lower lip.

"Really, I am." R-Bar stood up and nodded at them. "See."

"Sister, your wound. You are . . . changed, altered."

Messenger touched Tinker's arm and nodded. "She has been. Other strands of power, all intertwined. Still, she is who she was."

R-Bar stepped close to Tinker and looked up at him. "No taller."

"Nope. Same height, but filthier. You need a bath. And

some new clothes. Your smock is ripped again."

Soft lips brushed over his cheek, Raft sighed in passing. "We could go to Doth Lamex."

R-Bar laughed. And wrinkled her eyes at him.

Tinker frowned. "Who is Doth Lamex?"

Raft peeked at him from the other side of Fair Morn, who was holstering her weapon. "A land of pleasure."

"Oh, boy," said Messenger. "Let's go."

"**HALT!**" snapped Tinker. With one finger he lifted R-Bar's chin and asked her, very sternly. "What kind of pleasure did you have in mind, short and sneaky?"

"Bathing, eating, drinking, sleeping, resting, relaxing, talking. I am not short."

"No little tricks up your dark witch's sleeves?"

R-Bar pouted. "You don't trust me. And I am not short."

"Right. Two times."

"We don't have to go there." Her pout deepened.

"Sister," snapped Raft, standing next to R-Bar. "Don't let this bully, bully you. Hex him." She nudged her sister with one arm.

"I won't."

Raft started to say something.

A bolt cracked between her and Tinker.

"**OW!**" Raft rubbed her side. "That hurt."

"Sister, they are still protected."

"I forgot."

"And one more thing." R-Bar yanked her sister's arm to tilt her head down so she could whisper in her ear.

Raft's eyes widened. "Hum, hum, hum, hum!"

R-Bar turned back and looked at Tinker, then at the rest, and explained, "No one will do anything that they don't want to do. It is a safe place. No thing would dare violate Doth Lamex. No thing could. All put protection upon it. Can we go, Tink? Please?" Her hand gently touched his arm.

Tinker looked over the top of R-Bar's head. "Group?"

Chicken and Fair Horn nodded their heads.

Yes, MindMate.

"Oh, boy!" Messenger grinned. "An adventure to not have to worry about."

R-Bar swung them into and out.

Star Kragt Gate. Midnight Dark Time.

The implosion sucked everything away.

The explosion gouted flame and a wildly tumbling body through the air.

The flames scorched the soaring trees not sucked into the angry maw.

The body banged down, coming to rest in a tree top in a tangled heap of broken limbs, tree and human.

Blood dripped, pattering on lower stem leaves. Harsh breathing indicated some life was still there, but that it was rapidly fading.

The unbroken arm and hand clenched the end of a long, ornately carved rod. The hand of something else still clenched around the other end of the rod.

Slowly, painfully, she inched the rod upward until she could clench her teeth around it, freeing her still working hand. Then she reached into somewhere seeking the items she needed.

Something night black flapped down and landed on the bare back and took a tentative nibble, just to see whether this carrion was edible. Tilting its head to one side, it carefully tasted its find.

Then it bend forward, pressing the long beak down and slipped a hollow feeding tube into this prize and began to drain the valued moisture away.

Rapidly numbing fingers touched, grasped, and twisted.

The tree limbs, the body, the creature and other parts of the tree disappeared.

As had, a mere few moments before, the village of

Nowise.

Doth Lamex. Soft Gentle Time of Day.

They stood on polished stone, smooth polished to a high sheen stone. It was a gigantic circle, the outer edge ring of closely spaced stone columns tapering into points. It was the gateway to Doth Lamex.

"Two football fields at least," said Tinker.

A great mass of eyes and tentacles of a faint pink hue halted to a stop in front of them.

"Welcome to Doth Lamex," it boomed. It had a pleasant, well modulated voice. "Welcome back to Doth Lamex, Raft and R-Bar."

"Hayou, Dree'a'am," said R-Bar. "This is John Tinker, called Lord, called The Chosen one. This is The Noble Princess Chicken, his Queen. This is Smoke. This is Fair Morn, magic created. And this is Messenger, urh-Witch. And this is Dree'a'am, our host."

"Welcome, welcome, welcome, welcome, welcome," said their host.

A large number of eyes looked at R-Bar. "May I suggest a bath and some clothes cleaning, first?"

"Right," agreed Tinker.

One tentacle pointed. A path appeared between two of the stone columns. "What kind of bath?"

"Large," said Smoke.

"Gigantic," suggested Messenger.

"Warm," stated Chicken.

"That way," said Dree'a'am. "Someone will gather and return your garments."

Raft waved at them from between the columns, and called, "**THIS WAY!**"

They strolled down the indicated path and soon reached a branch in it. On every side were park-like settings of flowering shrubs, trees and neatly trimmed grass.

"Have a good time." Tinker took the other path, away from Raft and R-Bar. He didn't notice R-Bar glaring at him as he turned in the opposite direction.

The pool was immense, more lake than pool, steam drifting across its surface. By the time Tinker slipped into the water, Smoke was already far away, chin deep, and Fair Morn was moving toward her, slowly unfurling her wings.

Messenger surged to the surface next to Smoke beaming happily and splashing gaily.

"Be'damn'd boot," snarled Chicken from the bank.

Tinker looked over. "Problem?"

"My Lord, wouldst pick most miserable knot free?"

He waded over and reached for her foot. "O. K., hold still." He began to worry the knot. And after a long time it came loose. "Ta dum, you are free." He stepped back into deeper water.

Chicken yanked the rest of her clothes off and dropped into the pool. And sighed happily. "Pleasantly warm, Our Verra Own Prince." And bobbled next to him, water lapping around her neck.

"You, betcha."

"Tink?" said a very small voice. "May we join you?"

R-Bar and Raft stood near the pool, side by side. The two sisters were doing their best to look lonely.

"Please?"

Tinker's lower lip pushed out, a not kindly expression forming on his face. He looked at Chicken who was unsuccessfully suppressing a smile.

"Fair Prince, me'thinks thee would be most safe. Protect thee we will."

He sighed and sank a little lower in the water. "O.K., kids. Jump in."

Raft's clothes fluttered down into a heap. Her head burst to the surface in front of him. "I am no child either."

R-Bar turned away and peeled off her blouse. Crusted

blood coated her shoulder and side.

"Mess, mess, mess," said Raft, moving toward the deeper, further away parts of the pool. She wanted to see what the others were doing.

R-Bar leaped into the water. She lightly brushed past his side and popped to the surface, gurgling happily. "Hum, hum, hum."

Chicken pushed him to a shallower area and tickled his back with her fingernails. "Here there be scrubbing cloth. Would my back do?"

He turned around. "Sure. Ready?"

"In . . . deed, My Lord."

As he worked, he saw their clothes gathered up and carried away. He wondered how long it would be before they got them back again.

And time drifted away.

Chicken was leaning back against him. He was thinking about giving her a little pinch, here and there, when R-Bar came up to them.

"Princess," she asked shyly. "May he scrub my back? Please?"

"My Lord, this mooning witch does dearly a'scrubbing need. Ugly mess does not remove from mere soaking alone. Will thee so do?"

Tinker sighed softly and blew warm breath into Chicken's ear.

"O. K. Where'd that scrubber get to?"

R-Bar's hand shot above the surface of the water. "I have one."

Chicken reached back and tickled him and said to the witch. "You do in good hands be."

She started across the pool.

"Turn around grungy. You sure that you are all right?"

R-Bar turned, gurgling happily back over her shoulder at him. "It was a gift from Palos."

"Rough way to get a gift."

R-Bar spun back around, stood taller, and pointed. "There was no damage. See?" On the left pectoral were two small blue marks. She arched her back, threw her shoulder's back, and grinned. "Pretty nice, aren't they?"

"Turn around, shorty. I came to scrub your back not to admire your bod." He squeezed a torrent of water on top of her head. "Your hair needs washing too."

Snarling, she turned her back to him. And decided that he wasn't very nice after all.

"Maybe if I had a whip," mumbled Tinker to himself, gently washing her back, the soft current in the pool carrying away the spreading stain.

R-Bar rolled her shoulders forward. But, she decided, he was very gentle. And calming.

Off to one side, far across the pool the water erupted in loud splashing. R-Bar and Tinker both snapped their heads in that direction. Someone was tumbling through the air to crash heavily on their back, sending a great wave in all directions.

"Now what?" Tinker went back to work. "Don't wiggle." He lifted her left arm and began washing her side.

"It tickles." She wiggled. Just a little.

Raft's head popped to the surface in front of her sister. "Rak, rak, rak, rak, rak!" she snapped, looking very, very unhappy.

"Now what's going on?" asked Tinker, letting go of R-Bar's arm.

"Your, hum, Smoke grabbed me and threw me away."

"She grabbed you? How?" R-Bar wasn't ready to believe that.

She moves slow in water, MindMate.

Tinker smiled. "What were you doing over there?"

Raft pouted. "I was going to help."

"Do what?"

"Scrub the wings."

"Wings?" R-Bar frowned at Raft.

"Sister, that one, Fair Morn, has wings."

R-Bar turned to look at Tinker.

"Right," he said. "She is just a big moth."

R-Bar backed away, bumping into her sister. "Cho . . . Chosen One . . ." She thrust her arms in front of herself, warding him off. "Do . . . don't. Please?" And crouched low in the water.

He frowned at her, then at her sister. "Now what?"

"Move," snarled R-Bar, pushing at Raft. "Move, move!"

"You guys wanna tell me what's going on? This time." He sank down until the water lapped under his chin. "Please?"

"Don't touch me," snapped R-Bar. "Don't touch us." She backed further away.

"O.K., O.K. I won't. Promise." His hand thrust toward the sky. "Scout's honor. Now tell me what the problem is."

"I do not want to be made into a moth," stated R-Bar her eyes fastened on his. Unwavering. Dark. Watching carefully. She couldn't use magic here to defend herself, not in Doth Lamex. And wondered what kind of honor a scout had.

Tinker laughed.

"Ugly sense of humor," hissed Raft. "What's a scout?"

"Ladies," said Tinker. "I can't do that, turn you guys into moths. I didn't do that. That was the way that she came equipped."

They both frowned darkly at him. He had called them Ladies. Again.

He started to back away from them. "O. K., so don't believe me. Just go ask them." He stood and waved them away, his arms flailing wildly. "Go on. Go. **SHOO!**" Then he fell backward and closed his eyes. And floated.

The sisters started for the wildly splashing mob across the pool.

Both wondered how it could be true, even if Fair Morn had said so, back in Bahn Duhr Tohr.

Dawla of Snark's Fen. A Rather Nice Day.

Turintor and her ever silent companion were strolling casually, casually for witches, down one of the narrow streets of this small village. Nodding now and then as a witch or warlock of one of the various witch clans passed them headed the other way.

The pair stopped to read a poster plastered to a rock wall.

"Perhaps?"

Her companion shrugged.

"A small Foregather of two days on Quata."

Her companion waggled one hand.

"They list a booth specializing in Seek Spells."

Her companion nodded.

With a soft sigh of black they were gone.

Bahn Duhr Tohr. The Royal City. Mid-Morning. Court Business In Session.

Macabre, Gyre, Goose, and Chen appeared in the great courtyard. The servants, now accustomed to the sudden appearances of new guests of the Queen and the King, escorted them to the quarters of The Queen's Advisors.

The Queen was, at the moment in the Royal Hall, involved in resolving the issue between three contenting Princes as to which spot should be whose camp. Everyone, of course, thought that the other's spot had greater status. She eventually settled the argument and sent them on their way.

Macabre had just begun to explain to Ripple why they were here in Bahn Duhr Tohr when the ceiling erupted.

Leaves, twigs, limbs, pieces of vines, flowers, a battered figure, and a strange creature with wings tumbled into the room. The winged beast soared up, crashed into the ceiling, and thumped to the floor where it lay twitching violently. And emptied the contents of its stomach.

"Bloody hell," cried Goose, leaping to one side.

Ripple jumped into the tangle, throwing tree limbs and branches in all directions, and gently touched the crumpled form. The woman wore the tatters of some black garb. Firmly clenched in her teeth was strange rod with the hand of something holding one end.

"Rotak, let it go. It is me! Ripple."

One eye opened to a pain filled slit. The jaws relaxed. The rod fell into Ripple's hand.

"I . . . ," said Rotak.

"Gyre," commanded Macabre. "MedSection." Gyre and Rotak disappeared.

Ripple surged toward him, her finger's curling. Vague formed around her.

"Do not do anything. Or you will surely die, Madame." Macabre held an ugly weapon in each hand. He stood calmly, waiting for her reaction.

Ripple saw no fear in those watching eyes, nor any indication that what he said was not true.

"Where is my sister?" she demanded.

"On my ship. She needed medical care, instantly. If I had not acted as I did, she would never have reached the end of her sentence."

Gyre appeared and stated, "Very bad, inside and outside."

"How bad?" Macabre kept his full attention on Ripple.

"Med Section was unsure."

"How unsure?"

"In four hours, twenty-two minutes, thirty-two seconds, it will know whether she will survive. There are many, many damaged parts."

Gyre stopped speaking, listened, and continued. "Her mind is clear. First good sign."

"Praps," interrupted Goose. "This mess we might a'cleanin' be?"

Ripple unbent and waved one hand. Everything was

gone. Except for the strange rod and a large stain on the floor. "Husband, did you recognize any of that?"

"No," said Hanred. "Where ever she had been, it was not one of the many places I've seen." He stepped next to Ripple and slipped an arm around her shoulders. "I don't remember Rotak from The Aunt's place."

"She was not there. So, we have no way of knowing where she had been, or what she was doing there."

Macabre slipped his weapons into their holsters, and stated, "MedSection is beyond compare. If she can be repaired, it will be done. For a short time we must wait."

Ripple waved them toward a number of chairs. "Then, wait we will. And while we do, start over. Tell us why you have come here? And what is this thing you call ship?"

Macabre did.

"They are gone," said Ripple.

Macabre told her of his trip to Tinker's world and why they had come to Bahn Duhr Tohr.

Gyre explained the disturbances they had seen.

And then Macabre explained Gyreship, Gyre, and Med Section.

Hanred watched them carefully. He was fully accustomed to the oft times strange behavior, calm and very agitated, of Ripple's clan and sisters and the general witch behavior, but he was very uneasy with this large, heavyset man whose eyes twinkled so happily and whose presence emitted such murderous intent.

Ripple had been carefully, with small movements and whispered words, weaving a powerful protection spell around her husband and herself.

Finally she felt ready.

"Here and there, we, my sisters and I, have heard of The Destroyer. Slight rumors, no more, for no one had ever witnessed what had transpired. Only unbelievable tales of travel to a place erased from the surface of the soil. Or an elseplace no longer there. You are The Destroyer?"

Macabre smiled at her, patted his stomach, and said, "I am." He had just turned on a protective field.

Chen placed a hand on one of Goose's arms. She felt the building tension in the room. So did Goose. He acted first.

"Dark Advisor, we must our Lord Tinker find. Be there no manner pon which you might call for seekin' news. Tis problem most vexin' for this warrior simple."

Lightning crackled overhead.

All heads jerked up.

A small scroll tumbled into Ripple's lap.

She nodded. "Prince Goose, you seem to be favored." Untying the ribbon, she quickly read the message.

Hanred peered over her shoulder, but he couldn't see anything. Just blank surface. "Very interesting," he said.

"The Aunts tell me of many finds that suggest a great vileness which may explain what happened to Rotak. They also tell me that your Lord and his ladies and two of my sisters are resting on Doth Lamex, an elseplace of relaxation and pleasant surroundings."

Hanred grinned.

Ripple said to him, "When we are done."

Macabre flicked his eyes at Gyre who made the most imperceptible of nods. Ship library began the search for information about that world. He said, "We would normally leave right away but your sister cannot. Do you think we might stay here, somewhere? Or should we return to Ship?"

"The palace has many rooms," said Hanred. "The suite where Tinker and his group resided is open." He smiled at Goose. "And I feel certain that the Prince would wish to speak with his brother, The King, while we wait."

"Jolly good." Goose stood. "Whither go we?"

Ripple waved one hand. And send them to the appropriate places. And then busied herself with other, more arcane matters. For some time.

And much later, Hanred sat sprawling on the very large, very long couch trying to read. He had dragged another dusty tome from the other room and was carefully reading, or trying to read, something. The large volume rested on his stomach.

Ripple was more or less on his lap, legs propped on the arm of the couch. He was using that same arm of the couch as a backrest. Her ankles were just touching his shoulder. She was peering over the upper edge of the book.

Hanred pulled his lips one way, then the other. And then gave up trying to read. "Dusky Delight, what is it?"

"I am deeply bothered, Husband."

"A strange condition for you." He began to ease the book to the floor."What would dare bother you?" The book thumped heavily on the floor and belched a cloud of dust.

"I spoke with The Aunts. Asked them to notify my sisters that they were to leave the things they are finding with us."

Hanred held her hands in his. "And what manner of things are they bringing? You face speaks volumes to me, of something."

"Evil," hissed Ripple. "A great evil." She slipped her hands free and pulling her legs down, leaned forward and slipped her arms around him.

"Ripple, Witch of Witches, you are scaring me. I have never felt this before."

"Husband, my own life and love, there are things that even the witch dreads." Her arms tightened, her face pressed against his chest. "And I am bringing it home."

She sat up and looked deep into his eyes, tears glistening. "I want you to go away. Far, far away. I shall send Willawa and her King to the furthest reaches of the kingdom. You can travel in disguises."

A multi-limbed dar-bush entangled her in its sucker-lined tentacles and pinned her in place. **"WIFE! NO!"**

Hanred smiled at her. "And I mean it." He kissed the tears from her cheeks. "If anyone saw those tears, your nasty reputation would be soiled forever."

He nodded toward a doorway. "There are many volumes in there filled with arcane knowledge and dark secrets. What do we need?"

Ripple's lips caressed his. Then she told him, in the faintest of faint whispers.

The blood drained from his face, he tried to speak.

She grabbed his shoulders and shook him violently. "Husband?"

Hanred blinked, inhaled deeply, and breathed out. "I am all right." He whipped his arms around her and held her tight. "Your clan does continually manage to amaze me, though."

Another Suite of Rooms.

"I couldn't hear what she told him," said Gyre.

Macabre looked up. "This place probably doesn't know about doughnuts. What would frighten her?"

"What is disturbing so much? I could go up and bring some down?"

Macabre smiled. Gyre returned to ship.

Goose slumped, relaxed, in his chair.

Chen sat on the couch, her legs tucked under, deep in thought.

Goose nodded at Macabre. "There do be more in this place than do the eye see."

"That Ripple is a devious one. We may need a special weapon."

Gyre reappeared, holding a large tray covered with several layers of doughnuts. "What kind?"

Macabre beamed at her. "I'll take one of those." He grabbed his choice and took a big bite.

As Macabre chewed thoughtfully, Gyre offered the tray

to Goose.

"Tight field," said Macabre, quickly swallowing the last bite. He leaned forward and selected one covered in powered sugar. The tray sat on a low table between them.

Gyre offered around coffee, a food stuff she had copied from Tinker's world.

Brushing sugar from his mouth, Macabre added, "Hand held." And smiled warmly at Gyre.

Goose stared at Macabre.

Chen walked over and nudged him to keep him from staring.

Gyre handed Macabre a jelly-filled doughnut.

"Thought activated," he said.

On ship, Design Section turned on. Manufacturing activated Test Bay. Tool Bots warmed up and units were rearranged. Weapon construction began. It would take time. This design, the new design, was very compact.

"May we enter?" asked a voice.

"Our pleasure," answered Goose rising to his feet.

Ripple and Hanred appeared.

"The Queen and her King are free of their Royal Duties, Prince. He is most anxious to see you and your Lady Chen."

"Go visit," said Macabre, offering the tray to Ripple and Hanred.

"Doughnut? A confection from Tinker's world."

Hanred took one and then a careful bite.

Ripple hesitated.

"Delightful." Hanred picked up another and handed it to Ripple.

She took a tentative nibble, and watched her husband for signs of adverse reaction.

"Would you release the preparation scroll to the Royal Kitchen?" asked Hanred. "This is a treat fit for a Queen."

"We will fetch it down the next time we visit Ship," said Macabre.

Gyre nodded. The message was clear. She would bring down Rotak, the doughnut recipe, and the new weapon, if it was finished.

On ship more and more sections were activated. The latest acquisition had some unique thoughts. The work space was enlarged.

"Prince?" Ripple waved the door open. "Lady?"

Goose snatched a doughnut in passing.

Chen took his free hand.

They followed Ripple and Hanred down the hall to the Royal Quarters.

It was a short walk.

Doth Lamex. Warm, Pleasant Afternoon.

My Lord?

Tinker opened his eyes, momentarily confused, floating on his back. He had been dreaming of sleeping in the warm sun at home, on the thick, comfortable grass of the back field in northeastern Oregon. He sank. Up to his neck.

Huh? What?

Thee do them greatly frighten.

Who?

The witchy pair.

Princess, I didn't do anything. They misunderstood.

Sweet Prince, most gentle be. T'ween thee and great Smoke, these witches be most nervous. We did be'speak in soothing ways and even now they thee do approach. One protecting t'other. Be kind, my love.

Tinker felt their minds turning away, giving him privacy. He stood up and saw R-Bar and Raft approaching carefully. Raft was well behind her sister, watching intently.

"Chosen One?" It was a tentative question. It was soft. R-Bar was ready to bolt.

"What happened to Tink, short stuff?" He smiled at her

and sank up to his chin again.

R-Bar came closer. "Your Queen explained." She exhaled loudly, face flushing slightly. "This is very hard."

"Com'mer Kid." He reached out and gently took one of her hands and pulled her close. "Don't look so serious. It puts wrinkles in your face."

R-Bar nodded, a nervous nod.

Gently he brushed the hair back from her forehead. "I really am just a fairly normal person." He grinned. "Considering everything. Do you know what the problem really is?"

"No," said R-Bar in a little voice, still very, very cautious.

"Legends. It is all that stuff about legends. You have been hearing wild stories and believing them. I suspect that they are fairly over-exaggerated." He slipped one arm around her neck. "You and Raft are the witches, not us. You two can cast spells, not us. Well, except for Messenger. Although maybe not. We don't really know what it is that she does. Neither does anyone else that we have met."

R-Bar slid her arms around him, pressed her cheek against his chest. She mumbled softly, "Tink, can we still be friends? Please?"

He kissed her hair. "Sure, kid. Why not?"

She leaned back and looked at him, her eyes glistening wetly. And whispered harshly, "Because witches do not have friends. The strongest might. But it is a rare thing. They do not feel that need."

"I have never had a witch for a friend. We could try it. Shall we?"

R-Bar grinned broadly. "Let's." She hung on.

"O. K." He looked over her head at Raft, still staying well away.

"Tink," whispered R-Bar. "I will tell you my secret."

"What?" he whispered back.

"I am the only one."

"One, what?"

"That feels lonely. None of my sisters do. Witches are self contained, self-assured. Only their mate-for-life is allowed in." Her expression saddened. "Except for me, the runt."

He bent forward and kissed her gently, then said softly as he held her. "You are really a large person in a short body." Then he laughed. "And not all that short, actually. Messenger is just a few inches taller. Maybe less. You two could almost be sisters."

R-Bar laughed. And quickly coughed to hide it.

Raft pushed across the pool to visit with Fair Morn who was flailing the water with her wings. And wondered about her sister. Witches didn't laugh. Especially in public.

R-Bar ducked under the water and surged upward, wrapping her arms around his neck, her legs around his waist.

He lurched backward. "Watch it."

"Hum, hum, hum!" she sang.

"If we fall over, we will drown."

"Tink, you are mine."

"No, I am not."

R-Bar stared at him. "But you just said you were."

"Wrong thought, Shorty."

She gurgled deep in her throat and slipped down, dragging him over, forming an air bubble around their heads as they settled to the bottom of the pool.

Bahn Duhr Tohr. The Royal City.

Time passed slowly on Bahn Duhr Tohr.

For Macabre .

Goose and Chen enjoyed visiting with Willawa and Toucan.

The passage of time had little meaning for Gyre except as a reference point to mark events.

Hanred spent the days getting dusty, calling Ripple to

read this or that passage, as he searched for just the correct spell incantation.

Ranna passed through for a short visit, leaving the two items she had. She had flirted outrageously with Hanred, who had been standing by a table. She had leered over his shoulder as he tried to study, and had managed to get his shirt half off before Ripple slammed a heavy, and dusty, tome against her backside. Hissing elder sister threats, Ranna departed.

Ripple emptied one room of all furnishings and placed the things in the center of the floor. Then she spent the following day setting watches and guardians all around, over, and under, steadily building a container to hold the creature that she feared.

"Husband, you are dustier than your books."

He laughed, white teeth flashing, a dust coated chimney sweep librarian.

"Before you study any more, allow me to clean everything."

Hanred stepped close and carefully began to leave dusty hand-prints on the back of her clothes. "A very nice thought for as dark a witch as there is. I do believe that collection oozes dust. I think it has something to do with the strength of the ideas contained therein. Or something." He stepped back, cocked his head to one side. "A nice pattern, don't you think?"

"Erotic."

"Of course." His hand slipped over her hip. "I am famished."

"Bath first," said Ripple, bringing in a meal and listening to the low splash from their tub.

"LOOK AT THE OPEN PAGES!" called Hanred.

Ripple stared down at the large volume lying open on the table.

The multi-colored script glowed, the border decoration writhed, pulsating to the beat of an alien heart.

She began to read, testing, tasting the instructions. And faded into the magic.

Two hands slipped around her rib cage, a body pressed against her back. "Darkest Delight, why so long? I am washed and dried. The food is cold."

"I was deep inside this spell. It feels correct. After we satisfy our appetites, we will begin."

In the main room, they sat down to their meal. It was a new meal.

Rekel popped in, yanked a chair over, and joined them.

"This is for you," she said through a mouth full of food, handing a package to Ripple, hitching her chair closer to Hanred, slipping one hand onto his thigh while she ate with the other.

Hanred looked across the table at Ripple who gave him a slow wink.

Rekel was looking in one of the serving containers and complimenting Ripple upon her choice of foods.

Hanred spun in his chair, and leaned toward Rekel, staring into her eyes. He reached over and slid his hand across her mid-section, caressing her. Her eyes flew wide. She was gone.

Ripple held Hanred in place. "Nicely done, lecherous mate."

"Speaking of which." He stood. "I have been frolicking with only those volumes for days."

"Only four," said Ripple. "I think you are drooling."

Gyre appeared.

"Wife, I feel as if we are in the middle of one of the town squares."

"Med Section reports that your sister will live. Repairs are proceeding. Arm, ribs, pelvis, leg are knitting. Foreign enzymes are being flushed away."

Gyre disappeared.

"Good news," said Hanred, standing behind her and

gently kneading the muscles at the base of Ripple's neck. "I think."

She tilted her head back against him. "A day for it. Are you planning on molesting me?"

He grinned. "Perhaps. A passing thought."

"Please do."

Space. 47.24.99.66. QBD. In Ship's Notation.

"The damaged witch is recovering."

"Good. The sooner we can send her down, the sooner we can leave."

They stood in one of the large areas on ship. Macabre had been checking the new weapon and making suggestions upon the design.

Down below, Goose, Chen, Willawa, and Toucan were on a state visit to a near-by, but minor kingdom.

Doth Lamex. Pleasant Morning.

Tinker's eyes popped open. He couldn't see anything. Something smooth covered his face. He pushed up with his left hand, his right arm was held down.

Fair Morn mumbled into his right ear and shifted her weight. She was sleeping mostly face down using his arm and shoulder for a pillow. It was her left wings that were covering his face.

An arm snaked around his waist from the other side and pressed down as she sat up and beamed happily at him. "Hayou, Tink." The wing tent covered her as well.

Tinker rolled his eyes at her. "Shhhhhhh. I like it quiet in the morning, not boisterous good cheer."

R-Bar ran her hand up and down his chest and whispered. "What do you want to do today?"

The wings swung away as Fair Morn rolled onto her side. "Let's have breakfast."

Smoke leaned over the witch mashing her against him.

"I like that idea."

"OOOF."

"Me'thinks t'were one aye vote," said Chicken, standing up.

"It was not. I was, I am, being crushed."

"Heavy weighs the head that wears the crown, My Lord."

"It is my stomach that is being weighed upon."

Chicken bent down and peered at him. She had to brush aside R-Bar's hair to see his face. "Fair Bright Morn, Sweet Our Prince."

"It was. Off, off, off!" He pushed at Smoke and R-Bar.

R-Bar gurgled. "You are nice and warm comfortable."

"Merde," mumbled Tinker.

"Fair foul," said Chicken tickling the end of his nose.

"It is going to get worse if you guys don't get off."

Fair Morn stood and began to fold and fold and fold her wings.

Messenger settled next to Chicken and looked at Smoke. "Morning, mom. What are you doing to them, MyTinker?"

"Nothing."

"Oh." She smiled at Chicken. "Looks like something to me."

Tinker collapsed. "I quit."

"I am hungry," said Fair Morn. "Let's order breakfast."

"What manner of delight this morn?" asked Chicken.

"Lots," answered Smoke, sitting back. She tapped the witch on the shoulder. "Clothes."

R-Bar sat up and waved one hand. They were all dressed.

"So, order the food, before those two carnivores attack someone," said Tinker.

"I am not a carnivore," said Fair Morn, heading for the table covered with breakfast.

"I am." Smoke leaped up and followed her.

Soon they were all seated around the table, sampling the new variety of tastes and textures.

"Who pays for all this?" Tinker waved his arm, indicating everything in Doth Lamex.

"Everyone," said R-Bar. "As we can. I donated a spell the last time."

Messenger refilled Tinker's cup. "What shall we do today?"

"Leave."

"One?" Fair Morn looked over her cup at him, dragging one of the serving dishes closer with her other hand.

"I think that we have had enough R and R. Let's go find Ramp and Hard, J. C., and Mirf."

"Do we have to?" R-Bar's lower lip pushed out. "And when did we eat R and R?"

"Yep. It is why we left home. So, as soon as we are done, let's check our gear, thank our host, and be on our way." He winked at the witch. "We can always come back, can't we?"

She nodded. "Yes, we can." And nodded at Smoke.

"Rest and relaxation," said Smoke.

"Then off we go. Right?" said Tinker.

"Right."

"Finish your breakfast, shorty."

"Right, Tink."

"Where's Raft?"

R-Bar looked sideways at him. "Gone. She left during the party, We are traveling too slow for her."

They finished and then waited for Fair Morn to finish eating the rest of something. Everything. While she was doing that, Smoke brought the packs over and the weapons.

Tinker took his weaponkin from the corner and swung it onto its place.

Fair Morn dabbed at her lips with her napkin. "I am ready."

"Where are we going?" asked Messenger.

"Bahn Duhr Tohr," replied R-Bar, leading them down the correct path, to the main gate, and twisted them away.

Bahn Duhr Tohr. The Royal City. Afternoon.

Gyre and Macabre knocked on the door to the Royal Advisors suite.

Hanred opened it. He was very dusty, smudged and stained.

"Doing a little research." He ushered them inside.

"It is nice to have people knock first," Ripple said. She was standing staring at a large table heaped with ingredients. The stuff surrounded an ancient volume that was lying open. Another volume was sitting next to it, closed. She glanced up, back to the open pages, then back up again and stated, "Go away, we are busy!" She began to study the page again.

Macabre nodded. Once.

Gyre said. "Your sister is repaired." And vanished.

"What?" hissed Ripple, looking up.

Gyre reappeared, a woman of medium height, an easy smile on her face, standing next to her.

"ROTAK!"

"Hayou, Ripple. You look well. Dusty, mauled, but well."

"Ahem," said Hanred.

"This is Hanred," said Ripple, looking down again, realizing now that she had dusty patches on her clothes. "He is the one that mauls."

"We are leaving," said Macabre.

They did.

"I didn't have a chance to gift them," said Rotak.

"Gift? You would gift The Destroyer?" Ripple looked askance at her older sister.

"Him?" Rotak shrugged. "I am alive, not destroyed. I owe a gift for such a gift, do I not?"

"Yes," said Ripple, conceding the point unwillingly.

"Come. Sit. Tell me what happened."

Rotak told of receiving the call on the way world. She was being taught a story that she had heard of a magician who was being stalked by a nameless thing of many parts. Later, in a shop in the village of Nowise, she had persuaded the shop keeper to show her the relic when an enfolding had swallowed everything. She had hurtled a detar response to escape. Then she was only aware of reaching for the key as death took her far.

"Almost, sister, almost," said Ripple. "The Destroyer snatched you from us saying you would be repaired. His ba'tha took you. What did they do?"

"I vaguely remember being swallowed by swarming things of many joints. Then of sleeping, deep dreamless sleep. Now I am here, stiff in many places. New feeling in many places. But whole." She unwound the garment and stared at the red lines in patches and clusters on her body.

"Looks pretty good, discounting the scars," mumbled Rotak as she looked up at Hanred. "What do you think, pretty?"

"I think that you are fortunate. Pretty."

"Hum, hum." Rotak refolded her garb. "Where is the relic?"

"In a guarded room. With others."

"You have more?"

Ripple explained the scattering of the clan and what she had been hearing from The Aunts.

The air ripped open.

Bodies rained down.

A black figure landed lightly on her feet. "Hayou, Ripple," she called gaily. She spun and stared. "ROTAK! What happened to you?"

"A long story, child. For later."

R-Bar drew herself up. "I am no child."

"Hum, hum, hum, hum. So I can see. Well grown, in

many ways."

"These are my friends. John Tinker, Princess Chicken, Smoke, Messenger, Fair Morn."

Rotak gasped. "Friends?" And gurgled.

Ripple made soothing noises and said to Rotak, "She has always been a little different. You were away too much to notice."

"What are we doing here?" asked Tinker, looking around the room.

"Unloading," replied R-Bar, handing the objects to Ripple. "We are not staying long, just passing through."

The little witch danced around Ripple and kissed Hanred on the cheek. "Well journey," she sang gaily And twisted out. Taking her group with her.

Rotak blinked. "Ripple?"

"I can not say as I do not know." She looked at Hanred. "Do you?"

Hanred smiled. "Not I. But she was bubbling much more than normal. I would say she is having a very good time, a very good time."

"Hum, hum, hum."

Hanred slipped his arm around Ripple's shoulders. "Makes me rather uneasy." And hugged her.

"What?"

"A happy witch. Especially one that leaves things like that behind."

Ripple slipped free and headed for the guarded room. "These belong in there with the others."

She pointed at the open book. "Rotak, see what you think. Hanred will explain. This will take some time." She unlocked the door and shut it behind her.

Rotak walked over and began to read the pages. A small puff of green smoke floated up. She jumped back.

"Didn't do that before," said Hanred. "Did you say something?"

"No."

"Um. That is a strange one. Ripple thinks it will hold. What do you see?" He edged away.

Rotak leaned forward and took another look, a cautious look, a wary look. "Hum. Hum, hum! Subtle. Internally folded. Nine-ways twisted." She stepped back, turned and looked at Hanred, her eyes half-lidded, her expression dark. He took an involuntary step backward.

"Of all the sisters, Ripple was the blackest, Ripple was the most adept." Behind Rotak another puff of smoke headed for the ceiling.

She hissed. "Rangle."

A door thumped.

"Who is rangle? Husband, did you start?"

Green smoke was seeping from both of the open pages. Small fingers were poking out, trying to free themselves from the closed volume.

"No. It all just started when she took a look."

Ripple quickly walked around the table and peered down at the open pages, striking the busy fingers with a purple wand. "Hum, hum, hum. This one is a self-starter. You two will assist me. Husband, on my right. Sister, on my left."

She turned her head and smiled at Hanred. "You hand me the ingredients when I ask for them, as I name them."

To her sister she said. "You sing the under. See the marks?"

Rotak nodded.

Ripple began.

From the locked room they heard things thudding against the door, trying to escape, trying to reach them.

Fringloe's Tar. Late Afternoon.

Many hands thrust him from the back of the crowd to the front.

"I am Will Begood," he said.

"Hello, Will," said Ramp from the depths of her hood.

"Magician," replied Will Begood.

"I would like to talk with you. Somewhere else."

Will indicated the door with his chin. "Outside. My hom."

Mirf crowded on his heels as they stepped outside, grabbing one of his arms in a firm grip, and said, indicating Mountain, "Don't worry about him, he is with us."

Mountain hung his cudgel on his belt. And glared down at Mirf. "BY DUMPF, you are a trouble maker." He patted the timbers back into place, a crumpled patch of splintered wood.

"Gimble," mumbled Mirf.

"Maybe they could use a skylight? Let in lots of light." suggested J. C.

Ramp slipped an arm through Will's free arm. "Which way, Will. The town has changed since I was last here." They started walking down the street.

Hard tripped over some small thing, took a hop, a skip, and ambled alongside J. C.

"Klutzy as ever," mumbled Mirf, staring around Will at Ramp.

"Rampeleh, is this person safe?"

"Quite."

Mirf released Will, who waggled his arm, restoring the circulation in it. Mirf waited for J. C. and Hard to catch up with her, then walked with them. She rolled her eyes at Hard who had just dodged a tall post rising next to one of the buildings they were passing.

She nudged J. C. "So, big hunk, what do you think?"

"Certainly glad Mountain was with us. He is pretty handy to have a around."

"Right-o-rooney. Never know when you might need a building cracked open."

J. C. looked at her, waggled his head, and grinned. "Right-o-rooney?"

"So, do I make fun of the way you speak, bubeleh?"

J. C. ignored the question and took a careful look at their surroundings. "I wonder if they have a drinking fountain around, a large drinking fountain?"

"Ha. Ha."

"You thirsty?" asked Hard, looking from Mirf to J. C.

"I'll tell you later," said J. C.

"What?"

"Boychick," hissed Mirf. "Don't start with the endless questions?"

"Huh?" said Hard.

"Why?" asked J. C.

"**RAZ BAZ!**" snarled Mirf.

"Where?" asked Mountain, snatching his great club from his belt.

"Meshuggeners, one and all," grumbled Mirf. "It is my fate. I am doomed. Always meshuggeners. Always."

J. C. leaned sideways and whispered in her ear. "Raz baz."

Mirf's eyes rolled toward the sky. "Why me?"

"Cause you are a luscious morsel, said the Papa Bear," replied J. C., still whispering.

"I think that there must be something in the water in your elseplace, cute stuff." She jabbed a thumb toward Hard. "I thought that it was just him. Now it's you."

J. C. panted heavily. "It is just walking in the moonlight with you, cute stuff."

Mirf slipped her arm through one of J. C.'s. "You are all right. But. It is late afternoon."

He patted her hand. "You too. For a Chief Inspector. Shhhhh, we're there. So what?"

Will unlocked the door and pulled it open, waving Ramp inside.

Hard followed.

Mirf grunted and said to J .C., "Big hunk, while I take it

as a compliment, auf miene tokkes."

"What?"

"Stop fondling my backside."

"Mirf, I only have two hands." He waggled the fingers of his free hand at her and looked back and down over her shoulder. "Don't move. Just stand very still, very, very still." Releasing her hand, he stepped back.

Mirf hissed softly through her teeth.

"It looks like a large slug of some sort." J. C. batted it off.

It didn't come off.

"Don't move Mirf." He slapped the thing hard.

It wobbled.

Just a little.

Mirf twisted her head around and tried to see. "What's happening?"

"It doesn't seem to want to come off. Guess you'll just have to take your trousers off."

Mountain leaned over and peered at the slug. "BY DUMPF, that is ugly."

He mashed it between his thumb and forefinger. A soft pop/squish. And wiped his hand on his pant leg. He turned and dropped to the pavement with a dull thud and leaned back against the house wall. "I will sit out here."

Mirf and J. C. went inside.

"Turn around, to the right. Stop." She did.

J. C. cocked his head to one side and stared at her.

"J. C.?"

"Pretty nice." He grinned as she frowned. "OH, and that thing's head or mouth is still attached." Crouching down he poked at it with one finger. "I'd say that it was chewing through the material."

He took a knife from his pocket, opened it, and worked the body part loose. "O.K., babe, now you can sit again. Pretty strange wildlife they have around here."

Voices came from the next room. They followed the sound. Ramp, Will, and Hard sat around a large table, Ramp and Will in deep, animated conversation.

Mirf and J. C. sat on the large bench against one wall. He swung an arm around her shoulders and slumped a little.

"What are you doing?"

"Just being friendly."

She jabbed him not too lightly in the ribs with an elbow. "When I want friendly, I'll ask."

J. C. took his arm back, looked at her, puffed out his cheeks, rolled his eyes, and stuck out his tongue, and then said, "That is an editorial comment."

"So, be friendly. A little." She grinned.

He smiled. And slipped his arm back. "That's better, Boss."

"**BY DUMPF!**" Mountain's bellow rattled dishes on the shelves.

"**DUMPF, DUMPF, DUMPF, DUMPF!**"

Mirf and J. C. ran outside, banging the outer door back against the wall.

Mountain was stomping one leg up and down, systematically tromping upon something. His foot slipped sideways in the gelatinous mess.

"There," he announced with a final stomp. "A veritable army litching up the road. They make little grunting noises." He held two fingers close together and peered through the slit at Mirf and J. C. "**DAR DUMPFING** things."

Will, Ramp and Hard joined them on the street.

For reasons having more to do with the urge not to get involved than politeness, no lights came on, no neighbors came outside to see what all the commotion was about.

"What is it," asked Ramp.

Mountain explained. Then J. C. added to the story.

Will became very agitated, closed the door, opened it, urged them inside, changed his mind, slammed the door, and pointed toward a small side street.

Ramp touched his shoulder and stilled his panic. "We will leave now. It will be best." She gently led him inside the house and returned. "Mirf, can you find us a node? Quickly?"

Mirf snapped her head back and forth. She pointed at the same small side street that Will had indicated. "In there, not far. I can smell it."

She tapped the side of her nose. "A little hob-goblin comes in handy."

They hurried to the intersection and down the narrow, twisting lane. It wasn't a run, just a very fast walk.

"**HUMPF!**" Mountain didn't like this place at all.

"Bingo." Mirf pointed to an old foundation filled with black water. It appeared to be a bottomless pit surrounded by slime coated walls. Soft sucking noises, faint chittering, the glitter of tiny eyes watching them.

"You have got to be kidding." J. C. peered over the edge, carefully not touching anything.

"Really nasty looking." Hard stared at the water.

"Mirf?" asked Ramp.

"JUMP," announced Mirf, yanking J. C. with her, her fingers tightly clenching his belt.

They disappeared.

No splash.

No sound.

Gone.

"Gulp," gulped Hard. His fingers circled one of Ramp's wrists in as tight a grip as he could make. They jumped.

"**BY DUMPF!**" The great shape hurtled after them.

Pled Sweider. Late Afternoon. Early Evening.

"UFDA!" cried J. C. as they stumbled and crashed into the trash can in the city park.

Somehow, he wound up more or less on the bottom, covered with Mirf and gaily colored refuse.

"Klutz kopf," snarled Mirf, creating a new term, sitting up and scattering the debris over an even wider area.

"I do believe, My Dear," said the very proper British Gentleman, giving her a hard shove to the side. She had been sitting on his stomach. "That you grabbed me by the belt."

"Bizzle." Mirf stood and tossed the trash can into the reflecting pond.

J. C. sat up, leaned forward, and leered at her. "If you will bend down, luscious money tender, I'll lick the condiment from your forehead. Food dappled foreheads are sooooo sexy. Heh, heh, heh, heh." He was breathing heavily.

Mirf bent over and lifted him to his feet. Then used a sleeve, one of his, to wipe her forehead. "Let's get out of here, heavy breath."

They hurried down a neatly groomed path. Park guardians hurried past, scurrying toward the shambles scattered over a rather wide area.

"A little faster," urged Mirf, watching the park guardians over her shoulder.

They walked, very, very fast, out of the park and around the first corner they came to.

Mirf was almost dragging J. C.

On all sides of the park, tall buildings in various sizes and shapes, pointed toward the pink-tinged sky.

"Where are we?"

"This, boychick, is Pled Sweider. And before you should ask, the klutz , the magician, and the giant went elsewhere. And before you should also esk, I don't know where, either. Hookay?" She released his wrist.

"Right-o-rooney," beamed J. C., brushing loose a few stray decorations whose stains and food traces had stuck to his clothes. He licked at a smear on the back of his hand. "Not bad, not bad at all. Where we going, Chief?"

"Rather than putz around, we will just step into the local office, get some gelt, and check into a nice place. O.K. by you?"

"Your humble servant," said the very proper English Gentleman.

So, that is what they did.

Mirf received a large chunk of change from the Monetary Control Office 62-PS-S09-Al-1L-4900862, MTPS. The gold disc she carried and waved as she entered the office brought everyone to their feet, rigidly standing at attention, anxious to be of service, carefully not staring too pointedly at her clothes.

"My, my, my," chortled J. C. once they were back outside on the sidewalk again and headed somewhere.

Mirf was leading.

"My, my, my, yourself," she mumbled. Two blocks later, she asked. "So, what's my, my, my?"

"You are." J. C. laughed. "Glad I work for you."

Mirf whirled around, grabbed him by the neck of his shirt and pulled him forward and over until their noses were touching. "Meshuggener, you do not work **FOR** me. You are working **WITH** me. A free agent."

J. C. blinked. "You really are really beautiful when your eyes go all buggy like that. Crazy pupils, funky orange-green color." He kissed her nose. "So then, O. K., you can work for me. A deal?"

Mirf hissed and let him go.

J. C. threw an arm around her. "Did you know that I have this great, sexual fetish about radiators. If you keep hissing like that I won't be able to control myself."

Mirf sucked in a great, deep breath of air.

"Wonderful." J. C. sighed heavily, rolling his eyes dramatically as he ogled her chest. "That is pretty dramatic and overwhelming as well."

"J. C. ?" It was a quiet, soft question.

"Mirf?"

"O.K.?"

"O.K." He let go but tucked one of her arms under his. "Which way?"

Mirf tugged him in the correct direction, the chosen direction. "There is, not far from here, a very, very expensive restaurant. Let's spend a bunch of the agency's money. With our finances they won't mind our attire."

"Oh," said the very proper English gentleman. "Jolly good idea."

"And," she added. "Enough with the fancy accent."

"Sure," said J. C. as J. C.

Mirf disengaged her arm and slipped it around his waist. "Much better."

"I agree." He put his arm over her shoulders. "This place have pretty good food?"

"You better believe it, hunkeleh. And remember, he that eats well does his work well, Old Ed Gayton, 1654."

Mirf was correct.

Leaving the restaurant, headed for the lodging of Mirf's choice, J. C. groaned genteelly, and patted his stomach. "Think we will ever come this way again?"

"Who knows, bubee? We might."

"This hotel going to be on the same order as that restaurant?"

"Bingo."

"It's the agency's money, right?"

"They have lots. And I have the authority. So why not spend a little?"

"A little?"

"Eh? A little? A lot? So who's to argue?" She aimed him at the correct building.

And soon they were ushered into their rooms.

"This is decadent."

They were standing on a balcony, high above the city, admiring the view. A servant hovered just out of sight, ready to spring forward at the slightest hint of a need or a want. They had their drinks sitting on the wide top of the railing. The stuff was purple, continued to froth, and tasted wonderful. The balcony curved around, out of sight, in either direction.

"I like it," said Mirf. She had her boots and socks off and was flexing her toes in the deep material covering the floor.

J. C. was staring at the great city and the strange architectural styles of this place. Up this high, there was only the faintest of sound from the city below. He turned, leaned back against the railing, and sipped. "A few questions?"

"Shoot."

"Why are we here? Where did the others go?"

Mirf waved an arm, beckoning the servant. "We won't be needing anything until morning." Then she waited until the servant was gone.

"We have to see a certain citizen and ask a few questions. I heard what Will Begood told Ramp. Will didn't have the name but we might get lucky. Ah, J. C., no insult or anything, but you might want to stay here while I talk with this low lifer."

"Nope."

"And, I do not know where they went, like I said in the park, or where ever. I think, I hope, Ramp directed them to where she wanted to go. But we won't know that until we meet again, if we do."

J . C. stared through her until she stepped closer and touched the end of his nose with one finger.

"Ramp is very capable. So, don't worry, be happy."

J. C. eyes refocused. He took another sip. "Sure." His free arm swung around and tugged her closer.

"J. C.?"

And closer.

"J. C.?"

He set his cup down and unfastened the top button of her shirt.

Then the next.

Then the next.

"Don't worry," he said. "Be happy."

Mirf yanked his shirt loose and slid her hands up his back.

He froze, then bent his head close to her neck, and whispered. "There is someone in the living room."

"What?"

"I think there is someone in there. I swear that I saw something move."

Mirf's eyes glittered dangerously. "I told the servants to leave. Let's visit our visitor. You go right. I will go left." She turned and walked into the living room and turned left. J. C. turned right.

There was no one there .

Mirf stopped and slowly turned her head, listening intently.

Suddenly all her attention focused upon one spot, near one of the large pieces of furniture. J .C. followed her stare. And saw it.

In the soft, thick floor covering, there were two depressions. Something was standing there, pressing down the thick material.

Something that he couldn't see. It wasn't moving.

Mirf sprang, hurtling through the air, right over the twin depressions, her arms swinging around it. "**GOTCHA!**" And struggled to hold onto whatever it was.

J. C. jumped into the fray, wrapping his arms around Mirf and something. He could feel it flailing around. They staggered and fell, rolling, tumbling, crashing into tables and furniture of various forms and shapes. Then the fight was over.

Mirf had one hand clenched around something.

"So, sneak, I give you a choice. Show yourself or die."

The creature appeared.

J. C. rolled away and leaped to his feet. "A frog with teeth? What the hell is that thing?"

"A gonif. And one that I know, don't I?" She released her grip around its throat. "Grizmek."

"**ULP**," it said.

Mirf stood up and banged the creature on top of the head with her fist. "J. C., this light-fingered thief is Grizmek, the Grizmek. They are a race of thieves. And Grizmek the Gracile is one of the best of the bunch."

She wacked the frog thief again. "Dumbkopf, what are doing in here, stealing from me?"

Grizmek stood up, adjusted his clothes, and said, "**ULP**."

"Ulp me no ulps, dragle bait."

"Just picking up a few things, ulp. I didn't know anyone was staying here."

"Well, guess what?"

"**ULP?**"

Mirf dragged some coins from a pocket and wrapped one of Grizmek's hands around them. "You are working for me, thief."

"Standard contract?"

"With bonuses."

Grizmek put the coins into a deep pocket, retrieved a small statue and placed it back on the table and looked at J. C. "What's this?"

"This," answered Mirf, "is J. C. Remember Hard, Ramp's husband? He is from the same elseplace."

"Oh, ulp, one of those."

"Right," said J. C. "One of those."

"So," said Mirf to Grizmek. "Come back in the morning."

"Ulp. I will." Grizmek walked from the room, it was a rather strange, bounding stride.

"Really strange," said J. C.

"I told you that this trip would be instructional."

J. C. dropped onto and sank deeply into one of the

pieces of furniture. "I don't remember you saying anything about instructional. Would you like me to tell you what you said."

Mirf sank down next to him. "Sure."

J. C. smiled. "You said, and here I quote directly. It's an adventure, bubeleh, a chance to see new worlds. Maybe make a fortune even. Or two. Then you rubbed your fingers together like this." He demonstrated.

"I said adventure?" Mirf dragged his arm around her shoulders and nudged him gently.

"Right."

"Not instructional?" She turned and began to undo the buttons on his shirt.

"Not ever." His fingers traced the hollow from her throat to her shoulder.

"J. C.?"

"Yes." He tried to return the favor but her arm was at the wrong angle, tickling his stomach.

"Do you remember our conversation in Mountain's house?"

"Sure."

"Something about a debt?"

"Yes." He smiled and kissed her.

"What did I say?" This time the shirt slipped away.

He pulled his head back. "You want me to repeat that?"

"Meshuggener, did I not ask?"

"You said." He swallowed nosily. "Quote, Mountain must have a monstrous bed. You want to put it to me? End of a very crude quote."

She shoved him sideways. "Offer still stands."

"My, my," he said.

"Not too zaftik?"

"Nope. Actually, you are rather statuesque."

"Nice word choice." She rolled him sideways.

"An amazing piece of furniture."

"J. C., enough with the words, O. K.?"

"Sure," he said.

Later.

"Have a drink." Mirf handed him the bottle. "Eat, drink, and love, the rest's not worth a fillip. Byron, 1821."

It was night. They stood once again on the balcony, looking out at the city lights. Mirf wore a table cloth wrapped toga style around herself. J. C. had done the same thing. It was Mirf's idea. They were drinking from a bottle that they had taken from one of the many cabinets.

"Quite a place." He handed the bottle back to her.

"The money center. The market center. The business center. It is why we have an office here. Let's try another room." She walked back through the living room and out a far door.

This room had a soft, green-blue glow of its own.

"I was referring to these rooms." J . C. loosened her shoulder knot. "I'll bet you look even better in candlelight."

"So, we'll order some." She shoved him backward onto a deep pad. "Tomorrow."

"Mirf . Enough with the words, O. K.?"

"Sure," she said.

Early Morning.

The morning light streamed through the many windows and doors and bounced from the many faceted walls, dotting colors on everything.

Mirf leaned forward and smiled.

J. C.'s hand was tracing slowly across the many colors. "Interesting effect, those colors." He tugged her closer. "Morning in Pled Sweider."

Mirf kissed him gently. "Certainly is."

Servants brought them breakfast. Then the sun was at the proper angle. They were lounging in the fourth balcony bay watching the long shadow cast by the hotel slowly shorten.

Mirf spread green stuff on a bread of some kind and offered J. C. the first bite. She was nestling in his arms. He took a bite.

"That remind you of anything, J. C.?"

"No," he mumbled.

The furniture was easing them backward. Mirf hastily got rid of the bread.

Mid-Morning.

"Partner," said Mirf, her lips brushing the base of his throat. "We ought to finish and get back to work. The gonif is waiting in the main room and the sun is high in the sky."

His hand brushed her hair. "Partner. You are right, we ought to do that."

Arching her back, she smiled at him. "He can wait."

Late Morning.

Grizmek was sitting on his haunches when they entered the room.

They had showered, dressed, and eaten the new breakfast ordered by Mirf.

"ULP."

"Grizmek, remember me?"

The frog-thief looked her over. "No. Ulp. Other than you hired me yesterday, standard contract with bonuses."

"I gave you a special coin so you could retire."

Grizmek stepped closer, reached out and ran his hands over her. "You don't look or feel like a hob-goblin."

"I am not. Mostly. I am me. Mirf." She batted at his hands. "Enough already with the hands."

In one swift motion, Grizmek unfastened her shirt, reached in, and grabbed her. "Mirf wasn't like this. This is no hob-goblin."

Her blow struck the frog-thief in the middle of the

forehead, driving him backward, eyes glazing, knees buckling.

Mirf leaped forward, grabbed him by the throat, and banged his head on the floor. "I am going to feed you to the Lamia's servants if you don't pay attention. You do remember them, don't you? Grizmek?" She shook his head from side to side.

Then she stopped and stared into his eyes. "It is me. The real me, not that accursed hob-goblin that those ugly beyond belief Mud Brothers, may they forever rot in hell, which is where they are, put on me."

Grizmek's eyes refocused. "Ulp. You sound like Mirf and you act like Mirf."

"Then I must be Mirf, right?"

"Ulp."

She thumped him one more time, not too lightly, on the side of the head. "Yes or no?"

"Ulp. Yes."

"Sure?"

"Yes. Yes."

"Good. Two yeses." Mirf stepped back, stood and began to button her shirt and winked at J. C. "Never thought that I'd be fondled by a frog. Of a sort."

Grizmek wobbled to his feet. "Where are we going?"

"Tell you when we get there. Wouldn't want you running off."

"We have a contract. Ulp."

"Indeed we do." Mirf stepped toward him. Grizmek winced. She yanked her hand from her pocket, grabbed one of his, and dumped a fistful of gold coins into his palm. "First payment. Let's go." She headed for the door.

Grizmek bounded to her side as she stepped into the elevator. "Mirf, are you going to lay eggs? There is a nice lake on the other side of the business district." The door closed, the elevator dropped.

"**NO!**" snapped Mirf .

"I heard all the noise in the running water this morning, ulp. I was early, ulp, ulp."

J. C. covered his laughter with a loud cough.

"**NO!** Enough already with the laying of eggs."

The elevator door opened.

"Ground floor, everyone out. Wait here. I have some small business to attend to, then we will leave."

Mirf hurtled across the lobby and engaged the floor manager in conversation.

"Ulp." Grizmek looked at J. C. "It sounded like a mating dance to me?"

"Sort of," said J. C. "But I think that I would drop that subject for conversation, if I were you."

"Ulp."

J. C. assumed that meant agreement.

Mirf returned, smiling happily. "So, let's go." She turned and headed for the outside.

It was a long hike.

Then they ate lunch.

And hiked some more until they finally arrived.

The three of them stood on one of the less elegant streets of Pled Swieder. It was shabby. It was unclean. Litter shifted uneasily in the soft breeze shouldering its way through the narrow way. It didn't smell all that good either.

"Pretty dingy. Which one?" asked J. C.

"The door with the peeling green skin, Partner. You want to wait out here?"

"Nope."

"Ulp."

"You are coming with us," snapped Mirf at Grizmek. "But first, hop over there and open that door."

Grizmek did. In one long, soaring hop. And then, in a moment, the door yielded to his adept fingers. He eased the door open, ready to leap aside.

"He got that door open almost as fast as your shirt."

"Bizzle!" Mirf started for the open doorway. J. C. trailed behind. As far as he could tell, no one was watching them.

Inside, in the soft dimness, the door closing behind them, they stood and waited, listening to the silence. Mirf twisted her head back and forth, and then slipped silently along one of the three halls.

Outside the selected door, they paused. A crack of light shone below the door. It pulsated. Mirf pulled J. C.'s head down until her lips brushed against his ear. "We have to grab this guy fast. O.K.?"

He nodded and straightened up, ready to charge.

Mirf slowly settled her hand on the door mechanism and with almost imperceptible movements, edged it open.

She nodded, inhaled, and hurtled into the room, her shoulder banging the door back against the wall.

"**CHARGE!**" bellowed J. C. "**GO GET 'EM, RINNIE!**"

They both hit the room's occupant at the same time, collapsing a small table, and crashing in a heap on the floor.

Their victim didn't struggle at all. He merely said, in a voice, silky smooth. "It is Mirf, erm, is it not? How nice of you to drop in."

Mirf sat up, both knees pinning the arm she was holding to the floor. "If he moves or blinks, rip his heart out."

J. C. snarled in his most guttural manner. "Yah sure, Mirf, rip is art out."

"Ulp." It was Grizmek, carefully peering into the room from the shattered doorway.

Mirf grabbed the man by the throat. "Do you give your most solemn and sacred promise to bring no harm to me or my associates?"

"I do."

"Say it."

"I promise no harm to you or your associates. Erm, may I rise? Now?"

Mirf released his arm and his throat.

J. C. let go of the arm he was holding.

The small man rose and began to dust himself off. He was wearing a long shirt-like garment of many layers of flowing material, each layer a different color. Over this he wore a great coat that hung to his knees. A chain of glittering links hung around his neck.

"J. C., this Quam Tanle. He is not as innocent as he appears."

"Truibble," said Quam, looking at each of them in turn, carefully. "Erm, it is Grizmek the Gracile, is it not?"

"Ulp." Grizmek slid carefully into the room.

"And your name is Jay Cee?"

"Right."

"An associate of Mirf's?"

"Right."

"From the Monetary Control, erm?"

"Nope."

"You didn't look the type. I like your voice better this way."

"Vunderbar," interjected Mirf. "Enough questions already."

Quam shoved the pieces of the table to one side with a foot and sat in a chair. "What do you want? Mirf?"

She grabbed a chair and sat facing him. "I want some information."

"Perhaps you will get it."

Mirf leaned forward and told Quam of the threat to Ramp and what little else she knew.

All during her presentation, Quam watched her face. He added an "erm" here and there, now and then.

"That's the story. So who is it?"

"Erm," said Quam. "It is ancient history, clan rivalry, carefully maintained hate."

"So, tell us."

For a long time they sat in silence, then Quam decided. "I will. If you are able to halt this, I might even forgive you." He flashed her a smile and blushed.

"Don't get too daring," grumbled Mirf.

"Long ago, Ramp's grandmother, Paarz, demolished a clan of witches. One female, one male survived. Ramp's mother, Qader, married the male, a powerful warlock. They produced twelve children, all sisters. The father fled far into out there when Qader died, was killed. The killer was the single son produced by the sister. As you may, or perhaps, may not, know, a magician birth or a male birth stops the reproductive process in the females among these creatures. Should Ramp, the magician, successfully produce offspring, it will trigger some, or many, of her sisters. The clan will multiply. That single male out there, hating them, is the reproductive dead end of his clan. The witch magic flows down through the females only. His mother filled him with hate, a three generational hate."

Mirf hissed loudly. "The Desolation of Paarz."

"Precisely," said Quam.

"OI!" Mirf leaned back. "Such a thing."

"The killer son works for a larger desolation."

"His name?"

"A secret, carefully kept, never uttered."

"Where does this nogoodnik live?"

"Erm," said Quam, steepling his fingers in front of his mouth and looking at Mirf through lidded eyes. "Erm."

Mirf shifted uneasily in her chair. Her teeth made grinding noises. "Price?" Her voice was harsh, rasping.

"Erm."

"Worse and worse," mumbled Mirf.

Grizmek carefully drifted around the room, staying to the outer edges, keeping an eye on Quam.

"Do you play poker?" asked J. C.

"Poker?" asked Quam.

"A gambling game."

"I do not believe that I have ever heard of it."

"Oh. Just wondered."

"So. O.K., what is the price?" snapped Mirf.

Quam held up one finger. "Two hundred, thirty-one gold."

"Grizmek," snarled Mirf. "Paper and something to write with."

Grizmek bounded over and handed her the requested items. Mirf scribbled and handed him the paper. "Take this to the local office and return."

Grizmek leaped out the door.

"He was getting nervous," explained Mirf.

"Erm."

"So?"

Quam held up another finger. Mirf grumbled.

"Clean my record."

"Done," snapped Mirf.

A third finger joined the first two. Mirf made sizzling noises.

"I wish to be able to speak to a certain legend being held captive in a certain museum."

"Five minutes. Max!"

"Erm. Done."

A fourth finger rose. Mirf hissed.

"I do not want any of Ripple's witch kin coming here. I am not involved. I do not want to be involved in this."

"Quam. I can only speak to Ramp. I don't think the rest would listen to me."

"Erm. Done."

A fifth finger joined the four.

"Enough fingers already," growled Mirf.

"The last, Chief Inspector, the last."

"A deal?"

"Exactly."

"Make the best of a bad bargain. John Ray," mumbled Mirf. "So?"

"Erm . . . I wish to see the witch sister named Reep. And, erm, I do not want to die."

Mirf leaped to her feet. "How can I do that? I don't even know her."

"You can speak to the magician. All the witches care for their youngest sister."

"I can only ask."

"Done!"

Mirf looked at J. C. "You got all that?" He winked at her. "Of course."

"My secretary," explained Mirf.

Grizmek leaped into the room, handed Mirf a bag and slipped to the outer edges of the room.

Mirf handed the bag to Quam. "Here."

He dropped it to the floor next to his chair. "Erm."

"So, where is this witch-begotten son?"

"Lean close, Mirf. This is a three leap. Each spot more hazardous as you proceed. I will speak the names, you will seek them. Perhaps you will survive, perhaps you will not."

Mirf leaned close. Quam whispered in her ear. It took a long time.

Mirf pushed her chair back and stood. "Time to go."

"Erm?"

"What?"

"A favor."

She squinted at Quam, suspicious, untrusting. "What kind of a favor?"

"Harmless."

"So, what is this harmless?"

"Remove your upper coverings."

"BRANGLE LEAVINGS!"

"It is harmless," whispered J. C. in her ear.

"A favor?" she asked.

"Erm."

"You will owe me?"

"Erm."

Mirf sighed. "The things I have to do on this job." She unbuttoned her shirt and yanked it off. "So?"

Quam sat silent, unmoving, looking at her. "Thank you, Mirf. You may leave." Quam shut his eyes.

She headed for the door. "Let's go." She waved her arms at Grizmek. "What are you gawking at?" she snarled at J. C.

J. C. grinned. "Pretty nice."

"Raz baz!" She yanked on her shirt, angrily stuffing it into her trousers .

Outside, back on the street, she finished the buttoning up.

J. C. looked up at the sky. "Night?"

"Boychick, when you deal with Quam, you lose a lot of time. I am hungry. Let's go get something to eat. It is late." Over dessert, she explained Quam to J. C. While she did, J. C. carefully didn't watch Grizmek. The frog-thief's dessert seemed to wiggle.

"So you see, boychick, that little guy is big trouble. That is why we had to get his promise. We are safe, from him."

"One minor bit of curiosity." J. C. was struggling, and succeeding, in stifling an overwhelming urge to grin.

"Such as?"

"Such as, what was that mammary voyeurism all about?"

"Jealous?"

"Nope. Curious."

"Boychick, you are not very flattering."

"What?"

"The gracile fingers cop a big feel and you don't do anything."

"You beat me to it."

"That creepy Quam oogles my superb physique and you just join in the staring contest."

"You agreed to it, not me. How come, Monetary Queen?"

"You might find this hard to believe."

J. C. waggled his eyes at Grizmek and back.

Mirf smiled. "So maybe you won't." She shoved the pot toward him and waited until he refilled his cup and took a sip.

"Quam comes from a very different race of folk. His male portion lusts after me. His female portion lusts after other things. The other portion works out the details. So, he finally got a look. It is all he is ever going to get."

"Well," laughed J. C. "It certainly has been instructional."

She laughed with him. "Let's get back to the digs, partner."

"Right." He pushed his chair back and stood. "Partner."

Mirf slipped an arm through one of his and said over her shoulder. "Come on, Grizmek, you too."

"Could be even more instructional," murmured J. C.

She hurried them along.

The door slid open to sorta green.

"These are your quarters, gonif. Order what you wish. In the morning, we will do a deep pocket search."

"Ulp."

The door closed.

The elevator shot upward.

J. C.'s stomach shot downward.

"Last floor," announced Mirf. "Close your eyes, partner."

He did. The door opened.

She led him through the central room. "Surprise!"

He opened his eyes. The golden light, soft golden light was everywhere. Dozens of candles, carefully arranged, flooded the room with warm tones.

"It is a big wow, Mirf."

She spun around and faced him. "Ordered this morning. Just for you."

He slowly undid the buttons and slipped her shirt back from her shoulders. "Right. Lovely in candlelight."

Far Light. A Small Town On A Hill.

Clan Head Clamar of the Mirmar witch Clan sat and stared at their visitor. The visitor sat in one of the many chairs arranged around the circular Audience Room and stared back. Of course, Clamar wasn't exactly sure about that. The darkness inside the visitor's hood completely prevented anyone from knowing where she might be looking or what she might be thinking.

"You wish us," asked Clamar, "to teach you history, ancient arcane history?"

"It is what this one asks."

"You are named Lady Night-Reaper?"

"This one is so named."

Clamar waved one hand at the wall covered with shelving and stuffed with books, boxes of parchments and stacks of loose paper and bundles of scrolls. "We know much of ancient and arcane history." She sat up straighter. "Which history are you interested in learning about?"

The response caused Clamar's two most senior clan members, standing behind her chair, to jerk. And then to rapidly calm themselves.

"A very ancient piece of history. It will take some time, some long time, to work through the, um, literature, ah, documents. If we chose to allow that."

"This one has that time."

Clamar nodded.

"Much gold will be paid. The Divineal would owe debt."

Clamar heard two soft gasps from behind her chair. "Ummmm," she said, covering the sound. "Agreed."

Lady Night-Reaper flowed to her feet. "This one would have lodgings here as well."

Clamar stood and nodded. "Agreed. Carran will find you a room. It will be rather, ah, bare."

"This one has few requirements." She followed Carran from the room.

Kaina cleared her throat.

"Yesssss?"

"All must be warned of our, ah, guest."

"See to it. Find a room where she can read and study the materials. Assign Firdir to be The Lady's assistant. It will be good training. And caution her to tred softly, We do not want to lose her."

Kaina hurried from the room.

Clamar sank back in her chair and wondered about the survival of her clan. Perhaps she should send the rest of the seniors and the clan records and books elseplace. She would wait and see what Firdir reported over time. But she would begin to prepare

And Here and There.

"Poor J. C." Hard was running his hand gently over his wife's stomach. "You seem to be poking out quite a bit more."

"It is a fast process, for us, husband. Why?"

"What?"

"Poor J. C.?"

"He is with Mirf. I think. Isn't he?"

"Most probably. We came here. They went elsewhere."

"And Mountain, ah, here."

"Ummmm," said Ramp, gently stopping his hand with her's.

"Where?"

"I do not know." Ramp smiled at him and rolled onto her side.

"Poor J. C.?"

"Right," agreed Hard.

"Why poor J. C.?"

"He is going with Mirf, ah, not exactly going with her, but going along with Mirf, ah, traveling with him. HER! Her."

"So?"

"Well, from the parts I remember, Mirf is foul-tempered, foulmouthed, coarse, unpleasant, violent, mean, nasty, pig-headed, overbearing, rude, and, an all together not-nice person."

"She was a hob-goblin, then."

"True."

"She is a lady now."

"I doubt that."

"What?"

"A lady."

"A very beautiful lady."

"No lady, I'll bet."

"And you feel sorry for J. C. who has to travel with this female person who isn't a very nice lady?"

"Yep. I certainly would be."

"What would you be?"

"Sorry if I had to travel with Mirf."

"You were. You did."

"I mean alone. Travel alone. You saw how she acted. It felt like hob-goblin to me."

Ramp threw an arm around him. "I think that I shall hold my judgement until I can speak with your friend."

"Well, I'll bet he is sorry. J. C. really has a pretty low tolerance for excessive authority."

Ramp yawned very politely.

It caused Hard to yawn. "Boy, I am tired."

"We used much energy to get here. Sleep."

"Where are we?"

"The forest elseplace, Kemel Platse."

"O.K." He pulled her close and drifted to sleep.

In his tent, Mountain had long before eaten and gone to sleep.

In the morning, after breakfast, Ramp waved everything away.

They stood and looked at the small meadow where they had camped, deciding which way to go.

"**BY DUMPF**, it is much more pleasant traveling with you two than with John Tinker. Good food, pleasant accommodations."

Hard looked up. "Didn't Tinker feed you?"

"**ROCKS AND STONES!** We did too much sleeping on hard ground and going without meals, we did." He stepped toward the edge of the meadow.

"He didn't mention that," said Hard.

"I can do both, **BY DUMPF**, I just do not like to do it, either one."

Ramp had been consulting something. She pointed, "Shall we walk?"

"Lovely weather," said Mountain, strolling rapidly in the indicated direction.

The sun poured into the opening. It was hot, getting hotter.

Taking Hard's hand, Ramp followed Mountain. "It will be cooler in the forest." She changed their clothes into loose, billowing, light material.

Hard smiled at her. "No robe?"

"Not until we reach Ver Meek."

Ver Meek.

The brother and the sister Ter Trp were very nervous.

"I can feel her coming."

"What shall we do?"

"Pack and leave."

"She won't hurt us."

"He will."

"Don't tell her."

"How?"

"Hurry, brother, hurry."

Takle Woods.

"We have to rush," said Ramp.

"What?"

"We are felt."

Hard looked confused.

"Mountain," called Ramp. "Come back here, please."

Mountain stopped and slowly turned. "**BY DUMPF**, have I gone in the wrong direction?"

"**NO!** We have to travel faster."

He walked over and bent down. "I can easily carry you both and run."

Ramp smiled into the large face. "There are faster ways. Take one of my hands and one of Hard's."

Mountain very carefully did. Holding their hands with his thumbs and forefingers.

"My hand, husband. Nobody let go."

She said something.

Ver Meek.

It was a small town built around an irregular grass-covered space with widely spaced trees dotted here and there. The tops of the trees were taller than the tallest buildings.

"Ver Meek," said Ramp.

"**BY DUMPF!**" Mountain stared around and down at her.

"What?" asked Hard. He looked at the building they were standing directly in front of and wondered what Mountain was making noise about. Behind them, across a wide, open meadow began the edge of Takle Woods.

"Open the door. The one in front of us."

Hard stared at the door.

"Husband, I dare not touch it. They are still in there."

"Too late."

"I know."

Hard pushed at the door. It wouldn't open. He jerked and kicked at it.

Mountain pushed him to one side and jambed the head of his cudgle through the entrance, crushing the door, most of the door jamb, and pieces of the wall.

"There, **BY DUMPF.**" He stepped back.

Ramp said, "Watch the street." She stepped through the debris, tugging Hard with her.

A man and a woman stood in the center of the room, arms around each other's shoulders, staring at them.

"You were running?" asked Ramp.

"Yes."

"Yes."

"Why?" Ramp threw the hood of her robe back. She was now dressed in the proper attire for a magician of her clan.

"Frightened."

"Scared."

"Husband, this is the brother and sister Ter Trp. They are of the race, M'lok, a very ancient line."

Hard looked at the pair. Their skin tones were vaguely blue. Their faces were broad with high cheek bones, large eyes. They were dressed in clothes of some soft texture and color, rust orange, pale green.

"Tir Trp, he is called Hard. Mine!"

Four eyes focused upon Hard's face. He could feel something touch him, something wet and moist. The eyes blinked. The sensation went away.

"We don't want to."

"Tell you anything."

"You must," said Ramp.
"Someone is trying to kill her," said Hard.

"We know."

"We know."

"You do?"
"Shhhhh," said Ramp, pointing at four chairs equally spaced around a circular table, just created.

She walked over to the table and beckoned everyone over, and said to Hard, "You sit across from me, and do nothing until I say otherwise."

"Oh, sure," said Hard, dropping into the proper place.

Ramp wiggled at finger at Ter Trp.

They pouted and reluctantly sat.

Ramp placed her palm in the center of the table and lifted it up, drawing a gleaming jewel from the surface. Then folding her hands, one over the other, she nodded her head.

The jewel pulsated with a gentle red fire. The color rose in a thin column, touched the ceiling and umbrella spilled around them.

"You know?" asked Ramp softly.

"We."

"Do."

"Who, or what, is it?"

Ter Trp looked at other, eyes locking, speaking to each other and sighed, a low exhalation of breath and surrender.

"Clan enemy."

"Clan hater."

"Clan history."

"Clan pain."

"Who is it?" demanded Ramp.

"BY DOUBLE DUMPF!" bellowed Mountain from the outside. **"RUN, RUN!"**

Destruction shattered the building, blowing fragments throughout the town and surrounding countryside. The outer edge of the forest tumbled, along with Mountain who was charging into it.

Inside the house they sat unharmed, protected by the faint red fire.

"Tell me," said Ramp.

Ter Trp's eyes spoke to each other. They nodded. Once.

"The Desolation."

"Of Paarz."

Ramp nodded. "I have heard that tale about my grandmother. So?"

"The mother's."

"Daughter's."

"Son."

"Attacks you."

Ramp gasped. And stared at them. "There is such a person?"

"Yes."

"Yes."

"Hate filled."

"To kill your birthing."

"Is all."

"He thinks."

Ramp looked from side to side, from one to the other. "Do you know how? Using what?"

"Twisted forces."

"The Nameless Demon."

Ramp tossed each of them a ring made of green stone. "Wear these always."

"The son calls himself."

"Ra'aa'zar."

Ramp sat silent as the destruction swirled around their protective umbrella. All they could hear was the soft sound of vague shapes tumbling around and around them. Inside their protection all was still and calm.

"I have a sudden urge for bab-sauce." Ramp smiled at Hard. "Shhhhh," she said as he started to speak.

Ter Trp looked at her, eyes roving from her face downward. They smiled at her.

"We have said."

"All there is to say."

"Away, away," replied Ramp.

Ter Trp reached across the table and intertwined their fingers.

And disappeared.

The fire lifted and sank into the jewel.

Hard cried out. They were sitting in the middle of great heaps of shattered wood.

"We are safe," said Ramp. "For now."

At the edge of the ripped and torn forest, trees were heaved aside as Mountain stood, as he rose from his protective crouch.

"**RAR RUMPFING DOUBLE DUMPF.**" He stomped over to where they were sitting, kicking debris left and right. "**SAND AND PEBBLES**, worse and worse."

All through the town, structures lay tumbled, twisted into kindling. Town folk were standing in small groups, staring and pointing. A few groups were beginning to dig into the smashed ruins, seeking survivors.

Mountain opened a path for Ramp and Hard and waited until they were clear of the destroyed area before relaxing. "**BY DUMPF,** magician, what did you do?"

"Nothing. We were attacked." She pointed at the far side of town, which faced still standing trees. "A node is just there. We must hurry." She ran for the spot.

Hard charged after her, lengthening his stride to stay by her side. "Should you be running?"

"Yes. We must hurry."

"In your condition?"

"They are safe. I am safe. Now we must be safe."

Ramp led them between two shattered warehouses. At the end of the narrow alleyway, she pointed at a tilted rock wall. "There."

"Where?"

"The wall. We step into it."

"BY DUMPF!"

"Link hands."

They did.

She stepped into the wall, pulling them with her.

Hard closed his eyes.

Bebarrah. Night. A Time Of Quiet.

Multi-moons shed three shadow light upon the sleeping town.

Pilgrims, merchants, visitors, and the rest of the inhabitants dreamed of tomorrow, the An Day of Celebration.

Red twinkling, red glow, seeped from the cave mouth, slipping silently down the twisting path, passing under shrubs and through the grass, following the after image. The glowing stream frightened two scavengers digging among the discarded foodstuffs, and one prowling tanpra.

The stream poured into the town and along one of the streets and brushed against one of the buildings. The door of their destination was tightly shut and finely fitted all around. The stream poured up the wall and around a corner and flowed in through the open window.

Duff's eyes popped open. She sat up and tapped $1.98 lightly on the forehead.

His eyes flew wide, she ducked. The bolt crackled through the air.

"WHAT?"

"Quiet, Dear." She brushed the hair from his face and kissed him gently. He relaxed.

"What?"

"We have visitors."

"Who?" His hand reached out and grabbed the long, black wand.

It crackled.

Duff sat up and rapped his chest with one knuckle. "Put that away."

He did and sat up. And stared. "What are they doing here?"

A twinkling red blanket hung from the window sill and dripped onto the floor.

"I don't know." She leaned sideways and looked down. "The floor is covered with them."

He grabbed the wand back.

"$1. 98, it will not work on them."

"It won't?"

"No. That much I learned from our contact."

Red jewels crept up over the edges of the bed.

"Lay down and hold me," ordered Duff, pushing on his chest.

He did. Wrapping his arms tightly around her.

Glowing scarlet enveloped them, smothering his gasp, her moan, sparkling red layers binding the heaving bodies until all movement ceased.

Morning. Early Celebration. Excitement.

Sorrowful was leaning on the window sill, watching the crowds and the milling throng in the street below. It was long past morning. He had allowed Tears to run downstairs to observe at first hand, merely cautioning him to stay not too long.

Not too long had passed, some time ago and Sorrowful was scanning the surging mobs for some sign of his grandson.

The door to their rooms flew open, Tears ran in, eyes sparkling with excitement. "Today," he reported, "is the An Day of Celebration. All the pilgrims will go up to the Cavern of Delight and perform the Ritual Call. Then the An Bas will assign each a place, in The Order, and one by one, evening after evening, they will go up there and wait. And on the final day, they will have a great feast and end the event until next year. Where are Duff and $1.98?"

"You have learned much, Tears, in a small amount of time. Still sleeping, I suppose."

Tears stepped close to Sorrowful and whispered, "How can they still be sleeping, with all the noise and excitement just outside their window?"

Sorrowful laughed. "In five or six more years, maybe more, you will know, I think."

"What will he know?"

It was $1.98 leaning heavily against the door jamb.

"About growing up. Are you ill?" Sorrowful watched the magician drop heavily into a chair.

"No. Exhausted. Have you had breakfast?"

Tears jumped for the outside door. "I will order for you."

"Make it for two," said Duff, walking into the room, carefully closing their bedroom door. She stopped and kissed $1.98 on the cheek, ruffled his hair and sat on his lap, legs thrown over one arm of the chair. "Two large breakfasts."

Tears ran downstairs to speak to the kitchen.

"He wanted to know why you were sleeping late." Sorrowful smiled. "I told him that he would know when he grows older."

Duff laid her head on $1.98's chest with her eyes closed. "We had visitors late last night."

Sorrowful sat straighter. "Visitors? I did not waken. How did they get in, the door was barred?"

"Window," said $1.98. He folded his arms around Duff. "They came in through the window. We left it open."

Sorrowful jumped up and ran to the window and leaned way out. Then he pulled back and spun around. "It is a four story flat wall with no projections of any kind. How?"

Duff mumbled. And said, "Crawled. The entire horde. The room was knee-deep on $1.98 with them."

"Them?" Sorrowful walked over to their room to take a look.

Duff's head snapped up. "**DO NOT!** Not until we decide what to do."

Sorrowful walked back to his chair, sat, and stared at them.

"Them? What? Who? What kind of visitor did you have, do we have, here? In there?"

"Zeedar." Duff pulled her legs into a tight tuck and sighed.

The outer door popped open and Tears ushered in hotel staff with two huge breakfasts. They rapidly set the two large meals next to $1.98 and Duff and left.

"Well done," said Sorrowful, smiling at Tears.

"Many thanks." $1.98 handed a mug to Duff, who took it and sipped noisily.

She looked over the lip of her mug at Sorrowful. "It is the Zeedar, the red jewel creatures. They poured into the room and swarmed over us. Skin and nerves become hyper-sensitive, the pleasure centers of your brain run wild. There is no way to adequately explain what we felt. Zeedar, what the pilgrims seek."

"The festival is going to be a disappointment." $1.98 balanced a large plate in one hand while Duff ate from it.

"Why?" Sorrowful looked at the pair.

"May I see them?" Tears sat on the edge of his chair.

"**NO!** Stay away from that room." It was a command. Duff's face was firm, stern, demanding. "They want to go home."

"Home?" Sorrowful looked puzzled. "They do not live there, in that cavern?"

"Not from what they told Duff," said $1.98. She held the

plate while he ate.

She nodded. "They, or it, I am not sure whether it is many, or just one with many parts, said that they were shoved here when a horrible force took their world. And then passed on. They swap the sensation for food. At one time it was a form of defense against predation."

Duff offered $1.98 a special morsel from the meal. "We would have died enveloped in sensation, going happily, except he managed to slip a cloak around us."

$1.98 smiled wanly. "I am drained, quite literally and quite figuratively. We must sleep and rest, in your room. The Zeedar will stay where they are. Wake us for meals." He set the dishes aside and stood, Duff still cradled in his arms, and moved to the adjoining bedroom.

"Come, Tears." Sorrowful walked to the outer door. "Let us see this festival close up. We will return for meals."

They left and headed down the stairs to see, to record everything about this carnival.

Sorrowful, as they passed through the lobby, ordered a late brunch and a very late evening meal.

And then it was a very late evening meal that they were finishing. Both $1.98 and Duff appeared rested and refreshed.

"How do you feel."

"Like another day." $1.98 smiled at Sorrowful.

"Let's roll in the Zeedar." Duff patted $1.98 gently on the leg as he twitched. "Just a small joke, Dear."

He slumped back in his chair. "I really do not think we ever want to do that again. No telling what the damages would be. Or was."

Tears looked at Duff. "Are they really going to come with us?"

She nodded.

"How? There are too many to carry."

"Yes." Sorrowful looked at the pair. "What will we do?"

Duff shoved her plate aside. "Tonight we will wander

the streets with the crowds and locate the closest node. Tomorrow night while the town sleeps, we will go there and pour the horde through. We will go first, you and Tears will come last. Between $1.98 and myself, we can sleep spell a large enough area to ensure that no one will see us depart."

"It will ruin this town," said Sorrowful.

Duff smiled. "They will just have to do whatever they were doing before the Zeedar arrived. Let's go find that node."

When they returned to their rooms, Sorrowful offered the two magicians his and Tears' room. They could sleep on the couches.

"Not so hasty." Duff walked over to the other bedroom, threw open the door and snatched up one of the Zeedar, slamming the door shut before they could start to move.

"Duff?"

"Shhhh, Dear. One of them is only a tickle. We have to come to an understanding between them and us." She closed her eyes, cupped her hands together, trapping the Zeedar between her palms, and began the process. Instantly sweat began to pour from her body.

"Stop that," she mumbled. "Stop it. Stop. **STOP!**" She sighed. "That's better."

$1.98 hovered around her, nervous, ready to burst in, unsure of what to do. The air began to crackle as he walked back and forth. He was mumbling to himself.

Duff opened one eye. "Stop that, Dear. It is distracting." The eye closed.

$1.98 sat on a chair. Right on the edge of the seat, leaned forward. And watched her. Carefully.

Finally, Duff bent forward and set the jewel creature on the floor, walked over and opened the bedroom door. It slipped in to join the others. When they touched, all the Zeedar knew.

Duff walked over and took one of $1.98's hands in one of her's and tugged him to his feet. "We can sleep in our own bed, Dear. They will not touch us."

The red carpet flowed across the floor and around them, leaving a narrow space around their feet.

"Let's go. Just step, they are fast enough that we won't be able to step on them." She pulled him into motion.

And she was correct. The Zeedar did manage to not be stepped upon. But it was disconcerting. $1.98 found that if he didn't look down, it worked just fine.

"Breakfast at the normal time," called Duff, closing the door behind them. All the Zeedar were inside the room with them.

As $1.98 tugged the covers up, she nudged him. "Hold me, Dear."

He sat up violently. "**WHAT?** They're coming? **AGAIN?**"

She tickled his ribs. "Shhhhhh! No. I just want to be held."

$1.98 flopped backwards, fixed the blankets, and did as he was told. And ordered the lights to go out.

A small fireworks display erupted near the ceiling.

Duff put it out. "Just hold me, Dear. I will take care of the lights." Slowly the lights dimmed as she wiggled into a more comfortable position. "There."

The next day, they wandered the town. Following the crowd, listening to the conversations. Everyone was talking about the bad luck of the first pilgrim. Nothing had happened although he had reported strange noises coming from one of the many openings in the back wall of the cavern.

Tears looked at Sorrowful. "I wonder what that was?"

"Imagination, perhaps."

"Falsity," suggested Duff.

"Something else lives in there. I saw something, not Zeedar." $1.98 frowned.

Duff laughed. "It could be the start of a new festival."

They ate an early mid-day meal, returned to their

rooms, and took a nap. Then they had a early supper, and slept again. They wanted to be rested for this evening.

Late evening and they were preparing.

"Best I could do." $1.98 looked at the hole smoldering in the center of the table. "It should keep them asleep, though."

Duff dropped some coins next to the hole. "We should pay for the damages. It looked good."

"Yes." $1.98 nodded, the spell had. "The spell was good. The affected townfolk would probably sleep through most of the next day."

"Shall we go?" Sorrowful stood. The Zeedar were surging in slow swells as they poured into the main room.

"We'd better." Duff hurried to the door.

They hurried down the stairs, walking as quietly as they could. They passed through the lobby and saw the night clerk. He was snoring, head on the counter top. The red tide flowed along with them, the leading edge of the mass staying just even with Duff.

"Hold the door open, Dear. We do not want to trap any of them inside."

$1.98 stood aside and held the door and waited until he saw the last glittering red creature slip past. He waited, wondering if any of them would be stragglers. After awhile, when none had appeared, he decided all were outside. Then he ran up the street to rejoin the group now standing in a tight cluster, waiting for him.

Duff pointed at the node. "This should be interesting. Stay inside the Zeedar, Sorrowful, Tears, and come through just before the last of them." She grabbed $1.98's arm. "Ready, Dear?"

He nodded.

They stepped into the node followed by a thick torrent of red glow. Sorrowful and Tears hurried forward to get in before the last of the jewel creatures disappeared.

Somewhere. Unknown. Unpleasant. Late Day.

The slightly built, hooded figure drifted silently around the clearing. She recognized the slight flattening as the place where Ramp had put her tent-shape. The faint residue was definitely her youngest sister's spore.

Around and around she moved until she found it. One thin, alien thread. Slowly, carefully, with delicate touch and gentle fingers, she lifted it. And then began to wind it onto one end of an ebony and white wand. And then it was firmly attached.

"Hum, hum, hum," she said to herself as she gently tugged on the magical strand. It resisted. Good. It would lead back its owner. She was one of a very few that were able to see the magical strands left behind whenever a magic user traveled in and out.

The watcher, placed there for unwanted visitors, surged forward, intend upon destroying, horribly, this visitor. It clutched her by the front of her robe, claws bunching up the material. Slowly it drew her toward slavering jaws, hanging wide, multi-toothed jaws.

She flowed forward, unresisting.

It stared at her and hesitated. This was strange. Things screamed and struggled. None came willingly. It peered into the darkness of the hood, snapping its jaws at its meal.

Two large, dark eyes sadly gazed out and into the being of the watcher.

And killed it.

The one who had placed the beast howled in anger and hurtled destruction down.

But there was nothing to destroy.

Reep had turned elsewhere.

Following a dangling thread.

Pled Sweider. Morning.

"So, guess what, hunkeleh?" Mirf was looking into his

face.

J .C. squinted up at her, the morning sun painting narrow stripes across her. The windows in this room were designed that way.

"Zebra?"

"Fumch! That's not a guess. That's a smart mouth."

"Ump."

"So, give a guess."

"It's morning."

"Nice try. Nope." She wiggled just a little lower.

"It is time to get out of bed or whatever this thing is called."

"Nope." She settled.

"Mirf."

"Nope."

"Stop that."

Mirf grinned. "No way."

J. C. wrapped his arms around her. "How am I supposed to play guessing games with you when you are doing that?"

Her legs brushed against his. "So? You are doing something to me. Give up?"

"Absolutely."

"Grizmek is waiting. And guess what?"

"I gave up."

"He is going to keep waiting. After a long shower." Mirf went to the far door and whispered to Grizmek.

And after a long shower, they joined the frog-thief for breakfast.

When Mirf went to the main door to speak to one of the servants, J. C. leaned sideways and said, "No comments about laying eggs, O.K.?"

Grizmek bobbled his head. "Ulp."

"So, let's eat."

Mirf returned and popped the lid from a container and

heaped some of the contents on J. C.'s plate. Then she shoved the container at the frog-thief after serving herself. "So, help yourself, gonif."

It was a leisurely meal.

And when they were finally finished Mirf pushed the last container to the middle of the table and looked over at Grizmek. "O.K., deep pockets, empty them. Just place the stuff on the table." She swept dishes and everything aside with one forearm. "Right there."

"Ulp."

"**NOW!**"

Grizmek bobbed his head. "Ulp." And started to unload his several pockets.

J. C. stared at the amount of stuff piling up. "This guy is worse than Harpo Marx. Where did all that stuff come from?"

"Flying fingers," explained Mirf.

"Ulp." It was agreement.

Grizmek stopped.

Mirf began to push and shove the many things around, using one finger. "So, sticky fingers, this all?"

"Ulp."

Mirf leaped to her feet and banged him on top of the head.

"Don't you ulp me. Where's the stuff you snaggled from Quam? Put this pile away."

Grizmek hastily removed everything from the table.

"Put that jug back," snapped Mirf.

The frog-thief ducked his head and did.

"And now, Quam's."

"I am still surprised we have any furniture," said J. C.

"Too big, ulp." Grizmek reached into yet another pocket and placed a small, gleaming crystal on the table.

It glowed blue orange green in the sun and seemed to be continually changing shape.

"Ho Boy! What else." Mirf chortled happily.

Grizmek set a small figurine next to the crystal.

J. C. bent forward to take a closer look at it. The thing looked vaguely insect-like but almost somewhat, mostly, human. He decided it was the large multi-faceted eyes set in the deep eye sockets, and the extra arms. It had three pairs crossed over its chest. It blinked at him. He jerked his head back.

"And," prompted Mirf.

"**ULP.** That is all." Grizmek set a curved rod on the table. The ends almost touched each other.

Mirf sizzled with happiness.

J. C. placed his hand on the back of her neck. "How do you do that?"

"What, partner?"

"Sound like bacon frying."

Mirf rolled one eye at him. "Left over hob-goblin." She arched her neck and rolled her head against his hand. "We can always send Grizmek on an errand."

"Ulp."

"I came with large appetites, partner."

J. C. smiled. "You didn't tell me that when I ran away from home."

"Ulp?"

"Didn't think that you needed to know that. Then."

"You part gypsy also?"

"All Mirf. Just pure Mirf. Mostly. Almost."

"Ulp?"

J. C. slid his hand around and down her ribs and tugged her closer. "Partner?"

"Yes?" She hissed softly.

"What race of being are you?"

"You really want to know?"

"After meeting the creatures, ah, races that you've introduced me to in the past few days, yes, I do."

"After what you have been doing, you want to know?"

"Absolutely."

"Ulp?"

"Human. That is it. I am a branch of your kind. Just far, far in your future, that's all."

She threw an arm around him and nudged him. "Of course, since my, um, accident, cursed forever may be those slimey Mud Brothers, Ko Lett and The Harken Ryder, I got a dose of hob-goblin."

"Ulp?"

"What happened to them?"

"They died. Wonderfully horribly."

"Ulp, ulp."

Mirf swung her head around to stare at Grizmek through her eye brows. "What?"

"Nothing. Ulp."

"Nothing? Why all the ulps?"

"Just joining the conversation. Ulp."

J. C. laughed. And laughed.

Mirf smacked him on the shoulder. "You have a weird sense of humor, J. C."

He giggled. "That's me, Mirf. Mostly human. Ulp."

Grizmek peered at J. C. "Ulp, ulp?"

"Just joking," said J. C. "So, Mirf partner, you are Homo sapiens?"

"More or less. You three are interesting, you know that?"

"Three?"

"The Chosen One, the Klutz for life, and you."

"How?"

"Grizmek, go steal something. This beautiful hunk of humanity and I have to have a private conversation. Get back in time for lunch."

"Ulp." Grizmek headed for the door and a certain shop he had seen when they were heading for the first destination.

Mirf walked away from the table and beckoned J. C. to

follow with one finger. He did. In another room, where she selected a large piece of furniture covered with multi-colored, iridescent patches and sat down. "Come here."

He did.

"Hold me."

He did.

"I am going to tell you a secret. The agency files tell us, the agents, lots of things so we can do our jobs. They now have a file on you, I made it."

J. C. tried to sit up.

Mirf wrapped her arms and legs around him and kept him from getting away. "Just listen."

"What are guys, Super Gestapo?"

"**NO!** I will explain that later. Let's just say, we keep tabs on the forces moving from elseplace to elseplace in the universes. Or on things of interest. You have become a thing of interest. So we have a file. These are very restricted files."

J. C. slipped one arm free. "I don't like being a file, restricted or otherwise."

"When you took the job, bubeleh, you made the file." Mirf brushed her lips across his. "There is no personal information in there. You are safe. We don't have to get married."

"I wasn't worried about that." He blinked. "Should I be?"

"Partner, it is a little late to start worrying about that."

"That's the secret?"

"No. I just wanted to tell you a few things about agency curiosity."

J. C. ran his finger down her back. "So, tell me."

"You seem to be a fairly unique being, living in such a backward elseplace in such an obscure corner of the universe of universes, in reacting to true strangers, true aliens."

She released her grip on him and rolled back. "Here you are, rolling in the hay with one hob-goblined Chief Inspector and not recoiling in horror. The klutz-for-life is married to a magician from a clan of witches whose ancestry we cannot trace as their home galaxy exploded eons ago just after that clan had moved away. In your terms, they are probably not human. But she is having his children, their children."

J .C. twisted around and rested his head on her pillow.

"The Chosen one has become a new thing, a new creature. He is an entity of parts, a polyorganism, none of the parts are capable of bearing children, as far as we can tell, except for him, of course."

He sat up and turned, looking at her. "Why not?"

Mirf turned her head away and stared elsewhere.

"Tell me, partner."

Mirf looked back, reached over and took one of his hands. "So, O.K., so I will you. Princess Chicken is a recreated fluff Easter Egg decoration, courtesy of Big Red, and thus has a unique body chemistry. Smoke is a telepathic carnivore, unchanged genetically, with a recreated form, also courtesy of Big Red. Fair Morn's created form, all myth magic, has, we suspect a rather unique interior. Again, courtesy of Big Red. Messenger's tribe, of which we know very little, they being a rather minor population on their world, raised her on a special diet and with special teachings. The diet, we feel, probably altered her body chemistry in strange ways we would like to know about but will probably never have the time to investigate, finding out what it is."

"And so?" He tickled her lightly.

"That entity will never reproduce."

J. C. pinned her in place. "And why is that of such interest to your agency?"

"Because, partner, you three don't seem to mind. You interact with extreme ease with beings entirely outside your normal experience, that is why. All our data suggests that your culture should be zenophobic to an extreme. So . . ."

"So . . . ?"

Mirf smiled. "So, I am thinking of opening an office there and seeing if there might be more like you. The agency can always use a few good creatures."

"Men."

"Whatever. We were an equal opportunity employer long before your bunch ever heard of such things." Mirf heaved J. C. aside. "And guess what?" She tumbled on top of him.

"What?" mumbled J. C.

"I might pull some rank and station myself there. What do you think about that?"

"Chief Inspector," said J. C., reaching up. "I think that it could be instructional, educational, and just plain good fun."

Eventually, Grizmek returned. They had lunch ready to serve.

"Find anything nice?" Mirf smiled at the frog-thief. It was a real smile. This time.

"Ulp." Grizmek reached into a pocket.

"Keep it." Mirf shoved a plate at him. "Eat, eat!"

When they finished, J. C. pointed to the three objects sitting the middle of the table. "What are those things?"

Mirf picked up the strange crystal. "A finder." She handed it to Grizmek and warned him to keep it where he could reach it quickly. "For the keys that we need."

"Ulp." The crystal disappeared into some pocket.

Mirf picked up the statue and handed it to J .C. "Here, keep this in your shirt pocket. It is a female. I think. Probably bite me in an embarrassing place if I kept it."

J. C. dropped it into his shirt pocket. "What is it?"

"A suk-dragon. You can tell from the three pair of arms and the fancy eyeballs."

J. C. felt a slight stirring and looked down. The statue was standing up, the top pair of arms crossed over the edge of his pocket, and looking around.

"Now that makes me nervous."

"Ulp," agreed Grizmek.

"She didn't take a bite. You're safe." Mirf picked up the bent rod and eased it around her neck. It made for a rather unusual looking necklace. "And a weapon for me."

She stood. "Shall we go? We have some traveling to do."

J .C. pushed back from the table and followed her toward the door.

"Where are we headed?"

"Tell you when we get there. The walls might have ears. Grizmek, don't dawdle."

She hurried them from the hotel, down the street, and eventually to a node.

Bongs. Afternoon.

They stepped from the node.

Mirf hissed, "Hide, hide!" And hurtled face forward into the deep grass and behind a large clump of shrubs.

J. C. leaped behind another clump and rolled over and over as something clamped itself around him. His arms, chest, waist and legs were being firmly held. He tried to turn his head, but something was pressing against him in such a manner that he couldn't. He could feel the heat radiating into his back.

"Mirf," he whispered. "Let go."

"Shhhh, they'll hear." Her voice came from somewhere else.

Certainly not from directly behind.

Then he could hear them.

Heavy foot steps. Harsh breathing. A number of large some things were passing by, close by.

J .C. began to regulate his breathing, slowing it down, practicing what Tinker had taught him. He realized that he had no choice. He might as well calm down.

The thumping footfalls began to fade away. He waited

for Mirf to release him. Other than the faint noises of insect buzzing, he couldn't hear anything.

"Over-sexed," said Mirf in his ear. "That's the secret. Your crowd is over-sexed. If it is female, you jump it."

"Partner," said J. C. "Something has me in its clutches and all you can do is start making crude remarks."

Mirf tickled the back of his neck and said to the something that had him in its clutches. "You can let him go now, glitter eyes. He is safe."

The bands released him. Mirf grabbed him by the shirt front and pulled him away and up to his feet. He turned as his captor rose and looked at him.

It was a her.

The lower pair of arms hung straight down and slightly back. The middle pair were akimbo, her hands on her hips. The upper pair were held behind her back, hands clasping each other. She looked at him, and blinked. "Chirp?"

"Nice bod," observed Mirf. "I thought that she was a female."

The creature's upper arms pulled her shoulders back.

"She likes you, partner. See, she is preening. Pretty nice pair, huh?"

"Mirf, I don't think that you had better open an another office after all. I don't think that anyone is ready for this." He stared at the statue grown large.

"Chirp?"

"He likes you, he likes you," said Mirf, stepping close to his side. "Tell her you like her," she hissed at him.

"Sure." J. C. smiled. "I like you."

"Chirp."

"**Right!**" boomed Mirf, agreeing with her. She spun around and called for Grizmek.

The frog-thief hopped from a dense thicket.

"Don't worry, sticky fingers, they don't eat frogs."

"Ulp." Grizmek stood behind J. C. and peered around

him at the suk-dragon. He had never seen one before.

Suddenly J.C. laughed, threw an arm around Mirf and yanked her close. "I am the first, the very first."

Grizmek leaped away, far to one side.

"Well," said Mirf slyly. "You could be. She is young, I think."

"Ethno-zenologist, Mirf, ethno-zenologist."

"Sounds dirty to me. Could we go behind those trees and have you show me." Mirf fiddled with his belt buckle.

J. C. slapped her hand. "Ethno-zenology, the study of alien forms of life. It is an expansion of anthropology, the study of Homo sapiens. I am the first one. How do you like that?"

Mirf grabbed his shoulders and spun him around. "**BINGO!** I knew the agency was lacking something." She let go and rubbed her hands together. "Money, money, money! A whole new division. Wonder why no-one ever thought of it before?"

Grinning broadly, she kissed him. "A new section of the agency. Ho boy! You can be the Chief, what? Chief Ethno-zenologist. Glad that I thought of it." Then her face fell. "Only one small problem."

"What's that?"

"We have to finish this job. First. And survive it."

"Chirp?"

"Ulp?"

"O.K., O.K., we will start in a moment."

"You speak those languages, don't you?"

"Sure, more or less. Part of my training. Or maybe some of that hob-goblin" She shrugged a shoulder. "Let's go."

J. C. began to stamp a flat spot in the grass. "How about we sit down first and have a little talk? First."

Mirf joined him. And as soon as the four of them were sitting down, she crossed her legs, leaned forward, and said to J. C., "So, what's to talk about?"

"Won't Quam be mad at Grizmek for stealing its

things?"

"Nope. He made a promise, remember?"

"Where are we? And why?"

"Bongs. We need to steal a key. It is what Quam told me."

"Doesn't she have a shirt?"

"Nope. They all run around that way. You will just have to restrain yourself."

"Chirp." The suk-dragon hitched closer to J. C.

Mirf winked at him. "She just said that it would be all right with her if you wanted to fondle her."

J .C. glared at the suk-dragon, then at Mirf. "You, partner, are getting out of line, again."

Mirf tried to look contrite. "Sorry, partner. I just couldn't resist. It was your expression." Then she leaned very close and said very softly. "You could consider it field work." She laughed.

"Ulp?"

"Chirp?"

"B. S.," said J. C.

"Good thing I am a polyglot," mumbled Mirf. "O.K., J. C., I'll stop. But you will have to get used to it. There are a whole lot of races here, there, and everywhere."

"I'll adjust. But Doc will find it hard to believe."

"Ah, partner."

"Yes."

"Secrecy Act. You can't. Not in your elseplace. It is still too isolated, not ready. Much too violent, much too exploitive."

"I didn't sign anything."

"J .C., you must promise. Even I can't break that rule."

"O.K. I promise."

Mirf fished the gold medallion from her pocket. "Press your thumb here, count to two, and release."

J. C. did as instructed. Mirf put the shield away and patted his hip.

"You can always talk to me. Or your friends. They'll understand."

She stood up. "Let's go. Before those things come back. O.K., J. C.?"

"Let's go, partner." He stood and took her am. "It is an adventure all right." He laughed. "And interesting and educational."

The road they were following had been beaten into the earth by the passage of many heavy feet. They crested a slight rise and stopped. Far below them, at the base of the shallow swale, was a scatter of misshapen structures.

"Looks like a dump. We have to go in there?"

"That's where Quam said the first key is."

"Did he, or she, or it, say in which hovel?"

"Nope."

"Did, ah, Quam, say what this key looked like?"

"Nope."

"I think he, or whatever, set you up."

Mirf started down the slope. J. C. trotted at her side, waving for the other two to come along.

"Mirf, what is her name?"

"Who?"

"That, ummm, suk-dragon."

"They don't use names. The recognize each other by scent and dermal patterning."

"Well I can't just say, hey you, can I?"

"You got her, bubee, you name her."

J. C. turned his head and called, "Come on, Grizmek, come on, Fred, don't lag behind like that."

"Messhuggener."

"It's a good name." J. C. laughed at her, with her, happily.

They walked down a crooked space between the haphazard constructions. The buildings appeared to be made from limbs and branches, tucked together, forming rounded domes about fifteen feet tall.

Mirf stepped to an entrance and peered inside. "We might as well start here. **ANYONE HOME?**"

Someone snarled.

She stalked inside. "We need to talk."

Something large and round smashed into her stomach, hurtling her up and through the flimsy wall to crash heavily against the adjoining building.

Grizmek took one bound and disappeared. J. C. ran to the crumpled figure and began to throw broken wood in all directions. Fred peered over his shoulder.

"Don't just stand there staring, Fred, help." The suk-dragon moved around him and rapidly removed all the debris.

Mirf was lying there looking very, very dead.

J .C. gently rolled her onto her back and felt for a pulse on the side of her neck. Her eyes fluttered open. "Ho boy, I keep forgetting that I am me, not that hob-goblin."

"Anything broken?"

She waggled her fingers and toes. "Nope. Help me up."

J. C. and Fred did.

"Chirp?"

"I'm fine, thank you." Mirf slowly unbent. There was a great black stain on the front of her shirt. She looked at it and mumbled.

"Time for Plan B." She yanked her necklace off.

"That was Plan A? Maybe you better explain Plan Band C."

"Sorry, partner. I told you when we started. I just make it up as I go along." Mirf held the bent rod at arms length, the open end pointed away from her. "Now if I can just remember how this thing works."

Something flashed. A large wedge of the house cluster blew pattering across the distance ground.

"Ho boy," grunted Mirf.

"Holy Cow," gasped J. C.

"Don't start calling them, they make me nervous."

Mirf waved her arms and blew the top off another of the structures and peered over the edge of the cut wall. "You ready to talk to me now?"

Something snarled.

She jabbed the weapon down the entry way.

Something screamed. And hurtled itself through the back wall. It scrambled on hands and feet around and toward them. "Mercy, mercy, mercy," it gurgled over and over.

"Enough with the mercy, mercy, mercy. Where's the key?"

The thing sat up. "Key?"

"Dirt pile," hissed Mirf. "No games."

"What is key?" One eye looked one way, the other eye looked somewhere else.

"**RAZ BAZ.**" Mirf was beginning to get a wild expression on her face.

J. C. touched her shoulder, gently. "Let's send Grizmek."

"Good idea. **GRIZMEK!**"

The frog-thief leaped from somewhere. "Ulp, ulp?"

"Start looking, gonif. Find something valuable."

Grizmek ducked into the nearest structure. And screamed as he was hurtled up though the roof.

"Oi," said Mirf, jabbing the weapon in that direction. Another part of the settlement blew out across the landscape.

"It is a bad plan that cannot be altered. A whole bunch of guys." She smiled at J. C. and asked, "So what's Plan C."

"Bribery."

"I should have thought of that." She tossed a gold coin in front of the still groveling creature. It snatched it up. "Listen you. For each, um, house we search, one gold. How's that?"

"Bong," agreed the thing.

"Grizmek, let's try that again." She tossed a gold coin

into a structure and waved Grizmek after it. The frog-thief nervously followed the coin. In a moment he shot out the door.

"Ulp."

"So O.K., we spend a little."

Mirf and Grizmek worked their way through the remainder of the standing structures. Grizmek fetched out two things. One was a very ugly clay statue, the other a bent and twisted piece of metal.

Mirf looked back to where J. C. and Fred were sitting.

"What's Plan D?"

"Sit and think."

"I'll sit. You think." Mirf dropped to the ground next to him and watched J. C. disappear. He really didn't, physically. Mirf leaned forward and waved her hand in front of his eyes. He didn't blink. J. C. was thinking. Mirf sat back and began to idly chew on the tip of one finger nail. It was an old hob-goblin habit from when she had talons.

"Chirp?"

"Where?" Mirf looked up at the top of the hill.

Several large things were standing up there and staring down at the wrecked dwellings. And at them.

"J. C.," hissed Mirf. "We've got to go. NOW!" Nothing happened.

"Partner?" No reaction. She yelled into one of his ears, "**HELLO IN THERE!** Speak to me." Mirf jumped to her feet, arm raised, ready to bang him on the side of the head. His eyes focused. Then he turned his head and looked at Grizmek. "Use the jewel. Search again."

"**QUICKLY!**" Mirf scattered gold coins in all directions. "Hop, hop, **HOP!**"

J. C. stood up. "What's all the excitement about?"

Fred pointed at the not too distant hill top, three times at once.

"OH," said J. C,. looking up.

"Definitely an understatement," hissed Mirf.

The monsters had started down the slope toward them.

"When I tell you to, you follow me." Mirf began to swivel her head from side to side, sniffing loudly. "Hee Hoo, we are in luck."

Grizmek shot from one of the dwellings. "Ulp, ulp, ulp, ulp, ulp."

"**RUN!**" screamed Mirf. "**FOLLOW ME!**" She shot down the road through the dwellings and straight at the monsters which were just entering the edge of the complex. "**RUN, RUN, RUN!**"

Grizmek bounded past J. C. in one bound. "Ulp, ulp, ulp, ulp."

Mirf slid to a frantic halt, her boots sliding on the wet clay soil. She pointed to an open pit. "In there."

She grabbed J. C.'s arm as he ran up and yanked him in with her. Fred hit them in mid air, arms wrapping around them. Grizmek flew past. "ULP!"

Dindar Din Dinde. Bright Sunny Day.

They stumbled across the flower bed, the lawn, and out onto the side walk.

Mirf batted at Fred's hands. "Let go, let go. If I require fondling, I will ask my partner."

"Chirp?"

"You betcha."

Fred released them.

Grizmek hopped over, brushing leaves from his clothes.

"I took a side trip. The hotel is just down there. The place with the fancy entrance. The agency has suites in there."

Mirf started down the sidewalk, took a few steps and started to crumple.

"Help me, partner, I don't feel so good." She stifled a groan.

J.C. leaped to her side, tugging her arm up and over his shoulder, sliding the other arm around her waist. "Fred, get the other side. Grizmek, you open the doors when we get there."

They walked as fast as they could to the chosen hotel. Grizmek whipped open the door and followed them to the front desk.

Mirf pulled her arms loose and leaned on the counter, and said, "The key to Suite 309." She shoved the golden emblem across the countertop.

The deskman hastily fetched the key and pushed it and the gold medallion at her. Then he stared, curled his lip, and sneered. "We don't let her kind in here."

"Chirp?"

Mirf slid one hand across the counter, gripped the far edge, and punched the deskman between the eyes. "Schmuck." She had put all her remaining strength into the blow.

He dropped from sight.

"Help me upstairs. They have an elevator." She started to release her grip, her knees buckling.

Mirf pushed the medallion at Grizmek. "You know where the office is, here?"

"Ulp."

"Take this and bring a healer, a doctor, or something like that. Tell them my name. And hurry. Please." Her eyes rolled up as she sagged limply.

"Let's go." said J. C. to Fred.

They had Mirf stretched out on one of the beds when Grizmek and a very large man burst into the room. The man pushed J. C. aside, bent over Mirf and began to undo her clothes.

He grunted when he saw the bruising, and growled at J .C. "You will never see the light of day again, assassin."

"Ulp?"

"And your miscreant helpers."

One of Mirf's eyes struggled open. "Dumbkopf. My partner. Stick . . . medicine."

"Go in the other room. And wait. I must fill out a report."

Mirf mumbled as they left. "Bureaucrap."

Finally the healer came out and asked J. C. a long series of questions and started to leave. As he headed out the door, J. C. stopped him. "Would you check on the guy behind the desk? Mirf might have hurt him."

The healer shook his head from side to side. "I will. Every time she passes through, there is trouble."

He left, headed downstairs

J. C. and the others slipped into the bedroom. Mirf was under the covers, only her face showing.

"Mirf?"

"Hiya, J. C."

"You all right?"

She tried to smile. "I've felt better. But I'll be fine. You get a vacation. Of a sort."

J .C. ran a palm over her cheek.

"I need to sleep, partner. Grizmek can show you the sights."

"What do we do with Fred? That guy on the desk was pretty serious about her."

"Got what he deserved. Make her wear a big, baggy something robe. Should . . . do . . . the . . . trick." Mirf fell asleep as someone knocked on their door.

J .C. went to see who their visitor was this time.

The healer glared at him. "I sent the deskman to a curing center. He will live." He turned and hurried away.

J. C. shut the door and turned to the others in the living room.

"Grizmek, you heard what Mirf said. Go buy Fred a robe or something else equally loose. Something appropriate for this culture."

Grizmek hopped out the door.

J. C. sat and waited.

Fred sat next to him, slipped three arms around him. And waited. "Chirp?"

"I suppose." It took some time. J. C. wished he had thought to pack a book.

Fred leaned her head on his shoulder and fell asleep. She buzzed softly.

Finally Grizmek popped back into suite.

Fred jerked awake, which woke J. C.

J. C. stood up and took the robe and held it out in front of himself, and turned it back and forth. "Not bad. Slip this on, Fred. Then we can take a stroll and see what this town is like."

Fred shook her head violently from side to side and folded all her arms over her chest.

"Robe or stay," stated J. C. firmly. "And only stick two arms outside."

Fred glared at him, grabbed the robe and slipped it over her head.

"Turn around. Let's see how it looks."

She did. The robe flared neatly and fell in gentle folds, ending just below her knees.

"Looks pretty good to me. What do you think, Grizmek?"

"Ulp. Good."

"Well then, let's go see the city. You lead the way. We will follow. Don't pout Fred, you can shed it when we get back inside."

And so it went.

For five days.

Each day, the healer arrived in the morning, visited Mirf, glared at J. C., and left.

And each day, they went sight-seeing. Grizmek managed to pick up a thing or two without Fred or J .C. noticing.

When they entered the suite at the end of yet another day of touring about, the eighth day, Mirf had supper waiting.

"Welcome back, partner. Having a good time?"

Fred hurtled her robe into a corner.

"Big city, partner. But I am getting bored just wandering around, killing time. How do you feel?"

"Fit as a fiddle, right as rain, raring to go." She leered at him. "We can leave in the morning. I ordered wine for our meal."

J .C. drank one glass during the meal.

Mirf a lot.

Grizmek preferred water.

Fred had a few. "Chirp?" And bobbled her head up and down.

"Pretty good, huh?" Mirf served the dessert. And refilled J. C.'s glass.

Fred sat next to J .C., tickled his ear, his ribs, and patted his thigh.

"Stop that."

She twittered.

"What does she want?" stated J. C., slowly and carefully.

"Better that you shouldn't know. Partner, your face is getting awfully red."

"Oh, oh." J. C. surged to his feet and canted heavily to one side. "Bed. I've got to get to bed." And headed for the bedroom.

Fred leaped after him and tilted him upright just before he would have smashed into the doorjamb.

He grinned lopsidedly. "Thanks, ladies," he said, counting all the hands helping him.

By the time he hit the bed he was sound asleep.

"Ho boy," said Mirf from the doorway. "Was that a bad idea."

Fred rolled him under the covers as Mirf went back to the living room.

His eyes popped open. He smelled breakfast, and sat

up. "Hey."

Mirf leaned in through the doorway. "Morning, partner. You hungry?"

"Yes. Where's my clothes?"

"Beats me. You were wearing them when you fell in there." She hissed loudly and spun around. "Fred, you sneak, what did you do with his clothes?" And disappeared into the living room. In a moment Mirf stomped back into bed. "Little minx was curious. Said that she had never seen anyone sleep that soundly." She dumped his clothes on the bed.

"Always happens. Low alcohol tolerance. Three drinks max!"

"Bizzle. Food's ready." Mirf carefully closed the door as she left.

They waited breakfast for him.

As soon as everyone was finished, Mirf looked around the table and announced, "Let's hit the road."

"Whoa there, pard."

"What?"

"We haven't checked to see whether Grizmek got the key or not."

"RIGHT!" Mirf looked at Grizmek. "So show us what you got."

Grizmek began to set things on the table.

"What's all this?" asked J. C.

"Looks like you have been shopping, so to speak," answered Mirf. "Which one is the key?"

Grizmek handed her a small rod and began to put away the rest of the stuff.

"How does he stay out of jail?"

"No one ever sees him do it," explained Mirf. "What sort of a key is this, I wonder." She rolled it back and forth between her palms, then handed it to J. C.

"Here, you keep it."

J. C. slipped it into a front pocket and said, "Next thing."

"What?"

"We need a weapon, or something. You almost died. And Quam said that the next two places would be worse."

"I am not good at weapons. How about you?"

"Not much experience, either."

Mirf nodded her head. "That settles that, then. We will just have to be sneaky. Put on your robe, Fred. We have to travel down the street in the broad daylight."

Mirf stood, walked to one wall, and opened a deep hole. Throwing a leather sack at Grizmek, she said, "Stash this somewhere, we might need it."

She smiled at J. C. "Ready, partner."

He stood and headed for the door. "O.K., let's go."

The Foregather at Quata.

Throughout the zone of the Foregather witches from many clans wandered about, often in groups of two or three.

Here and there a warlock strolled along, sometimes accompanied by a witch. Some of these pairs were bonded: mates-for-life. Every witch knew that it was best to politely, very politely, inquire as to the status of any of these males in such a pair.

A witch was fiercely protective of their mate and tended to be flash-ready to deliver chaos and mayhem on anything bothering their chosen.

The warlocks, for the most part, tended to be calmer as well as being a somewhat calming influence on any witch within their vicinity, mate or otherwise.

There were few disasters at a Foregather as all who attended knew the underlying values that allowed such a density of witches to coexist for these short periods of time. It was what made a Foregather possible.

Turintor arranged lodgings at the appropriate booth

and received a detailed map of the Foregather and the surrounding town as well as a list of the scheduled events, demonstrations, and spell displays.

"Let's get something to eat."

Her companion nodded.

So they sat at the small table of the first food place they came to and ordered food and beverage.

The beverage was green with black streaks and sang a soft song. The food was very tasty and well behaved.

As they were enjoying their meal a shadow was cast over their table. So they looked up. Turintor frowned. Her companion just looked.

The one who cast the shadow was tall and very broad shouldered. He was dressed in black clothes with just a hint in of faint grey in the ornate design that ran down the outside of each sleeve. His black boots were polished to a high shine, the bottom portion visible just below the edge of carefully tailored trousers.

"If it is permissible, this warlock would table share." He gestured at their surroundings. "There are no other unclaimed seats."

He stood the proper distance away from them and waited. The decision was up to them to make.

"Very polite," murmured Turintor to her companion whose eyes were still tightly focused upon this person who was bothering them, ever so little. Then she nodded.

He sat and said, "I am Motaiss, Talair witch Clan. Just arrived."

"Potri witch Turintor. My companion is unknown."

Motaiss jerked slightly. "Unknown?" Unknown witch clans were things of ancient myth reputed to be hazardous beyond beyond.

"A temporary condition," hissed Turintor. Her companion had slipped her hand up her left sleeve.

Motaiss nodded. He had felt the faint crackle of witch

spell developing. "May I buy, each, another beverage? It is told Quata Fruit Slick is very smooth."

They nodded.

So he did. And took a sip and decided to make a daring request.

"If it is permissible, I would share Foregather with both. I do travel mostly alone and have come far many with none to relax talk."

Turintor looked from Motaiss to her companion and then back to stare into the carefully hooded blue almost black eyes. "We would allow such company. Tell us of the Talair."

He did. It was the polite thing to do.

The Talair had lived in a somewhat isolated elseplace ever since the Great Event that had scattered the witches out into the universe of universes and had begun the many clans. The elseplace of the Talair was named after the original inhabitants of that land who named themselves and their elseplace, Tal.

The Talair mostly lived on Tal but sent a few, carefully trained, out into the many to seek knowledge. And cautiously, carefully, added to their clan knowledge.

"It is now named Talandra after the mid-day sky of the warm time."

"Talandra." Turintor frowned. "A not quite new word."

Motaiss carefully placed his hands on the table top, sitting still as still.

"It is said that the folk of Talandra are subtle beyond subtle, softer than soft," said Turintor.

He watched two carefully controlled witch expressions and cast every protection spell that he knew. Then he saw some slight expression flicker between them.

"The very polite, and subtle, Motaiss may join us during and for the Foregather. If such a warlock does so wish."

"Yesssssss." He nodded at them. "So I wish."

"We would first visit the Seek Spell booth."

"Eeeah." Motaisse stood. "Always a thing to learn, seek spells."

The trio wandered out into the Foregather.

Der'Cha'Ter'Der'Cha. Morning. Just Past Rising Sun.

Tinker looked up. The sky was a deep, dark blue. All around them the terrain was stark. Sandy and rocky. On the far horizon loomed a large something, artificial, constructed.

"O.K. Where are we?"

"The natives call this place, Der'Cha'Ter'Der'Cha," gurgled R-Bar. "We call it Larza Land. The folk are scally, like Larza beasts."

"A sere abode, My Lord."

"You've been here before, I gather."

"Oh, yes." R-Bar frowned. "We will have to walk from here. They get nervous if I just pop in."

"We can use the exercise, MindMate." Smoke stretched. "We have been laying about too much."

"Probably right in that. Shall we start?"

R-Bar walked to one side of the group. "The trail is over there. We have to walk in a single file. Local custom."

"You go first. If they see a familiar figure, it will be better than a stranger. Keep them from getting nervous."

Off they went, single file. Smoke brought up the rear, reaching out in all directions, her sensenet cast wide. Not much around, she thought, and too far from that structure. For the moment, they were safe.

"What are we doing here?" Tinker spoke to R-Bar's back.

"We are going to visit Penny Collect," she answered. "In this sector the person to see, hum, hum, hum."

Hum, hum, hum, My Lord?

Right. When these witches hum they are up to something.

I think she is nice.

I didn't say that she wasn't, kitten. Just that she is up to something.

Dark Sister?

Princess Queen, the witch minds are hard to see clearly. I am not used to them. But eventually.

Then we will wait and see.

Oh, Aye, My Lord.

One, did she say scally?

Larza, My Tinker?

Wait and see, gang.

They fell silent and walked along, each mind thinking its own thoughts. Finally, they were close enough for Smoke's sensenet to spread into the structure.

A great fortress. This is a frontier. We are walking out of their wilderness, their wild place, their vast unknown.

Friend or foe? Chicken popped her sword up and down in its scabbard .

Vague curiosity. I think that they do recognize the witch. No fear, no danger reaction.

Smoke pulled her sensenet in. *Too many minds.*

"It's immense," said Tinker.

"One of their smaller ones," said R-Bar. "Tink?" She turned and carefully watched his face.

"What?"

"Let me speak for the group. Please?"

"Sure, go ahead. You know this place, we don't."

They started walking again. Toward the great structure.

They slowly approached the gate. As they trudged up the incline, R-Bar waggled her arm in an ornate pattern. The gate lifted and they filed inside the entry portal. The gate slid down.

They were trapped inside a long stone hall with a gate at either end.

"Just checking," whispered R-Bar, heading for the far end.

The inner gate lifted.

"Let's go see Penny Collect," said the little witch.

The streets she led them through were narrow with many twists and turns. At places they were wide enough for four people to walk abreast. Then around a corner and the street was just wide enough for one person to walk, shoulders brushing either side. On some blocks the buildings were all one story tall. On the next sat structures that rose high overhead.

They passed through spaces that were open, large and small. These seemed to be the market places, the spots where shops and cafes were located. And it was in these places that they saw the bulk of the population.

The inhabitants were definitely reptilian in appearance. They were wide in the shoulder and thick in the body and legs. All their backs were bowed to some degree, varying from person to person. All the faces were more elongated than the human model. Faces and hands had a soft shine from the tiny scales that covered the skin with a color that ranged from light tan to dark rich red-brown

Smoke?

They see us as an inferior race of barbarians from the wilds. Not something to fear.

R-Bar led them deeper and deeper into the fortress city. "This is where the non-folk live," she explained.

The buildings here were of the same construction as the rest of the place, but they had an air of disrepair. Tinker noticed that there were at least a dozen different kind of folk in here, all hurrying about their business.

R-Bar ducked into a very narrow street and led them to the end.

They stood facing a solid wooden door. Gleaming letters arched over it announcing the owner's name

PEN' AA' ENE' KUL' LE' EKT

"Penny Collect," said R-Bar. She thumped the door knocker three times and pulled the door open. They followed her inside, Fair Morn pulled the door closed behind them.

They stood in a large room, a large cluttered room. Tables and cabinets, in no apparent order, stood awash in boxes, crates, and a jumble of artifacts made from every kind of material imaginable.

Everything wore a coat of dust. From inside the piles and heaps they could hear things rustling about. Overhead, objects of all sizes and shapes hung from the ceiling. Every available spot on the walls was festooned with more things.

R-Bar led them down a narrow aisle to a small door almost buried behind towers of stacked boxes. She rapped on it with one knuckle and waited.

Slowly the door opened and she stepped through followed by the others.

No sound.

No warning.

The bolt snapped down, from one upper corner, and tossed the witch sideways, crashing into a heap of metallic objects.

One blast and one silent flash removed a large section of this structure in the general area where the assassin had been. Messenger and Fair Morn leaped to either side of Tinker, ready to level the remainder of the place.

WAIT! Smoke only felt one other entity besides themselves. He was in small, dark space, frightened.

She turned her head and pointed to a packing crate in the far corner. It had other boxes piled on top of it.

Tinker hurtled artifacts in all directions and rolled the limp witch onto her back. There was a ragged hole just below her shoulder on the right hand side. Cradling her with one arm, he sat her up, using one leg as a prop. Chicken dropped onto her knees on the other side of R-Bar.

"Be she dead?"

Tinker was feeling for a pulse in her neck. R-Bar's head wobbled loosely. "Not quite."

"My Lord, she does have hole in lower back."

Tinker ripped R-Bar's smock open, using the hole in front as a starting place. "Lung shot, Princess. She has to stay upright and we need something to slap over the two openings."

"Oh, my," gasped Messenger. "She is leaking badly."

"First aid kits," snapped Tinker. "Quickly. Fair Morn, watch the door."

Smoke was tossing impediments away so she could reach whoever was hiding in the crate. Ripping the front panel away, she grabbed him by the throat, her minds overwhelming his.

Turning from the box, she dragged the limb body over to where Tinker and Chicken were trying to aid R-Bar.

R-Bar mumbled something as blood trickled from the corner of her mouth.

Messenger handed two large pads to Tinker.

"Here, Princess," he said, handing her one. "Press this over the hole in her back. Messenger, tape it in place." He ripped the paper covering away with his teeth, snatched out the pad and slapped it over the hole in front.

Chicken leaned over to do the same thing and gasped. "My Lord, her wound do wiggle most strangely." She sucked in a breath.

"What?"

"It do heal itself."

"Nonsense."

"Do see for thyself." Holding the pad in place, he bent around, Chicken holding the sagging witch upright. The wound was almost closed by red, coarse tissue. He jerked back, lifted the pad he held in place, and stared.

The front wound, smaller than the back one, was totally closed by a similar mass of pebbly material.

"Hold her up, Princess. Give me antiseptic, Messenger. At least we can sterilize the area." He began to gently wipe the blood away from the entry wound, being very generous with the antiseptic. Then he did the back. Satisfied that there was nothing else he could do, he sat back on his legs. And looked at what Smoke had dragged over.

"Is he dead?"

"No, MindMate, waiting."

"Wake him up."

Smoke reached in and yanked his consciousness to the surface.

The man's eyes popped open, the blood drained from his face, and he slumped sideways.

"It was painful," explained Smoke. She nudged him back.

"Who are you?" asked Tinker.

The man stared at R-Bar. "She called me Penny Collect."

"Why did you try to kill her?"

Penny Collect jerked. "Not me. **NEVER!** The witches would come."

"True," said Smoke.

Penny Collect's eyes darted up to see who was speaking and saw her eyes watching him.

"Ahhhhhhhh, da demon, a female da demon." He grabbed Tinker's arm. "Do not give me to her, I beg, I plead, do no, do not!"

"Who shot her?" Tinker stood.

"Him," whispered Penny Collect, rising to stand close to Tinker.

"Him, who?"

The answer was whispered even more softly. "Him, the warlock with no name. He set the trap and locked me in that crate. He laughed. He said she would come sooner or later. If it was later, maybe the smell wouldn't frighten her away. I couldn't get free. No one could hear me." He started to weep.

"Smoke, is there anything we can do for her?"

"No."

"My Lord, we must to node go." Chicken gently smoothed R-Bar's hair back with one hand.

"We don't know how to work it."

"Tis slim chance for success there. Do we here stay with chances none?"

Tinker leaned forward and shook the still weeping figure. "Penny, she came here looking for something. Do you have any idea what it would be?"

Penny Collect looked up, wiped his face on his sleeve, and gestured at the room. "There are many, many things here. She liked small amusements."

Tinker sighed. Then he scanned the room. "It would take forever."

"MyTinker, I could search."

"Try. "

Messenger walked off, clenching her wand in her right hand.

Penny Collect stared at it. Then he spoke softly to Tinker.

"How did she get that wand?"

"Recognize it?"

"Only the power."

"It was a gift."

Penny Collect stepped even closer to Tinker, beginning to feel less frightened. "How is it and who are you that travels with such females?"

"Just lucky, I guess." He nodded. "Name is Tinker, John Tinker," he replied in his best James Bond tone of voice. He was watching Messenger drifting up one narrow aisle and down the next, in and around the stacks.

"Smoke, how is R-Bar doing?"

"Still alive."

R-Bar mumbled, and drooled a red, muscous stream

from one corner of her mouth.

"We better get ready to leave."

"I will carry her, MindMate. Fair Morn has that weapon."

"Princess, you take the left side, I'll take the right. In the narrow places, I go first. Ready?"

"Indeed, My Lord."

"Fair Morn, you lead in front when the space is open enough. If anything tries to interfere, zap it."

Fair Morn nodded. "Yes, One."

He called, "Come on, Messenger, it is time to go."

She screamed. The dark corner lit up with a bright flash.

Tinker hurtled over piles, weaponkin in his hand.

Smoke was right behind him. Penny Collect dropped to the floor and huddled into as small a shape as he could.

They found Messenger, hunkering on top of a large box, pointing the wand at a head lying on the floor. It was part of a statue.

"Don't touch it, don't touch it."

"What is it?"

"Evil, evil, evil."

"What evil?"

"It is part of that thing. Like those pieces we found before."

Tinker lightly rubbed her back. "Kitten, how do we take it with us?"

"With us?"

"Yes. Back to Ripple."

"Ooooooooooh."

"Sssssssssssh." He held her in an awkward embrace. "How?"

"Use that green container." The head snapped its teeth at them.

"How?"

"The gold rod. Poke it with the gold rod."

Gingerly, working together, Messenger watching carefully, Tinker and Smoke shoved the head into the green container and fastened the latches. There was a carrying handle on the top. It was hollow.

They slipped the gold rod into it and latched the plate over the end.

"I will carry this thing," said Messenger, taping the case with her wand. White fire cascaded over the container and faded. She picked it up by the handle, using her left hand, never releasing her grip on the wand in her right hand.

As they gathered around the front door, Tinker turned to the shop owner. "Mr. Collect, what do we owe you for that thing?"

"Nothing. One thing."

"What?"

"Tell the witches, tell them, it was not my fault."

"I will tell her sister what happened."

Penny Collect squinted at Tinker. "Which one is that?"

"Ripple."

Penny Collect pulled at his hair and howled into the air, "I am a dead man, a dead man! Dead, dead!"

"Move somewhere else," suggested Tinker. "Let's go, gang."

Fair Morn pushed open the door.

As they passed through the foreigners' compound, they received many stares, but no one moved to interfer with them. Folk whispered to each other and pointed at the dark woman carrying the child and the dark stain slowly spreading downward between them.

Entering the main part of the fortress, they turned left, guided by Smoke whose mental map always remembered her route. The inhabitants stayed away. They didn't care what the strangers did as long as it didn't affect them.

Finally they stood in front of the first gate. And waited for it to rise.

Tinker grunted. "O. K., enough of this. Just the gate, Fair Morn."

They heard two soft clicks as she readjusted the levers on her weapon and saw a brilliant flash. Only a few edge pieces of the gate remained.

They walked toward and through the hall, having heard far gate sliding up.

As they passed outside, Tinker asked. "How is she doing?"

"Still alive, so far," said Smoke, shifting one of R-Bar's limbs a little. "But we need to hurry."

"You want to give her to Fair Morn, take a rest?"

"**NO!**"

"The far ridge?"

"Yes."

"Fast as possible, then."

They hurried as fast as they could down the narrow path, frequently cutting across the corners of the winding path as directed by Smoke.

"O.K.," said Tinker, turning around and around. "Where is it?"

"Here somewhere," said Smoke.

"Messenger, see anything?"

"No."

"Damn. Smoke, we have to wake her up or we are stuck here."

Smoke reached in and gently pushed. "**OUCH!** She has some kind of protection."

"Now what?" Tinker looked from face to face.

"I will remove it." Messenger brushed tears from her eyes. "Ready, mom?"

Smoke nodded.

Messenger stepped close, made adjustments, and struck R-Bar on the side of the head with her wand.

Smoke plunged through.

R-Bar's eyes popped open.

"Where's that damn node," snapped Tinker.

"Between . . . red rocks," gurgled the witch, dribbling crimson down Smoke's chest.

"Tell it to take us to Ripple," command Tinker, as he moved toward the proper place.

R-Bar managed to nod her head and mumbled something.

Smoke stepped into the node. The rest followed.

Bahn Duhr Tohr. The Royal City. Evening Meal.

They crashed into the room, collapsing tables, and scattering food and broken dishes everywhere. Only Smoke managed to stay on her feet.

Hanred tumbled into a wall. "**OOOOF!**"

Ripple leaped the other way, hissing and snarling and saw Hanred heave himself to his feet. The air crackled with dark energy. "You will die for this." She advanced slowly upon them.

Messenger stood up, stepped in front of Ripple, and yelled. "**SHUT UP!**"

Thunder rumbled overhead, the ceiling creaked.

Messenger jabbed her wand straight up. "**YOU ALSO!**" She swung her left arm around and slammed the green container into Ripple's stomach. "This is for you. R-Bar desperately needs help. **DO IT!** "

Ripple glared at Messenger and narrowed her eyes. She could feel the magic pouring in great streams from the agitated young woman standing in front of her.

"Calm yourself, powerful one. We do not need an accident."

Tinker stood, brushing food from his clothes. "R-Bar was shot by something. We brought her here. We didn't know what else to do."

Ripple's head snapped sideways. She stared at the burden Smoke carried and the gory mess she had become. "Husband," she snapped. "Take her into the spare room. We must be swift."

Hanred stepped up to Smoke and held out his arms. Smoke gently slipped R-Bar into them, and said, "Still alive." She grabbed a surviving chair and sat down.

Ripple opened the sealed room, set the container down, and backed out. Then she ran into the room that Hanred had entered and slammed the door behind herself.

They stood looking around the room.

Fair Morn picked up a few of the chairs that were still usable.

Chicken found an unopened jug and two metal goblets.

"I am very hungry," said Smoke.

Chicken handed her one of the filled goblets.

Messenger threw her arms around Tinker and leaned her head against his chest. "I'm sorry, MyTinker, but she made me angry. She was just being indignant and not paying any attention to her sister." She started to cry.

He held her tight. "Nothing to cry about. She deserved it."

Messenger looked up. "Will she live?"

"I don't know. We did all that we could do."

"My Lord, We shall sally Us forth and do some servant find. And fetch Ourselves a meal." Chicken walked to the door and threw it open.

"Who are you?" they both said.

"I am Rotak," said the woman shoving past Chicken.

Chicken grabbed her by the shoulder and spun her around. "And I am the Princess Chicken, Queen to Our Noble Lord Tinker, Sister to the Most Royal King Toucan. Fetch us some food, ill-mannered wench."

Rotak spun away from her, and kicked her way through the mess on the floor. "Fetch your own food! What has been happening in here?"

She glared at Smoke. "Who are you? Are you injured?" Then she saw Tinker holding Messenger.

Rotak leaped sideways. "What is that doing in here?"

The ceiling rumbled, thunder crackled.

"Oh!" said Rotak. She waved away the mess, restored the furniture, and covered the table with food stuffs.

"Never met you before." She stomped into the spare room to see if Ripple needed some help.

They sat and ate.

And waited.

And long after their meal was done, Ripple, Rotak, and Hanred came from the bed room.

Rotak twisted away to her rooms.

Ripple dropped into an empty chair and took a goblet from Hanred. Her hand shook from fatigue. She glanced at Tinker from half-lidded eyes. "She wants to see you."

"You are a mess," she said to Smoke and winked her away. The great splash from the tub room told everyone where Smoke had been sent.

"Bed," mumbled Ripple. She and Hanred disappeared.

Tinker walked over and into the spare bedroom.

R-Bar was sitting propped up by several thick pillows. Her pale witch complexion, even paler, was drained of what little color she normally had. She was wearing a robe of some dark fluffy material, open at the neck.

Tinker sat on the edge of the bed. Only her eyes moved, watching him. Her voice came all harsh whisper, "You saved my life, Tink." She stared into his eyes. "All of you."

He picked up one of her limp hands and held it. "That's what friends are for, kiddo."

R-Bar tried to smile. Tear's began to trickle down her cheeks.

He brushed them away. "Guess you are going to live, huh?"

"Yes," she whispered.

He stood up. "Look, I think you had better sleep now, O.K.? I will see you tomorrow."

"Kiss me . . . Tink."

He leaned over and did. And started to say something and stopped. She was sleeping.

They all headed for their bedroom.

In the morning, while they were all lounging in their rooms after breakfast, Ripple appeared. "She is awake and would like you to visit."

"Who?" asked Tinker.

"You."

"O. K." He stood. "See you later, gang. Let's go," he said to Ripple.

He was standing in R-Bar's bedroom. A palace servant was just removing a tray from her lap.

Tinker sat on the edge of the bed. "You look better. You going to be all right? How do you feel?"

The servant left.

"Alive. Do you want to feel me?" Her hand slowly raised her napkin to her mouth and slowly wiped away something red.

"You need lots of rest, you know."

"I need company. It is no fun staring at white walls."

"So what do you want to do?"

He heard Messenger giggle at something Smoke had suggested.

Go away, you guys. They did.

"Slight change around your eyes just then." R-Bar tried a slight smile.

"So what do you want to do?" he asked again.

"You didn't answer my question."

"Not going to."

"Talk to me."

"O.K. What about?"

"Yourself. Them. How you got to be what you are?"

"It is a very long story."

He bent down and unlaced and removed his boots. Then he heaved two pillows next to her's, plumped them up and lay on the bed, his back propped up at a comfortable angle. "Might as well get comfortable, don't you agree?"

"Oh, yes." She thought that it was a good idea

He carefully slipped an arm around her shoulders. "Now, this is how it all began."

The next morning, she said, "Tell me some more." And held his hand tightly.

"You feeling better?"

"Oh, yes. Much better."

So, he got comfortable, and continued the story.

The third morning, she said, "Don't leave without me, Tink."

"We can't. We don't know how you guys do that, move from place to place."

"Promise? Please?"

"O.K. We won't. Promise."

R-Bar patted the bed and grinned.

So, he got comfortable, and continued the story.

The fourth morning, R-Bar sat with her knees up. "I can get out of bed tomorrow and take walks."

"Good. I am running out of story to tell." He made himself comfortable.

She reached over and tickled him.

"Look, if you are going to do that, I will have to sit in a chair."

She pouted.

"Nice lower lip, kid." He continued the story.

On the fifth day, he found her standing in front of the mirror, dressed in her usual costume, twisting from side to side, and snarling at what she saw. "Dim, dim, dim, dim, dim, **DIM!**"

"What's the problem, short stuff?"

"I am not short. Or stuff." R-Bar whipped around and glared at him. "I have lost weight."

"Yep, certainly have. Makes your face even prettier. Not so chubby-cheeked. Nice cheek bones. Emphasizes those gorgeous eyes."

"You really think so?" She looked over her shoulder into the mirror. "I have lost weight everywhere."

"Happens when you are sick."

She turned sideways and inhaled.

"What are you doing?"

R-Bar stared down the front of her smock. "Now I look more like a child than before."

Tinker laughed.

She growled. And glared at him. He wasn't being nice.

"Looks pretty good to me. And to tell you the truth, I don't know any child that pokes out like that, kid."

R-Bar danced over to stand in front of him. "Really? You are not just saying that, are you, Tink?"

"Nope. Where are we walking to?"

She grabbed his arm. "Down to the main market and back."

"You sure you can do all that?"

R-Bar gurgled. "You can carry me if I collapse. I don't weight as much now." And wondered whether she ought to collapse. Not too far from the castle.

"Let's go."

Then she wondered whether he would really carry her.

They sat at a small cafe, outside, and watched people hurrying here and there. They were sipping from some local concoction, eating a local delicacy.

"Do they mind?"

"Who? Mind? What?"

"Them."

Tinker laughed. "Oh, they them. Who?"

R-Bar frowned at him. Witches weren't used to not being answered when they asked questions. Immediately. It was not healthy for the one asked to not answer. "Your Queen, Chicken. And the others," she stated firmly, firmly as only a witch could state firmly.

"Oh. About what?" He was suppressing a smile, hiding it by sipping from his cup.

"You being with me so much the last many days."

Of course not, My Lord.

"I don't think so."

MindMate, you know we do not.

R-Bar looked at him very carefully. "They don't wonder what you, we, might have been doing? In my bed? Alone? Just you and me?"

Tinker heard Messenger giggle. "Nope."

One, I think that you should tell her.

Indeed, My Lord, do.

Tinker sighed.

R-Bar looked worried. "Was I getting too personal?"

She hoped not. After all, he was strange. But, perhaps, a person one might associate with.

"Nope. Ummmmm. I need to explain something to you, ah, about us, me, err, me and them."

"They are angry with you, right?" She grabbed one of his hands, ready to defend him. The air crackled wildly. After all, he had saved her life. "I will tell them that we didn't do anything. Cause we didn't. They are angry, correct?"

He took another sip from his cup. "Ah, no. Look, this is a little hard to explain. Remember I told you how we all came together and all that?"

She nodded. "Yes."

"Well, there is something else, umm, that I didn't mention."

She frowned. "What?" Maybe he wasn't really a person but something else.

Tinker rubbed his chin and looked at her. "O. K., do this. Hold your hand out, either one, toward me. How many fingers?"

She released his hand and looked at her own. "Five." And looked up at him, puzzled.

"They are all part of your hand and your hand doesn't operate with only one finger, right?"

"Yes." Her frown deepened. Her eyes began to squint a little.

"Now think of them and me as your hand. We are like that."

She frowned. "You're not connected." And waggled her fingers at him.

He tapped his forehead. "In here, we are."

Her mouth dropped open. "They are all in there?"

"Sort of. We share, ah, we are all together, and separate, at some time. But we can be private, if we wish."

R-Bar leaned forward and whispered. "Are they listening now?"

"And seeing, if they wish."

"That is why your eyes go strange around the edges. It is when they are talking with you."

She stared into his eyes. Looking deep. She couldn't see anyone in there.

"I suppose."

"Hum, hum, hum." She waggled her fingers in front of his face. "Hayou, whoever is there!" And gurgled.

Tinker stood. "Maybe we ought to head back. You don't want to overdo the first day."

R-Bar flipped a coin to the waiter and grabbed Tinker's arm as they started back toward the castle. "Are we still friends, Tink?"

"Sure. Why?"

"If you are my friend, then they must be also. Correct?"

"Yep."

This time she laughed loudly. A most unwitch thing to do. And swung his arm vigorously as they strolled.

People stared at her. And worried. One rarely heard a laugh like that. Especially from a witch, And made space between themselves and this pair. Laughing witches were said to be on the edge of doing mayhem.

It was a long pleasant stroll, passed in silence.

As they entered the castle, R-Bar looked at him. "If I asked Princess Chicken, your Queen, something, would you know?"

"Only if you wished it to be so, or vice versa."

R-Bar grinned. Then she yawned.

He left her at her door. "Don't wake too early, you need rest."

The living room floor was covered with their gear, supplies, and other materials from their packs.

Smoke and Chicken were kneeling in the midst of everything, talking.

Messenger sat on a couch talking with Fair Morn as they sorted things.

"What's all this?"

"We did think to prepare, My Lord. Dark Sister does feel we do be most ready for travel."

"MindMate, she is almost healed. Her strength is rapidly rebuilding. And many are out there, searching."

Tinker sat next to Fair Morn. "I think you're right. Can't do much to help Ramp and Hard sitting around here. And I am beginning to worry about where J. C. and Mirf have gotten to. Or into. How much longer?"

"Two days," said Smoke.

"She is very nice," said Messenger looking over at Tinker.

"Certainly different than the others that we have met,"

added Fair Morn, stuffing items into her pack.

"I'll say. Those sisters are a surly lot, except for Ramp," said Tinker. "Must be all that witch stuff."

Suddenly he sat up and stared at Smoke. "**NO!**"

She blinked her eyes at him, once. **??**

He stood and tip-toed through the clutter. "Never mind, I am going to bed. That was a long walk."

Far Corner. A Sunny Day.

Abadoda wandered from shop to shop and quietly talked with the local folk that she met. She was polite and unassuming. From her garb everyone thought her to be a witch. From her behavior they thought her to be a very different kind of witch. Witches rarely visited this hardly ever visited corner of the universe of universes, but they had all heard about how witches behaved. And of course they had heard all about the group recently relocating here.

But she was polite and unassuming and her group had purchased and moved into that long ago abandoned rather sprawling edifice on the edge of town. They had repaired and refurbished that place and had pretty much stayed to themselves. Now and then, one of them would wander into town proper to shop and purchase this or that other thing.

All in all that group were so unobtrusive that soon the local folk no longer noticed their presence as being outsiders nor did they any longer discuss them as being different.

And this is exactly what the Sorcerer clan had wanted when they had decided to relocate to this elseplace.

Bahn Duhr Tohr. The Royal City. Fairly Early In the Morning.

They were standing in the main castle hall near a number of doors.

"So, short-stuff, where are we going today?"

R-Bar lifted up on her toes and kissed him.

"What is that for?"

"For being you."

She peered into his eyes. "For all being my friends."

She poked him gently in the side. "And I agree with you. I think that I am much prettier now. To a small bazaar on the other side of the main market."

She grabbed his hand and headed for the outside door, pulling him along.

It was very crowded. Although, as Tinker began to notice, the masses of people, all pushing and shoving, didn't seem to push or shove them nearly as much. He pointed this out to R-Bar.

Her happy expression fell, and she nodded, and said, softly, "It is because I am a witch. Everyone always is a little afraid. Of witches. If Ramp were here they wouldn't pay any attention to her. Or, at least, not as much."

"Well, your group is a little short tempered. And your clothes are a dead giveaway."

"Hum, hum, hum."

"Wear something else."

"I can't do that," she snapped. "It is not done! The Witches Code!" She shook her head.

"You are still recovering. I will protect you." He pointed at a shop along the edge of the market. "Find something pretty."

R-Bar gurgled and tilted her head to one side. "You had better not tell Ripple." And ran into the shop.

In a few moments she returned wearing bright red, floppy pants and a soft rose colored, very low cut, loose blouse of some soft material. The pants were draped over a pair of tan boots. She had the blouse tightly wrapped at her waist by her red belt.

"Very nice," offered Tinker by way of comment. "But pretty loud colors."

"I like red."

They had to push and shove their way across the

bazaar.

"Let's find a place to sit down," suggested Tinker after they had walked the twelve aisles and gawked at everything that was for sale.

They located a small refreshment booth and took a small table, sitting on the bench.

R-Bar slid up against his side. She beamed sideways at him and whispered in his ear. "Men keep looking down my blouse." She grinned wickedly.

"Could have worn something else." He sipped whatever they had ordered.

R-Bar pouted and swirled her finger around in her cup. He definitely wasn't a nice person. The beverage in her cup steamed. He was supposed to get jealous.

"Don't play with your food." He reached over and grabbed her lower lip gently between two of his fingers. "Why is this thing hanging out?" And let go.

"You don't mind!"

"What? Holding your lip? Behaving?"

She glanced down. "Men peeking down my blouse."

"Oh." He stood up. "Let's go," he snapped.

Startled, she quickly slid away from him. "Where?"

"To get you a different blouse. I can't have the entire male population of the capital city spending all their time oogling your chest even if you have shrunk some. Just won't do."

She started to laugh, stopped, and looked at him, "You are joking, aren't you?"

Tinker flopped back onto the bench. He rolled his eyes wildly and stared fixedly at her chest. "Yep. Let them ogle." He tugged her back and threw an arm over her shoulders. "Can I ask a question, sorta personal?"

"Hum," she said, snuggling closer, checking to see if he was looking down her blouse, which she was allowing to drape as open as possible.

"Hum, yourself. Do all witch wounds heal up the way your's did?"

"Oh, no." She leaned close and whispered very softly in his ear, her lips brushing lightly against him. "That was Palo's gift." Then puffed warm air into his ear. And did it again. And waited.

Tinker waved her away and turned to face her. "What are you doing? That tickles."

The pout returned. "The Princess, Your Queen, said I could."

He looked at her, a very suspicious look. "Do what?"

"She said that if I blew in your ear, you would follow me anywhere."

Damn it, you guys, stop!

He felt four female minds clamp down.

He stifled a laugh. "It was a bad joke, kiddo. Ready to start back?"

"May we take a side trip?"

"You up to a side trip?"

"You betcha."

"You betcha?"

"That is what they say, don't they?"

He frowned. "Yes, it is. Now what?"

"Tink?"

"Now what is going on?"

R-Bar shrugged. "Nothing. It is just a normal bazaar place." She looked around and nodded. "That is what it is."

Tinker sighed. "O. K., let's take a side trip."

The place was crowded, loud, noisy.

Tinker stared around. "What is this dive, anyway?"

R-Bar winked. "This is a place where big, handsome warriors take their wenches. Here they drink, get drunk, fondle their women, and have a boisterous good time." She tugged him further inside, clenching his arm firmly.

"Time to go, shorty." He stopped.

Her lower lip became very noticeable. "You said we could. And you are a big, handsome warrior."

"I am not big. And I do not want to get into a brawl."

He tugged at his arm. "Nor handsome either!"

She grabbed his arm in a tighter grip, using both hands. "Tink, none of them would dare, not with that blade monster riding on your back. See how they look at you. Slyly, indirectly. They know."

"O.K., sneak. One drink, but you are not a wench, witch."

She ducked her head, "Shhhhh. I am in disguise otherwise I couldn't come in here." And pulled him deeper inside. It wasn't exactly true. Witches went wherever they wished to go.

A large rough-hewn drink server hustled past them and banged down two large mugs on the counter in front of them. Tinker flipped a coin to him and received a curt nod in return.

R-Bar tugged him down so she could whisper in his ear. "I heard about this place from one of the servant girls."

"Did you plan this from the start?"

"No! Only after you made me change my clothes. So it is your fault." She banged the side of his foot with her boot. Then she nudged him in the ribs. "And you will have to put your arm around me in order to look proper for this place."

So he did. She gurgled happily and tugged the blouse off her shoulders, whispering happily, "I am looking wench-like, big warrior." She yanked the blouse even lower. "Hum, hum, hum." Something had to make him notice how beautiful she was.

"Shhhhhh, wench." He took another sip and listened to the conversations going on around them.

She stared at him. He was supposed to be looking at her.

The men were from the various armies encamped around the city. All the conversations dealt with the various contests and who had thumped whom. They were dressed in the various colors of their respective lords and princes.

Tinker's black attire made him the exception. As did the great two-handed sword lying flat against his back with no apparent support. Anyone standing close to them could hear the soft hum coming from it.

Tinker could feel the slight vibration. Ruffling her hair, he leaned over, kissed her cheek and said in a very, very low voice. "I hope these guys don't start anything. It is getting excited."

"What is?"

"The sword."

"Turn around. I want to see."

"Don't touch it. Ever."

"I won't."

He turned and she stared at the weaponkin, leaning close to listen. "Tink?"

He turned, leaned back against the bar and yanked her roughly against his side. "What?"

R-Bar gurgled happily. "That thing is impure, vile, brutal."

"Nothing to be happy about."

"Playing the wench." She really didn't think that things were impure or vile or brutal. As long as they behaved.

Tinker grinned back. The server banged down two filled mugs, took the empties, and received another coin.

"Better slow down, kiddo." He took a sip, wiped his mouth on his sleeve, and watched the action in the place.

R-Bar slipped an arm around his waist and leaned against him, holding the mug in her free hand.

Two warriors, one dressed in red and one dressed in pink and gold, were taking turns banging each other on the shoulder. Money was changing hands. The red army won.

A number of contests later, the score board read: RED 6; GREEN 5; PINK & GOLD 7; AZURE 8; BLUE & LAVENDER

4; YELLOW-ORANGE 2.

It was chalked on the wall. The rest of the bar's customers hadn't joined in.

"I think that it is time to head back." He pushed his empty mug away.

"Let's stay," she said, tilting her mug up, emptying it.

He looked at her face. There was a faint blush on her cheeks and a bright glitter in her eyes. "Wenchlette, I think you are getting sloushed."

"S'fun, Tink. B'sides," she said this very seriously, frowning heavily. "B'sides you haven't fondled me like all the other Warriors are doing with their wenches." She yanked her blouse even lower. She indicated the others with her chin.

"Be careful, you'll pop out. And forget it!"

"**WON'T!**" She glared up at him. He was supposed to do it.

"I knew this was a bad idea," he mumbled, reaching around and patting her on the hip. "There."

"Dim, dim, dim, dim, dim. **DIM!**"

"You keep that witchy temper under control or I will spank your butt. In public." He glowered at her and snarled back. "I mean it. Behave."

She kicked him on the side of the leg. He had better do what she told him to do.

"Damn it." Tinker grabbed her, lifted up and banged her down hard on top of the low counter and glowered at her. "I told you to behave! Stop acting like a spoiled child."

Tears started running down her cheeks. "I'm sorry, Tink. May we stay just a little longer? I will behave, I promise. Please?" She couldn't explain it. Not to him. Witches didn't cry. For anything.

"Ten gold." A warrior wearing purple and gold stood on the other side of R-Bar, his eyes roving over her body. "Give you ten gold for the quean." He reached into her blouse and grabbed her. "Nice. On the small size, but firm."

R-Bar hissed loudly and slammed her fist between his eyes, driving him stumbling backwards, wobbly in the knees. The air crackled around her.

A loud cheer rose from the crowd. No-one had heard the noise of her angry magic.

Tinker smiled at her, and said through his teeth, "Well, you got fondled. Happy?"

"He was rough." She tugged her blouse up, leaned forward, threw her arms around his neck and mashed her lips against his, tears wetting his face. He was so very comfortable feeling.

After a bit, Tinker realized someone was tapping him on the shoulder, very hard tapping on the shoulder. R-Bar released him. He turned and faced a very angry warrior with a rapidly discoloring blotch on his forehead. It was shaped like the front of a small fist.

"Have a drink," offered Tinker.

The warrior swung. Tinker stepped inside the blow and buried his fist in the warrior's mid-section, shoving him back with his free hand.

"Come on, wench, it is time to go." He turned to lift R-Bar down and heard the liquid slithering of a sword being pulled free, and gasped, "Oh, no!"

Tinker spun around, took one step sideways, away from the counter, away from R-Bar, and held his hands out in front of himself, making waving away gestures, and said, "Don't do it! Have a drink. Have two. Large drinks."

"You are unmanly," growled the warrior. "And your trull is birdig."

Tinker laughed and asked over his shoulder. "That is pretty bad, huh?"

"GUTTER KNAVE DIRT!" yelled R-Bar. She had heard the servant girls yell that at a merchant boy once.

"That sounds pretty bad too." He smiled at the large warrior. "Look fella, we are just going to slip out the door and be on our way. O.K.?"

The warrior roared and attacked.

Tinker's right hand flashed up and grabbed the hilt. The weaponkin took over. In a flash, Tinker danced to one side, the monstrous blade swinging out and around. Both parts of the attacking warrior tumbled against the counter front, spraying gore over the floor and some of the onlookers.

R-Bar yanked her legs up and away, gaping at what had happened.

Warriors leaped in all directions, shouting and cursing, leaving, making a wide space around Tinker and staring at the dark sword that danced so lightly, so hugely in one hand.

The sword sang, wanting more.

"Tink? Tink, let's go! Please?"

Slowly his arm lifted the great weapon and flopped it back over his shoulder and let go. The humming faded away. He turned toward her.

The server slammed two filled mugs on the bar top, and stated, "Fear not! All witnessed. His Lord will do none. No charge."

Tinker looked around. The body parts had already been removed, another layer of straw covered the spot. He grabbed his mug and took a deep swallow. Then he patted R-Bar on one leg as she unfolded them. She was still sitting on the counter. "Sorry, kiddo. I didn't mean to ruin your adventure."

Her eyes were still wide. She twitched nervously when he touched her. "I didn't . . . I didn't believe." Her face fell. She had made a big mistake. Even witches feared certain kinds of warriors.

"Hey, have a sip and don't look so sad. I couldn't do anything else. Really." Tinker tried a smile. She didn't smile back.

He sighed and spoke softly to her, "O.K., you win, wenchlette. You stand next to me and I will fondle you. Just a little. Then we will leave."

R-Bar didn't move.

He reached out and lifted her chin with his hand. And asked very gently, "What's the matter?"

She looked at him, face carefully held expressionless. Ready to bolt. "Are we really friends, Chosen One, or have you been playing with me?"

Gently he brushed the tear from her cheek. "We are really friends. I didn't, we don't, play those kind of games. And I am Tink to you, O.K.?"

She nodded. "O.K. Lift me down. Please?"

He set her down and shoved her mug over. "Here, have a drink, kid."

Behind them, he could hear the crowd noise returning to normal.

R-Bar slipped her arm around his waist and bumped him with her hip. She leaned her other elbow on the counter and played with her mug. "Tink?"

Tinker swung his arm around and ran his hand up her rib cage, under her arm, fingers tickling, touching her gently. She gurgled, way deep in her throat. This was much better.

Eventually they headed back toward the castle.

"It is a beautiful night, isn't it?" asked R-Bar.

"Yep."

They were approaching a small side gate to the castle. She had her arm slipped through one of his. It was later than anticipated.

They had stopped at the various bars along the road, bought a number of drinks and ate a lot of spicy foods. And he had treated her like a warrior's wench.

"It was a nice day except for that one thing."

"It was," agreed Tinker. "Don't dwell on it."

R-Bar tugged him into a dark shadow next to the gate. "Warrior, I am still your wench, for just a short while yet, and I demand that you still treat me like one." She reached up, threw her arms around his neck.

So he did.

When they stepped up to the side door, he pulled her into a shadow draped alcove. R-Bar giggled and fiddled with one of his shirt buttons.

"Time for you to get dressed," he said.

"I am dressed, more or less."

"You look like a wench, not a witch."

She gasped. "I forgot." Her clothing shimmered and transformed itself. "There. Now I am the kid witch again." She pouted.

Tinker smiled and reached for her. "Nice. On the small size but firm."

She wiggled and gurgled deep in her throat. He swung her around by the shoulders and pushed her toward the door, giving her a little pat. "Witch again, but no kid."

She opened the door, her happy gurgling echoing across the empty hall.

When they reached the door to his suite, she whispered. "Good sleep, Tink." And disappeared.

He fell asleep the instant he hit the bed.

Chicken leaned over him. "My Lord, tis near time for to sup."

"Umpf?"

Messenger tickled his ear. "Lunch time."

"Hummh?"

Smoke grabbed his ankles and dragged him part of the way from the bed, then tickled his stomach with one finger.

"Stop that"

Fair Morn began to unbutton his pajama top. "We are hungry and waiting for you, One."

Slapping at her hands, he sat up. "Get away, get away! I don't need any help."

Chicken dumped his clothes next to him and curtsied. "Indeed. Your humble servant, Me'Lord."

They left him and finished setting the table.

When he finally stepped from the bedroom, she beamed at him.

"Hayou, Tink, ready for lunch?"

"Sure." He sat on the chair that Fair Morn slid out. "What's going on? Now?"

"Nary a thing, Fair Prince."

"Nothing," intoned Messenger.

Smoke slid a plate in front of him.

Fair Morn served.

R-Bar gurgled happily.

Tinker looked at this sea of innocence, and sighed. "My hair will turn gray and I will get an ulcer."

"Sweet Lord, why speak thee so?"

"Cause you guys are up to something, cause when you guys get this way, I start to worry. And worry turns your hair gray and gives you an ulcer. That really coffee I smell?"

"Yes," said Smoke, filling his cup. "The kid witch made it."

Tinker waited for the outburst.

R-Bar beamed at Smoke.

He concentrated on his food. Waiting for the blow to fall.

The rest served themselves and began to eat.

He began to worry even more.

"Sweet Conqueror of Our Hearts," began Chicken.

"Two ulcers and bald," stated Tinker. He poured for himself.

"Our Own Verra True Love, Lord," she said.

"My teeth will fall out and I will go blind," he announced. "Get to the point. What no good plot has this group hatched out now, this time. Just be yourselves and stop all this fiddle-faddling."

"Fiddle-faddling?" Messenger looked at Smoke.

"MindMate, we loaned you to this witch," stated Smoke firmly, shrugging at Messenger.

"Just for the day," added Messenger.

"And night," amended Fair Morn, nodding at R-Bar.

"Only if thy Noble Self do so agree, My Leige," slipped in Chicken.

"What is this? You guys becoming a lending library with me as the only book? Past the coffee, Please?" He frowned, glared, and looked angry. And didn't convince anyone.

"My Lord, pon the morrow we journey do. Thus, did we agree final preparations to make this day whilst thee did naught but relax in most pleasant and fair company. Be this so mean?"

Smoke stood behind him and massaged his shoulders, Messenger pushed the coffee pot over.

"That's it, huh?" He pushed with his mind. They resisted.

Naughty, naughty, MyTinker.

"You win," cried Tinker. "I give up." He looked over at R-Bar. "What do you want to do today, kiddo. But no more warrior bars."

R-Bar gestured at the far corner of the room. "Leave that thing here. Please?"

"Witch Ripple did say thee would be most safe everyplace hereabouts."

Tinker stared at Chicken. "She is involved in this, also?"

R-Bar jerked.

Chicken violently shook her head. "Nay. Mere protective be."

Tinker pushed his chair back and nodded at R-Bar. "Let's go, kid. I know when I have been out maneuvered by experts."

As they passed through the main castle gate and out into the city, R-Bar asked, "Are you angry?"

"Not really. And they know it."

She slipped her arm under his. "Tink?" And held it

tight.

"UMMM?" He was still trying to see what they were up to. And finding out nothing. So he gave up.

"May I not be a witch today, like yesterday?" She carefully checked the street.

"No wenches."

Her clothes changed color and cut. Her blouse was V-necked and plunging, laced with a gold cord, the end tied at the top of the opening.

"What are you? Now?"

"Common citizen, standard garb."

"You sure?"

"Yes." She steered him into and down a long, wide street.

"So, what's on the agenda?"

"Outside the wall to watch the games, dinner, entertainment."

"Ah?"

"What?"

"You don't think we will be recognized by one of the warriors?"

R-Bar giggled. "I changed your clothes also. Now we don't look like a warrior and his wench. We are just two plain citizens. They won't even look at us."

He looked at his clothes and compared them to the folk they were passing. She was correct. They looked like plain citizens.

"O.K., smarty. What about Ripple?"

R-Bar whispered, "I won't tell if you don't."

He whispered back. "I won't. If you behave. And don't pout." She promised that she would try. It would be hard. To behave. Not pout.

Outside the wall, they bought refreshments and found a place to watch the games.

R-Bar stood in front of him, tugging his arms around

her. She leaned back. "Hum, hum, hum." He positively radiated comfort.

"Who do you think will win?"

"Orange and blue."

"Wanna bet?"

"Sure."

Later she asked, "Is Messenger your daughter?"

"Huh?"

"Your daughter?"

"No, why?"

"I heard her call the dark one, mother."

He threw an arm around her shoulders and hugged her. They were now sitting on a bench they had rented. "Nope, Smoke just sorta rebirthed her when she kept Messenger from dying. So now Smoke gets called mom. Once in a while." He gave her another hug. "Don't mention it to Smoke, will ya? She gets kinna touchy about being called mom."

R-Bar slipped her arm around his waist. "I won't. Hum, hum, hum."

He sniffed.

"What Tink?"

"Flowers. Really nice."

She looked around. "I don't see any."

He did the same. "Must be around here somewhere." And shrugged. And watched as the games continued.

The town walls were casting long shadows. The last game had ended. The town folk strolled away while the warriors prepared to soak aching bodies in nearby hot lakes.

"Hee, hee, hee," she cackled at him.

"Don't gloat."

"Nine to three. I won, Tink."

"I'll buy dinner. Know a good restaurant nearby?"

"I have heard of one."

He stopped walking and turned to face her. "Not from the servants, I hope."

"NO. I heard some of the Lords talking."

"Let's go."

She led him through a series of small streets and narrow alleys and then out into a broad avenue. "There it is."

"Looks fancy. Do we have enough money?"

"Of course."

He stopped walking. "Small point."

R-Bar looked up and down the street. "Where?" She didn't see any of those creatures hanging about.

"Wrong phrase. Do common folk go in there?"

She shook her head. "I don't think so. Why?"

"We are common folk."

"OH." R-Bar checked the street, and saw that no one was looking in their direction. "There. Now we are a Lord and his Lady." She had changed their clothes.

Tinker smiled. "You make a nice looking Lady, lady."

"Thanks, Mine Lord." She made a proper bow. And grinned. "See. I can do that correctly." And tugged him across the street. This time she felt that it was appropriate to be called lady.

It was a great meal. And Tinker told her so.

She smiled just so, being a very proper Lady, and said in just the correct tone of voice. "I am so delighted that you enjoyed it, Great Prince." And she meant it. He could hear it in her voice.

Servants whisked away plates and brought desserts. And wondered from which of the kingdoms this Prince and His Lady were from.

R-Bar ate two of the desserts and winked at him.

Tinker ordered an after dinner drink and relaxed while he was sipping it. "You been here before?"

"No." She leaned close and whispered. "They would get all fluffy if a witch came in. They couldn't do anything about it, but they would be stiff."

"The witches could do what we did," he suggested

softly.

"It is not proper," she huffed.

"You did."

She smiled at him, just so. "I guess I just am not proper."

"Hum, hum, hum," said Tinker.

R-Bar clamped her hand over his mouth, her eyes popping wide. "Shhhhh, don't do that," she whispered, letting go.

"Burgle, burgle, burgle," he said, holding up one finger.

A waiter hurried up with another drink. "My Lady will have one also."

"At once, Sir."

Tinker held up his glass as soon as her's arrived. "A toast."

R-Bar held up her glass.

He gently touched the glasses together. They made a faint chime. A faint perfume drifted from the liquid in their glasses. "To a very lovely, very Noble Lady and to a very nice, very special friend. And don't do that."

She blinked her eyes, a tear escaped. "We have to leave, Tink," she mumbled, dabbing at her eyes with a napkin.

"I just spoiled your evening." He kissed the tear away.

She grinned, carefully hiding it so no-one else could see. "No, we have a play to attend."

They took their seats, now dressed in proper play attending attire.

"This was written just for the games," explained R-Bar.

"Serious?"

"A comedy."

"Good." He was in the mood for funny, not serious.

The lights were put out, one by one. The play began.

As they pushed out with the rest of the crowd, she asked, "Did you enjoy it?"

"I missed some of the humor, but yes, I enjoyed it. Now what, tour guide?"

"A surprise."

"A series of surprise so far. Which way?"

"This way."

It was just down the block and around and in and through a narrow walkway.

"Nice place."

The light was soft, subdued, the music quiet, the booth very private. Refreshments were delivered silently, efficiently.

R-Bar nestled under his arm, clothes altered once again.

"That is quite a wardrobe you have. Much nicer than basic black." Her blouse was open to the waist.

"You look pretty good yourself." So was his.

"Thanks. How do we order?" She touched a small plate in the center of their table.

Empties were removed and replaced.

Tinker sighed, a long sigh of relaxation. And slumped lower on the comfortable curved seating. It had been a very relaxing day.

"Kiss me, Tink." She slipped onto his lap, her arms around his neck.

"Sure."

And after a while, she said, "Hum, hum, hum. Much nicer than being a wench."

He reached around and handed her one of the glasses and then sipped from the other. "Right." This beverage had a nice fruity tang that shifted into something else as you held it in your mouth.

She snapped her fingers and refreshed their drinks.

"That's handy."

"Ummmm!" she replied, sliding her hand over his chest and staring into his eyes when he reciprocated. "Ummmmmm. I like being kissed."

Their lips joined.

And eventually they went elsewhere.

Her hands held his and he held her as she leaned back

against him. Standing in front of the floor to ceiling windows, they looked out upon the city spreading below and before them. Full moonlight flooded the night. And the room.

R-Bar turned in his arms, her skin luminescent in the soft glow. Dark hair, dark eyes, other worldly being. "We are creatures of the moon." Her lips caressed his chest.

"Where are we, Moon Maid?"

"One of the Royal Guest Rooms, renown for the beds and things that the Royal Guests do in them."

"This was all planned, wasn't it?"

She looked up. "You are angry."

He shook his head. "I am flattered."

"You saved my life. Endless debt. Witch Word, Witch Oath. So it was, so it will be. Forever and forever. Witch Oath, Witch Word."

"Hum, hum, hum."

She lightly touched his chest. "You shouldn't do that. People will misunderstand."

His hand gently stroked her cheek.

"Tink, shall we use this bed again?"

"Hum, hum, hum." He winked at her.

Quawnder. Early Day.

They stepped into tall grass. Except for $1.98. On him it was merely deep.

"Where are we, Duff?"

"Not where we belong."

Sorrowful looked around and saw Tears leaning over, parting the grass with his hands.

"Tears?"

"Looking for the red jewels." He laughed. "There they are."

"Not where we belong?" $1.98 scanned their surroundings.

"Yes, dear. Something interfered. Looks like we are all

here, however. No one scattered, sent somewhere elseplace."
She patted the top of one of the traveling bags.

$1.98 pointed. "I think we ought to go that way."

She nodded and pushed through the grass to his side as
he started walking in the chosen direction. "That area with all
the trees?"

"Yes. And once we find out where we are, I think we
should go around-and-out rather than through a node. Mage
trav is better."

"You are just old . . . fashioned. But I agree." She patted
his hand. Walking along behind the two magicians, about
where they thought the trailing edge of the Zeedar were, Tears
looked at his grandfather.

"This is how your Great Tale was created, was it not?"

"Yes. Only we used that wondrous device created by
Big Red. Neither John Tinker nor I, nor any of the others, had
ever heard about these node spots. The portal was a special
guide as well. These things are just p'dindll doors."

Tears laughed at the image of the long toothed p'dindll
gnawing little holes between all these lands.

"Grandfather, are we going to visit with your other
friends?"

"It would be most pleasant if we do. But that I do not
know."

"You don't?"

"Tears," said Sorrowful very sternly. "A great teller of
tales does not mush his words together unless there is some
special reason, some special affect desired for the sake of The
Tale."

Tears ducked his head. Another lesson. Again.

"Strange." $1.98 stopped. The bags jostled up to his side.

The path began where the grass ended. The grass
stopped growing, abruptly, at the edge of the tree line.

"What are they doing?" asked Tears.

"Being cautious," answered Sorrowful. "On adventures

such as these, it pays to be very, very cautious. That is a hard thing to remember because so much is new, so much is exciting."

"Shall we?" Duff held a short purple wand in her right hand.

$1.98 nodded.

The path was wide enough for them to walk side by side. Duff looked behind them.

The Zeedar were splitting into two streams, flowing down either side of the path, staying in the grass, staying hidden.

"They are strange beasts."

$1.98 smiled at her. "Perhaps that is their natural way."

Sorrowful and Tears hurried after them and soon were walking just behind the magicians, just behind the traveling bags. The Zeedar had mostly disappeared, an occasional flash of red in the growth, the only thing that reminded the four of their strange traveling companions.

They had walked a long, long way, and with the exception of some small creature that hopped or flew as they approached, the group had seen no signs of life in this place.

"Dear, let's have something to eat. We have been walking all night even if it is day here."

"Here? Or should we wait until we find a village?"

"Here!" Duff pointed at the ground.

$1.98 slipped the sleeves of his robe back beyond his elbows and said something.

A table and four chairs appeared on the trail. The table was set and had food stuffs in bowls and cups waiting for them.

"Not bad," said Duff, seating herself and patting the chair next to her. Sorrowful and Tears sat opposite them, the table being long and narrow in order to fit upon the trail.

Duff pulled over a bowl and tasted the contents. "Interesting. But edible." She served $1.98, then herself.

It was a quiet meal, for all were feeling the effect of the lack of sleep and the long hike.

A small flying creature settled in the vegetation next to the trail and looked up at them. Suddenly it squawked and was sucked downward.

"Must be lunch time for them also," said Duff. She nudged $1.98 and indicated her cup. He poured. "Perhaps," she said, patting her lips with a napkin. "We could set up sleeping spaces over there, off the trail?"

$1.98 looked at the indicated space. "Let's look. Sorrowful, Tears?"

They all walked over to inspect the spot.

"Here?" asked $1.98.

"Big enough, Dear."

Sorrowful and Tears nodded their agreement.

"I'll give it a try." $1.98 stifled a yawn. Two dull brown tents appeared.

"Immmmmm." Duff was peering into one of the tents. She jerked her head back and snapped at $1.98, "I will do the insides."

Both tents lit up as something flashed in their interiors and blinked out.

"Let's go to bed." Duff erased the table and all. She stepped into the closest tent. $1.98 said, "Sleep well." And followed her inside.

As soon as Sorrowful and Tears entered their tent a soft rustling came from all sides. It was the Zeedar closing around the tents, waiting for their guides to reappear. A few more small creatures were absorbed.

"Nice colors" $1.98 stretched out, wiggling into a comfortable spot on the thick, soft layers of the sleeping accommodations.

Duff stretched out alongside him. "Thought that you would approve, Dear."

"Have I ever not?"

She rolled over and tickled his ear. "It seems to me that you have, now and occasionally."

He tickled her in return. "Flaming der-yellow was hard on the eyes."

She grabbed his hand and held it still. "Perhaps we ought to sleep?"

He yawned. "You are correct. Perhaps we should." Throwing his arm around her, he did, as she wiggled into a comfortable position.

One red jewel slipped under the tent flap and settled near the sleepers.

"OHHHHH." His arms flapped wildly, then wrapped tightly around her chest.

"$1.98! WAKE UP!"

His eyes popped open. "Morning?"

"Let go, Dear."

He did. "I think I just had a reaction to the other night."

She stood up and walked over to peek outside the tent. "Still night here."

She came back and began to rearrange the sleeping materials. "A time flep rapt!"

$1.98 lay on his side, head propped on one hand, and watched her as she finished straightening everything to her satisfaction. The light flared.

"I will take care of it, Dear."

The light began to dim.

"A magician's dream," he said, reaching for her as she settled next to him.

"Better than Rose Indam?"

"Much. You are . . . more . . . "

"Rounded? Pointed? Firm?"

"Nice," he said as the light went out.

They ate breakfast outside. Duff had selected the menu and waved away the tents.

As they finished, $1.98 said, "We can just turn out and

be on our way. No sense wandering around looking for one of the node spots."

"No, Dear, we have to follow the trail."

"Why? We are in the wrong elseplace and you told the Zeedar that you would take them home, which this place is not, I think."

"We must stay and find something or someone."

"Who, or what, are we looking for?"

Sorrowful looked from one magician to the other.

Duff shrugged

$1.98 stared at her. "DUFF?"

"The ring told me. So we stay and find it."

"OH." $1.98 stood. "Shall we?"

Duff waved everything away as they headed back to the trail.

As they walked along, Sorrowful reached forward and tapped her on the shoulder. "What ring?"

She slowed up and walked by his side and held up her hand. The ring glittered green fire in the morning sun. "The Guild gave it to us just before we started, remember? That is why I feel we must see what lies ahead. Perhaps it will give us some sense of direction. I feel a little lost, so far."

"Tears." Sorrowful beckoned his grandson forward. "Come up here and look at this ring. It is something you will need to remember."

Sorrowful hurried up to walk beside $1.98 so Tears could walk next to Duff. She stopped and let him take her hand and look at the ring. Once he had turned it around and around on her finger, they walked quickly after the others.

The trail wandered in gentle curves through the forest.

"Why do you think this trail started just at the edge of the forest?" asked Sorrowful.

"I suspect the grass just grew over it and covered it." $1.98 pointed to the edge of the trail. Things were beginning to grow over the edge, even here inside the forest.

"Strange. It appears well worn yet the grass was untrammeled."

They spent the day hiking along trail, only stopping for lunch, and then dinner. When they found a good spot the tents reappeared, ready for use.

"I am tired." Duff swung open the tent flap.

"Go ahead," said $1.98. "I think I will sit out here for just a short while."

"Don't do anything, please, Dear?"

"I will call, first."

The tent flap fell behind her.

$1.98 sat and leaned back against the sloping tent side, staring into nowhere, wondering.

Sorrowful and Tears retired for the night.

In the gathering dark, soft lights fluttered between the trees.

$1.98 sat and watched them for a long time.

The flap opened and Duff stepped out and leaned against him. "I couldn't sleep." In the dark, the ring made a green halo around her finger and hand.

$1.98 kissed her hand. "Didn't mean to keep you up."

She sat next to him. "What are those things?"

"I can't tell. They just flit from place to place."

"We could catch one?"

"We could leave them alone."

"We could go to bed." She nudged him.

He stood, picking her up in his arms. "We could do that." And stepped into the tent.

After lunch, two days later, as they were walking along, $1.98 suggested that they decide how much longer they would do this before turning away.

While they discussed this, they came to another grass covered area. The trail was visible, here and there, swinging to their left in a great, gliding arc.

"Strange," said Sorrowful.

"It is," agreed Duff. She winced and jerked her hand up to stare at the ring. "$1.98, please get ready."

The tall magician whipped the long, black wand from the sleeve of his robe. "What is it?"

"Stay right behind me, but don't do anything rash." She stared out into the grass zone.

Sorrowful reached down, his fingers gently closing around the handle of his dagger. He could feel the slight tremor as the weaponkin waited.

They stood well away from the forest and walked slowly forward. Then they saw someone coming toward them. As the distance closed between them, they saw that it was two someones, two rough and rudely shaped men. They both looked as if whoever had made them was not very good at their craft.

"Eeeee ho," said one.

"Ho eeee," said the other.

They were both carrying large weapons, many points glittered bright flashes as they were turned back and forth.

$1.98 stopped. "Careful, they are raf."

"**WAIT!**" Duff stepped slowly forward and then stopped, leaving a wide space between herself and $1.98.

The two beings also stopped. Then one crept toward her. He started to drool. "Slib tiv." He licked his lips, and leaped and thrust.

The weapon stopped just short, the tines pressing dents into the fabric of her blouse. "Slur mif."

"**DON'T!**" warned Duff, speaking to $1.98.

"**URK!**" The man jerked back one step, staring at the ground.

"**UB!**" He tried to lift one leg, then the other. Then he quivered, fingers twitching, dropping his weapon.

"**GAHHHHHHHH!**" He collapsed downward, thrashing wildly as red flowed up and over him. The shuddering mound stopped moving.

"**TIV URKGH!**" Screaming wildly, the other one charged, flaying the weapon from side to side. One foot came up dripping Zeedar, the other leg collapsed, spilling him face down, sliding into the grass.

Disappearing.

"Oh, my," said Sorrowful.

A soft red glow pulsated all around them and faded away.

$1.98 ran to her side, dropped to his knees. "Are you all right? Injured?"

"Yes. No. Not even a scratch."

"I wonder where those things came from?" Sorrowful was looking down their path.

"Or what they were," added Tears.

"Duff?" asked $1.98.

She shrugged a shoulder and started to walk down the trail.

$1.98 stood and hurried to her side. She shook her head. "Never saw anything like that before. Did you recognize the language?"

"No."

The grass appeared to reach to the far horizon. The longer they walked, the further it seemed to stretch before them.

Tears remained very close to Sorrowful.

$1.98 laid a restraining hand of Duff's shoulder. "Slow up. There is an opening ahead. It looks like a narrow canyon."

She did.

And soon, then after then, the four of them stood side by side and looked at the sight below. Some sort of a structure sprawled in disjointed fits and starts along the bottom of the draw.

"Strange building in a strange land," observed Sorrowful.

A sea of red began to seep over the edge and flow in a

broad sheet down the slope.

"It seems that they are going down there." Duff smiled.

"Be more cautious this time," commanded $1.98.

"Yes, Dear." She started down the slope. "Tears, you stay close to Sorrowful."

"I will." He looked at his grandfather. "Were all your adventures like this?"

"More or less," came the reply. "We kept running into monsters. But so far, we have not done that. Unless you count those two creatures back in the meadow."

"The Tale does not really bring out all the true happenings, does it?"

"No. If it were totally accurate, I am not sure there would be an audience. I think it would be badhard for most people to follow or understand or accept. So, as The Teller, one has to blend the events into what people will feel rather than reject. It is a fine line, Tears. Only through doing will you find the sense of touch, the feel of variation, the reality of audience."

"Will I ever?"

"I think so." Sorrowful smiled. "I really do. But for now, all you must do is remember, so that when the time comes, you will have all the pieces."

"I will try."

"No," corrected The Grand Master. "You will do."

Tears nodded.

"That way." $1.98 pointed at a larger lump of structure. "Feels like an entrance to me. We could just turn in."

"Door first," said Duff. Her hand was tingling from the ring.

They found it.

It was a door of some kind. More a hole than a door. Just pieces of material hanging from one wall.

Duff pushed light into the interior.

"I will go first." $1.98 stepped in front of her, thrusting

the door materials out of the way with one arm.

They passed into a small chamber, then into a larger one.

Then into an even larger one.

All these spaces were empty. No furniture. No inhabitants.

"Stranger than strange." Duff looked around. In this open space there were two other openings other than the one they had just stepped through. She looked at $1.98.

He pointed, then slowly approached his choice. And they stepped into a small chamber.

Then a large chamber.

A small chamber.

A smaller chamber.

Everywhere was bare.

Or abandoned.

Or something.

The Zeedar flowed along with them, following Duff, eddying in waves as the spaces opened and closed.

"Have you heard anything?"

"No, Dear, I have not." They had just stepped out into the largest chamber yet.

Tears pointed up at the ceiling, high overhead. "Look."

Dark things let go and rained down.

Sorrowful grabbed Tears and ran for a wall opening. He stumbled and fell, tumbling them into it.

Tears screamed, pain and fear intermingled.

The blast removed most of the upper walls and all of the ceiling.

Duff was cursing loudly. She was wreathed in green.

A number of creatures twitched and thrashed brokenly around her.

$1.98 stomped one under his boot and blasted another from his arm, punching a great hole in the far wall. And looked around.

Tears was standing in an entrance, blood running down his arm, dripping onto the floor, his right sleeve torn from shoulder to wrist. He was crying and staring at Sorrowful who was slumped against the wall next to him. Something had entered The Grand Master's back and exited from his side.

Sorrowful was fumbling with his belt. "Help me, Tears, help me. We must hurry."

With his left hand, Tears aided his grandfather in undoing the belt. Sorrowful yanked the dagger from its sheath, and holding it by the blade, offered it to Tears. "My Tale is about to finish, grandson." He rubbed the dagger hilt against his blood soaked shirt, coating it.

"Take it in your right hand quickly. Let our bloods mingle. I gift the weaponkin to you." Then he rubbed the blade in the gore dripping from Tears right hand.

Tears stared at Sorrowful.

"Do what I say," snapped The Grand Master. It was a command none would dare disobey.

Tears grabbed the dagger hilt and winced as the current passed up his arm, now jerking and twitching wildly under the forceful impact of the bonding, and into his shoulder.

"She is now your property, Tears. As you are her's. As you know from The Tale, there are only three weaponkin of which this is one. Wear it. And remember me."

Sorrowful looked up as Duff and $1.98 ran up to them. "Goodbye, lovely magician. Watch out for him." He nodded to Duff and slipped down the wall to the floor, and slumped sideways.

$1.98 dropped on his knees next to the still form. "Duff?"

"No," she whispered.

$1 98 threw his hood over his head and sat.

Duff could feel the sorrow pouring from him, knowing she could do nothing but wait.

"Put that thing of your's in its sheath, Tears, and let me

see your arm." She didn't dare touch him until the dagger rested in its scabbard.

After he did what she ordered, she examined his arm. "Not too bad. You will live." She pulled Tears into her arms.

"I am so sorry. But we could do nothing." The spell flowed from her and sealed his wound and eased his pain. Duff didn't try to touch his sorrow. She merely held him until the shaking stopped.

Then she stepped back, wiped his cheeks with her sleeve, and smiled gently. "You will be all right. I know that it doesn't feel like that now. But it is true."

Duff turned away and laid a long, gold wand on Sorrowful's chest and bound him in a golden shroud.

Straightening up, she spoke to Tears. "Sorrowful doesn't deserve to be left in this strange place. $1.98 will send him home. He can send you along, if you wish."

Tears shook his head. "NO! I will remain to record it all." He blinked away the last of the tears trickling down his cheeks. For now.

Gently laying one hand on $1.98's shoulder, she asked even more gently, "Dear?"

Slowly, ever so slowly, $1.98 straightened up and stood. The hood fell away. Tears gasped. Two deep lines of sorrow cut down the magician's face.

Duff threw her arms around $1.98 and began to cry.

"Duff," he whispered. "Don't cry. Please? You know it hurts me so."

She sniffed loudly. "Yes, Dear." And let him go, wiping her eyes with an already moist sleeve. "Send him! Tears is staying with us."

$1.98 stared one last time at their friend and said something.

Sorrowful went home.

The Foregather At Quata.

Turintor bought a Seek Spell at the appropriate booth but suggested to Motaiss and her silent companion, after both had examined it, that she didn't think it would be very useful.

Now they sat finishing the evening meal, ordered and paid for by Motaiss, and watching the light fade from the sky into night, knowing that there would be displays later on. Some Foregathers ran all night but the short ones tended to not do this.

"Would it be permitted," began Motaiss very carefully, having already layered on protection, "to ask whether some small aid might be offered?"

"It is a thought," suggested Turintor. "We sent a Dark Caster some time past. It seems to have failed."

"A Dark Caster!' gasped Motaiss. "Ap do tah!"

"Mildly coarse," observed Turintor.

"Surprise startled," explained Motaiss.

Turintor looked at her companion, nodded, turned back to stare at the warlock, and nodded again.

"I will tell our tale, Motaiss, Talair warlock. If you feel some aid offer afterwards, then we would accept." And then she told Motaiss everything that had happened and all that they had done.

She leaned back and took a sip from her beverage, ordered by Motaiss as he had listened to the tale, and stared at him.

The air hissed around the warlock.

Few witches, witch companions, or warlocks passing by, would walk within thirty feet of the trio sitting at the table. All recognized the sound of a very strong hazard building and all hoped that the trio would contain themselves. One worked very hard at a Foregather to behave and not cause too great a commotion.

"Some person, some thing, most needs killing," growled Motaiss.

"Settle, settle," grumbled Turintor at him.

He did.

The air quieted.

He nodded. "I cannot speak for Talair, but for myself only." And leaned forward. "I would do wander with Turintor and the silent one to assist in all ways." He smiled. It was a pure witch smile that offered death and destruction.

He hastily altered his expression as witches of every color fled in all directions from the immediate vicinity of that table where the trio sat. A smile like that promised spell flare of the worse type.

Turintor gently touched her companion's hand. "Our wander has great hazard, Warlock Motaiss."

He waggled one hand. "Of small concern."

"Then you may."

He nodded. And stood. "There is a Green Glow display on the far side."

The trio headed that way.

The Land Where Godami Aroses. Lovely Day. Lunch Time.

"Where are we?"

Ramp looked around and smiled. "This elseplace is called The Land Where Godomi Aroses. As you will soon see, it is a place of tiny villages all connected to each other by wide causeways of stone. Each village specializes in just one thing."

"BY DUMPF. Who does food?" Mountain's stomach gave a low gurgling rumble.

Hard's head snapped around.

"We are hungry," explained the giant.

Ramp laughed. "We are only two away. Let's walk down this street."

She guided them through the maze and out of the small cluster of houses and businesses. The next cluster could be seen in the near distance, the causeway shooting arrow-straight between them.

Hard pointed at a figure walking down the street ahead of them. "Is that a witch? In that   really dark forest green?"

The figure wore a hooded robe that flared widely at the lower edge, just skimming above the road surface. The robe was a deep dark green almost black. In one hand the person held a short gold staff.

"Don't point!" hissed Ramp.

Hard jerked to stare at her. Mountain frowned.

"They do not even like to be stared at," she said. "She is one of The Divineal of Thantala. They worship The Lady of Death and are deeply studied into the Lord Of Thantos. Death itself."

The robed figure turned a corner. All the folk on the road relaxed.

It was but a short time before they arrived at the food cluster. None of the inhabitants appeared to pay much attention to these visitors.

"A very cosmopolitan elseplace," explained Ramp. "Often visited by folk from many wheres. Shall we eat here?"

The place she selected was on the edge of the cluster which stood about thirty feet higher than the surrounding fields.

"Everyone of these has a different level?" asked Hard.

"Indeed, husband, they do. Although I have never understood what the significance of the levels are. But it is very important to the folk here."

"Food," enthused Mountain, his stomach rumbling happily and loudly as he sat on the pavement. **"DE-DUMPFING DELIGHTFUL!"**

"Do we have enough money to feed him?" Hard stood close to Ramp and whispered to her and looked anxiously at Mountain.

"Have no fear." She handed him a leather bag.

The air crackled.

And exploded.

Ramp grabbed Hard by a sleeve and yanked him behind herself.

Mountain lurched to his feet, the gigantic club springing into his hand. **"DUMPF!"** A chair and a table were thrown crashing to one side.

"Dim, dim, dim dim!" snarled one of the figures, dropping to the surface of the street, staring around. "This is not Trail's Lett."

"What happened, kid?"

"My Lord, peer thee yonder."

"IT'S TINKER!" shouted Hard.

"BY DUMPFING DUMPF, John Tinker."

Tinker whipped an arm around R-Bar's shoulders. "Calm down, shorty. We just met up with some friends of mine."

R-Bar stared at the great hulk approaching them, rehanging the immense cudgle on his belt. Then she gurgled happily and ran forward.

"Sister. Ramp magician."

Ramp laughed lightly but backed around behind Hard. "I should have recognized the growling and the sound of your arrival. You are traveling with them?"

R-Bar grinned. "Yes. We are friends."

Ramp stared at her, frowning slightly. "Friends? Small witch, what has happened to you. I feel a difference, several differences."

"Mountain, what are you doing here?"

"I was about to eat, **BY DUMPF**, John Tinker, when you interrupted us."

"A good idea," said Fair Morn.

"We can talk while we eat," suggested Smoke.

"I nearly went far," said R-Bar to Ramp.

Tinker slowly herded them all into one area and got them settled down.

Mountain picked up the chair and table and reset them

in place.

Messenger stared at Ramp, especially at her middle.

Smoke nudged her sharply.

"Mom," said Messenger. "She is going to be a mom. Soon!"

Tinker looked over and smiled. "Well Hard, it has been a long time for you."

"Not much," said Hard.

R-Bar nodded while Ramp explained the accelerated gestation period of the Faan.

The food arrived.

"Better order lots more," said Tinker. "We have three large appetites."

And after several courses, Mountain started casting glances at Fair Morn.

"**BY DUMPF**, John Tinker, from what stumpf does she derive?"

Tinker laughed and introduced Mountain to Fair Morn, Messenger and R-Bar.

"Another witch," grumbled Mountain. "**FUMPFING FAIR** numbers of them."

"We are a large clan," explained Ramp. "She is not a witch!"

Mountain dumped large quantities of food on his plate.

"What's wrong with witches?" demanded R-Bar, glaring darkly at the gigantic man.

"Simmer down, attack dog," said Tinker.

R-Bar glared at him. "What manner of beast is that?"

Hard looked from face to face. "Whose dog attacked?"

"What?" asked Tinker.

"Indeed," said Chicken.

"I don't see a dog," said Messenger, searching their surroundings.

Fair Morn took another helping and shoved the remainder over at Mountain.

"I don't think that I like being called that!" growled R-Bar.

"What?" asked Tinker.

"What, what?" said Hard.

"My Lord, tis conversation of most dizzying aspect." Chicken poked his upper arm with her eating utensil.

Mountain shoved a platter over at Fair Morn. She had an appetite to admire. For a small folk. Almost civilized.

"She is growling," said Hard. "She does that a lot."

R-Bar was mumbling something under her breath. Dark shadows were beginning to form beneath her feet.

"**SISTER!**" cautioned Ramp.

"Where's J. C.?" Tinker looked at Hard. "We heard he was with you."

"We got separated. He is with Mirf somewhere. What are you guys doing here?"

"I think our guide took a wrong turn. Somewhere."

"She is your guide?" whispered Hard, watching R-Bar carefully.

"Yep. We don't have any idea about how to move from here to there. Witchy-poo seems to do it with some ease."

R-Bar hissed at him. "What was that?" He was really getting irritating.

"My Lord, cease thy jests. She does understand not thy quirks."

A short wand flashed into R-Bar's hand. "Where?" The air crackled loudly around her.

"What?" said Tinker and Hard simultaneously.

Ramp threw her hood over her head to hide her laughter.

Smoke grabbed R-Bar's wrist. "Be careful."

"Quirks are mean and nasty." R-Bar jerked her arm violently. "Let go!"

Tinker slumped deeper into his chair.

Fair Morn shoved a large cup over to him.

"Sweet Prince, have some drink." Chicken poured.

"This is getting too goofy for words." He took a sip, eyes sliding from face to face.

Messenger held out her cup. "May I have some?"

Chicken filled her cup, then drank the rest from the bottle.

"Fairly crude," observed Tinker.

"Hold out your hand, palm up," said Ramp to R-Bar.

R-Bar did.

Slowly Ramp stretched out her hand, palm down. And began to lower it toward R-Bar's.

"Don't, don't." R-Bar jerked her hand back.

"Sister," warned Ramp.

Slowly R-Bar put her hand back where it had been.

Ramp held her hand close. "Muchly changed."

"I was Palo gifted," stated R-Bar sternly.

"Altered," snapped Ramp grabbing R-Bar's hand.

"**GIB TAK!**" screamed R-Bar as she twitched violently, yanking her arm backwards, trying to get away before the clash of witch magic and mage magic destroyed them both along with a considerable piece of the local environment. A large black shape materialized next to her chair, snapping its teeth. The thing was as large as a Saint Bernard and covered with fur and scales. Smoke dribbled from nostrils set in a flat face. Slit eyes gleamed, pulsated with almost black red.

"Don't shoot!" barked Tinker.

Fair Mom had whipped her weapon out and was aiming across the table.

"What manner of beastie be that?"

"A helper, Princess." R-Bar stared at her hand, still tightly held by Ramp. "Nothing happened."

She stared at Ramp.

The beast disappeared.

"Altered," said Ramp.

"What's going on?" asked Tinker.

"Wife?" asked Hard.

"Witches may not touch magicians," explained R-Bar. "Most of the time."

"Not from the time they start growing into adulthood," added Ramp.

"Oh," said Messenger.

"Huh?" said Tinker.

Ramp nodded. "Our forces, though similar, are polar opposites. Direct physical contact could be lethal." Ramp's face fell. "When we were not child, not yet adult, they could run and play, push and shove, and roll and tumble with each other. I had to watch with my su-friend."

"We created it so she could have someone close. Only our mother could touch her." She reached out and placed her other hand on top of Ramp's, carefully.

"What has happened to me? Or is it you, sister? Does birthing do this to you?"

Ramp shook her head. "No, Young Witch, Young Woman. You have been . . . altered. That is the best word. What have you been doing?"

R-Bar looked puzzled. Then she looked at Tinker. "You?"

He shook his head. "Out of my class, kiddo. I don't know any of that stuff."

"OH, MY," gasped Messenger, covering her mouth with one hand.

All heads turned to look at her.

Messenger blushed.

"Kitten?" Smoke stared at her.

Her hand dropped. "She was so happy to have friends." Messenger hesitated, then continued. "And I saw we could not touch. And I wanted to be her friend also."

She blinked back tears. "I thought that it was just me."

Chicken threw her arm around Messenger. "What did thee do, clever ourself?"

Messenger looked down and stared at the table top and pushed her finger back and forth on the wooden surface, and whispered. "I bent it. Just a little."

R-Bar bounded from her chair hissing. "I have been bent?" She looked at her arms and legs, peered over her shoulder and down her back as best as she could. Then she snatched her blouse forward and peered inside.

"Explain," commanded Smoke.

Messenger moved closer to Chicken and said in a very small voice, "I just bend a few strands. So we could touch each other. She is as witch as before." She looked up at R-Bar. And smiled, a small quiet smile. "I wouldn't take that away."

The two sisters stared at her.

Ramp stood and walked around the table to stand next to Messenger. "May I touch you?"

"Oh sure." Messenger nodded at her.

Ramp did. And jerked her hand away.

"I didn't do anything." Messenger looked at Smoke.

"Ramp?" It was Hard .

She returned to her seat. "Just nervous, nothing else. She is a . . . controller."

R-Bar was still staring fixedly at Messenger, her mouth slightly open, her eyes wide, leaning slightly forward. "You could take it away?" she said hesitatingly. And asked, all harsh whisper, "What are you?"

Messenger looked at R-Bar. Her lips began to quiver as tears rolled down her cheeks. "I am The Messenger. I am part of us. And I don't know what I am." She began to wail. And turned inside Chicken's arms as Chicken hugged her tight.

Smoke's mind grabbed her and held her tight.

Careful, Smoke.

I have her, MindMate.

R-Bar ran around the table and threw her arms around Messenger and hugged her. "Don't, don't, don't, don't, don't cry." She was snuffling away a tear. Because her friend was crying.

Messenger hiccuped.

R-Bar giggled and kissed her cheek. "Are you all right?"

Messenger nodded. And hiccuped again.

R-Bar touched the end of Messenger's nose with her finger.

"There."

"Thanks."

"Whoosh," sighed Tinker.

"May we have dessert?" asked Fair Mom, looking around the table.

Tinker started to laugh and waved one hand. "Why not?"

They did.

R-Bar sat next to Messenger and took and held one of her hands.

They held a whispered conversation.

"My Lord?" Chicken pushed her plate away. "Praps we ought be a'foot?"

"**DUMPF**," agreed Mountain, staring at Fair Morn. She stared back at him. His girth had grown noticeably. Her waist was unchanged, She lightly touched the back handle of the weapon holstered on her thigh. "Are there no women where you live?"

"**HUMPF!** Of course. Else why would I exist?"

"Now what?" Tinker slipped lower in his chair, eyeing the two of them staring at each other.

"One," said Fair Morn. "This immense person keeps staring at my body. Should I take off my clothes?"

"**WHAT?**" His eyes darted toward Chicken.

"No," said Chicken. "That would be most unseemly."

Mountain leaned toward Fair Morn, his hand held out, one finger extended. "May I touch you?"

Her hand clasped the weapon. "Yes."

He gently touched her stomach with the tip of his finger,

and ever so gently pushed. Then he sat back. "**BY ALL THE ROCKS AND STONES, SAND AND GRAVEL!** Where does it all go?"

Tinker started to laugh. "Extremely high metabolic rate. Or some such thing."

"**DEE DO DUMPF!**" exclaimed Mountain.

"I guess," said Tinker.

Ramp had been restraining Hard who was bursting with questions.

She nudged him to go pay their bill.

As he did, the owner grinned broadly. Now his wife and sister-sister-sister would stop nagging. He could buy the nertle nextus.

While the bill was being settled, Ramp explained where she was headed and how to get there.

"We will go ahead," said Tinker. "And meet you there. Take care."

He waved at Hard as Hard walked back to the table. "See you later, buddy."

They started off, Smoke guiding them, following Ramp's directions.

They were just entering the second cluster to the left on the third one, straight ahead.

"Hey there, kiddo." Tinker violently fluffed R-Bar's hair.

"You have any idea why we are here?"

"No, Tink, I do not," growled the little witch, combing her hair back with her fingers.

Tinker stepped sideways and did the same thing to Fair Morn.

"You have been awfully quiet. How come?"

She grabbed him in an iron grasp and kissed him.

"**UMMMMMM?**"

When she finally released him, he said, "My, my!"

"One, I have just felt like being quiet. Why are you attacking us?"

"He do feel some unease," stated Chicken. "Thus do Our Love twitter about."

"I wonder what the specialty of this cluster is?" He looked around.

Holding Fair Morn just above the soft swelling of her hips. It was a small waist. He said, "No wonder Mountain wonders where all the food goes."

"Curios," said Smoke, answering his question about this cluster.

R-Bar was already wandering among the open shops, arm in arm with Messenger, inspecting the strange and wonderous things for sale.

"Sweet Prince?" asked Chicken, brushing soft lips across the back of his neck. "Shall we shop?"

"Until you drop," he replied, releasing Fair Morn. "Or until Hard, Ramp, and Mountain get here. Which ever comes first."

They scattered throughout the shops.

"Passing strange things." Chicken and Tinker were in a shop of small figurines.

"Yep. Haven't seen anything that I would want to take home."

They wandered next door, to a small booth.

"Rings and things," said Tinker.

"My Lord, we do wear all we do wish even now."

"Anyone here have any idea why we are here?"

"Nay. Sweet witch do be equally be'puzzled." She slipped an arm around his waist.

"Sweet witch?"

"Indeed, for hath thee not nibbled at fair confection and found it so?"

"Wasn't my idea," he grumbled, tossing an arm over her shoulders.

"T'were thy resistance not."

"Therapy," he suggested.

"Doctor Ours, would treat Us so?" She grinned at him.

"Heh, heh, heh," he said, leering dramatically at her..

She slipped from his arm, grabbed it and towed him into the next shop. "My Lord, it do seem a'Us, it do, that we ought by Ramp stay close for she does grow fastly."

"I think that you are right. Course they have Mountain with them."

"True."

This shop was littered with parts of things, the odd recognizable object appearing here and there among the obscure and the unknown.

Chicken's finger's suddenly dug into his arm. "In far corner," he hissed.

He looked.

A small green box sat on top of a pile of clothes.

"Tis most like t'other."

Tinker started forward.

She held him back. *Messenger, look. Here. Now.*

Messenger looked from her eyes at the box and started to hurry in their direction, pulling R-Bar by one arm.

"Dim, dim, dim!" she snarled. "What are you doing?"

Kitten?

Hurry, mom, hurry. Messenger stepped into the shop from the other door and indicated the box.

R-Bar hissed and crouched, her eyes darting up to the far corners. The air crackled. A large thing appeared, its eyes glowing, smoke pouring from its mouth.

"That is really ugly," said Messenger. "Really really!"

R-Bar slowly approached the green box.

The shop owner stepped from another door and spoke to them. "Of what might I sell you?" He gasped and pressed back against the cloth wall. "No beasts allowed!"

Smoke stepped through the entry just behind Chicken and Tinker.

"He is only the owner," said Smoke. "There is no else.

That box is cloudy."

The beast disappeared.

"We would like to purchase that box over there," said Tinker. "How much?"

"Four gold."

"One!" snapped Chicken.

Overhead they heard thumping, the roof sagged.

"Now what?" Tinker looked up.

One. It is I.

What are you doing on the roof?

Watching.

"Three?" said the owner.

"One," stated Chicken.

He looked forlorn. "Two?"

"SOLD!" Chicken tossed him two gold coins. "Take ugly box, R-Bar."

"Do you see anything," whispered the witch to Messenger, who was approaching the box from the other side, her wand in her hand.

"No," came the whispered reply. "But there is something nasty inside."

R-Bar hissed. And slowly reached for the carrying handle.

The roof split. A leg dropped through.

Soft spot.

R-Bar and Messenger both leaped backwards, brushing piles of stuff in all directions.

The shop owner started making strange noises, looking first at them and then at the leg being pulled upward.

Fair Morn peered down through the hole. "Tell him that I am sorry but that his roof is pretty rotten and needs repair."

Tinker tossed the owner another gold coin. "For your roof."

He watched R-Bar and Messenger stalking the green

box, and asked the owner, "How long have you had that green box?"

"Fifteen turns, I think."

Where did you get it?"

"Hocha, hum. Umm, bought it from, umm, a tall-dark man. Sold it cheap."

Finally R-Bar touched the carrying handle. Nothing happened.

She and Messenger took it outside. Footsteps slithered down the roof.

They gathered around the box.

"Open it," said Tinker. "Let's see what we bought."

R-Bar tugged at the door. It wouldn't budge. "Dim, dim!"

"Let me try." Tinker gave it a yank. "Stubborn devil."

Smoke knelt next to him. "MindMate?"

He moved aside. "Go ahead."

She grabbed the handle and pulled. The door squealed as frozen hinges began to release.

The blast blew her tumbling into the booth behind them.

"**AAAAAAAAHHHHHH!**" screamed R-Bar as the air broke and splittered around her, her beast ripping and tearing at something.

"**NOOOOOOO!**" howled Messenger, her wand erupting.

Fumes and dark swirling clouds billowed over everything.

Lightning flashed.

Surrounding booths and shops collapsed.

Chicken hurtled herself on top of Tinker. "My Lord!"

He saw a bright flash off to one side.

The air finally cleared. All around them were smoking ruins, a shambles of scattered and jumbled merchant's wares. One edge of the cluster was missing, sheared neatly away.

Fair Morn shoved her weapon back into its holster and

grabbed the dazed Messenger who was stumbling in erratic circles.

A mass of debris heaved. "Dim, dim, dim!" R-Bar shoved her way to the surface and lurched on one numb leg.

The green box lay undamaged, the door tightly shut.

Tinker rolled Chicken off. "You O.K., Princess?"

"Indeed, My Lord."

"Where's Smoke?"

She tugged him to his feet. "Yonder."

Smoke's arm was sticking out from under a jumble on the far side of the road. Her fingers were twitching.

They ran and began to dig her free.

Fair Morn pushed Messenger at R-Bar, ran over and joined them.

Finally Smoke was uncovered. Blood ran from her mouth, from her nose. One eye was mostly swollen shut.

Her blouse was ripped and torn. One pant leg split half way to her thigh. Tacky wet blotches spread dark red in a number of places.

He peered inside. She had closed off all the pain.

"Smoke?"

Her good eye opened and looked at him. "MindMate?"

"Tell me."

"Hit me . . . in the chest and stomach . . . I hear the Evening Chant."

"Oh no you don't. **R-BAR, GET OVER HERE!**"

The witch hurried over, leading the still incoherent Messenger by the hand.

"Take us back to Ripple. **NOW!**"

R-Bar gave Messenger to Tinker.

Fair Mom picked up Smoke.

They twisted away.

Just as the others arrived at the far edge.

They stopped and stared at the shambles that was this cluster.

"**BY DUMPF!**" Mountain waggled his cudgel in his right hand. "**BY DOUBLE DUMPF!**"

"What happened here?" asked Hard to no one in particular.

Ramp stared around and saw the marks. "Magic, witch and evil. And something else. Splashed in all directions."

Slowly they worked their way around and among the debris, searching for someone alive, someone who could tell them what had happened here.

They found him, sitting in a chair, a somehow undamaged chair, holding his head in his hands, staring at what had been his shop.

"Shop keeper, what happened here?" Ramp spoke very gently.

He looked up. "I have nothing. Nothing. Nothing to sell, nothing to barter."

Hard tripped over something. He bent down and picked it up. It was a small figurine.

"You may keep it," said the shop keeper.

"Is it yours?"

"Yes."

Hard handed it to him. "There are probably lots more buried in the rubble, don't you think?"

"Shop keeper, we need to know what manner of event occurred here. Do you know?"

He nodded. And told them.

When he had finished, Hard turned his gaze to Ramp. "Where did they go?"

"Back to Ripple, perhaps."

"Then so should we."

"Perhaps."

"Wife," said Hard, trying to look stern. "We ought to go back to Ripple's."

Ramp suppressed her smile. "I believe you are correct, Husband. But, we have to find a node. And this place has been destroyed. We can look in the next cluster."

"Then let's go!" Suddenly Hard was very anxious to get away from here.

Mountain hung his cudgel on his belt. "**DUMPFING** good idea. Which way?"

Ramp nudged Hard. "Over here. We shall have to go to the cluster on this side."

Soon they were hurrying along the causeway and far from the earshot of curious folk.

"What they found could have killed them all," explained Ramp.

Hard was frowning, deeper and deeper. "He said one was dead and that one was driven mad."

"**BY DUMPF**, this person must be pounded into dusty dust. He seems all evil." Mountain was glowering at everything.

"That clan was evil. Witches tend to be self-centered and short-tempered when they are in are best of moods, but that clan had gone wrong. Now grandmother's error threatens universes of innocents."

"What error?" asked Hard.

"Husband, she let one live."

"Two, including your father."

Ramp clenched his arm. "Husband, it all flows through the female line. Our father did not transmit such bent nature to his daughters."

Hard smiled. "I'm glad, else we would not be married, would we?"

She laughed, gently. "No, I suppose not."

"**STAR-STUMPFING** strange families these witch clans are," rumbled Mountain, appreciating his family life more and more.

"Not to us," suggested Ramp.

Hard looked at her. "Well, Ripple doesn't seem all that bad to me, not any more. Just pushy, and, um, mean-tempered, and, um, aggressive. But nice." He smiled. "Um, sort of."

"Rangle."

"What?"

"Ripple is rangle, very rangle."

Hard shrugged. "Oh, I suppose." He looked at her. "Is that a bad word?"

"Bad?"

"You know. Obscenity, swear word, cussing?"

Ramp pointed across the way. "There is a node. No, it is just a descriptive word."

"Oh, ugh!" Hard looked down into the node. "Tell me, before we jump. Why are these things always so strange, most of the time?"

The node was green, a gray-green. It looked like something that had escaped from a food container long forgotten in a refrigerator.

"No one knows. In fact, no one knows how they came into existence. Myths tell of a great wizard who caused them to be. A wizard with a very warped mind."

"I guess so." Hard stared at the node.

"Ready? Mountain?" Ramp looked from one to the other.

"I am," said Hard, taking her hand.

"**DAR DUMPFING**, I am." One great hand enveloped her free hand.

"Jump," commanded Ramp.

Murklan Obscuratan. A Place Never Visited.

Lady Grimtouch, Glimmer of the Divineal of Thantala, shook her hood back and looked at the still forms gathered around the gold platform upon which rested *The Book of Death* now open to *The Chapter of Inquisition*. Her eyes flowed from face to face and then up to peer at the face of The Lady of Death looming high into the shadows above.

"Our past and our future are blurring together. Lady

Fairdeath, Lady Dawnmort, and Lady Nightreaper search deep into past mysteries for answers to the question we have posed."

Stepping from behind the gold platform, she stopped in front of each still figure, handed them a scroll, and kissed them on the forehead, before moving on to the next. And finally returned to her place.

"The Face of Death is rarely seen. Which is as it should be. The Voice of Death is but a passing whisper. Which is as it should be. The Touch of Death is but a light caress. Which is as it should be. The Passage of Death is but a soft shadow. Which is as it should be."

She pulled her hood up and over her head until nothing but the darkness within could be see.

All those gathered did the same thing.

"Yet will we speak to The Lady and seek that which is inscribed."

She watched the silent figures slip silently from the room. Then she closed the great volume and walked down to the main floor to stand and gaze upward at The Lady of Death.

Well, You Never Know.

Quawnder. Mid-Day.

It was a large, lopsided room. The floor tilted one way, the ceiling the other. Every wall canted in several directions at once and bent into strange angles at the corners. There were many walls and many corners.

The ring on her finger flickered, green magic flashed verdant tones off the floor.

"In here somewhere," whispered Duff.

It came hurtling from a corner. The ring snapped at the attacker. None of them had a chance to react.

Duff was thrown into $1.98 and Tears. Tears went down, $1.98 staggered sideways over him, and tripped over the traveling bags.

Duff landed on top of the heap.

"$1.98?"

"I am all right. Get off."

She stood and offered them a hand up.

They stood close together and looked at the crumpled form on the floor. A fist-sized round hole had been punched through the chest. The severed edges smoldered green fumes.

The wall behind was shattered, jagged green lines slowly cracked open, bits and pieces tumbling out, pattering to the floor.

"Who was that?"

"Dear, I do not know."

$1.98 bent over and peered at the object still clenched in one warped hand. It was a wand fashioned from thin jagged cylinders of uneven lengths, bound by narrow brown strands.

"You ever see a wand like that?"

Duff shook her head. "Never?"

He poked at it with one finger tip. Nothing happened.

$1.98 slipped the great black wand from his sleeve and handed it to Duff. "Hold this, I am going to pick it up."

"Careful, careful!" snapped Duff, taking the Black Snake from $1.98.

"I am. Always."

Duff stepped away from him, gently holding his wand as far away from her body as she could. "Yes, Dear. TEARS, get over here."

When she felt they were at a safe enough distance from $1.98, she said, "You may proceed." And snapped a protective wall around herself and Tears.

$1.98 slowly reached down and tugged at the strange wand with two fingers, slipping it from rapidly stiffening fingers.

Nothing happened.

He gently, softly, set his hand down on top of it.

Nothing happened.

Exhaling, a whisper of breath, $1.98 picked it up.

Nothing happened.

He turned and smiled at Duff and Tears. "Seems safe enough."

The room exploded.

The heat was intense. He could feel his cheeks drying. He opened his eyes. He was lying on one steep slope of the narrow canyon. Not far away, somewhat downhill from where he lay, flames were roaring into the sky. The warped and bent structure was burning. Then he realized that he had been burning as well. A number of spots on his robe were still smoking.

Duff was tugging on one shoulder. Tears was pulling on the other. Each had a firm grip on his robe and were slowly yanking him, in fits and starts, up the hill.

"Duff?"

She stopped, dropped to her knees and kissed his face. "I thought you went over. And never to return."

"What happened?"

"That wand did it."

"It did." He sat up, reached over with his left hand and pulled his right sleeve back from his right hand, and waggled his right hand from the wrist. He was still clenching the strange wand. He was having trouble letting go, his fingers were so stiff.

"Seems harmless enough now," he said. "I didn't say anything. Or feel, anything."

$1.98 lurched to his feet and started staggering toward the upper edge of the canyon. As he lurched upward he managed to place the wand somewhere. "Duff, let's leave, let's leave this place."

They stood up there, at the edge of the canyon, and looked down at the burning structure. It had become mostly ruins and embers.

$1.98 swung an arm around each of them. "Where are the Zeedar? What happened to them?"

Duff shook her head. "I do not know, Dear. All I saw was you burning, and that place coming down around us. Tears and I tried so hard to drag you free. He is very brave."

$1.98 hugged them both tightly. "Both of you. Both."

"You are very heavy," said Tears. He whispered to $1.98, "She said awful things."

$1.98 smiled. "She does that, at times."

"Nothing would work in there, Dear, nothing. I have never felt that before."

"Nothing?" $1.98 stared harder at the jumble of burned timbers. "What manner of place was that? Why were we here?"

Duff rubbed the back of his hand on her cheek. "I do not

know, Dear. Either one."

Tears had walked off to one side and stood looking into the now mostly empty space below, silently crying for his grandfather, for his loss. And in his mind, ever so gently trained by that Grand Master Teller of Tales, he heard Sorrowful telling him all the things that he needed to know.

And, after some time had passed, when they had judged the moment right, Duff walked over to him. "It is time for us to leave this place. We must travel on."

Tears nodded, threw back his shoulders, and patted the dagger hanging from his belt, and stated," In many ways Grandfather will be with me always. It is the Tale Teller's gift."

Duff slipped an arm around him and hugged him close. "Good." She held him for long moments. "Ready?"

Tears nodded. "Yes, we have an adventure to tell." And straightened his shoulders.

They rejoined $1.98, who was standing in a certain spot only he could see. The traveling bags jostled each other, eager to follow, their sides battered, torn, and scorched, but still holding their contents intact.

"This way," said $1.98, taking a step and turning.

Bahn Duhr Tohr. The Royal City. Evening.

The air ripped open.

Ripple sat up and hastily began to stuff her blouse into her trouser's, snarling loudly. "SISTER, that is really bad manners and really bad timing!"

Hanred sat up. "Hayou, R-Bar."

"Help us," cried the small witch. "**PLEASE?**"

Smoke's head hung backwards, loose.

Fair Morn looked at Ripple. "She is badly injured."

"Come with me," snapped Ripple, walking swiftly into the adjoining room.

Tinker stood there holding Messenger. She was mumbling something, the black wand still held tightly in her hand. It crackled menacingly.

"Her also?" Hanred stared at them.

"Yes," said Tinker. "Her also."

R-Bar set the green box on the table. "Don't touch it."

Hanred walked over and bent to look at it. "Just like the other one."

Rotak burst into the room. "What is happening in here?" She leaped sideways, skidding away from Tinker and what he held in his arms.

"She is injured," said R-Bar. "Help her."

Rotak shook her head. "I can not. I dare not touch her."

"Then tell me. I will." R-Bar glared at her sister.

Rotak hissed at her. "You will die. Horribly, horribly. Magic clash ripped."

"Tell me, tell me, **TELL ME!**" screamed R-Bar grabbing Messenger's hand, wand and all.

"**DON'T!**" Rotak howled and crouched, covering her face with her hands, calling down all the protection she knew.

"Tell me. Please?"

Rotak opened the fingers of one hand and peered out at her younger sister. "How?"

"We can talk about that later. Hurry."

Rotak stood and headed for another room. "Bring her in here."

Tinker and R-Bar followed her.

Hanred waved Chicken into a chair and grabbed a jug and two glasses. "I think we can use a little something. What happened? This time?"

Chicken told him everything.

"I think that she will become a terror among terrors."

"Who?"

"R-Bar. That runt is growing in all directions, many never before imagined by the witch clan. Rotak is already frightened by her."

"True?"

He nodded. "Yes, Princess, very true. Even Ripple will have much to ponder once she has time to think about it."

"Have you knowledge pon J. C. and loud Mirf?"

Hanred shook his head, and refilled their glasses. "They just disappeared into the elsewheres. None of the sisters have reported seeing them."

Tinker entered the room and joined them at the table.

Hanred shoved another glass over to him, the liquid sloshing back and forth in the container. "Restorative. What is in that box?"

Tinker shrugged. "I never got a chance to see. I think only R-Bar and Messenger know. What a mess." He shuddered, face muscles twitching.

Chicken stood and stepped behind him, throwing her arms around him, her mind reaching in, intertwining with his. "Oh My Lord, it hurts so."

"Is there anything that I might do?" Hanred looked from face to face.

"POUR!" said Tinker harshly.

They emptied the bottle.

Hanred was sitting on the couch, reading, when Ripple came from the adjoining room.

Tinker was asleep on the other couch, Chicken wrapped in his arms.

The great weaponkin lay on the floor beside them.

"This is getting brutal, husband."

"And strange."

She pushed the book and his hands out of his lap. "I am worried. And you are not to tell anyone that."

"Never." Settling the book on his chest, he asked, "You want to sleep?"

"No. I though that I heard Rotak come in?"

"You did. She is in the other room with R-Bar."

Ripple hissed. "Again? How bad was it? This time?"

"I am unharmed." R-Bar and Rotak came into the room.

Ripple frowned and looked at the other couch.

Fair Morn was stretched out, sound asleep.

Ripple's face went blank.

"Umm, oh," whispered Hanred.

"That one?" Ripple looked at R-Bar and Rotak. "Is it bad? Can she self-cure? I will fetch the court-help."

"No need," stated R-Bar. "She is mending. Rotak had the perfect spell."

Ripple carefully examined Rotak. "What good?"

"I did it!" stated R-Bar.

Ripple frowned.

"I watched her do it," said Rotak, dropping heavily into an empty chair. "I saw . . ." She beckoned a new, full jug and a glass over and poured and drank. "I saw . . ." She refilled the glass.

Ripple beckoned R-Bar over with one finger. "Come here."

R-Bar stepped close and stared defiantly at her older sister.

"Hum, hum, hum, hum." Ripple reached out and with great hesitation, with great caution, touched her. "You are still you."

"Of course," snapped R-Bar.

"Hum, hum, hum." Ripple's eyes bored deep. "Of course." She held one of R-Bar's hands gently, carefully. "You look very tired, little sister. Rest."

"How is Smoke?"

"Sleeping," said Fair Morn, rising, walking over, sitting on the end of the couch, making two pairs of legs move out of the way. "Now we owe you a debt." She smiled. "Think upon it." She leaned back and fell back asleep.

"We all need to do that," said Ripple. "Sleep."

Rotak nodded her head and disappeared.

"I will sit and read for awhile," said Hanred.

"No, you will not. You will hold me." Ripple grabbed

one of his hands. They disappeared.

The book thumped on the floor. A cloud of dust drifted from it.

R-Bar stretched out on the now empty couch, dimmed the lights, and fell asleep.

In the soft light of as new day, Tinker yawned and stretched. "OOOOP, sorry, Princess, I forgot."

"Ummm, Our Prince."

His mind reached wide. "We are still whole." He sighed, and then grumbled at her, "Why do we keep doing this?"

"Thee did a'promise make."

"Yah, I know. Think I will ever learn?" He rolled onto his side and kissed her. "Good morning, Noble Queen, Fair Princess, Fierce Warrior, Old Yellar." He smiled, and gave her a quick kiss.

"Who wert last?"

"Joke."

"Yellow tis most pleasing a'color." She yawned and wiggled. "Thou art being most familiar."

"Uh huh."

"Tis nay sport for spectators, Loverly."

"What?"

"First Day meal time," announced R-Bar cheerily, sitting up.

"Damn kid," mumbled Tinker. He gave Chicken another quick kiss and sat up, to turn and glare across the room. "Don't you guys ever knock?"

R-Bar's happy face faded. "I slept here, just in case." And looked unhappy at him.

Chicken sat up and buttoned her blouse. "He do be naught but mighty grouch in fair morn. Tis a most pleasing spread thee did lay."

Chicken joined R-Bar at the table, gave her a hug, and whispered in her ear. "Thee must wait till he does wake most fully." She served them both after they sat, and shoved a coffee cup at Tinker as he joined them.

"Thanks," he mumbled, looking at the two faces looking at him. "Morning, R-Bar." Then he slowly let the day seep in.

By the end of breakfast, he had moved around and was sitting next to R-Bar, teasing her. She was gurgling, softly.

My Tinker?

He jumped up and hurried into Messenger's room, Chicken and R-Bar right behind him. "What?"

"May I get out of bed? I am hungry."

"Sure."

"I can't."

R-Bar waved one hand, did something. "We had to keep you in bed."

Messenger sat up. *Mom? MOM?*

Not so loud. It hurts.

Tears started running down Messenger's cheeks. "I couldn't feel her."

"Thee do be a'mending yet," said Chicken.

They went back into the central room, Chicken and R-Bar helping Messenger.

"It was horrid," said Messenger.

"What's in the box?" asked Tinker.

"A heart," replied R-Bar. "A black stone heart."

"IT is alive," whispered Messenger. "Beating!"

Tinker pushed a cup in front of her. "Eat your breakfast, kitten, we can talk about it later. We will be here awhile."

Chicken set a tray down, then she and R-Bar went to visit Smoke.

"How are you feeling?"

"All right." Messenger smiled at him.

Tinker sat next to her and bumped her gently with his shoulder. "We owe R-Bar a whole lot. If it hadn't been for her we wouldn't been able to get back here. And from what I understood, you couldn't have been healed."

"She is our friend."

He took one of Messenger's hands in his. "A rather special friend."

"Good," announced Fair Morn, strolling from Smoke's room. "Breakfast." She dragged a languid hand over Messenger's back and shoulder. "You should eat, build up your strength."

Tinker released Messenger's hand. "Don't let me stop you." He pushed a platter toward Messenger and served her. "Before super appetite consumes everything. Good thing the dishes aren't edible."

Fair Morn looked at him, picked up a clean plate, and took a bite out of it, and calmly chewed. "Not very tasty, One."

"Every day in every way, I get smarter and smarter," mumbled Tinker.

Fair Morn spit the glob into her mug. "Not very nutritious, either."

"I am glad. Food is less expensive. Here." He poured Fair Morn a mug of coffee in a different mug. He didn't see her wink at Messenger.

"Fair morn, Fair Morn," said Chicken as they returned.

"Hayou," said R-Bar. "What happened to that plate?"

"Ask the moth," said Tinker. "And while she is explaining that one, we need to talk." He guided Chicken out the door into the hall.

"T'was but mere jest, My Lord. Fair Morn did mean naught."

"I know." He wandered down the hall, Chicken at his side.

"Our Prince?"

"It is turning bad, Princess, We are beginning to spend more time here than we are accomplishing anything. We can't keep getting battered like this. And we are separated from them again."

"Most true."

"We owe her."

"Most true also. As Fairest of Morns did say."

"We. Not me!"

"Most true again." Chicken stopped him and pushed him against the wall. "We do know that." She grinned wickedly and fiddled with the buttons on his shirt.

"Princess?" he cautioned.

"Lord Love?" She tickled his chest and inched closer.

He grabbed her and started walking, yanking her along. "Not this time, you don't."

"My Lord?"

"You are as sneaky as a witch."

"Hee, hee, hee," she cackled most witch-like, swinging his arm back and forth, a light bounce in her step.

"I think we are getting close," said R-Bar frowning at Chicken witch sounds. "To that monster after Ramp."

"How can you tell?" asked Messenger.

"Yes?" said Fair Morn, peeking into a covered bowl and taking a helping of whatever it was. "How can you tell?"

"Just a feeling."

I am still hungry.

Fair Morn left the table and returned with the tray and began to pile it with food. Then she left.

R-Bar watched her, then sat next to Messenger and whispered into her ear. "It is true, isn't it? What Tink told me about you? One complex organism? I saw her listen, I did."

Messenger took hold of R-Bar's hand and nodded. "Yes."

"How did you become a part?"

"I was dying. Smoke saved my life by joining me with them."

R-Bar squeezed her hand tightly. "Did it hurt?"

"Oh, no. It was like growing in another direction, seeing and hearing and learning and feeling, four ways at once, or one at a time."

"Four? There are five?"

Messenger blushed. "That was my fault. Didn't he tell you about that?"

R-Bar frowned. "I think he left out a lot of things."

So Messenger told her how she had broken the magical strands holding Fair Morn to Big Red and how this had changed her from being a magical jest into a live, free person. Fair Morn had been so sad and so unhappy that she just couldn't resist helping her.

"Didn't that red magician become angry? He is said to be terrible." R-Bar's eyes darted around the room. She had heard all kinds of stories about that one, The Great Red Magician. He had trained Ramp.

"He likes MyTinker."

"So do I." R-Bar nodded and asked, "May I call you kitten, also?"

Messenger nodded back. "Sure."

"You may call me kid, if you wish. I really won't mind." She leaned closer to Messenger. "Hold still, I want to see."

Messenger sat very still while R-Bar carefully checked the spell bits. She ducked her head. "One day more. You will be as good as ever by tonight, kitten."

Messenger exhaled loudly. "Thanks, kid." She smiled. And kissed her on the cheek.

R-Bar gasped. Witches didn't do things like that.

Fair Morn returned. "She wants to see you, little witch."

R-Bar bounded into Smoke's room.

Fair Morn smiled at Messenger. "If we sit on the roof of the northeast eave, we can watch the armies play games below the wall. I will keep you from falling."

"Let's," said Messenger, standing up.

They left.

And hurried to the far end of the hallway.

Smoke was propped up, just a little.

R-Bar was feeding her. "Ripple is very talented," said the small witch.

Smoke nodded, her mouth was full.

"Fair Morn said you were in my debt as I was in your's."

Smoke swallowed loudly. "We are. A double death may well have been a lethal shock."

R-Bar's eyes went wide. "They would have died also?"

"Could have. I have seen it happen. Some died instantly, some went mad first, then died."

R-Bar lightly touched one of Smoke's arms. "I have never met anyone like you before."

The golden eyes fastened upon her's. "Me? Or us?"

R-Bar couldn't pull her eyes away. "Both. Especially the whole."

"My people are a rare race. And I am now part of a rarer thing."

R-Bar leaned close. "What is it like?"

The great eyes seemed to grow and grow, the vertical pupils widening, pulling her in. "Would you like to experience us?"

"May I? Please?"

"Hold my hands. You will be safe." Smoke's hands folded over R-Bar's. "Just for a little. I am weak."

R-Bar felt the wind tostling her hair. She was sitting on the roof watching the army games. Messenger looked at her and smiled.

Isn't it nice?

She felt the urge to unfurl her wings.

Don't do that, cautioned Fair Morn.

For just a moment, she felt Tinker's hands sliding over her body.

And her response.

Smoke smiled at her. "Here we are. We don't intrude upon the others during private times."

R-Bar leaned forward and kissed her. "Thank you."

"I need to sleep now."

R-Bar removed the tray and quietly closed the door as she left the room.

"Sister, we need to talk." Ripple was seated at the table.

Hanred winked at R-Bar.

Twilight was transforming itself into night by the time Tinker and Chicken returned to the rooms.

Messenger, Fair Morn, and Hanred were already there. He was reading.

Fair Morn was rubbing some medicine, provided by the Royal Staff on Messenger's face. She had gotten rather sunburned.

"Hayou, John Tinker, Princess," said Hanred, setting his book aside, making another dust patch on the rug.

"How's the patient?" asked Tinker.

"Recovering nicely. And this one, except for the reddened face, is as good as she ever was." He beckoned Tinker over as Chicken walked over to look at Messenger's face.

Tugging Tinker closer as he bend over, Hanred said very softly. "Those . . . ladies of your's are an, ah, very interesting, um, assortment. I was rubbing in her, Smoke's, medicine." Hanred held up his hands. They were stained a deep green. "And while I was doing that, she made deep rumbling sounds, purring she called it."

"What he means to say," interrupted Ripple, leaning over, one hand on Tinker's back. "Is that it occurred while he was merrily fondling her chest."

"Ebony Delight, you exaggerate."

"Hum, hum," said Ripple. "Perhaps I should return the favor without the green?"

Tinker straightened up and stepped sideways. "How is Smoke?"

"She may take short walks starting tomorrow. She will have new scars among those old scars."

Ripple looked across the room. "The other is cured.

Shall we have dinner?"

The table rearranged itself.

As they took their places, Ripple pointed at Messenger. "You sit over there. Not too close."

Chicken looked around, and then at Ripple. "Where be your sisters?"

"Rotak gets nervous being around her." Ripple gestured with her fork at Messenger. "I think my sister hasn't fully recovered and may still need some treatment." She nudged Hanred. "You may help. "

Hanred grinned and poured Ripple's mug full.

"And R-Bar?" asked Fair Morn.

"Visiting The Aunts," snapped Ripple.

Green Ghost. Just After Sunrise.

Standing on the beach, they looked around. Fred threw off her robe and dashed into the water, rolling and splashing. Grizmek scooped up the garment and stuffed it into a pocket.

"Welcome to Green Ghost," announced Mirf, sweeping her arms in a wide, expansive gesture.

J. C. admired the wide, gently sloping beach and the waves rolling in. They started a long, long way off shore. Surfing paradise, he thought. The sand was packed hard, even where they stood, high above the water line. It was purple-blue. So was the water. And the sky.

As he stared at the far horizon, everything merged and blurred into a seamless whole. It was disconcerting.

The other side of the beach, at least four hundred feet away, ended abruptly into a mass of growth that rose high into the air.

Things flitted and jumped from plant to plant. In spite of the clear sky, the temperature was quite mild.

"Nice place."

Fred surged from the water.

J. C. thought that she looked very happy although she

never seemed to have much of a facial expression.

"They like water," explained Mirf as Fred circled around them and then hurtled back into and through the surf.

"Where are we going?"

Mirf pointed down the beach. "There."

By squinting, and cupping his hands around his eyes, J. C. could just make out a faint line crossing the beach. It seemed to stretch out to sea.

"Shall we?' said Mirf.

J. C. waved Fred back out of the water and hurried down the beach.

Mirf called at his rapidly receding back. "Slow down, partner. No need to hurry. Enjoy the day. Enjoy!"

So they strolled down the beach.

Mirf explained, as they walked, that all the towns here were built out over the water. It was the only way to keep out the vegetation. It could not, it would not, grow over the beach. The early settlements had been rapidly swallowed up whenever they tried to establish themselves inside the thick growth.

No-one knew anything about the interior as it was impossible to cut a road that far in before it disappeared behind you. And from the air, it was all green, a thick mass of tangled green. If there were openings in it, they were hidden from the air, and anything else. And if there was a population of something living out there, they were hidden also.

The towns harvested and exported exotic fruits and vegetables collected from the fringes of the growth. The climate was mild, the work hard. The people who came here to live and to work used any name that they wished and no one asked any questions. This was a frontier elseplace.

"So, you see, blue eyes, we can be as sneaky as everyone else. And I'll tell you something else, the food and the drink and the lodgings are very nice." She grinned at him.

"Been here before, huh?"

"You betcha, bubee, But I was in disguise. Checking on some currency fiddling."

Fred ran past them, turned sharply and then leaped back into the water.

J. C. smiled. "Maybe we should call her Golden Retriever?"

"Stick with Fred."

Eventually they stopped for lunch.

They sat near the dense growth eating things that Mirf had plucked and snapped from limbs and vines.

J. C. pointed down the beach. "A lot longer away than it looks."

"Distances are deceiving here," mumbled Mirf, purple juice dribbling from one corner of her mouth.

When they finished eating, she grabbed a handful of sand and washed her hands and face with it. She was instantly clean. None of the sand adhered to her skin.

J. C. bent over and peered closely at the sand, poking at it with one finger. "Interesting stuff."

She had to wack him on the back with the flat of her hand to get his attention. "Let's go, let's go. Night is not a good time to be on the beach."

J. C. looked up. It was a moment before he saw her. "Sure, Mirf. Let's go."

They did.

Go.

Down the beach.

The sun was hugging the horizon, a large, yellow sphere suddenly cut across the lower edge by dark purple-blue. Not far away, the town causeway marched on pilings out to sea. Figures were moving here and there along the pier-like structure.

"Hold up for a moment, J. C."

They stopped. Mirf unbuttoned her shirt, yanked it off and handed it to Grizmek. "Hang on to this." Then she reached over and tugged J. C.'s shirt loose. "Take it off, partner."

"Mirf?"

"Local custom. All the human-types dress this way. The other forms however. Fred will fit right in."

"I see." He grinned at her.

"No jokes," snapped Mirf. "When a woman once begins to be ashamed of what she ought not be ashamed of, she will not be ashamed of what she ought." She grinned broadly back at him. "Thank you, Cato the Censor."

"Feels pretty good," said J. C. "Looks pretty good."

"Comfort is comfort. Let's go." She led the way to the stairs.

And undid the intricate locking mechanism, then relocked it after they had passed through. At the top of the stairs, they stepped out onto the main concourse.

"When in Rome," said J. C.

"Head out to sea," stated Mirf.

"That is not the quote."

"That is the direction, partner. We want to find food and lodgings. If that place isn't full." She pointed toward the far end. "I am hungry."

"Let's go," said J. C.

"Ulp."

"Chirp."

"Well, we are all agreed on that." Mirf led them along the upward sloping deck until they reached the level stretch. It shot arrow straight into the darkness.

Far ahead they could see a cluster of twinkling yellow lights.

"That's the town," said Mirf, walking faster.

No one paid any attention to them.

At least, not yet.

Town was a maze of passageways that took them to a wide deck area lined with open shops on one side, the sea on the other. A few structures were cantilevered out over the water.

"That place." She pointed at one of the more extremely cantilevered places. A small sign near the door read, *DIR*. "I'll sign us in," said Mirf pushing through the door ahead of them. She did, adding after their names: *PAK EO COP*.

Stacking a glittering column of coins on the counter, Mirf smiled at the owner, Dir. "Take the best when the company pays."

"Yar so," said Dir, scooping the gold into a pocket and handing her two yellow tags. "Drar and Ser."

Mirf led her party down a stairwell and into a long narrow corridor. At the end, she took one of the tags and hung it on a hook near one of two doors, then threw it open. "Grizmek, Fred, this is your room. Our rooms are the ones next door. They interconnect."

Yanking J. C. sideways, Mirf hung the other tag next to the other door and pushed him inside. It was a large round room. She pointed.

"That door opens to the rooms next door. We will eat in here, Dir will bring a real feast." She jabbed one finger. "Big tub in there. Bed in there."

Someone kicked on their door. It was Dir. And his helpers, two young women. As they set the table, the younger one eyed J. C. and smiled softly. Mirf opened the connecting door and called Grizmek and Fred to join them for their meal. Dir and helpers left.

As they ate, Mirf nudged J. C. "Oh, one more thing partner. The female human-types here are rather forward and aggressive. The males are not. So, watch it."

J. C. nudged Mirf back. "The taller one was rather cute. Beautiful light green eyes."

"Bizzle." Mirf shoved a jug at him. "Sure that it was the eyes you were admiring? Eat. Drink. Tomorrow will be a busy day. Pak Eo Cop is our company name. We specialize in importing exotic food stuffs. A very big company, a very wealthy company, a very big, very wealthy company. So, we have lots of reason to be wandering around and talking to the folk. By mid-morning, everyone will know us."

"Very clever."

"Very sneaky."

Mirf heaped everyone's plate full of the many kinds of food available. It was a slow, casual meal, that eventually ended with all feeling quite stuffed.

Grizmek and Fred returned to their rooms.

Mirf dragged J. C. to the other room to show him the bed. It seemed to float in a bubble attached to the side of the structure and was entered from their main room.

"The only one like it here. Wholly private," she said some time later. "Different, huh?"

"Mirf, working with you is an ongoing series of surprises."

"J. C ., for you, I have become a tsatske."

"A what?"

"A plaything, a girl who fools around with studs like you. A kept woman, only I am doing the keeping."

"Two dolla, G. I.," said J. C.

"Meshuggener monzer, pay attention! I am being serious."

J. C. tickled her, just a bit. "So, be serious. See if I care."

"Ummmm, you are a hazard to my health."

He laughed. "I'd say, First Chief Inspector, Monetary Control, that you are the healthiest woman I have ever known."

Mirf shoved him onto his back and sprawled on top of him. "Listen partner. STOP THAT! Just listen. DON'T! Hey, listen . . . listen."

"O. K., I'll listen. Don't giggle, either."

Mirf pinched his cheek. "You gonna listen?" And waggled his head.

"Sure."

"When we finish here, I am going to send you home."

"WHAT? Oh no, you are not."

Mirf sat up and smiled at him. "Not here. This elseplace."

J. C. shook his head. "Still no."

"I'll come and visit, open an office, drag you into dark alleys."

"NO!"

She stopped smiling. "I am afraid, J. C."

"You?"

"That you are going to get killed, if you stay with me."

"What about you? If I hadn't been, there you would be, already. Dead."

"So? I thanked you."

"Don't be a hard ass."

Mirf leaned forward and lay on his chest, her arms holding him. "Go home, partner. Please? OI, I said that, me? Please?"

J. C. rolled sideways and lay there staring into those strange looking eyes. "Even with a touch of hob-goblin, you are very attractive. And not only that, you are a nice person as well. So, I am going to stay. I am a big boy."

She winked at him. "I'll say. OH, EM! You did that deliberately."

"Captain, my Captain, a good leader makes a good company, so I say, lead on."

"J. C."

"In the morning. For now, let's just enjoy the view."

"You betcha, bubee."

They watched the sky, the last stars fade away, as mist clouds hazed the sky.

"How are we going to find the second key?"

"I don't know, Just schmei around, shmoos here and there, maybe shmeer a few palms."

He sat up and looked at her. "And be careful, right?

Along with those other things?"

She reached over and grabbed him. "And be sneaky."

"Right. Sneaky." He nodded.

A number of warm hands pattered lightly over his back. "Chirp?"

"Fred, what are you doing in here?"

Mirf let go. J. C. turned around.

"Chirp?"

Mirf laughed. "She wants to get in bed with you, us."

"Not a good idea, Fred."

Mirf threw back the covers. "Hop in."

Fred did.

"MIRF!" J. C. jerked up and glared at her.

"She is lonely, J. C.," cooed Mirf. "So, lay down, sleep a little."

"It's still early." He lay back. Mirf tugged up the blankets. "I don't know about this," said J. C. "She going to behave? What do you know about suk-dragons anyway?" He sat up.

Mirf tugged the covers back up, putting her hands behind her head, staring up at the sky. "Lay down, partner, relax. I will tell you all that I know."

J. C. laid back. And felt the warmth radiating from Fred.

Mirf snorted. "All in all, she is just a lovely young female with just a few extra parts, being mainly her arms. An interesting articulation in the skeleton. You have already admired her chest. Her eyes are like one of your dragon flies except that they sit in eye sockets."

J. C. sat up again. "I can see all that. I saw all that."

Mirf yanked up the blanket. Again.

Fred lay there and watched him, one pair of arms at her sides, one pair folded over her stomach, the other pair trying to drag the covers up to her chin.

He flopped back down.

"And be careful how you kiss her, darlink, she has

poisonous fangs."

J. C. jerked upright. "**WHAT?**" Yanking the covers down again. "**DO WHAT?**"

Fred lifted her upper lip with her fingers and showed him. There were two of them, side by side, on the top jaw where each canine ought to be. A third, on the lower jaw, slid between the uppers, nesting between them.

Mirf laughed. "Don't worry, partner. She has total control over her poison glands. Accidental nips are harmless. Go to sleep." She dragged the blanket back, rolled onto her side, faced out to sea. "So give a little experiment. I won't mind. She won't mind."

J. C. rolled onto his side, facing Fred.

"Chirp."

"Go to sleep," he mumbled, trying to do the same thing.

The Foregather At Quata.

The Foregather had ended. Booths were being taken down and removed to the appropriate storage areas until the next Foregather. Witches and warlocks of various clans still lingered in the few refreshments booths, those still standing and open, holding soft conversations.

In a small beverage place in a far corner the trio sat and pondered what they had been told by a witch of the Rantan clan at the end of a Dark Hallow display. She had suggested, very gently suggested, that a Franzak on Nonnap might help the witches call in a cure spell.

"The Franzak are ugly bent," stated Motaiss.

"Um um." Turintor flicked her eyes at her companion. Who shrugged.

"Yessss," said Turintor.

"We will be subtle cautious?" Motaiss frowned at the pair as he watched the hazard build around them.

The two witches stood and looked at him.

He stood. And nodded.

They swirled out in a soft puff of black.

Leaving two gold coins on the tabletop.

Green Ghost. Morning.

The sun was high overhead when J. C's eyes opened. The upper edge of the bubble glowed yellow. Warm hands were fluttering over him. Multi-lensed eyes were peering into his eyes.

"Fred, stop that." He reached up to push her away. "OOP."

Her hands held his in place. She smiled and leaned closer, arms slipping around his waist.

"Fred, behave yourself." He pushed. To no avail. She was stronger than she looked.

Warm, soft lips brushed over his.

"Impf."

"Breakfast, in ten minutes," called Mirf, from the other room.

Fred released his hands and pressed herself against his chest. J. C. managed to lurch into a sitting position and found himself with Fred straddling his lap, arms around his waist, chest, and neck, leaning back, looking into his face. She blinked.

"**MIRF!**"

"Five minutes," she called back. "Gonna have'ta hurry."

"You hear that? Let me go." J. C. tried to escape again. It did no good.

Fred leaned forward and kissed him.

"You men are all alike," chortled Mirf from the doorway.

J. C. fell backward. Fred nuzzled his neck. "Mirf, this is not funny. Get her off. I am out numbered, three to one. Damn it, Fred, stop. **STOP THAT!**"

Mirf laughed. "Discounting certain differences, I don't see how you can resist."

"Cause I do not chase everything that happens to be handy, that's why," yelled J. C. "Fred, if you don't let me go, I am going to give you away."

Fred sat up and looked at him, her large eyes blinked, her lips trembled.

"I didn't really mean it," said J. C. "Honestly."

She fell against his chest and held him, tightly.

"But," he gasped. "You have got to behave yourself." He patted her back. "Let's go eat breakfast, shall we? And don't hold so tight."

Fred sat up, fished her trousers from the jumbled bed covers, turned around and demurely yanked them on, and walked over to stand next to Mirf.

Mirf threw an arm around her. "Let's go set the table, glitter eyes." And led her into the other room.

They were sitting, waiting for him, when he stepped into the main room, Breakfast was very elaborate.

"Compliments of Dir," explained Mirf.

Grizmek was already eating. Mirf and Fred had waited for J. C. Fred sat with her hands folded in her lap, head tilted down, chin resting on her chest.

"Chirp?" she said softly.

"Tell her that you are not angry with her, J. C."

J. C. slid his hands over the top of Fred's shoulders. "I am not angry with you, Fred. But you have to understand that you cannot just attack people that way."

Her big eyes stared at him, facets glittering in the bright light.

J. C. leaned close and kissed her. "O.K."

"Chirp." She kissed him back.

Mirf grinned at him. "You do have a way with the ladies, big hunk." She shoved her chair sideways and dragged another over. "Here, you can sit between us."

He did.

During breakfast, Mirf told him what they would be

doing this day. She was all business, giving each of them detailed instructions, especially to Grizmek, who was to go first and to work on his own. Then Mirf banged down her coffee cup, or whatever the beverage really was. "SO! We ready to go?"

"Sure," said J. C.

"Ulp."

"Chirp."

"Vunderbar." Mirf jumped up and herded them outside.

And there they were, outside, on one of the main streets, hurrying along. And then, at a certain spot, carefully selected by Mirf, they parted company. Grizmek disappeared into the crowd. Mirf directed them down the street, slipping her arm under one of J. C.'s. Fred looked over and slipped one of her's under his other arm.

"Family bizarre."

"Only for one of your backward elseplace," said Mirf.

"It has been interesting," agreed J. C. He winked at Fred. She winked back.

"You want interesting, you take her to bed," mumbled Mirf.

"Don't be so crude."

"Such an opportunity you have never had."

"Such an opportunity I do not need," stated J. C. firmly.

"Ho boy," replied Mirf, "an echo. Of a sort."

"No insult intended, Fred," stated J. C.

They stepped into the first of the many business places that Mirf had decided that they would visit.

"I talk, you listen," advised Mirf.

And that is just what they did.

All day long.

Place after place.

J. C. lay on his face. Fred sat on his back. She was massaging his neck, shoulder, and back muscles. Mirf was watching. They had returned late, eaten dinner, and now they were relaxing. Grizmek and Mirf had discussed their respective day's activities and then the frog-thief had retired for the night.

Mirf sprawled on the floor next to J. C. "Me too."

Fred gave J. C. a few final pats and changed position.

"Hoooooo boy," sighed Mirf.

J. C. sat on the couch and stretched out his legs. "She has a real career there."

"Vunderbar," agreed Mirf.

Finally, Fred patted her and stood. Mirf rolled over and up.

"Come on, kiddolink. You too, J. C." She led them into the bubble and onto the bed.

"Mirf?"

"Relax." She pushed a button. The back edge of the bed raised and transformed the bed into a gigantic lounge. Mirf pushed another button and a panel opened. She grabbed a container and three mugs, poured and handed them around. Then she sat, stretched her legs out and stared out at the sea. "Sit, sit."

J. C. did. So did Fred. Mirf nestled against him. Fred got the other side.

"Cheers," said Mirf, taking a big swallow.

"Cheers."

"Chirp."

They watched the last of the sun disappear.

Mirf nudged him. "The weary sun hath made a golden set, and by the bright track of his firey care, gives sign of a goodly day tomorrow. King Richard III, by Old Will himself."

"You are amazing, Mirf." J. C. took another sip. "Pretty good stuff." He smiled. "Now I know how Tinker feels." He looked right, then left.

"Could be worse."

"How?"

"Could be four."

"I don't see how he does it."

"Different organism."

"What?"

Mirf explained, again, adding some more details.

J. C. shook his head. "Boy, did he leave out a lot of stuff."

Mirf refilled his mug and then Fred's. And her own. "When we hit the bottom of the bottle, it is time for bed. Tomorrow is another big day."

They watched the stars appear. Fred rolled her head back and looked up into the dark reaches of the wall.

Suddenly, many hands grabbed J. C. and tossed him to the far end of the bed.

The bolt of fire snapped through the bed where he had been sitting.

"**HEEEEEEY!**" He bounced. Rolled. And sat up. And saw Fred as she crawled up the wall, all arms spread wide, fingers and toes finding small purchases here and there. She swarmed into the darkness.

Someone screamed in terror.

"**DON'T KILL HIM!**" yelled Mirf.

A body tumbled to the floor, arms and legs thrashing violently.

Fred dropped, landing in a crouch, arms arched, body leaning forward, head low, thrust forward. She glared at the now still form, green froth bubbling from her between her lips. Slowly she scanned the rest of the dark spaces in the room.

"Too late," sighed Mirf, pouring a bottle of something into the smoldering hole where J. C. had been sitting. She touched a button and watched the bed flatten. Then walked over to the body and looked down at it.

"Must be getting close." She bent and riffled through the dead man's pockets. "No help there." Grabbing a wrist, she said, "Give me a hand, if you'll pardon the pun. We need to get rid of this."

J. C. helped her drag the dead man through the central room and over to a small hatch in one wall. They shoved the body through and heard the splash when it hit the sea.

J. C. whispered to Mirf. "She bit him?"

"Sure did."

He straightened up. Fred slipped up to him, her hands running lightly over his body.

"I am all right. Thanks." J. C. pulled her close and kissed her, seriously this time.

"You are learning, partner." Mirf tapped them both on a shoulder. "Break time. Bed time. To sleep, to sleep." And headed back into the bubble, towing J. C. and Fred with her.

Kicking the covers around, Mirf yanked off her clothes and tumbled under the blankets. "Going to be closer together than last night. Unless someone wants to sleep over that hole."

J. C. joined her as did Fred.

"And," cautioned Mirf. "No hanky-panky. We will need to be bright-eyed and bushy tailed tomorrow."

J .C. rolled onto his side and kissed Mirf goodnight. Fred nestled against his back, kissed his neck, and dropped her arms lightly over him.

"O. K.," said Mirf, as they ate a late lunch. The restaurant was far across the town from their lodgings. They had been wandering from place to place all morning. "We've got him."

"Ulp?" Grizmek had met them at this restaurant as had been prearranged.

"You are sure?" asked J. C.

"You betcha, bubee. It is sneaky time cause this guy is going to be plenty nervous since a certain henchman has dropped, ha ha, out of sight."

J. C. rolled his head sideways. "And we are going to be very, very careful, are we not?"

"Don't kvetch!" Mirf banged him on the shoulder and then rapidly told each of them what they were to do, what her plan was. She nudged J. C. with her shoulder. "And we will be careful."

He set his hand on Fred's upper right forearm. "You too."

Fred slipped from the table and out the door.

They waited for her to get into position.

Then Mirf stood. "Grizmek, you have that crystal handy?"

"Ulp."

"Good. Let's go." She led them outside and down the street.

They stood in front of the shop, one of the many many along this street, and peered in the window.

"Grizmek, you keep your hand on that crystal. We need to know the moment we get next to that key." She tapped him on the chest.

"Ulp." Grizmek nodded.

Mirf stepped over and pushed open the front door. "Let's shop." She grabbed J. C.'s arm.

As the owner approached, she said loudly, "I want to buy something."

"Yes, Dear," said J. C., meekly.

Grizmek hovered behind them. "Our servant," explained J. C. apologetically to the shop keeper, wringing his hands, and wobbling a weak smile onto his face.

Mirf curled her lip at J. C. "You know what I want, look over there." She beamed at the owner. "And you may show me those lovely things in that case." She pointed.

J. C. and Grizmek began the search while Mirf looked at every expensive thing in the shop, jingling the bag of gold coins from time to time, just as a reminder that she had much to spend.

And some time later, as she bargained over a small ring, J. C. and Grizmek joined her.

"Nope," he said quietly.

She glared at him. "There must be something here, somewhere." She handed the owner his price and snatched the ring from his hand. "I'll take it." Then, batting her eyes at him, she said. "Perhaps in back? Some special thing. Or two?"

He nodded. "Just step this way. Perhaps some small thing not on display?"

"Exactly," she said, taking his arm in her's.

As they entered the high-ceilinged back room, a large figure loomed up from the shadows. "My assistant," said the shop owner.

The assistant held a weapon of some kind in one hand. It was pointed at Mirf.

"Oh dear," she said, still in character.

"Ulp," said Grizmek, still being Grizmek.

J. C. watched and waited and wondered if he could jerk Mirf out of the way fast enough.

"Ulp, ulp," ulped Grizmek. The crystal was reacting to something nearby. His eyes darted everywhere. And then he saw it. It was a small brown sphere. It wobbled slightly, reacting to the crystal. Slowly, the frog-thief eased his hands from his pockets, eyes calculating the distance.

Mirf stepped sideways, glanced at J. C. and Grizmek, recognized the Grizmek look, and said, loudly, waving her hands. "What does this mean?"

"It means, Mirf," said the shop owner. "That you are about to feed the sea dwellers. Our Master wishes you dead."

She nodded. "So, that was your boy."

"Kill her," rasped the owner. "Then, them."

A shadow dropped from an overhead girder, arms and legs wrapping around the assistant, fangs plunging deep into his neck. He fired.

The steel bolt creased his back as J. C. turned, bent, and bowled over Mirf.

Grizmek dropped under a table.

Fred bounded through the air, driving the owner onto

his face.

"**NO!**" shouted Mirf from the floor.

The thrashing of the assistant collapsed two tables sending art objects rattling and banging loudly, dust puffing in soft billows everywhere.

Fred's teeth clapped together loudly as she jerked her head back, reacting to Mirf's scream. She lifted the terrified owner to his feet. She held his arms behind his back, crushed his neck, and held his head up by the hair.

Mirf struggled to her feet, walked over and snarled in his face. "Tell me who this master of your's is."

"**NEVER!**" he screamed, slashing at her with a blade that snapped from one boot. Mirf leaped sideways and caught the blow with a large metal pot.

Fred dropped the convulsing body and shook her head from side to side.

"Just the two," stated Mirf. "We had better get out of here. Grizmek?"

The frog-thief eased himself out from under the table. "Ulp. Got it."

"HO BOY! Let's go!" She ran for the outside door. "There is a node just around the corner."

Doth Lamex, Warm, Mid-Morning. Pleasant.

The party of four arrived at the circle entry. The host drifted silently over to greet them. "Welcome," it boomed. "Rest and relax. May I have your names for our register? This is your first time here."

"Prince Goose, Lady Chen, Gyre and Macabre. Who are you?" asked Macabre.

"I am the host of Doth Lamex, Land of Pleasure, Comfort, and Relaxation, Dree'a'am. May I suggest a light snack? First?"

Macabre lifted his hands from the butts of the weapons hung on his belt. "First we would prefer to meet up with the rest of our party. Then we will decide what to do."

"Certainly. Name me their names and I will path you to them."

"John Tinker. Start there."

"That party of six left five and two boltic past. One left a mispta earlier."

"Approximately one earth day," translated Gyre.

"Host, what wasss their destination from here," asked Chen.

"They left no forwarding address," replied Dree'a'am. "Many do not."

"Tis most wild a'goose we do chase," said Goose. He giggled. "T'was nary a pun intended."

Gyre looked at their host. "If I give you the formula, are you able to make a certain foodstuff?"

"Certainly. Anything."

She did. Nudging Macabre gently, she said, "Your adrenaline is elevated."

"I am getting irritated."

"We have time for a cup of coffee and a doughnut."

"Follow that path," announced Dree'a'am. He floated away.

"Jolly good idea," said Goose, slipping his arm around Chen, heading over to and then down the path.

Soon they were sitting around the table, relaxing.

Goose and Chen were relaxed.

Macabre was starting to relax.

Gyre just was.

"Only one thing to do," stated Macabre, snapping a large piece from the side of a chocolate covered doughnut.

"Ummmmm?" replied Goose. His mouth full.

"We will have to hang around that witch until she hears where they are. Gyre, your portal part must be ready to take us to wherever they are. Pump all the energy you can into it. I have a bad feeling, very bad."

"The disturbances are widely scattered, with no apparent pattern. Yet," stated Gyre. "In addition, some massive force is ripping across and from the furthest reaches. Plotting its trajectory only indicates a number of possible impact points, one of which is Bahn Duhr Tohr. I cannot tell what this thing is. It is unknown to the data banks."

Macabre patted her hand gently. "Wait and wait, Gyre. Wait and wait." He took another doughnut.

Bahn Duhr Tohr. The Royal City. Late Afternoon.

"Hum, hum, hum."

"Humming handful, what is it?" Hanred looked over the top of the volume he was reading at Ripple who was, as was her custom, sprawling across his lap.

"That thing in the spellbox is growing together. The heart must have been a key fragment."

"And?" he prompted.

"And," she said, lifting the book from his hands. "I think we might consider relocating our quarters as this set of rooms has become too much of a crossroads. Folk are coming and going at inopportune times."

"I see," he said, recognizing that certain glint in her eyes.

Her smile grew more wicked. "I see that you do."

"And your patient?"

"Two more days."

"We are back," announced Macabre.

Ripple sat up, pushing her husband's hands away, mumbling coarse things under her breath.

"Two more days?" said Hanred sotto voce.

"Why?" demanded Ripple, turning toward her visitors. "Are you back? Here?"

"He wasn't there," stated Macabre.

"And we did decide, we did, that this most Noble Castle do be most busy a'hub, hence a'waitin' here we do be," added

Goose.

"Certainly getting to be that way," observed Hanred.

"What are you four doing here?"

They all spun around to face this new speaker. Chen jumped sideways and then to her side. "Great Smoke, what isss the matter?"

Smoke was leaning heavily on the doorjamb, one hand clenching it.

"Nothing now, thanks to that glowering witch. But I haven't totally recuperated."

"You get back in that bed," snarled Ripple. "NOW!" And pointed.

Smoke grabbed Chen's arm for support and turned back into her room.

"Pears, Macabre, we did find them. Where tis Smoke, tis all, me'thinks." Goose was smiling broadly.

"Oh, sit down, all of you," growled Ripple. "They are off to town and will not return until dark." She stomped over and dropped into a chair next to the table. "DRINK!" she commanded.

Hanred handed around the cups that had appeared on the table and poured from one of the bottles. "Allow me." He put one of the bottles in Ripple's hand, a cup in the other. "Here. This one is all your's."

Then, ever so carefully, he pulled her up from the chair and over to the couch. There he propped up his legs, making a spot for her to sprawl. He banged her cup with his. "Don't drink it all." His free hand popped the top button loose on her blouse. One corner af her mouth twitched as she poured his cup full.

"Husband, you are a sly devil." She leaned forward.

Leering outrageously down her blouse, he said softly, "Have to be." Then he whispered so that only she could hear. "Did you know that there is a secret room very high up on the south side of the east turret, just by the outside corner, east, with a small and private balcony just below the highest peak?"

"Hum, hum, hum," she said.

"Just you and me and a few refreshments. And no traffic."

They disappeared.

"By George," said Goose. "They do pop off be'times."

Macabre handed Goose a small device. "Call me when John Tinker arrives. We will be in ship." He nodded at Gyre.

They disappeared.

Goose shrugged, stood and walked over to an open doorway. Knocking softly on the door, he leaned in and said, "Might I enter, Ladies?" He was carrying bottles and cups. "People just do be a'disappearin' left and right."

Outside, the sun had set.

Inside, Smoke said, "They have just entered the castle and are on their way here. I didn't tell them you are here."

Goose was singing a bawdy song, one that The Guard liked to sing, not too clearly, not too loud. Stopped and cleared his throat. "Jolly good. Bit of a surprise."

He was now stretched out on the bed, pillows propping him up, next to Smoke. Chen sat on a chair on the opposite side of the bed.

Mostly they had been talking. Mostly Goose had been sampling various of the beverages provided by the castle, first sitting in a chair, then sprawling on the bed. And listening to them talk.

Smoke had described their various adventures and offered to show them her recent wounds. Goose had blushed. Lady Chen had demurred. For them both. Then Smoke and Chen had started a long discussion about the witch, R-Bar. Sometime during this convoluted discussion Goose had fetched yet another bottle and had decided to make himself more comfortable, carefully pointing out that Chen was in the room, that Smoke was under the bed covers, while he was on top of those same bed covers.

"Shhhhhhh, shhhhhh, shhhhhh," said Goose. "I do hear them a'clumpin' now."

The outer door opened and four happy voices bubbled inside.

"Dark Sister?" called Chicken.

"Mom, are you awake?" called Messenger. "We brought you something."

"I am," replied Smoke, grumbling just a little.

Chicken and Messenger headed for Smoke's room. Tinker and Fair Morn sat at the table.

"Just the thing after a long walk," said Tinker, grabbing one of the bottles from the collection on the table top.

Fair Morn, stood, tostled his hair, and started for the outside door.

"Aaaaargh!" He smoothed his hair back into place. "What's up?"

"Me. Soon. One, I need to stretch and fly. It is getting dark and I shall be careful. I doubt the folk here spend a lot of time staring upward."

"Have a good time."

She winked at him and slipped out the door and down the outside hall headed for a balcony, one that she had noticed earlier at the far end of this same hall.

Chicken jumped back and gasped, "Ga'zooks, Brother! What be thee a'doing in Our Sister's bed?"

Tinker jumped to his feet and hurried over to see what the commotion was this time. "Now what?"

As he stepped into the room, he heard Goose say, not too clearly, "Most Noble Sister Queen, we did but wait pon thy arrival, doin' some small tipplin' as fair time did pass most slowly." His smile was very lopsided.

Then he waved one arm grandly. "Nay cause for complaint for this Dark Lady do lie beneath guardin' bed clothes whilst I do meself be'lie above. And she do be most well protected, nay guarded, by most fierce dragon who would defend the honor of the weak against all comers." He hiccuped genteelly. And bowed grandly, elegantly to Chicken, forgetting that he was still lying flat on the bed.

Tinker stepped up behind Chicken, gently held her upper arms, and looked over her shoulder at Goose and Chen. "How did you two get there?"

Goose twisted and swung his feet to the floor and lurched upright, tilting heavily to one side. "Sire. Mine Lady and I did a'journey go inst Macabre's vessel. We have been most long a time do a'searchin' for thee and thine. T'was most unkingly a deed thee did so done . . . "

Chen had hurried around, bowed to Tinker, and grabbed her Prince as he leaned too far.

Tinker laughed. "Good night, Goose, Chen. See you in the morning."

"By your leave, Sire." He saluted rather vaguely in the general direction of Tinker and Chicken.

Tinker winked at the pair. "We can all sit and talk tomorrow. We are not going anywhere."

Chen and Goose left and headed for their quarters.

Messenger handed Smoke the package she had been holding. "Open it."

Smoke smiled at her and did. And held it up against herself. It was a black blouse of some soft material. An intricate pattern was woven into the material.

"Your other one was messy," explained Messenger.

"I will wear it tomorrow."

"See," explained Messenger as she showed Smoke how it fastened. She ran her finger down an offset seam. The blouse parted. Then she overlapped the edges and ran her finger up. They stuck together again.

"Neat, huh?' said Tinker.

"You did let us know not," grumbled Chicken, frowning at Smoke.

"Surprise." Smoke winked at her.

"Oh, mom." Messenger hugged her. "EEEEEK!"

"What?" asked three voices in unison.

"You are green." Messenger was staring at the open space at the throat of Smoke's robe. "Really really green."

"I am told that tomorrow's dose will be the last one. I heard Ripple tell Hanred that in a very loud voice." She winked at Tinker. "He enjoys his work. I am coming with you on your walk tomorrow. I need the exercise."

"O. K. See you at breakfast." He walked over and kissed her goodnight.

As did Chicken and Messenger.

Good night, mom. They felt the air flowing over the great wings as Fair Morn sailed high into the night sky.

Everyone headed for bed.

And sleep.

"Nice spot, huh?"

They sat on a high knoll, picnic materials scattered around them. From here, they could watch the army games in comfort and were out of the dust drifting down into the lower fields of the great grass plain.

Smoke was wearing her new blouse. The rest of them, other than Tinker, had just decided that after they finished lunch, they would all have to purchase matching designs, in different colors, of course.

The last of the food was consumed, mainly by Fair Morn, who said, "One, did you know that there is a small balcony just below the roof on one of the towers?"

"Hadn't noticed. Why?"

She leaned close and whispered in his ear. "I saw Ripple and Hanred up there." Then she hastily added. "They didn't see me." Fair Morn blushed.

Tinker nudged her with an elbow. "I don't think that I would mention it to them."

"OH NO! I immediately went a different way."

"Ready, My Lord?" Chicken was standing. And smiling.

"For what?"

"Shopping," chorused the others.

"Sure. Sounds like fun." He didn't sound like he really meant it.

Smoke dropped a hand on his shoulder. "You could stay here, watch the rest of the games. We wouldn't be out of range."

"Nope. Coming with you guys. Someone has to keep you out of trouble."

They gathered up what they had scattered around and headed back into town. And the shop that Messenger had discovered.

"Nice," said Tinker. "Beautiful! Wonderful! My, my, my!"

The four of them turned this way and that way, around and around, for his inspection, showing him the various styles and patterns.

"One," said Fair Morn, holding up a pastel blue shirt with a delicate white design. "They make men's shirts also."

"Buy it, buy it," bubbled Messenger.

"Try it, MindMate."

"Would be most Princely," added Chicken.

Fair Morn handed the shirt to him.

"O.K., O. K. But, these things are for leisure not, ah, work, right?"

Everyone agreed with that. So, he took off his shirt and put the new one on.

When he turned around they all agreed that he had to buy it. And wear it for the rest of the day.

So he did.

Mid-afternoon and all had returned to their quarters.

Smoke was taking a nap.

Tinker was enveloped. Sitting on the couch. Fair Morn on one side, Chicken on the other. Messenger had claimed his lap, her legs draped over Fair Morn's lap as well. She was leaning a bit upon Chicken. All three were intent on poking, prodding, and, in general, mildly harassing him. They thought that it was good fun.

Tinker was trying to ignore them. They knew that he was. And he knew that they knew that he was. And around and around went their interconnected minds. Smoke had self-isolated in order to get to sleep.

"Stop it," growled Tinker. "Or I will have to get mean."

Chicken cringed dramatically. "Mercy, Great King, mercy!" She cringed too far and toppled Messenger backward, who grabbed him around the neck as she went.

"Yargh!"

Fair Morn pulled them upright. "I never heard that word before."

"I have never had to use it before," replied Tinker.

"Piffle," suggested Chicken.

"That one either," added Fair Morn.

"Just expanding your vocabulary left and right, today," mumbled Tinker. "Oversized bug."

Fair Morn buzzed in his ear, "Buzz, buzz, buzz."

"You are not a bee."

"Generic bug noises."

"Piffle."

"Use thy own words." Chicken poked him in the side. "Utterance thief."

The air ripped open, A small figure tumbled down, crashing to the floor on hands and knees. She struggled to push herself upright. "Dim, dim, dim!" And collapsed.

Chicken leaped to her side and crashed into a sitting position, rolled her over and cradled the witch in her arms.

R-Bar's eyes fluttered open and looked at her. "Hayou, Princess."

Fair Morn lifted her from Chicken's arms and set her on the couch. "One, she has lost some weight."

Tinker knelt next to the couch, shocked at the deep lines

in her face. "You look kinna beat up, kiddo. What have you been doing?"

Messenger ran from the other room, clenching blankets in her arms, and helped Fair Morn cover R-Bar and then sit her up, tucking pillows here and there. "Would you like something to eat? We showed the castle cook how to make a sort of pizza."

R-Bar nodded, and thought that whatever it was it might be all right to eat. After all, they had eaten some of it. "I am starving. Thank you. What is it?"

Messenger handed her a slice. "It is not too bad."

Tinker pulled over a chair and waited until everyone was settled, again. He sat on it backwards, folding his arms over the back, leaning his head upon his arms, and looked at her.

R-Bar tentatively took a bite from the wedge of the stuff she was holding and then quickly devoured the rest.

"There's lots," said Messenger, bringing her a plate heaped with more slices of the pizza, such as it was.

"You keep losing weight, kid, and you won't be there at all." He frowned at her.

"I will eat and eat, I promise," she said meekly, for a witch. "May I have some of that drink also?"

Chicken handed her a cup, Fair Morn poured.

R-Bar grinned at them. "I like being waited upon."

"Enjoy it while ye may," said Tinker. "It will be short lived."

R-Bar shrugged.

"So," demanded Tinker. "What have you been doing?"

Chicken tapped him on the shoulder. "My Lord, she does need bath and rest. First."

"Are kind of dirty," observed Messenger. "I'll fill the tub."

R-Bar ate the rest of the pizza and smiled happily at them, pushed the pillows and blankets aside, and stood up.

Her legs gave out, tumbling her back onto the couch.

Fair Morn picked her up and headed for the tub room.

R-Bar called over Fair Morn's shoulder. "Scrub my, back, Tink?"

Chicken followed them. "We will Ourself scrub all that do require a'scrubbing. You do now require rest in fair quantities."

"Spoil sport," said Tinker, winking at R-Bar as she peered over Fair Morn's shoulder. She grinned at him.

Sometime during the night, someone squirmed between him and Chicken. "I am cold."

In the morning, he was woken by someone tickling his ribs.

"Kitten, stop that!" Tinker jerked up the covers.

A sleepy voice mumbled from the other side. "What?"

Tinker lifted the covers and peered under them. And snarled, "What are you doing in here?"

"Trying to sleep, My Lord."

"Not you, Princess."

"I was cold."

"Piffle," announced Fair Morn pulling a pillow over her head.

"And what exactly is going on," growled Smoke, standing at the foot of the bed.

R-Bar peeked out at her, holding the covers just below her eyes. "Hayou," she said weakly into that stern gaze with the eyes that seemed to grow and grow, larger and larger.

"Someone claims that they were cold," grumbled Tinker. "And now that we are all awake, we might as well get up and have some breakfast. It ready?"

"That is a very beautiful blouse. Where did you get it?" asked R-Bar, sitting up, smiling at Smoke, who was now smiling at her.

"A shop in town."

"We all bought one," said Messenger, slipping from the

bed, somehow dragging most of the covers with her.

"I want one too," said R-Bar yanking desperately at the blankets slipping away.

"We'll go shopping," said Messenger, snatching her clothes from a chair. "Together."

"OH?" said Tinker, staring at the ceiling, pondering, not for the first time, the wisdom of his life style and life.

"Indeed, My Lord." Chicken leaned on him and kissed him.

Far Corner. Late At Night.

Tananapa, a Two Rank Sorcerer, had arrived from an extended wander, rested, and was now standing in the small room reporting to Netanada, Elixa Sorceress, Head of the Phylota, and Abadoda, the Three Rank Sorceress.

"They prowl widely do these ones, The Sisters of Death. They are seeking Dark Knowledge from those that know of these things. Never before has it been known why they wander as they do."

Netanada looked down at his report, her finger lightly touching the names written there. And then looked up. "They are actually doing this?"

"Yessssss."

"There is no doubt?" Abadoda frowned at him and at his report.

"It is so. One of them lived with a Mage of the Sluba Guild for several seasons. Another did the same with a witch clan. Yet another delved deep into a library of the darkest dark. All seek to learn Old Knowledge, Ancient Knowledge, knowledge of the almost before before."

Netanada stared at him. "And these that they visit still live?"

"It is so."

"Then it is time for us to search deep in our own archives and to seek what the most feared are intent upon. You shall have none else but this." She nodded at him. "And you may ask any you wish to assist in this. We must learn of this thing."

Tananapa frowned deeply, nodded, and hurried away.

"What think you?"

Abadoda sighed. "I believe it has something to do with that strange organism. Before that one appeared those Dark Ones never approached any other in such a manner."

"Watch that one carefully."

Abadoda nodded and hurried away.

Netanada opened the Ancient Book of Songs and carefully added to it the report. And began sketching a great protection spell that would take all their skills to spin. And hoped that it would be strong enough.

Bahn Duhr Tohr. The Royal City. Fairly Early Morning.

After breakfast, they went shopping.

"They will pack nicely in our packs," said Smoke as she looked about the shop.

"The Princess said we can't find clothes like these in Grandeville," explained Fair Morn to Tinker while holding a green shirt against him which she thought he would look nice wearing while they were shopping.

"Right."

"Pretty nice, don't you think so, Tink?" R-Bar spun around, a flare of bright red.

"Certainly eye-catching. I thought you guys favored black?"

"Hum, hum, hum. I like other colors also, especially red." She bounced up and down in front of him. "Don't you remember?"

"Looks good with that dark hair and pale skin."

R-Bar laughed, kissed him, and spun away to look at another collection.

The woman who owned the shop came over and stood

by his side. "That design is an exclusive only with me." And worried about a laughing witch and wondered whether this group could control her.

"Really?"

"Absolutely true, Great Lord." The owner had decided he must be a great Lord to be able to afford such Ladies as these. And so many, even a witch. She leaned close and told him confidentially. "It is my sister who is so clever. I am a mere shop owner."

"You are pretty lucky. That is a good combination." He smiled at her.

R-Bar popped from behind a tall cabinet. "May I buy two, please?"

Chicken walked from somewhere. "Three. We did decide that mere three more would nary a' problem be, we did, for a' packing and a' traveling."

"OH BOY," called Messenger from somewhere in the depths of the shop. "Aren't you glad we bought you a gift, mom?"

Smoke growled at her. She was trying, unsuccessfully, so far, to stop Messenger and Fair Morn from calling her mom.

A yellow shirt flew from somewhere and hit Tinker. "For thee, Our Prince."

"Gee, thanks, Princess."

Smoke strolled from another corner of the shop, "We are done, MindMate."

"You are sure?"

"Indeed, we do be," stated Chicken, stepping out from behind a tall divider and smiling at him.

"We are, Tink, we are," said R-Bar, walking over to him arm in arm with Messenger.

"Finished," announced Fair Morn. "One, you have your shirts?"

"Wouldn't leave home without them."

Five pair of eyes stared at him. Then Messenger giggled.

The shop owner presented her bill. Chicken paid it. Which confused the shop owner. Lords paid. Ladies played.

"Praps," asked Chicken. "You could us direct to restaurant fine, nearby?"

She received detailed instructions.

"Good," said Smoke. "I am famished."

"How do you do," said Tinker. "I am Tinker." The shop owner goggled at them.

"My Lord, be thee light-headed?"

"Shopping fatigue. Let's go."

They left the shop, each carrying their gaily decorated, gaily wrapped packages. Messenger waved goodbye.

The shop owner wondered from which far flung corner of the kingdoms they had traveled from. It must be a very strange place.

They had a large table to themselves. Fair Morn claimed a chair on one side of Tinker, Messenger the other. R-Bar glared at them, to no avail.

"So, Big Bird, how was night flying?"

"Very nice, One. Here they do not have aerial devices cluttering up the air. And few people look up. And it is a much quieter land. Red is a nice color for her, don't you think?"

"Yep. But I wonder how the witches are going to like it. Black seems to be the proper color, the only color for them to wear."

"MyTinker," whispered Messenger, leaning close. "She has changed, or she has been changed."

"Into what?" he whispered back.

Messenger stared at him for a moment, then said, "Not that way. The witch strands are altered. Other kinds are intertwined all around her."

"And you don't think that comes from being bitten, ahhh, gifted by her friend Or whatever that was?"

Messenger shook her head. *No, MyTinker. She wasn't this way before she went to the Aunts.*

Why are we speaking inside?

I don't want her to read our lips.

Why not?

One, our kitten fears for that witch.

WHAT?

Whish, gentle, My Lord, wilt us all headache give.

What is going on, kitten? This time?

He saw a tear forming in one of Messenger's eyes, then the other. *Don't.*

I'm sorry, MyTinker. But I like her, and she was so lonely, and she is not just pure witch any more and when we leave she will be even more outside their group. And alone.

NO!

She doesn't have to be us. She could just live with us. In her own room.

The rest crowded in.

Breath deep, Sweet Prince, thee does jitter so.

MindMate, push it deep.

Oh my, oh my. I am sorry, MyTinker, I am so sorry.

Fair Morn pushed a cup into his hand and wrapped his fingers around it. "Drink it. It is lime tea."

He did. And blinked his eyes and watched the room come back into focus. Then he set down the cup and took one of Messenger's hands in his. *We can't keep doing that. There are too many people in too many worlds. And don't cry, kitten.*

R-Bar nudged Chicken. "You are all doing it, aren't you? I can see it going on."

Chicken smiled at her. "What, pray tell?"

"A single person. You just became a single person. Now you are not. Again." Her eyes watched Chicken's face, carefully, intently. "I am correct."

Chicken nodded. "Indeed."

R-Bar turned back to her dinner, looked at her plate, then up, her eyes darting from face to face around the table.

Slowly she pushed her chair back, stood, and twisted away.

She was gone.

"Now what?" He stared around the table.

"Back to castle, she did go." Chicken linked with Smoke and Smoke reached and pushed, hard.

R-Bar reappeared, wiping her face on the sleeve of her blouse. Through puffy eyes she looked at Tinker. "I am sorry, Tink. I just felt pushed aside. Alone, again." She sat down, and stared at the table top.

Ooooooo . . . Messenger struggled to hold back her tears.

Chicken threw an arm around R-Bar's shoulders and pulled her close, their chairs banging together. Then she kissed R-Bar on the forehead and said in such a low voice that only the witch could hear, "Do not worry, young witch, we . . ."

Princess!

Chicken hugged R-Bar and winked at her and tostled her hair and sat back.

"My Lord?"

"Ahhhhh, nothing. Pass that platter, will you?" He glared at Chicken.

"Dim, dim, dim!" snarled the witch, smoothing her hair back in place. When Tinker turned aside to speak to Fair Morn, R-Bar winked back at Chicken, Then she asked the table at large. "May we go to a play after we eat?"

They did.

"Where are they?" demanded Macabre.

Macabre and Gyre had materialized in the living room. Goose and Chen were sitting at a table playing cribbage, a game Tinker had taught them.

"All did go a'shoppin' in town, they did." Goose waved idly in the general direction of the center of town.

Macabre yanked out a chair and sat down. "But not away from here?"

"No," said Chen, pegging out and winning 6 games to 2. "We visited with the King and Queen, watched the gamesss, and now wait here until they return."

Gyre stood next to Macabre, one hand on his shoulder. "Sensors indicate they are wandering in this general direction. Slowly."

Goose shoved the cribbage board to one side. "I say, Macabre old nasty, wouldst card game learn?"

"Is it lethal?"

Goose giggled. "Praps. In some maner of speakin'. T'was Our Lord Tinker did teach us all, it. It be named *Hearts* and does some nasty tricks contain."

Macabre nodded. "Join us Gyre. This might prove interesting."

She sat down. Goose explained the rules and began to deal.

"I am not sure this is such a good idea," said Tinker as they left the fourth place, nudging Chicken gently in the side.

"Sweet My Lord, is this not what thee did describe, once, that Sport from Merry Olde England borrowed?"

"Princess, I also said that students did this and they certainly didn't pub crawl in alien cultures."

"Piffle," commented Fair Morn. She was walking on his other side.

They were now all wearing their new shirts. The once gaily decorated packages were now showing heavy signs of wear and tear. Crumpled and battered they were, tucked under one arm or another.

Up ahead of them, Tinker and Chicken saw R-Bar, Messenger, Fair Morn, and Smoke turn into the next place.

"Whose idea was this, anyway?"

"My Lord, We Ourselves do believe thee did so speak a'us pon this very thing while we did intermission wait and talk."

"Maybe I'll stop talking to you guys," he grumbled.

"Prince!" Macabre frowned darkly at Goose as Goose

pulled in the last trick of the hand. It contained one heart. "That is the third time you have done that."

"Tis naught but fair nasty part I did mention err we did start. Tis your shuffle." He stacked the cards in front of Macabre and stood. "Praps some small libation wilt we imbibe while we do a'wait pon their arrival?"

"Let's," agreed Macabre. "Where are they?"

"Sensors indicate a slowing down in their progress. They appear to be stopping frequently as they weave in this general direction."

"Passin' strange," said Goose, offering his fellow card players a choice of bottles provided by the Royal Steward in charge of such matters. "King's compliments."

"Mothra," said Tinker to Fair Morn as he pulled Smoke over to her. "You and the big hunk are designated guides. You guys think you can get this mob back to the castle soon? Three of us are getting fuzzy-eyed and I suspect that the kid witch is getting that way too."

"MindMate, R-Bar is the lightest. Can you carry her?"

"Sure."

"Then I will carry Messenger and Fair Morn can tote your Queen, our sister."

"What?"

"If it comes to that."

"Right," he shoved his mug away.

They headed for the next place.

A very noisy mob burst in upon the card game. They were playing pinochle now.

Fair Morn gently laid Chicken on the couch.

"Heavy seas," mumbled Chicken.

Smoke, cradling Messenger in her arms, carried her into one of the bedrooms.

Tinker staggered in, R-Bar draped over one shoulder, his arms wrapped around her thighs. "GOOSE, give me a hand. Do you know how many steps it is up to here." He slipped the witch from his shoulders and into Goose's arms. "Put her with Messenger. Whew." He dropped into a vacant chair and grabbed a mug. "Who's pouring?"

"We will talk in the morning," said Macabre standing up.

"Ahhhhh, mid-morning. Please?"

Gyre took Macabre back to ship.

Goose gathered up the scattered cards and put them away. "Morning it be, Sire." He and Chen left.

Smoke came in, banged him comradely on the back, and headed for her room. "I am bushed. Good night." The door banged shut.

"One?" Fair Morn had entered the room.

Tinker stood. "Don't move," he commanded as he stepped in front of her and put a finger on her collar.

"What?" Her eyes tried to see what it was that was crawling on her.

"Nothing," he said, slowly sliding the finger tip down the shirt seam, watching the garment fall open. "Really nice."

She slid her finger down his shirt. "Yep."

He woke, draped with soft wings. Fair Morn's arm was flung over his chest. From the living room came the sounds of morning and a number of voices.

"One?"

Tinker moved her arm, reached over, and with both hands lifted her straight up. She smiled down at him.

"I am always amazed at how light you are."

Her wings lifted.

"You're not going to flap those things in here, are you?"

"No. Just moving them out of the way."

"Such a clever rascal," he said lowering her back down.

"I am." Her lips closed over his.

Chicken, sprawling on the couch, had been threatening Goose with a number of foul actions until Macabre and Gyre appeared bearing powdered doughnuts and pots of coffee.

Chen had merely nodded, now and then, during the lengthily tirade.

"Your custom, I believe," said Macabre, pouring their cups full. They sat at the table with Chen and Goose. Chicken joined them.

"How fare them all?" she asked Goose.

He shrugged his shoulders. "Until thee did wake, Noble Queen, t'was most quiet here abouts."

She looked into themselves. Tinker and Fair Morn had locked themselves aside. Smoke was rising, she had smelled the coffee. Messenger was stirring. A little.

"We will rest this day, travel on the morrow," stated Chicken.

"Whither?" asked Goose.

"Where?" asked Macabre.

"Unknown," replied Chicken.

Macabre took another doughnut. "Who was the child that John toted in last night?"

"I am not a child," grumbled R-Bar. She stood glaring at them from the doorway, bare toes digging into the rug. She had pulled on her trousers. Her blouse was balled up and clenched in one hand.

"My, my," observed Macabre. "Certainly not."

"By George!" gasped Goose.

"Cloth thyself, brazen wench!" snapped Chicken.

R-Bar slipped her arms into the shirt and slid her finger up the seam, closing it. "Dim, dim, dim!" She stalked to the table, grabbed a cup and dropped into a chair.

"We will speak later, we will," commanded Chicken.

Goose poured coffee into the witch's cup. Gyre slid a platter over to her.

R-Bar glared at the table top.

"We will," insisted Chicken.

R-Bar looked up, moving only her eyes, And nodded once.

"Has anyone ordered breakfast?" Smoke walked in, pulled up a chair and sat, pulling over the doughnut platter and smiling at Goose as he filled her mug.

Messenger started to wander into the room from the bedroom, saw visitors and jumped back, slamming the door. "WHOOPSIE!"

Chicken smiled at R-Bar.

"Where's Tink?"

"Still in bed," said Smoke. "What are you up to these days?" She looked at Macabre.

"Oh," he said airily, waving a doughnut, scattering sugar dust here and there. "Same old job, killing things."

R-Bar choked and began to cough, quickly taking several swallows from her cup. She stared at Macabre, looking for the joke. And saw that he wasn't joking. "You are a friend?"

"Yes. We have worked together several times before. And this time he will need all the help that I can give. There is something very, very wrong going on and who ever or what ever is responsible for that needs to die, wonderfully horribly." Macabre smiled.

R-Bar reached into somewhere for a wand.

"Sensors show disturbances in many, many places," explained Gyre. "We were heading for the nearest one when we decided to pay John Tinker a visit. He was gone, but Prince Goose remembered what Ramp had said. We came here and tried to meet him more than once."

"What kind of help," asked R-Bar, glancing around the table.

Macabre reached for another doughnut. "Oh, just a little thing." He shrugged a shoulder. "A hand held material crusher. Need some place to test it."

"It will work," stated Gyre.

"Of course," agreed Macabre.

"May we come in?" A voice spoke to them from the ceiling. It was Ripple. She was intent on starting a new custom, ask before entering.

"Indeed," answered Chicken.

Ripple and Hanred appeared. He did a double-take at R-Bar's shirt, and quickly said, "Doughnuts. How delightful."

Ripple stared at her younger sister. "What . . . is that thing . . . you . . . are . . . wearing?"

"A present." R-Bar pointed at Chicken and Smoke. "They bought it for me, yesterday."

"It . . . is . . . red."

"Tink said that I looked good in red." R-Bar glared back at her older sister. "I am tired of black."

Ripple stalked around the table ready to rip the garment from her sister's back. And reached. Something crackled around R-Bar. Ripple quickly snatched her hand back. "How?"

"The Old Aunts," stated R-Bar.

"Look at me."

R-Bar did.

"Weight loss."

"The Old Aunts."

Ripple leaned closer and looked into R-Bar's eyes. "Muchly grown changed."

"The Old Aunts."

"Rangle, rangle, rangle!"

"The Old Aunts! The Old Aunts! The Old Aunts!"

Ripple's face relaxed, changed expression, softening. Hanred sucked in a silent breath, stifling his surprise. This was a private, intimate thing never done in the open.

"What have you become, favorite one?" murmured Ripple.

"Just me," whispered R-Bar. "Just me."

"Morning, morning, morning," bubbled Messenger as she came into the room. She was bare footed having noticed that R-Bar was. She sat next to R-Bar and said, "I had a wonderful time last night." And dropped her hand on the witch's shoulder.

Ripple leaped backward, black crackling around, protecting herself.

Messenger stared at the display. "Oh, my!"

It died as Ripple advanced and carefully reached out to touch her sister. As her fingertip gently stroked R-Bar's check, Ripple looked deeper and deeper into her sister's eyes. "Hum, hum, hum. The Old Aunts are most devious, yet this tastes most un-aunt."

"I am just me," whispered R-Bar, looking very worried and miserable.

Ripple's face became very hard and public and whispered, "You are still my favorite one. But red? And black?"

R-Bar nodded. "I like it."

"Hum." Ripple sat in a chair, backbone very straight and commanded breakfast to appear. "I am hungry. And you need to regain lost." She nodded at R-Bar.

Hanred smiled at Smoke. "How is my patient?"

"Green," replied Smoke. "Ready to travel."

"Morning," said Tinker, entering the room. He yawned and stretched. "You could have waited."

"My Lord," said Chicken, suppressing a smile. "We did know not how long thee would be . . . a'sleeping."

"I'm hungry," announced Fair Morn, walking in, eyeing everything on the table.

"Violent exercise do have that affect," said Chicken sweetly.

Tinker chose to ignore her and took a seat next to Hanred and reached for the coffee pot and said to him, "You had better eat before she gets started." He had a feeling that this was going to be a very long day.

Dark Yozquae. Mist Soft Day Dim.

"What kind of a place is this?" J. C. stared at it and their surroundings.

Broken rock, deep canyons running ragged to the horizon. Shades of grey, shades of black. Mist curled from below and tickled over sharp edges to fade soft drifting feather forms. Ahead, piled high on the tip of a peninsula, peering out into vast deepness, a citadel.

"Ulp?" Grizmek stood behind J. C. and peered cautiously at the looming structure.

"A third key place, partner. A dump like this is, I wouldn't wish on anyone. Almost."

"Let's sit behind this rock pile and do a little planning," said J. C., yanking Mirf around behind the jagged mass. Grizmek was there in one bound.

J. C. sat.

Mirf joined him, back against the rocky surface. "So we are sitting already. What?"

"Chirp?" Fred sat next to J. C. on his other side. She had moved Grizmek over.

"I don't know. But standing out there in the open didn't strike me as a very clever idea."

"Right," agreed Mirf. She slid one arm around his back. "Bend forward."

J. C. looked at her. "What?"

"Bend forward, I want to see. Your back is sticky." Mirf pulled her hand back and wiped it on her thigh.

J. C. stared, then bent forward.

"You need a new shirt." Mirf ripped it further open.

"HEY!"

"Don't kvetch! I need to see." She saw a long red slash running diagonally across his back. "Not too bad. Starting to clot already."

Fred leaned over to take a look and sat back. She began to spit into one pair of her hands.

"Yuck Fred." J. C. stared at her.

She was spitting something that was brownish-grey slimy. Then she leaned behind him and rapidly wiped the goo over his wound.

J. C. jerked. Then he realized that the pain had left his wound. "MIRF? What is she doing?"

"Chirp," said Fred.

"Wound healer." Mirf watched the bubbly, frothing stuff dribbling down his back. Then she ripped a piece from his shirt and wiped his back clean. The wound had crusted over, stopped bleeding.

"Ho Boy," laughed Mirf.

"What?"

"How do you feel?"

J. C. sat back, held himself upright. "No pain. Why? What did she do?" He squinted at Mirf. "What did she do, Partner?"

"Fixed it. Wonder if the color will be permanent?"

J. C. glared at Mirf. "What color?"

Fred sat back, hands lightly fluttering over J. C.'s face, her eyes watching his.

"It is blue. That rip across your back turned blue when she sealed it."

"Blue?"

"Yep."

Fred waggled the left middle forearm in front of his face. A jagged blue line ran up it.

He sighed. "I think that I have just been tatooed."

"The women in your elseplace will get all hot and bothered when they see it. They will be dragging you into their beds to find out how you got it." Mirf grinned at him.

"Mirf," cautioned J. C.

"Oooooooooooooo, J. C.," cooed Mirf. She panted heavily at him.

"Knock it off, lady."

"I ain't no lady. I am your partner, big hunk." Mirf glared back at him. Then she kissed him on the cheek. "So what's a little blue line among friends?" She started to unbutton her blouse. "You want to see my scars? Again? Much more fun than looking at etchings."

"HEY!"

Mirf stopped and pouted. "So, I am rejected?" "STOP!"

"I'm heart broken." Mirf tried to look sad.

"Enough, already."

"That an ethnic slur?" demanded Mirf.

"All right, all right. Partner."

"So, no more worry about blue lines?"

"I will never mention it again."

Mirf grabbed one of his arms and leaned against his side. "Any ideas?" Fred clutched his other arm.

"No. This is your profession, not mine."

"Bingo," said Mirf. "So, we'll make a sneak, right?"

"How are you going to do that. The front is wide open."

"Send the gonif. He is the sneakiest thing we have." Mirf smiled at Grizmek.

"ULP."

Mirf leaned further forward and peered past Fred at Grizmek who was trying to hide behind the suk-dragon. Unsuccessfully. "Ulp me no ulps. Get in there and find that key."

"Chirp. Chirp."

"Positively verbose," noted J. C.

"If you think you can glitter eyes, give it a try."

Fred slipped away, followed by Grizmek.

Mirf and J. C. peeked from behind their rock pile to watch. Fred and Grizmek were nowhere to be seen.

"See. Very sneaky. Now, where were we?"

"Nowhere," answered J. C.

"Wrong-o-rooney. You were going to come up and see my scars, Big Boy."

"Mirf, get serious. This is neither the time nor the place for that."

"You bring a deck of cards?"

"Partner?"

"Yessssssssss?"

J. C. stood. He was still well hidden. The rock they were behind was more than big enough in all directions, if they didn't move around too much.

"Assuming Grizmek and Fred make it out alive, maybe we ought to find the escape route now?"

Mirf bounded to her feet and started sniffing loudly, slowly turning this way and that way. She wandered off, away from their target and stopped to peer into a large opening under a rock overhang. "**HERE!** We just run in here and away we goooo."

J. C. looked into the open space. "You sure?"

Mirf nodded. "Yep." She pointed into it. "This is way out." Then she walked past him, back toward their rock. "Come on, let's sit. And wait."

It was a long wait. The already depressing atmosphere became even more depressing as the light dimmed. Mirf began to fidget.

"Calm down, partner."

"I am calm, I am calm. I am just nervous."

"They must be doing all right. No one has sounded an alarm."

"I don't wait well." Mirf stood up. And sat down. She jumped to her feet, took a step out, then back, sat down. "Maybe we should go and take a peek. See if they need any help?"

"No weapons."

"Bizzle blak."

He peered at her face. "Your eyes are getting more funny looking."

"Hob-goblin," she explained.

"Shhhhhhhh." He placed a hand over her mouth.

Neither moved. Both listened. A stone rattled out there. Another small noise.

Something was headed their way.

Mirf jerked away and handed J. C. a large stone. She held another in her other hand. Slowly they moved around to see what they could.

Fred slipped from the gloom. She had Grizmek draped over one shoulder. He was a very pale green, about as pale as a Grizmek can get.

"Ulp," he whispered.

"He got it!" explained Mirf. "What's wrong with the gonif?"

"Chirp." Fred slid Grizmek to the ground.

Mirf propped the sagging frog-thief up and leaned him back against their rock. "I have never seen him that frightened." She held her hands out, making a small bowl with them. "Give me the other key and the crystal."

Grizmek dug in his pockets and dropped them into her hands. The crystal, the keys.

Mirf handed them to J. C. and leaned forward. "So Grizmek, listen to me carefully. Our contract is finished. I am sending you home. Keep the bag of gold. Can you travel?"

Grizmek leaned forward and stood on wobbly legs and bobbled his head up and down.

"Come with me." Mirf led him away and shoved him through the node.

"What about Fred?" asked J. C., when Mirf returned. Six arms wrapped themselves around various parts of him.

"She stays. Good company makes the way seem shorter, Goldsmith, 1768. Let's go."

"Where?"

Mirf smiled, a very humorless smile. "To see what these keys unlock."

Nonnap. A Rather Dreary Appearing Place.

They stood in front of the cavern dwelling castle wherein the Franzak lived. And very carefully checked their surroundings. Especially the gaping entrance to this place.

"Nothing," stated Motaiss. He pointed. "With the exception of that, this is a benign elseplace."

Turintor looked at her silent companion.

She nodded and stared for the entrance.

And deep inside they stood and stared.

Everything they could see appeared quite ordinary. Although the room was on the large size, it was rather plain in decoration and furnishing.

"You expected gawdy?" asked a soft voice from behind them.

Then he strolled around and stopped in front of them and smiled. "Three magical ones from three different witch clans. Most strange. Rarely ever see something like this. Why?"

The speaker appeared to be just as ordinary as his surroundings. His clothes were a soft green color.

"Shall we sit?" He gestured casually. A table and four chairs appeared.

He sat. And waited.

So they sat.

"We seek information," stated Turintor.

"Why?"

So she explained. Everything. In some detail. Everything that they had done. And everything that had been done to herself and her companion. And of the willingness of Motaiss to help them in this endeavor.

The Franzak filled their cups and took a sip from his. And carefully looked from face to face to face.

"What do you offer? For my help, assistance, aid? In your endeavor, search, seeking?"

"Perhaps little. Perhaps much," stated Turintor. "Clan debt of two clans." She indicated herself and her companion.

"I may not speak for my clan," said Motaiss. "Only for myself."

"Not much," suggested the Franzak.

Turintor nodded. "Then we thank you for your beverage and for your time."

The Franzak waggled a finger at her. "Ah, ah, ah. Perhaps there is some small thing you would give?"

"Such?"

"I would receive a small touch of your magic. From each." He shrugged. "It is the nature of the Franzak to do so. At times."

"What get we?"

"A way to return to yourselves. To be once again whole. And to finally be able to rid the universe of universes of the abomination that caused this thing to happen." He nodded at the two witches. "I will also help once you know."

Turintor nodded and looked at her companions. Each nodded in turn.

The Franzak stood and pointed at the witch in black. "You first." His eyes darted from her to each of the others. "None to react."

Then he stepped over and touched her on the forehead with one finger.

She shivered, and collapsed.

"Next."

Turintor stood.

And the process was repeated.

Motaiss stood.

And the process was repeated.

And then, some time after some time had passed, the four sat at the table, sipping restorative beverages.

"Now," said the Franzak. "I will send you deep into the Dark Under. You will be gone for long. But down there you will find that which you seek. Here will I wait your return."

And with a wave of one hand he send them down.

The Unnamed Place. Dark. Dark. Dark.

The slightly built, hooded figure dressed in black stood

and stared at the great wall. This was the destination. Silently she spoke the words.

Inside the structure, the disturbance readied the hordes and smiled happily.

They were eager to rend and tear their way to the victim. She would appear in The Great Open. He had suffered many loses, but this event would occur, there was no other path for her to follow. Everything was too well planned. And no one else could pass that way, only her. And her abomination.

With her end, he would terminate that clan. They would all finish screaming in agony, one by one, singing his favorite song just for his ears only. It was a joy to anticipate, an event to treasure always. He would do anything to rid the elseplaces of her and her spawn. He had already done much.

Ra'aa'zar raked his claws through his hair, eyes flashing madness.

And thought happy thoughts.

Zink Two. Mid-Morning.

Rumtah and Reptar dropped what they were doing. The two sisters picked themselves up, ran screaming into the next room, leaping wildly over the shattered remains of the room.

"So," said Rumtah. "The Silent One has found the beast."

"Those two were involved." Reptar jabbed her finger at a wall and watched it bulge and shatter, filling the adjacent room with flying debris.

"No longer. Come." Rumtah took Reptar's hand and turned away.

To follow the call.

Prandal's Dalk. Nighttime.

Rekel released Pantrap and watched him slide down the wall, his magic bent and broken.

"The city can always use another beggar," she whispered.

And followed the call.

Goeasy Llow. Afternoon. Market Time.

Ranna smiled at the shop keeper who cringed behind his counter.

The shop was filled with smoke and acrid fumes that eddied from the smoldering heaps of trade goods

"You are about to become unemployed," she said. "Your master has been found."

She disappeared.

To follow the call.

Oraon. Rest Day Noon.

Raft flashed through the great hall. The Wizards Guild of Oraon ran in full panic. Bodies fell and bodies piled up near all the exits.

The Least of the Least huddled near a corner with one of his fellow juniors. "I told you that it was a mistake. No power is worth this."

"You were correct," said Raft as she hurtled his friend over the balcony railing. Lifting The Least by the throat, she stopped, tilting her head to one side. "Maybe next time.

She was gone.

To follow the call.

Bahn Duhr Tohr. The Royal City. Night.

Rotak hurtled into Ripple's room, yanking bedclothes in all directions.

Ripple leaped from the bed, hissing wildly. Then stopped. They both ran from the room. Ripple charged back and yanked Hanred with her.

"What is it?" He stared around the living room, seeking the cause of all this turmoil.

Ripple's eyes glittered. "We are going to return that thing. It is whole and hungry." She waved their clothes on and handed Hanred a list. "I require these things."

He snatched the list from her hand, quickly scanned it, and ran from the room.

Ripple was getting ready to follow the call.

The Unnamed Place. Dark. Dark. Dark.

R-Bar took them all.

Following the call.

They stood between the second and third walls. Their gear pattered down around them.

"Now what?" Tinker looked at the narrow open space. "Now what's going on?" And yawned.

Five pair of eyes focused upon the small witch.

"It was here," she hissed. "Under our very noses." And disappeared.

Tinker began to strip off his pajamas and put on his dark clothes. The great sword hummed as he swung it into place.

The others hastily followed his example, dressing for battle.

Fair Morn fastened the holster to her right thigh and yanked the weapon free, rapidly setting the levers.

Bahn Duhr Tohr. The Royal City. Night.

Willawa leaped from the bed and ran to the corner and began to prepare her armor. Toucan followed her, dressing hastily, yanking on his boots. He ran from the room pulling his shirt on as he went, calling for the Palace Guard.

And soon, in the broad fields outside the city walls, trumpets began to blare, calling all the armies to their feet, calling the men to arms.

The games had honed their skills to a fine degree. They were ready to do battle.

To follow the call.

Space. 47.24.99.66, QBD. In Ship's Notation.

Macabre woke instantly.

Gyre had a screen on, the target centered in the aiming device.

"Very clever." Macabre nodded his head. "We ready?"

"We will not be able to use The Weapon," said Gyre.

"Not from up here." He reached for his battle gear.

Bahn Duhr Tohr. The Royal City. Night.

Goose ran into the courtyard, Chen at his side. They could hear the thunder of departing armies. "We must follow them, My Lady."

Chen nodded.

A cloud swirled around them as they lifted into the night sky.

Servants stared at the empty courtyard and the great dragon soaring up and beyond the city walls and hurried back inside, slamming the doors and latching them firmly.

The Unnamed Place. Dark. Dark. Dark.

"So, O. K., there must be a door or something in this wall somewhere. Those keys fit something."

Fred pointed to their left.

J. C. handed Mirf the keys and the crystal.

"Suk-dragon night vision," explained Mirf as she walked that way, squinting and finally bending over as she found the correct spot. She held the crystal rod and began to search the small door for a round opening of the correct size.

The Desolation of Paarz. Night Dark. Quiet.

"BY DUMPF!"

They stood in the center of a great open plain on an open patch of sand. Twelve black pillars formed a line off to one side, evenly and widely spaced. Far away, shrouded by night, they could just discern a great stone structure. From somewhere in the center of it, light flashed and pulsated.

Twisted Castle.

$1.98 pulled them into a dark shadow space. "Duff, this place reeks."

She nodded. The madness rankled her nose. The ring sheeted them in pale green glow.

Tear's dagger sang an angry hum.

"Where are we, Dear?"

$1.98 shrugged. "Here." The strange wand in his hand crackled softly."

"Careful, careful," she said, wrapping them in soft unseen.

They began a stealthy search.

Twisted Castle.

Mirf shoved the rod in and heaved on the door. It silently swung open. "Ho Boy," she whispered. "That's one." Touching J. C., she ducked into the long hall that passed down the interior of the wall.

Fred danced nervously behind them.

The door closed with a soft *click*.

Something started to brush past them. Six arms snapped out, and held it.

"Suk being, release me. I am not your enemy." It was soft shadow whisper, almost no voice at all.

Mirf shoved J. C. behind herself. "Who are you, shiksa?"

The hooded figure stood motionless, unresisting in Fred's many armed grip. "I am Reep. Of the Faan. I also seek the enemy."

Mirf hissed. "Oi vay, it is one of them!"

"We have no quarrel, Chief Inspector. Reptar pushes much."

J. C. stepped around from behind Mirf and snapped, "Fred, let her go."

Fred did.

"Do you have the keys?" sighed Reep. "These doors are locked by generations of hate. I could do nothing."

"Yes." J. C. nodded at her.

"How did you get here?" asked Mirf.

"I followed the thread. He is powerful. And careless. Come." Reep drifted silently ahead of them, down the corridor.

They followed her.

Desolation of Paarz. Night Dark. Quiet.

"HUSBAND, run for your life. We stand in The Desolation of Paarz." Ramp shoved at Hard violently and called, "Run, Mountain, run."

They didn't get far.

"**ROCKS AND STONES!**" Mountain bounced back from something unseen, his arms flailing wildly

"Trapped," hissed Ramp. She gathered in the forces. The ground split open sending a jagged crevice across the clearing. It banged into the shield and stopped. Ramp gasped and staggered sideways.

"CAREFUL!" Hard leaped to her side, throwing his arms around her.

"Too strong. I couldn't break free."

"Stop trying, stop trying," screamed Hard. "You'll injure yourself."

"BY DUMPF," grumbled Mountain, waggling his great club in one hand. "Some thing needs to be pounded into dusty dust."

But there was nothing around.

Twisted Castle.

"MindMate, this door is stuck."

Smoke stepped back from the wall. "Perhaps further

around?"

"Who's in there?"

She shook her head. "Totally blocked. I have never felt such strength."

Messenger stared at the wall, tracing the intricate binding, the complicated knots of magic.

R-Bar appeared. "Can't we get inside?"

Desolation of Paarz. Night Dark. Quiet.

Rekel crept along the outer wall of the vast structure and stopped. Far out on the plain she saw them.

"Ramp," she hissed and ran toward them.

A thread of lightning snaked from a pillar and flashed around her, snapping back.

Struggling, snarling, spell blasts arcing wildly, she was bound to the pillar. Nothing she tried worked.

The light in the center of the great stone structure flashed brighter.

"What's happening?" Hard stared at the struggling figure.

"It is Rekel. He has got her." Ramp began to weave a thick cover around Hard. "I will not let him kill you, My Husband."

Twisted Castle.

The boom echoed between the walls.

"Just what we need, a storm." Tinker looked up at the night sky.

"Magic blast," corrected R-Bar.

"Blow it open," commanded Tinker.

Fair Morn did.

The door and part of the wall disappeared.

A pillar of flame arced high into the air overhead screaming angrily downward toward them.

"**INSIDE!**" howled the witch.

They charged through the hole and down the corridor. It lit up with the glow of fire striking and then faded.

"Close, My Lord." Chicken lightly touched his arm, a reassuring gesture.

Desolation of Paaraz. Night Dark.

They stepped out and killed the creeping beast. It had started out toward Ramp. Then they saw Rekel twisting angrily. And ran toward her.

The ground flashed around them, snapping them off their feet.

"Hee, hee, hee," chanted a disembodied voice as Rumteh and Reptar slammed into their pillars. "That is three."

Twisted Castle.

"Well, here goes nothing." Mirf shoved the sphere into the opening. The ramp crashed down. They hurried through. It stayed down.

"Where are we going?" asked J. C.

"Deeper and deeper," answered Mirf. "Mysteries are born of mysteries, Sam Tuke, 1663."

"Mirf," whispered J. C. "What are we going to do when we get there? We don't have any weapons?"

"Sa'good question, bubee. Ask me again, when we get there."

$1.98 ripped a hole in the covering. The fierce power of the multi-rodded wand was beginning to alter him. Tears stared. Duff clapped an iron grasp on Tears' arm.

"Silence," she commanded, seeing the questions forming on his young face.

$1.98's eyes had darkened and sunk deeper into their sockets. A strange light flared in there.

They followed him into a small room. It was a cluttered library.

"Evil, evil, evil, evil," muttered $1.98, igniting everything he found.

Space. 47.24.99.66, QBD. In Ship's Notation.

"Macabre, all the disturbances have stopped. Only that one great force still hurtles this way. Everything else is focused below."

"Ho, ho, ho, ho, ho, ho, ho." He strapped on the last section and tucked the latest design under his arm. "I am in the mood to do a little disturbing myself." He carefully examined the image on the screen and tapped one finger at a selected place.

"Gyre, my own, put us down right there. We will just watch and wait, a little."

Gyre nodded.

They stood to one side and looked at the gigantic building and then out across the field, sensors slowly scanning, identifying the trapping tendrils by their energy flow.

"A very nasty one lives here." Macabre slipped silently away, Gyre at his side. They moved just far enough to be out of the trap way.

Desolation of Paarz. Night Dark.

Ranna prowled around the outer edge seeking some way to break the bindings. She was a low shadow close to the ground.

Ramp sensed her presence and shouted. "**AWAY, AWAY, FLEE, FLEE!**"

A blinding flash of light, a scream of rage. Ranna blasted wide sections of turf clean as she was dragged slowly to her imprisoning pillar.

Twisted Castle.

"This place is a maze," said Tinker.

"He is in here somewhere," snarled R-Bar.

Messenger pointed. "That way, it is stronger that. way."

They took that passageway.

Tinker's weaponkin hummed louder. The great two-handed sword floated lightly in his hand.

R-Bar stayed carefully away from it, standing as far to one side as she could get.

"Well partner, here goes nothing." Mirf shoved the third key into the wall. Nothing happened. "A dud?"

J. C. looked at her.

The wall shimmered and folded open.

Mirf stepped through first.

"YOU!"

"Yes," said Quam, the franta. "It is I."

"What are you doing here?" she demanded.

"Helping. You should have died."

Fred leaped at him.

Quam kicked the small statue across the floor. "Dumb beast."

J. C. leaped around Mirf and lunged, fist striking just as he had been taught by John Tinker. He caught Quam on the side of the jaw and knocked him stumbling back into a small table.

"Nice punch," observed Mirf.

The franta leaped to his feet and ripped something from a pocket.

"**DUCK!**, screamed Mirf, shoving J. C. to one side.

Quam stopped and stared past them at the still, silent figure that had just drifted into the room. "You!"

She drifted up to him and stood, still as death.

Quam turned, ran to the wall, bent down, grabbed something, hurried back to shove it into Mirf's hand. "You did it."

Mirf handed the statue to J. C. and smiled at Quam. "So did you. Have a good time." She mumbled under her breath,

"And often treachery kicks back at its author."

"What?" asked Quam.

Reep looked. Quam stared into those deep, dark eyes, and smiled happily. And died.

"Double dealer," hissed Mirf. "You should have known La Fontaine. Let's go this way." She tugged on J. C.'s sleeve.

Desolation of Paarz. Dark Night Beginning to Lighten Into Faint Dawn.

Ripple, Rotak and Hanred stood near the outer wall in deep shadow. They could see the witch sisters twisting and turning, snarling, struggling vainly to break free from their fastenings.

In the center of the great clearing stood Ramp and her's, guarded by a gigantic figure carrying a monstrous club. They watched while he walked over and jabbed the weapon against something which flashed and refused to let him pass through.

"Hum, hum, hum. A great luretrap. Be wary, Husband, be wary. You also."

Rotak snarled.

Hanred asked, "How do we free them?"

"They will be free as soon as we kill the one responsible," growled Ripple.

Rotak stepped on a tendril.

The ground flashed as she was yanked into the trap.

Ripple leaped sideways, lightning flashing, bolts igniting, exploding, and releasing the struggling figure being pulled across the ground. Ripple ran over and yanked her sister to her feet. "Careful."

She turned and stepped away, speaking to Hanred. "Don't you move at all."

It unfolded, wrapping her in silence and snapped to a pillar.

Rotak was snatched backward as she hurtled a bolt to kill it.

Hanred didn't move, for long moments, he didn't move. Then he carefully stepped backward and circled far out and around, until he was directly behind Ripple. Slowly, ever so slowly he slipped up until he was close enough to touch her. He tried to break the bonds holding her in place. Nothing worked. He could see her lips moving, but no sound escaped her prison.

Twisted Castle.

Ra'aa'zar released the hordes. They poured from the gate, gibbering, scampering, each anxious to be the first to pull down the magician.

They didn't feel the ground vibrating under their feet.

And if they did, they thought it was from their passage. They didn't hear the soft thunder approaching in the near distance.

They flowed into the open field intent upon only one thing.

Death to the magician.

"My Lord, most great storm does approach."

They could hear the dull rumble, feel it through the soles of their feet.

Messenger pointed. "That way."

They eased into the designated corridor and slipped as quiet as they could toward the far end.

Tinker halted them and gathered them in. *I am going first. If there are just one or two guards, the weaponkin will be better, much more quiet. There is no sense in you guys blowing out walls and announcing our presence that way. We need surprise on our side.*

He started forward, Chicken hurrying at his side, her blade swishing back and forth. *And We, My Lord.*

Messenger whispered in R-Bar's ear, telling her what he had just said.

Desolation of Paarz. Faint Dawn Light.

The combined armies of Bahn Duhr Tohr, formed in a great crescent, broke around the central spot, and thrust into the side ranks of the demon hordes charging toward Ramp.

"**NO QUARTER OFFERED!**" shouted Toucan at the head of the left wing.

"**NO QUARTER GIVEN!**" commanded The Queen from the front of the right. Her armor gleamed white in the first light of dawn. Her sword flashed.

The horde was ripped into two wheeling mobs, the greater, the main force found itself attacked from all sides. The multicolor army continued to roar into the battle. A large unit smashed through the front gate of the great stone structure and plunged deep into the interior of the first ring wall, hacking and slashing their way forward. Other units swung wide, attacking any opening they could find.

Warriors stormed into the building from all sides.

Twisted Castle.

Macabre carefully blew away the few remaining gates and trundled into the second ring wall.

"We had better hurry. Wouldn't want to get caught up in all that."

They trotted along a jagged corridor. The roar of battle fading behind them as they passed deeper and deeper through the massive structure.

"Strangely empty," mumbled Macabre. "In here."

"Sensors indicate there are two other parties ahead of us, closer to the center. They are at divergent angles to us. Proceed slowly." She pointed and indicated the places where these others were.

"Ho, ho, ho, ho, ho. Good." He fired, just a tickle. And ripped a hole to the interior. "We will just have to go direct."

They ran into the space between the second and third ring walls.

Slipping up to the closed door on cat silent feet, he listened and moved them forward.

Tears was frightened.

$1.98 had become something else.

Now the magician's shoulders were broader, but more rolled forward. His eyes pulsated with an ember glow. Greenish-grey smoke was seeping from the seams of his robe. His hands had become more claw-like, knobby, hard. Even the wand now appeared more menacing.

"HE is inside, here," sighed $1.98, power crackling down his arm, charging the wand. He gently shoved the door open and slipped inside.

He stared into the viewing space and watched the witches struggle and snarl. It was a pretty sight. They deserved it. And more. But that would have to come later, a little later. Just now he had to do something about that army. It was destroying his horde and battering through the several ring walls toward him.

The spell took shape in his hand. It had to kill them all but not touch the horde. It was getting difficult to discriminate one from the other, they were so intermingled and twisted together. And there were so many more enemies hurtling into the fray.

He shrugged one shoulder. Oh well, then they would all die.

Whipping his arm back, he started the chant, and twisted around, to launch the spell.

The bolt ripped through his shoulder an instant before he let go, shriveling the arm, altering the spell, now on its way.

Howling in rage, he spun to face whatever had dared to attack him in his own center. The curse he threw ripped away the wall, floor, and ceiling, exploding outward. Everything rained down far into the adjoining forest.

He grinned and stared into the night silence. The armies,

the hordes, lay in tangled, still heaps.

How nice. Now it was time to visit the witches, it was time to play. Time to slowly pull that one apart.

But, Ripple would be the first.

He stepped out onto the field.

"Locate that explosion."

"Off to the side." Gyre pointed.

"Aim me." Macabre swivelled his weapon toward where he felt that explosion had originated.

"Right. Right. He is still there. Right. Left, just a touch. FIRE!"

The weapon sizzled, a low humming buzz. A wide hole snapped through the structure, through the center, and on and on, cutting a swath through the adjoining forest, and through the far distant hills.

The beam was tight. It barely widened as it passed out into space.

The weapon snapped off.

"He moved," said Gyre.

"Where?"

"Into that field we saw."

Macabre spun around and trotted down the hall. Much better, he thought, out in the open.

Smoke heard the bolt pass through the structure not far ahead of them. She grabbed Tinker, and spoke to the others. *HALT*.

Messenger stopped R-Bar. "Wait," she whispered.

Tinker and Smoke eased their way around the corner and stopped to stare at the sight.

A large round tunnel passed through the building. The walls were smooth. It was about ten feet in diameter. Tinker walked up to it and cautiously touched the inside. It was warm.

"What did that?"

Chicken peeked around the corner. "My Lord, do be most careful. Praps t'will act again, this thing."

Tinker yanked his hand back. "Good thought. We'll have to go around."

R-Bar stood next to him, head cocked slightly, listening to a voice speak to her. "Outside. He is threatening Ripple." She disappeared.

Tinker started to run back down the corridor, headed for the outside.

They ran with him.

Mirf pushed open a door and dropped into a crouch, then cautiously peered around the edge. "My, my, looks like a small treasure room with no-one home." She stood up and strode inside.

The guard leaped, claws flashing, at Mirf.

J. C. leaped at it.

But he didn't have claws.

The three of them tumbled across the floor, arms and legs flailing.

Reep waited. Patiently she waited.

The tangle crashed into a tall cabinet, the doors sprang open spilling ornaments, jewels, and ornate daggers down upon them.

J. C. grabbed a knife and plunged it into the beast's side. It hesitated, claws deep in Mirf's flesh, teeth poised to rip out her throat.

Reep reached down and yanked the thing's head around by one ear, twisting it tightly. The guard looked up. And died. Sagging over its intended victims.

J. C. struggled and managed to heave the dead weight off them by pushing with his feet and finally managed to sit up. Mirf was still slumped in a loose heap.

"DAMN, DAMN!" He yanked a dagger from his thigh

and threw it across the room. "You want to give me a hand, lady." He glared at the witch.

Reep reached down and lifted him to his feet.

"Ummmm, stronger than you look."

"I am no lady," came the feather soft reply. "And you are welcome, pretty one. Hum, hum, hum."

J. C. hauled the dead beast to one side and eased Mirf over onto her back. Blood dripped onto her chest. He looked up at the ceiling.

"It is you partner. You are a mess."

J. C. looked down. "Me?" He dripped on her again.

"Very piratical. There are three furrows running from your left temple to the side of your cheek. And now you really need a new shirt."

He stood and ripped the remains of the shirt off, twirled it into a thick band, and wound it around his upper right leg, tying a large knot to hold the makeshift bandage in place.

"J. C., how bad is it?"

"Not too bad. It only went in a little way, And it only hurts when I laugh."

"Dumbkopf. Me!"

"Oh." He stepped back, winced, and gasped. "You're not too bad. One eye closed and all puffy. Cracked lips. Your shirt is pretty well shredded all down one side. Hold still." Carefully bending over, he pulled the bloody tatter's away. "Breath deep."

She did.

"Guess you didn't break any ribs. Pretty badly clawed though."

He helped Mirf to her feet and started to brush the hair from her forehead.

"OUCH!"

The hair was matted and tacky.

"Sizable bump and a couple of cuts," he reported. Then he nudged that thing on the floor with one boot tip. "She killed it."

"You?" Mirf looked at the still figure.

"It needed killing," breathed the shadows.

"Ho Boy." Mirf looked from the large carcass to the slight figure. "What did you use?"

Darkness whispered, "I looked."

Mirf lurched away from J. C. and dropped heavily into a gilded throne. She dragged her left leg stiffly. "Twisted something."

J. C. pulled over a table and sat on it and looked from Mirf to Reep. "What's next?"

"We sit for awhile," answered Mirf.

"O. K. How come?"

"Listen. What do you hear?"

J. C. stopped breathing and listened. "Nothing. I don't hear anything."

"Bingo. No noise, no shouting, no explosions, now no nothing. For me, that is a bad sign."

J. C. stood and limped across the room, bent over, picked up some things, and came back. "Here." He handed Mirf one of the jewel encrusted daggers. "Fancy, but sharp."

"So?" She looked up at him as she took it.

"If you can hobble, let's go take a look."

Mirf carefully eased herself to her feet. "Oh boy, am I ever glad I asked you to come along. Two stumbling wrecks, beaten, abused and bleeding. And what does he want to do? Go take a look." She stood next to him, turned and swung an arm around his neck. "Slowly, please."

Then she jerked away. "Not yet, boychick."

"Why not?"

Mirf stepped in front of him and gently brushed his lips with hers, wincing. "J. C., when we first started, I suggested something, and here we are."

"What?" He flinched as her lips touched the side of his mouth.

Mirf stepped back and grinned. With her swollen face it was a very lopsided grin. "A fortune or two. So, take something, take a bunch. Take whatever you fancy, you deserve it."

He grinned back at her and turned to hunt through the jumble. After he slipped a few items into his pocket, he turned back and said, "Hold out your hand, partner."

She frowned at him, and did.

J. C. grabbed her hand, separated the fingers, and slipped a gold and black ring on her finger.

"For you."

Mirf threw her arms around his waist, nearly toppling them over. "Does this mean we are engaged?" She slid her hand over his back, carefully avoiding the diagonal wound. "Say yes, J. C., I have never been engaged before."

He laughed softly. "Think your career can handle it?"

"Trifler. Things can always be arranged."

"Yes," said J. C. carefully enfolding her in his arms.

"HO BOY. Another first. You wanna know something?"

J. C. grinned. "You lost a lot of shirt back there."

"OUCH!"

"Sorry. What?"

"I really like you, J. C."

"You are pretty nice, also."

Reep found a book of spells which she slipped into her pocket. "Hum, hum, hum," sighed the shadows. Her eyes slid up and down J. C.'s body, a frank appraising glance.

"Partner," sighed Mirf. "There is very little of me you may caress without causing pain. And you are leaking from a number of places. So let's go take a look before we both fall over. But slowly."

They started down the hall that they hoped would lead them to the outside.

"Wouldn't have it any other way, Schweety," lisped Humphrey Bogart.

"Messhuggener."

Desolation of Paarz. Lightening Dawn.

Ra'aa'zar stood in front of her and carefully described, in extreme detail, what he was going to do to her.

Ripple glared at him.

"And then, the rest, one by one, piece by writhing piece. And she is last." He jabbed his left hand at Ramp, the right arm hung useless, limp, swinging loosely by his side.

Someone appeared from behind the pillar and stepped between him and Ripple.

"Who are you, fool?"

"I am Hanred." He grabbed something from a small sack hanging from his belt and hurtled it at Ra'aa'zar's feet.

The explosion blew Ra'aa'zar backwards to sprawl on the grass.

"A feeble toy," gurgled Ra'aa'zar as he lurched to his feet, pointing, hurtling the Master Illusionist far across the field. He walked over and reached for Ripple.

Twisted Castle.

Chicken gasped and jolted to a halt.

Messenger screamed.

The corridor was full of bodies, tumbled and entangled.

Smoke grabbed Tinker's shoulder. "Some of them are still alive. But it is hard to see." She jerked her head from side to side.

STOP.

"Yes, MindMate," she said meekly, her minds clamping down.

Tinker pointed. "Fair Morn, punch a hole that way. We need a short cut."

Fair Morn fired.

Desolation of Paarz. Dawn Streaked Plain.

Something growled behind him.

Ra'aa'zar whirled around.

She grabbed him. And threw him against the nearest empty pillar.

Swiftly, the creature sliced away Ripple's bonds with her long claws, spun away and charged their enemy, her long legs kicking, talons digging into the turf, fangs gleaming.

Ra'aa'zar thrust out his good hand. The force picked up the creature and smashed it back against the barrier containing Ramp.

The thing tumbled to the ground, twitched and lay still.

Tossing aside the cut bindings, Ripple reached into somewhere and yanked it down.

The ground shuddered beneath its feet.

Ra'aa'zar screamed and scrabbled sideways, his good hand clenching the pillar, holding himself upright.

The Demon With No Name slowly turned its head from side to side, a cruel grin splitting its stone face, its fingers clenching and unclenching, passing the rod from hand to hand.

"THERE!" commanded Ripple, pointing at Ra'aa'zar.

"**THERE!**" She howled the command into the night

sky.

"**THERE!**" She screamed.

Blue light poured from the demon's eye sockets as it searched for its victim. It opened its mouth to speak.

The universe began to split open.

"**NO!**" The voice thundered down around them.

"**NO, YOU MAY NOT DO THAT!**"

He stood in front of the monster and struck it with his fist, a single blow. He struck it with his fist and shattered it into a thousand shards. And scattered them into a thousand universes. Turning, ignoring the snarling witch, he stomped across the field, his feet leaving deep holes, the air whirling and shrieking around him.

He stopped and stared. Then he snatched Ra'aa'zar from the ground by the neck and smashed him against the pillar. "I should have killed you a long time ago."

He dumped the groaning body to the ground and stomped. And stomped. And then there was nothing but deeply churned soil beneath his feet.

Tinker and company charged from the far side of the field, fanning out, weapons at the ready, ready to attack whatever he was.

The man ignored them and walked over to the small, crumpled, strangely shaped figure lying on the ground wearing a crimson shirt. Bending over, he picked her up and held her cradled in his arms. "I will speak to The Aunts about this." His voice boomed through across the great open space, blowing leaves from the trees.

Then he gently stroked the battered creature with one finger tip. The creature shimmered and became a small witch again.

She opened her eyes and smiled, a very crooked smile at him. "Hayou, Father."

Tinker jerked to a halt, stared up at this person, and leaned on his weaponkin, the point pressed into the soil. He was breathing heavily from his run. "Father?"

The dark man gently set R-Bar down. She smiled happily at Tinker. "Tink, this is our father. He is a warlock."

Raft stood next to Tinker, next to R-Bar. "Hayou Father."

Reep drifted up to them.

"Now are you, Silent One?" boomed the great voice.

"I am fine," returned the gentlest of whispers.

He turned, reached out and snapped all the bonds, breaking all the barriers, smiling as Ramp approached him.

"Brave and foolish daughters, one and all. But not too close, Magician. We have no desire to injure your children yet to be born."

Ramp stood and looked up into his face, tears streaming down her cheeks.

He smiled gently and said, very, very quietly, "Perhaps, sometime, I will visit. Just to see my grandchildren."

One arm reached down and lifted R-Bar in the crook of his arm. "And you mischievous one, you have become unique." He winked at her. "And very nice."

He kissed her on the forehead, touched her with his thumb on the same spot, and then set her down. "And very rangle."

Then he stepped away, said something to Ripple only she could hear, then he touched each of his witch daughters in turn. And walked up into the night sky.

In and among the jumbled heaps of bodies, the live ones struggled to free themselves. The spell had been greatly damaged. Many had survived.

A figure clad in badly stained white armor staggered toward the other wing of her army, her left arm hanging limply, her right dragging a gore encrusted sword. Searching.

Castan Forest.

In the shattered forest, Duff hitched herself over broken stone and splintered tree remains, crawling painfully forward.

Tear's sat crying and shaking a robed figure. One traveling bag stood next to him, its contents hanging loose from a long rip down one side.

"Tears," gasped Duff. "Hand me that black wand." She sprawled on the torn soil, one hand reaching, stretching as far in front of herself as she could reach. "Hurry, Dear."

Dol Spar. Mirf's Home. Mid-Morning Bright Sunny Day.

"Where are we?"

"This is my home."

"Really?"

"You betcha, bubee."

"How did we get here?" J. C. looked around, admiring the decor.

"That witch, Reep, did it." Mirf cast a sly glance at him. "I thought that you wouldn't get angry and that it would be best if you healed up first before going back to your elseplace."

J. C smiled, using one side of his face. "O. K, partner. I won't get angry."

Mirf threw open the windows. "Good. All's well that ends well, as the Bard would say. Needs to air out."

Then she turned and kissed him carefully. "I'll even let you make love to Fred. I promise I won't get jealous."

Six arms wrapped around J .C. from behind his back. "Chirp?"

"STOP THAT!"

Desolation of Paarz. Dawn, Brightening Into Day.

Macabre had watched the various events unfold in the great field.

Behind them, another round hole radiated out from the badly shattered structure. He stood with one arm around Gyre. "The weapon worked very well. Pity he arrived. Killing that thing would have been a rare pleasure."

"There will be others."

"There always are. Can MedSection build a small mobile unit? With a forget circuit? Quickly? These brave kingdoms are close to becoming depopulated of their males unless rapid healing is instituted."

Gyre started the various sections to work. "It will be ready soon after this world has its full sunrise."

"Take us up. I want to shed this armor and hang this little toy on the wall."

They disappeared.

Battle Plain, Once Called the Desolation of Paarz. Morning.

They were all sitting in loose clusters watching the sun rise, flooding the open plain with light.

The witches sat in a group around Ripple, who held Hanred cradled in her arms.

Ramp sat a proper distance from them, Hard by her side. Mountain sat next to them while Tinker and the others sat off to one side of the two groupings.

R-Bar sat near Tinker's side, one arm thrown around Messenger's waist and watched Tinker. Chicken and Smoke were talking in low tones. Fair Morn held one of Tinker's hands, and watched everyone else, and held her weapon ready.

Hanred's eyes slowly opened and focused. "Dusky Delight," he croaked. "You are alive."

"More so than you, Husband." Ripple barely had the strength to hold him in her arms. She had been pouring her life into him all through the dark hours and was now wobbling badly.

"Witch wife?" He breathed softly. "Am I as bad looking as you?"

She peered into the wan, lined face. "No. You are beautiful." Ripple had convinced her sisters to send them back to the castle, to their rooms. And to ask before entering.

Ramp led Hard over to where Tinker and company were sitting, clenching Hard's arm tightly.

Mountain now lay on his side, his stomach rumbling loudly.

Hard asked Tinker, "Have you seen J. C. anywhere?"

"Nope."

"I hope that he is all right."

Tinker laughed. "Knowing J. C., I am sure that he is."

Hard smiled. "You are probably correct."

Ramp suddenly doubled over and grunted.

"RAMP!" Hard's face lost its color. "What's wrong?"

Slowly she straightened up. "We had better go home. Now! Your children are coming."

R-Bar leaped to her feet. "Stay where you are, Sister." She ran over to the witch sister group now beginning to think about going in their own directions, and held a hurried conversation with them. They all joined hands, and stared at Ramp.

She grabbed Hard's hand and held it tight.

They vanished.

Goose and Chen came walking across the field toward Tinker and group.

As they approached, the witches twisted away, one by one by one, each in their own fashion.

"The weird sisters do leave," observed Goose.

"Yep." Tinker nodded, standing.

Goose swayed from side to side. He and Chen had been helping the wounded and sick, sorting the dead from the dying all through the early hours of before morning dark.

"Sire, we would here for some months remain. Mine Brother Toucan, The King, will be a'mendin' long and long. And given great carnage, the kingdoms, large and small, will be most astir, politic rife. The Noble Queen Willawa, most badly battered, has need for aid in maintainin' this fair world's order."

Tinker interrupted the dissertation. "Stop. I am convinced, Goose. I agree." He pointed at a box-like device that was drifting among the wreckage of the great army. "What's that thing?"

"As fair sun did march up and across battered field did appear Macabre and fair silver Lady Gyre and it. Tis medico and does rapidly heal all not yet dead."

Chicken joined them, slipped an arm around Tinker. "My Lord, it does appear foul and fearsome Macabre does some soft spot under hard shell have."

Tinker smiled at her. "Don't tell him, Princess."

"Oh, aye." She pulled away and threw her arms around Goose and kissed him on one cheek. "Rest, Brother, rest. That Queen does require hale and hardy advisors to stem fierce tide of disorder as great Princes and greater Lords still alive do soon tussle for position."

Not too far away, not too close, she peered out from the dense vegetation that survived the warfare, vegetation dense to most folk, but not to her. Tiny Rosebud stared at the destruction and wondered whether following that one was a good idea after all. How he could do something like that was beyond belief. She watched the several groups out there for some time, trying to decide when it would be the best moment to step forth and plead the case for the Garden Gnomes.

Elsewhere, not too far away, another pair of eyes also watched everything. Flerlan the Observer observed the one of concern as he talked to this one or that one. And he wondered why the smallest Garden Gnome he had ever seen was also staring so intently at the one of concern.

He tickled his beast just to tell it to remain quiet, and smiled to himself. Garden Gnomes were also very good at watching from concealment. And he was amazed at the ability of the one of concern to continually become enmeshed in events of such great chaos.

R-Bar ran over and rejoined the group.

Tinker threw an arm around her and said softly, "It is time for us to go home, kiddo. I think the kingdom could use a little help from you also."

She smiled. "Goodbye, Tink." With a wave of her hand, she sent them one way, Mountain another. Then she turned. "Prince Goose. I have some traveling to do as well."

R-Bar twisted away.

Grandeville. Tinker's Place. Morning.

They dropped their gear anywhere, happy to be home again.

Tinker fell back into the couch. "At least this time getting back was easy."

Chicken reached over, ruffled his hair, and left to change her clothes. Into pajamas.

Messenger followed her.

Smoke announced that she was going to cook as Chen had left a note saying that he was staying in town for a day or two.

Fair Morn sat on the floor and yanked her boots off. Then she did the same for him. She was in the process of pulling her shirt off when a small figure danced into the room from somewhere.

"Hayou, Tink," she laughed. "Guess who came to visit?"

www.ingramcontent.com/pod-product-compliance
Lightning Source LLC
Chambersburg PA
CBHW030843030726

47495CB00005B/1349